DAMAGED

Simon Conway

CANONGATE

First published in Great Britain
in 1998 by Canongate Books Ltd,
14 High Street, Edinburgh EH1 1TE

Copyright © Simon Conway 1998

The moral rights of the author have been asserted.

British Library Cataloguing in Publication Data
A catalogue record for this book is available on
request from the British Library

ISBN 0 86241 760 0

Typeset by Palimpsest Book Production Limited,
Polmont, Stirlingshire

Printed in Finland by WSOY

DAMAGED

ABOUT THE AUTHOR

Simon Conway was born in Sacramento, California in 1967. He was brought up in Thailand and Beirut, and witnessed the Syrian invasion of Lebanon in 1976. He was educated in England and at the University of Edinburgh. He went on to work as a bartender on the Lower East Side in New York, and as a roadie for the Butthole Surfers' 1987 tour. He participated in the Tomkin's Square Riots the following year. He left New York to join the British Army, and served in a Highland Regiment in Belfast and after that in Medicine Hat, Canada, where he was part of a training unit that was the subject of a parliamentary investigation due to its high casualty rate. He was suspended from duty for a year pending court martial, but the case was dropped for lack of evidence and he was subsequently promoted. Since leaving the army he has worked as a postman, a blacksmith and a private investigator. He lives with his wife and two children on a Scottish island.

For Paddy and Paula

With thanks to

Marshall, Steve, James, Phil, Jamie, Kate, Auden,
Iomhar, Organ, Zoë, Mike, Ian, Head, Cat, Gus, Jo,
Rowan, Helen, Toby, Jim and Graeme

BOOK ONE

THE LONG-HAIRED ACHAEANS

November 1995–January 1996

I am so glutted with resentment that I ache
War Music, Christopher Logue

1

Calum Bean woke at the radio-alarm's insistence, reluctantly lifted his eyelids and found himself staring across a Dutch hotel room into the crackling eye of the television, remembering fragments of a drunken spree at the Terneuzen bierfest. It felt like a stack of bulkheads were tumbling through the interior of his skull.

'Nevermore,' he croaked.

'Repent,' advised Leonard Cohen from the radio.

Cal spun the dial, searching the frequencies for the shipping forecast. Finding it, he cursed out loud: there were stormfronts gathering out in Dogger and German Bight. Awful retribution.

He stood under the shower for an extra five minutes, hunching his body to get his head under the shower-head, ate two Paracetamols, tied his dreadlocks in a loose bun and skipped a monotonous breakfast that was fried and greasy.

He was on the water with the rest of the crew inside half an hour.

He brought the Zodiac in a wide arc across the shipping lane, steering between the black hulks of container ships bound for Antwerp. It was raining hard and he had the drawstring on the hood of his waterproofs drawn tight so that there was only a small aperture, but still the icy needles of water struck the bridge of his nose and his cheeks and stung his eyes. The well of the boat was awash with foaming water and he had his steel-capped boots jammed tightly in the stirrup-loops to brace him against the rolling bow-waves.

The rig was out here somewhere. He scanned the horizon for the single blinking light on her superstructure.

She wasn't much of a drilling rig, nothing more, really, than a raft of welded steel pontoons standing on four hydraulic legs. Her deck was loaded with a derrick, a crane, water and guagum and diesel tanks, a Volvo powerpack, and a couple of freight containers serving as a workshop and a tea hut. Not much to speak of, but a home of sorts for the last six months, first off the coast of Gaza and now here in a Dutch shipping lane.

Then he saw her. The blinking light, and after it, her skeletal outline.

She was dangerously low in the water. She was standing in forty metres of water with her legs fully extended, only one steel lug showing above the leg bearings, and the tops of the waves from the shipping lane were breaking across the deck, balls of spume roiling between the tanks and the stacks of drill pipes.

Fearful of being swept on to the deck, he held off as far as he could and the ongoing and offgoing crews were forced to jump the gap. As he was attempting to hold her steady, he glanced at the crane.

Odd. He rubbed the salt out of his eyes.

The previous evening, at the end of the shift, he had taken the time to realign the crane with the edge of the platform. He had dozed for a few minutes in the cramped and heated cab, until the nodding of his head against the dash had woken him. He remembered sitting for a minute or so, staring straight ahead at the winking lights on the gantries and metal corsetry of the chemical factory on the north shore. Now, looking up at it, he saw that, although the crane was still flush with the edge of the platform, the cab no longer faced the chemical factory.

The rig was drifting.

Implications not quite grasped made him uneasy and he turned them over in his mind, despite the best efforts of his hangover, as he ferried the nightshift back to shore: if the rig was drifting in the deep mud, there was no telling what the stresses would be like on legs that were already overextended. The rig had been designed to work in a depth of no more than thirty metres; the extra ten-metre leg sections had only been added because their previous job, surveying for a new port off the Gaza Strip, had required them. The money had required them. He'd thought nothing of it. Adding leg sections was just more welding. He'd been told to do it, so he'd done it. Besides, the weather in the Med had been a lot calmer.

Here it was terrible. Half the Netherlands was flooded; the hotel where he spent his off-duty hours was filled with families who'd been forced to abandon their homes.

The Westershelde job had been last-minute, a fast one, pulled on them just as they were approaching England. A radio signal. A new destination, a new geologist, everyone on the rig to stay put and await further instructions. The instructions duly came: they were contracted to undertake a site investigation for a proposed tunnel connecting Terneuzen with Zuid-Beveland on the north shore.

Cal had been part of the maintenance crew that had travelled with the rig as it was towed back from Gaza across the Mediterranean, with the legs dismantled into sections and stacked on the deck. It was logical that he stay on for the Terneuzen job, but, more than that, he had his own reason for not wanting to leave the rig; namely, it allowed him to keep a close eye on the leg section that contained ten kilos of pressed Lebanese hashish in a watertight welded-steel box. The leg section that was now thirty metres down in the mud.

He had arranged to offload the hash at Plymouth docks, the rig's final destination. It was already a week overdue. All sorts of heavy people were breathing down his neck. This new job, and the consequent delay, was beginning to scare him. The rig had only been in place for two days, and at no time had the weather improved beyond a murky greyness. Now it seemed as if she might be about to drift away.

If he lost the hash he was likely to lose his kneecaps.

The tide was fast flowing out of the Westershelde as he cautiously approached the blinking light on the superstructure for the second time. The deck was no longer awash with water and the tops of the legs were revealed. For the second time that morning he had the feeling that something was wrong.

The Motorola handset in his jacket pocket was howling white noise. Maybe someone was shouting, maybe not. He couldn't distinguish a word over the roaring of the boat's seventy-five-horsepower Suzuki engine and the ships sounding in the ragged fog that lay tight against the water. His bare hands were numb and bluing. Each wave seemed to strike him harder than the one before.

The crew in their fluorescent yellow waterproofs were running around the edge of the platform and waving frantically at him. He coaxed more power out of the engine and brought the Zodiac alongside. It wallowed in a sudden trough and was nearly swept under the rig. A heavy coil of rope slammed into the bottom of the boat. Yvonne, the foreman, was leaning far out over the handrail, shouting at him and pointing out into the shipping lane. Cal cursed, and fumbled with numb fingers for the Motorola. He cupped it awkwardly against his ear. The radio hissed, and screamed, and then he got it clearly.

'Git that fuckin' leg!'

The rig was standing on only three legs; one had ripped out of its bearing. He hadn't noticed. He looked out in the direction that they were frantically signalling. The missing leg was heading at about four knots into the shipping lane, aimed like a torpedo directly at an inbound container ship.

'Jesusfuckshitefuck,' he shouted, but the wind whipped the words out of his mouth. He opened out the engine and chased after the steel leg, the boat slamming into the waves as he accelerated towards it.

Yvonne stomped into the tea hut, dropped into one of the plastic chairs and slammed her steel-capped boots down on the splintering, paint-spattered workbench. She swept the hood of her waterproofs back and started shaking her pale fingers vigorously to coax some life back into them.

The last one in hauled the door closed against the wind, and they all stood for a few seconds, savouring the respite from the weather. The space heater roared in the corner. Naked women and men, torn from magazines, sprawled on the walls.

'What the fuck ur we gannae dae now?' Yvonne asked nobody in particular.

'Cup of tea?' suggested Dave, the second mate, who was squatting in front of the heater, massaging his hands.

'Sharrup ya mash basturt,' she replied.

Dave shrugged good-naturedly. His earrings glowed red in the light from the heater.

'Let's get off this rig,' suggested the geologist, who had a savage hangover, 'before the tide comes back in.'

'Well auf ye fuckin gae, then,' snarled Yvonne.

Recovering the leg had been the easy part. A coastguard tug, which had been monitoring the radio net, had intercepted the leg at the same time as the Zodiac, and together they had managed to tow it out of the shipping lane before it collided with the container ship. It was now chained to the side of the platform.

Meanwhile the platform was drifting slowly with the tide, dragging its remaining legs through the thick mud. The crew had been left with the task of trying to assess the damage without letting the coastguard or the Dutch maritime authorities know the full extent of it; a penalty clause in the contract required the company to remove all plant at the end of the contract. Yvonne had let them know, in characteristically crude terms, that a major salvage bill would wreck the company. They would lose all the money earned in Gaza.

They surfed the radio net as they clambered round the rig, hopping channels to outwit any listeners. A cursory examination revealed that the situation was bad but not yet disastrous. The drill pipe was lost, sheared completely away, and the condition of the legs was unknown. Because of the tide the water-level had dropped five metres and half the top section of each leg was exposed.

They looked all right.

Dutch divers dispatched by the coastguard to inspect the rig were unable to go deeper than ten metres, but what they could see of the legs appeared undamaged. Distracted by their concern for the legs, the divers had not noticed that the drilling pipe was gone. There was still a chance.

'I've a suggestion.' Cal was leaning, slightly apart from the others, with the back of his head resting against the wall of the container. A habitual pose.

Yvonne studied him with her small, suspicious eyes. There was a frisson of unstated dislike between them. She wasn't keen on educated crew-members. It made her suspicious. She seemed to think that Cal had something to hide – correctly, as it happened. Besides which, Calum was tall and Yvonne was a bantam with a healthy-sized chip on her shoulder.

'Awright, Mr University smart cunt, wat is it?'

Cal had perfected a half-hearted shrug that was designed to infuriate her. He offered his suggestion without enthusiasm. 'Bring one up.'

'Bring one up?'

'Aye, jack one up, and take a look.'

'Which one?'

Calum knew exactly which one. He unfolded himself batlike off the wall. Yvonne locked her fingers together, turned down her palms, and cracked the joints.

The Volvo powerpack squealed, and the handle on the hydraulic ram began to twist in Cal's hands, the collar mashing the lugs. The whole leg was bending like forge-work as it came up out of the bearing. There was a stripped-bare moment of silent astonishment, then Cal began to run, slipping and sliding across the grillwork on the deck. Everyone ran.

The powerpack seized. The ram fractured and shattered, spraying shrapnel and scalding hydraulic oil across the deck. The protruding leg shuddered above them like a sapling in a storm. There was a rending sound as welds began to crack inside the bearing and the individual sections began to twist and tear.

Somewhere, Dave was screaming in pain.

Cal lay clinging to the deck and life, his mouth full of seawater. Around him Dave's screams and the whistle of splinters seemed to swell and recede and swell again.

In the course of those few seconds Cal experienced an important insight; he did not welcome it, although it came as no surprise. The insight was that he had no courage. For over two years, and with casual arrogance, he had striven through hard physical labour to put behind him an act of cowardice. Cowering on the deck, he realised that he was no further from that act of capitulation than he had ever been.

The leg snapped. The rig groaned and staggered like a drunkard.

Cal looked out from between his fingers. The upper two sections remained wedged at an angle out of the top of the bearing, but the lower two sections had fallen away and sunk into the water. The hash was gone.

He ran across the deck to the powerpack and hit the STOP button. Turning, he saw that Yvonne was standing over Dave and shouting at him. She was stocky like the rig, a box-shaped woman as wide as she was tall; her voice as big as she tried to be.

'Wat's yer fuckin name, son?'

Calum went across to them. Dave was a sickly grey-green colour and he was having trouble focusing. Shock.

Yvonne bellowed, 'Wat's yer fuckin name?'

Dave looked confused. He shook his head. 'Dave,' he said at last.

'Welcome back.' Yvonne knelt down beside him and for one brief, tender moment she rested the back of her hand against his cheek. She looked up briefly at Cal. 'Gae fir the stretcher. I ken the wee tube has broken his pelvis.'

'Cheers,' Dave said. 'Cheers very much'.

'I'm dead,' Cal announced; an agonising appraisal.

'Never mind that,' Yvonne told him. 'Let's jus git oaf this rig – and fuckin pronto.'

Five hours later, bone-tired and sodden, Cal staggered back across the hotel car-park past a once metallic-blue Ford Escort Cosworth that was now splattered with fan-tails of glutinous mud, and parked, or rather discarded, diagonally across two clearly delineated parking spaces. He climbed the steps and went into the striplit foyer. The balding receptionist glared at him with bulbous eyes as he squelched past, leaving muddy footprints on the bright linoleum.

The door to his room had been kicked open – the wood panelling was cracked and splintered – and inside he found his cousin Sebastian MacCoinneach stretched out on the bed, fully clothed, with his mud-caked cowboy boots on the twisted sheet, a tumbler full of Scotch in one hand and a cigarette in the other.

'Flew into Schiphol,' Seb explained. He inhaled, then blew a thin plume of smoke in Cal's direction. 'A few hours to kill. I'd heard you were here so I thought I'd come and see you. You look like shit.'

Cal didn't bother asking how Seb had found him; he knew that he wouldn't get an answer. Seb removed his sunglasses; the whites of his startling azure eyes were streaked with threads of red. Stoned. Cal hadn't seen him for two years, not since a Monday morning in a layby on the M4.

'Well?' Seb demanded.

'I thought that if I saw you again there'd be trouble,' Cal said.

'And now you're seeing me again.'

'That's right.'

'And there's trouble?'

'The rig sank,' Cal explained. 'I've spent the last two hours being grilled by the coastguard. The company I work for has gone bankrupt – and by the way I'm dead.'

'You're exaggerating.' Seb jumped up off the bed. 'Here, sit down.'

Cal sank heavily on to the bed, and rested his head in his hands. Seb watched him from the dressing-table. Cal sighed, and rubbed his face with his palms.

'Where have you been?' he asked, trying to make conversation.

'Moscow,' Seb replied, with enthusiasm. 'Making deals with expatriate Chechen gangsters.'

This meant nothing to Cal, who hadn't read a broadsheet for months.

Seb explained as he squeezed droplets from a plastic vial on to his contact lenses, 'Chechens from Chechnya. Pesky republic in the Caucasus. Not a good place to be right now. Boris Yeltsin is busy bombing the shit out of it as we speak. The wisest rats have fled to brighter climes. Cyprus, for instance.'

Cal frowned. 'Not work, then?'

'Definitely not. This is something else entirely. More your line. Moving weight, I mean.'

The telephone rang. Cal answered it; it was Byron.

Byron owned the hash. The hash that was now lost at the bottom of the sea. 'I thought I'd come on over. I heard you had a few problems.' He said it in a flat menacing tone, as a statement not a question. Cal was shocked: news travelled fast.

Seb was unimpressed, opening and closing his eyes, bright tears on the harsh planes of his face. 'Let him come, mate. I'll show him. You'll see.'

'Where would you be without me?' Seb said accusingly. 'You'd be down there on the floor like him.' This was their relationship, through and through. Seb's face was terrible, exultant. There was blood on the mirrored panes of his aviator Ray-Bans, bright-red on bronze in the striplight; and on the cloth of his button-down blue oxford shirt.

He touched the left hand corner of his mouth and then the right. 'I'll slice you quick,' he spat.

Byron, turtled on the ground and already badly beaten, turned backwards in a panicking flail of arms and legs. Seb, after three breathtaking strides, caught him, turned his Purdey blade flat and opened Byron's right cheek and then his left.

'Like orange peel.' He stopped, then whispered: 'I can hear your heart.'

If it was in the nature of their relationship that Seb hauled Cal out of the shit, the trade-off was that Seb's methods could be without bounds. Suddenly he smiled, revealing rows of razor-bright teeth; and reached out and laid a hand on Cal's shoulder and squeezed.

'Excellent, lover.' The same voice, but beguiling now; his spirits were back. *The knife* – that slice of malignant vigour in his character that worked on the blind side of reasonable behaviour – never showed for long. Cal wondered briefly, and with no reason that he could later fathom, if Seb might try and kiss him.

Instead: 'How much fur duh nigguh?'

Seb stepped away, over Byron's slowly twisting body, flicking his black hair away from his face and lighting a Silk Cut. The gleaming bronze Zippo left a draft of petrol fumes in his wake.

'Come on, Calum, get a grip,' Seb commanded, without looking at him. 'What did you lose? What do you owe the man?'

'Ten kilos of hash. I'm not really sure.'

'Is that all?'

He spun round and strode back across the room, like a panther in a small cage, exactly, Cal imagined, as he had carried himself after the Provos threw a nailbomb at him, or after he'd cleared a bunker of Iraqis with white phosphorus. He scooped up the Karrimor rucksack that he had discarded at the onset of violence. It was bulky and full. He unclipped the lid, half-tipped it and loosed a waterfall of twenty-dollar bills that rained down on Byron's body. Thousands of dollars' worth. They clung to Byron's bloody cotton shirt and to his hands, which were cupped over his face.

'One of these knives is worth all this heap,' Seb announced – obviously quoting though Cal didn't recognise the source. Seb leant over the bloody body, his face pleasant and his tone matter-of-fact, 'Your pound of salt, fuckwit.'

He kicked Byron so hard that the sound of breaking ribs could be heard above the rasping noise issuing from his throat. 'Whadyathink?'

Calum shook his head.

'*Robinson Crusoe*,' Seb explained. He had a seemingly inexhaustible supply of quotes.

The rucksack was still brimming with money. He clipped it shut and flung it on the divan bed. 'I think I'll wash my hands.'

A few minutes later he stepped dripping from the bathroom. His torso and upper arms were a manuscript of Celtic designwork, blue-black ink tattoos, shield-roundels and knotwork torques, serpents eating themselves, and wrestling saints. His warrior signs. He balled up his bloodstained shirt and stuffed it in the rucksack on top of the money. He dragged his black leather jacket off the bed, slipped it on and zipped it up to the throat.

Cal said, 'What now?'

'We leave,' Seb told him.

Together, they watched Byron's slow progression across the carpet. He was heading for a corner, and had left a trail of stray notes and bloody handprints behind him. He was breathing heavily, like a blunt saw in a log.

Seb said, 'You want to go home?'

Cal hadn't been home for two years. 'I suppose so.'

'I need you there, mate,' Seb said, and then, with a change of tack, 'It's your brother's wedding next month.'

Cal considered this. He hadn't known.

Seb ground the heel of his boot down on the side of Byron's head. He said, 'You'll do me the courtesy of paying me your full attention, Byron. This money, the money that I have paid you, is dirty. Really dirty. So dirty, in fact, that if you try to spend it here you'll have every law-enforcement agency in Europe on your case so fast you won't even have time to breathe, and right on their heels will come the FBI, and after them all sorts of heavy people. So clean the money before you spend it. Do I make myself clear? Or should I kick the fuck out of you again? Do I make myself clear?'

'Yes,' Byron whispered.

Seb looked across at Cal. 'Does this guy know where you live?'

'No.'

'What about the company?'

Cal let out a strangled laugh. 'What company? They'll have shredded everything by now and run for the Caribbean.'

'And the coastguard?'

'I gave them a false name and address. I said my passport went down with the rig.'

'Did it?'

'No.'

Seb nodded, apparently satisfied. 'Good man. You're learning.' Then he added, 'Have you got any money?'

'No.'

'Here.' Seb reached into the back pocket of his jeans and pulled out a silver money clip. He selected five crisp notes and held them out to Cal. Cal stared at them, and at Seb's freshly scrubbed fingers.

'Don't worry,' Seb said, knowingly, 'They've been through the washing-machine.' And then that brilliant, infectious smile, the luminous halo in his azure eyes. 'Come on, mate, let's go to Amsterdam. I've got a monster hire car.'

'A thrust, mate, with a sharp blade into the corridors of wealth.' He jabbed two fingers at Cal, across the top of the tall glasses of lager, trailing smoke and ash from the coffee-shop skunk joint wedged between them. 'That's my dream. Stick it in, twist it and pull it out. Quick.' He pulled his fingers back, and downed a mouthful of beer, then unselfconsciously wiped his lips with the back of his hand. 'That's what I want. No hanging around. A lightning crusade, a pre-emptive strike if you like, while the market is still wide open, and before the London dealers have moved in.' He held out his cupped hands as if they held something precious. 'Ulster. The new market place. It's like the Berlin Wall coming down: the opening of a closed market that for too long has been dominated by IRA Marxist-lunatics. Everybody wants a piece of the action. I mean, Sainsbury's is opening new stores. It's the future.' He paused, grim-faced. 'A carefully selected team of operators. A cell-structure. A tight plan. I mean *so fucking secure'* – a rictus of threatened violence on his face. 'We swamp the province with drugs, and earn enough money never to have to do it again. Once it's done, we walk away with our hearts softened and grateful and our pockets full of spondoolicks.

'Listen to me. I've read Howard Marks, the boyo from the valleys and all that shite. Know this. He had to build himself up: he might have been to Oxford but he wasn't connected for a one-time job, not like me. He had to put the apparatus in place, set up a logistic chain. Once he'd set it up the temptation was to go on using it. He was too successful too many times. I'm not saying he was greedy – after all he believed in what he was doing. He just overdid it, and the maxim holds true: they'll get you in the end. I don't want any of that.'

He was burning. It was like basking in the glow of an atomic reaction, you could feel the heat of his intent. It had always been this way. Cal loved him for it. They played pool in Hunter's bar, and Seb didn't stop talking, leaning far over the cue, always with a joint hanging off his lip, his eyes never leaving the table.

'Never flinch from the power of money. You said it yourself: the Freedom To Live . . .'

Cal's words. Five years old now. Clinging to the scaffolding on the clock face of the North British Hotel on a crisp February night with Princes Street Gardens beneath them and Edinburgh all around them, and older blackened masses, the castle, Salisbury Crags and the sphinx-shape of Arthur's Seat, the old volcano, driving wedges up through the city's sodium light; and the full moon above them, white as bone; shouting those very words: the Freedom To Live.

'Listen to this. Nothing in use by man, for power of ill, can equal money. Whadyathink?'

Cal shrugged. It was a game they played. Name that quote. He said slowly, 'It's all Greek to me.'

'Very good,' Seb said. 'Sophocles, in fact.' He paused. 'We're the same, you and I. Just different ends of the political spectrum. I'm a libertarian, you're an anarchist, but we believe the same thing. Everything is permitted, right?'

Everything? It was a source of constant bafflement to Cal that Seb saw no apparent contradiction between his private conduct and his public persona.

'Not everything,' Cal said, eyeing the table, his chin resting on the tip of the cue.

There was a pause.

Seb laughed disconcertingly. He relished the disconcerting. 'Sure, of course not everything,' he said. He keenly watched the effect his words had on listeners, and he was always eager to talk. It was a feature of command. 'Cannabis – you've said it yourself – should be made available to everyone.'

'You're not frightened of getting caught?'

He laughed. 'I'm a redeemed soul. The Lord wouldn't cast me away.'

Cal shook his head, suppressing a smile. 'So who benefits?'

'We do.'

'Over there?'

It took Seb a few seconds to understand. 'In Ulster? Don't worry about it. People like us. Think about it, an engine for peace.'

They parted at Schiphol airport, in the departure lounge, Seb taking a flight for Cyprus while Cal waited for a later flight to London. Seb was wearing a brand-new shirt from one of the airport boutiques, and still carrying his rucksack full of money.

'En route to the Limassol launderette,' he explained. 'Chechens like their money laundered in Cyprus. See ya.'

Cal rode out the flight from Schiphol curled up in his seat, whitening beneath the bleaching glare of the bulkhead striplights. He slept for a short time and woke on the runway at Heathrow. It was just after dawn. There was a dull ache in his head and in the upper arch of his jaw. The mark of his beating. He scoured the ridgelines of hard plastic with the tip of his tongue.

When the plane was almost empty he retrieved his rucksack, which was his only luggage, from the overhead bins, smiled halfheartedly at the attendants, whose eyes flicked across him without interest, and followed the arrivals signs through the maze of antiseptic-smelling corridors. He went through passport control swiftly and passed baggage reclaim and all the milling passengers. He was stopped at customs, in the blue channel, the customs officer gesturing to him across the broad, deserted channel. He went through Cal's bag and found nothing but dirty clothes and his blow-torches and hoses and dog-eared books and notebooks.

He held up the shank of Cal's welding torch. 'What is this?'

'It's a welding tool.'

The customs officer put it down gently, on the surface of the desk right next to the bag. 'Is that what you do?'

Cal smiled faintly and shrugged. 'It looks that way.'

The customs officer clicked his teeth and looked up from rummaging in the bag. 'You're an activist.'

'What makes you say that?'

The man didn't bother to reply. 'You can go,' he said. He watched carefully as Cal repacked his bag, an expression of barely concealed contempt on his face.

Cal travelled on the Underground from Heathrow. He dozed between switching trains. It was light when he reached Stoke Newington, and beginning to snow. The squat was on the Kingsmead estate, on the third floor of a dismal-grey block of flats. The concrete stairwell was slick with yellow-green fungus and blurred graffiti, and the steps so deep in crushed glass and slush that it was as if he was rising through a subterranean waterfall.

The party had been going for two days, the heavy Dub sound beating in the stairwell. The lock was splintered and the rivets hanging out of the thin steel plate on the door. He ducked his head as he entered the hallway, and picked his way through the people crouched there. He felt as if he was gliding. The main room was full of heaving bodies and the sound system, and a jury-rigged strobe light. Girls in lycra and boots. Ecstasy. He slid between them. He spotted Kelly weaving drunkenly towards him, a bottle of Tesco scotch in her hand. She was wearing Doc Martens, black tights and a short red tartan skirt. There were threaders of beads in her hair.

She saw him and screamed, 'Calum!'

She grabbed him around the neck and shouted drunkenly in his ear, 'Happy new year!' though it was still November. She crushed her lips against his and her tongue went into the roof of his mouth. She smelt of whisky and cigarettes. He gently lifted her away and set her down and she stumbled away with the bottle gripped firmly in her hand.

He crossed the kitchen through a group of men, two Rastas and three white guys, one of whom he knew vaguely, a plumber from Leith. He was spraying WD40 on his scuffed para boots and dancing around. The others were reeling back and forth watching him; a chillum was being passed round, coils of white smoke drifting up from it. Calum begged a hit and raised the clay funnel, gripped between his cupped hands, to his forehead and then to his lips and inhaled deeply. He nodded, his eyes watering, and passed the pipe. He blew the smoke out of his nose. He staggered slightly. He felt better now, more in tune with his surroundings, the pain in his mouth receding.

He found Al in a bedroom. Four guys and a skinny girl were

sitting on the floor beside a mattress strewn with coats and intertwined bodies. Cal stood in the doorway watching them, Al bending over the square of aluminium foil with his tatty black locks tied away from his face with a rubber band, running the lighter back and forth beneath the heroin, dragging the smoke up through a foil tube.

When he was done he lifted his red-rimmed eyes to Calum and nodded slowly, 'Awright there, big yin?'

'Aye.'

'You wanna hit?'

Cal shook his head.

'Please yersel.'

Al's jaw drifted down onto his chest and he seemed to pass out.

Seconds later his head jerked back up again and he smiled, his mouth filled with yellowed stubs of teeth. 'I saw yer fren Seb and some auld Provo fucker,' he said, 'jus a cupil ae months ago. Fucker dissed me.'

'Aye.'

'He's a cunt.'

'Aye.'

Cal could well imagine. Seb despised heroin and wasn't afraid to direct his fury at anyone he found using it. Heroin was Seb's bugbear, his one passionate dislike. Seb's elder brother Rory had died after taking an overdose.

'Thir's werk fir ya,' Al said, 'at Claremont Road.'

'I see.'

Al drifted away again. One of the guys on the floor was glaring up at him; he had a thin, sharp nose and his eyes seemed too close together. Cal shifted the weight on the balls of his feet and stuck his chin out. The guy dropped his head and stared at the frayed brown and black carpet.

Cal went looking for Kelly. He found her slumped in a corner with her hands still on the bottle. He prised it gently from her fingers, took a swig and handed it to the nearest person. He lifted her on to his shoulder and carried her to her bedroom, laying her down on the pile of blankets on the mattress in the corner of the room. He looked around, and snowflakes wafted over him, borne through the open window on a cold gust of wind. Kelly had started to snore. He went to the window and pounded at it, and the window loosened in its frame and slid shut with a bang. He paused, resting his forehead against the cold glass, watching the falling snow melting on the pavement outside. Then he pulled a blanket from under Kelly, and got down beside her and dragged the thin, coarse blanket over them both. She mumbled and shifted on the bed. He put his cheek against hers, and listened to the firm cadences of her breathing. Her flesh was cold. He put his arms round her and held her to try to make her warm.

·

2

Cal fed the last of the rod into the molten pool, chased the white-hot metal to the end of the weld, splashed fire across the two surfaces, and lifted the torch away, pushing his goggles up on his blackened, grimy forehead. He turned down the acetylene and then the oxygen, listening for the pop as the flame was extinguished.

'Hello, Cal,' said a voice behind him.

Lieutenant Sebastian Raasay MacCoinneach stood, like Achilles before the gates of Troy, a congruence of perfect health and coordinated strength, surveying the preparations for battle taking place around him: the steel barricades, the piles of car tyres, and shopping trolleys embedded in cement.

Claremont Road.

Cal had heard the explosion, and seen the pall of dust, out on the cordon half an hour before. They all had. They had wondered if it marked the onset of the eviction. Now he had a nasty suspicion that the bomber was closer to hand.

'Here for the fall of the Reichstag? You've dug yourselves in well, mate. I've been looking around. What a sight.' Seb grinned, a huge, wide-open grin, bright white in the gloaming.

At Seb's shoulder stood Ed Crowe, one of his regular phalanx. Ed maintained an office in Soho staffed by teams of girls with home-counties accents, and made irregular forays into the world of TV production. He travelled internationally, 'raising money'.

He offered Cal an asthmatic inhaler. 'Toot?'

'No, thanks,' Cal replied. He rarely touched cocaine.

'I heard you'd be here,' Seb explained, 'so I came down for a recce. FIBUA, we call it, fighting in built-up areas. This is better than anything I've ever seen. Underground passages. Rat runs.'

The stark, rubble-filled and fortified row of terraced houses loomed above them, as did the huge floodlit banner on the hundred-foot scaffold tower that brandished its words at the two-hundred-strong contingent of riot police and the twenty or more bailiffs waiting beyond the perimeter: 'Claremont Road, E11, says No to the M11 link'.

'Do you get paid for this?' Ed asked.

'I'm a volunteer,' Cal explained. Ed looked disgusted.

'They should teach this down at Warminster,' Seb observed, looking around.

Donga tribespeople scrambled across the netting strung between the houses and the trees. Everywhere there was frantic last-minute activity.

He turned his attention to Calum. 'You've been keeping busy.'

Cal, at six foot three, was three inches taller than Seb; it made him feel awkward and gangling. 'How did you get in through the cordon?' he asked.

'Trick of the trade,' Seb drawled. He was wearing ripped, mud-stained jeans, a black leather jacket and a black wool skull-cap. There were silver hoops in his ears. He called it security and survival – his 'double life'. Most off-duty army officers can be identified at a hundred paces by their manners, their haircuts, their clothes and the shine on their shoes. Not Seb – his armour adapted chameleon-like to his surroundings.

There was a thick cone-shaped Indica blunt poking from between his index finger and forefinger. Away from the army, away from his bespoke tweed suits and sporting interests, he was rarely without a joint.

Cal confronted him. 'Did you set off a bomb?'

Seb frowned, his eyes fixed on an unknown horizon. 'Don't be like that. It was just something to kick up dust.'

'A firework,' Ed said, 'nothing more.'

Cal groaned. He was tired and exasperated. He hadn't slept for two days and his arms ached from holding steady while welding. 'It doesn't exactly help our cause.'

Seb lifted the joint to his lips and inhaled, the dim coal flaring brightly. 'I didn't know you cared about roads?'

Cal removed his leather gauntlets and flexed his fingers. 'It's not just roads, it's them taking liberties.'

'Kill the Bill?' mused Seb. 'Kill the pigs.'

Sometimes Seb could be truly wide of the mark.

Cal asked, 'What are you doing here?'

The smoke rushed out of Seb's nose and mouth. 'Our last day of freedom,' he said eventually. 'It looks like you're going to gaol for a public-order offence and I'm going back to school.' He looked straight at Cal. 'You're supposed to be in Scotland. I need you.'

Calum asked flatly, 'Why?'

He was grinning, the mischief in him glinting like parhelion in his eyes. That infectious, dangerous grin. 'It's happening . . .'

Calum shook his head. 'What's happening?'

'It, you fool, it.' Seb was laughing. 'The Freedom To Live.'

'At Her Majesty's pleasure?' asked Cal cynically.

Seb replied with a brief curl of the mouth that suggested contempt. He said, 'At our own pleasure.'

'You're serious,' Cal observed, studying his face.

'Never been more so.' The shade of contempt was just as suddenly gone. 'A golden opportunity. Everything is in place. I couldn't say that when we spoke before. There were loose ends to tie. Cyprus, for instance. Now everything is set up.'

Cal looked away from him, out across the steel barricades he'd been working on for the last two days. Already gangs of protesters were struggling against the encroaching darkness, pouring the concrete that would set them in the road. Bonfires were being lit around them.

'You're finished here,' Seb said, echoing his thoughts. 'You've done your bit. It's good, but it won't take the police more than a couple of days to dismantle it.'

'There's other places,' Cal protested. 'The Pollok Free State.'

'And keep losing?'

'Maybe.'

'You'd be set up for life,' Seb countered. 'An eternal protester. Think of it. No more shitty oil-rig jobs to tide you over. No more McJobs. No more working for the enemy.'

Calum shrugged.

'Listen to me,' Seb persisted. 'You've been there since the beginning. The Freedom To Live. You gave it its name.'

One drunken night a long time ago.

'What about the army?'

'What?' he sneered, genuinely outraged. 'Fuck the army. It's finished. Dull, penny-pinching and visionless. I have a real vision.'

'And what exactly do you want me to do?'

'Go home to Scotland and see my sister,' Seb said, and jabbed a couple of fingers at him. 'Keep an eye on her while I'm away. Don't fuck her.'

Cal rewarded him with a wide grin – as an occasional lover of Madelene des Esseintes, Seb's wildly unpredictable and absurdly beautiful half-sister, Cal had developed a philosophical attitude to her behaviour – but some shade of anger on Seb's face made him modify his expression.

'Sort Dougie Hogg out,' Seb continued, coldly. 'Pay him cash for his boat. We need it to bring the merchandise ashore.'

'Merchandise?'

'Sure. Merchandise, weight, whatever. Get Dougie to deliver the boat to the cove on the estate. Seal his lips. That's all, for now. More to follow later.'

Seb glanced at his watch, a Rolex. He claimed that it was a Hong Kong fake, but Cal suspected it was real. He added, 'There's clean money waiting for you, you know where.'

'Where are you going?' Cal asked.

'Back to school, mate, like I said. Belfast. To keep the peace. I'm flying tomorrow.'

'He's a man with a plan,' Ed Crowe said.

Calum nodded slowly. 'Well, give us a toke on that. I'm gasping.'

Cal waited a week. He watched from safety while the police and the bailiffs moved in and dismantled the fortifications at Claremont Road. He turned down the offer of other protests. He slept late in the day. Sometimes he tried to imagine Seb in Belfast, but it seemed too large a leap of the imagination. That side of Seb's life was entirely closed to him.

Eventually he gave up fighting it, and decided to go back to Scotland.

Al and Kelly accompanied him to Victoria Station. They were stoned, and staggered slightly as they fought against the wind from the Underground station to the coach station. It was snowing again, though it seemed that there was little prospect of it settling, and cars churned past them spraying tailfeathers of slush. Al was limping, dragging his pinned and plated leg, the result of a motorcycle accident. That morning Cal had asked him why he was doing heroin.

'Fer the pain,' Al explained. 'It stops the pain makin us violent.'

They drank coffee in the station café, next to the cavernous terminus building and ranks of coaches. Al stared at the scratched Formica table-top without speaking. There were beads of sweat running down his face and stinging his eyes. Kelly called him an asshole. Cal could never quite understand why she stuck by Al. It wasn't much of a relationship. She gave ten pence to a tramp.

'Ah've had enough of this shit,' she said.

'We'll go back together,' Cal suggested.

She shook her head. 'It's no better in Scotland. An what about him? Ay take him back and he'll start using needles for sure.'

Al grunted and sank further down in his seat.

'His problem is he suffahs fae reverse vertigo. He gits frightened if he's not high.'

'My bus,' Cal said.

'I'll chum yer,' she said, and, standing, hooked her arm through Calum's. They walked across the café floor, arm in arm, steering between the tables and out into the terminus, leaving Al asleep at the table. It was bitterly cold. The snow settled on her hair like powder. Their breath went out in front of their faces like steam.

They stopped in front of the Glasgow coach and he turned to face her and held her shivering body against his. Her nose was red and the hairs lining the moist tubes of her nostrils were frozen white.

'You're always special Cal.'

It surprised him.

'I missed you when you were gone,' she said.

They fumbled for each other's mouth, coming together in a clumsy, passionate kiss. Afterwards she searched his face, and he did not know if she had found whatever it was she was looking for. She pulled the zip of his jacket up to his throat.

'Take care,' she said, and seemed to skip away, slipping from his grasp and disappearing into the darkness – back to her boyfriend. He had the feeling that in one unguarded kiss he had ruined a friendship.

The coach was filled with roughnecks heading back to Aberdeen and a month on the rigs. They shared Buckfast and Special Brew and chain-smoked and abused the driver so that he nearly threw them all out – he eventually relented – and they arrived in

Glasgow the next morning with Calum having had no sleep at all.

He walked up and down Sauchiehall Street while waiting for his connection. The shops were shuttered and there were people slumped in the doorways beneath shreds of plastic and handout blankets.

The bus to Kennacraig was empty and he curled up on the wide row of seats at the back and slept until Inveraray, where the bus stopped briefly and he stretched his legs by walking out from the granite breakwater on to the wooden pier. He stared out across the choppy waters of Loch Fyne at the snow-covered mountains of Kintyre, and for the first time since his arrival from Holland his head felt clear.

He had a short wait at the ticket office at Kennacraig while they unloaded the Cual ferry. He drank coffee from the machine and acknowledged those people he recognised.

As he boarded the ferry, one of the crewmen called out to him from the upper deck. 'Are you coming back to work on the ferry, Calum?'

He just smiled and waved.

When the ferry had cleared the shelter of Loch Tarbert and was heading out into the gale, he borrowed a red Cal-Mac water-proof and went out on the deck. He worked his way round hand over hand through the spray, and stood against the railings on the balcony with the lighted windows of the bridge above him. The ship surged into a trough and a huge wave broke across the bow and swept the deck, throwing him against the superstructure. He grinned maniacally and staggered forward, looping his arms through the railings, holding on as the ship rose and fell.

He was going home.

Cual is the head and shoulders of a drunken hunchback, ravaged by too many years sleeping rough, and its companion island, Garbh, is his misshapen conical hat. Glaciers, volcanoes and Atlantic storms have etched their mark on the island's face. Its protuberant nose is veined with pink gneiss, foliated bands of sandstone known as the Rhinns of Cual; its single flared nostril is a deep sea loch, with the island's capital, Deochmore, at its root; its open mouth is a broad bay with ten kilometres of white sand beach known as the Big Strand; its stubbly jaw is the crags and inlets of the thickly forested coastline to the south-east and its bare chin is the huge granite outcrop known as the Og, with the island's cemetery at the rim of its cliffs and a whirlpool at its base. The convex curvature of the hunchback's spine is an expanse of open moor, its vertebrae the outcrops of dolerite and basalt haphazardly strewn amongst the heather.

Cal had grown up on the rocky ground overlooking Garbh, on a farm, an old Viking settlement, named Skurryvaig. His cousin Seb lived on the far side of the moor, on a secluded and heavily forested estate, Murbhach; it had become a kind of surrogate home to him.

After a couple of hours at sea Cal could just about make out the lumpen outline of the Og, and the raging surf of the whirlpool at the base of its cliffs.

On a good day you could see Antrim in Ireland from the ferry, but not today, and staring into a rent in the whiteness he thought of his friend Seb over the water in Ireland, and the fear was with him again, and a dull ache in his jaw. Then he saw the large metal sheds of the Port Claganach distillery.

He was offered a lift to Skurryvaig by one of the abattoir workers but decided instead, as he always did when he returned to Cual, to head for the Murbhach estate. He hitched a lift from one of the workers at the Clambrach distillery, who dropped him off at the head of the driveway to Murbhach.

MacCoinneach territory.

The entrance to the estate was flanked by two man-high granite gateposts surmounted with ancient disintegrating whale vertebrae that rose into the green darkness of a beech tree. The walk down the drive took about a quarter of an hour, through tangled thickets of rhododendron. There were deep ruts in the gravel, and the middle of the drive was thick with grass. A hare ran across almost under his feet and he braced himself for The MacCoinneach's dogs, but the woods were silent except for the rain.

He passed the shinty field, with its broken wooden goalposts and rotten netting and the charred ruin of the old house, Castle Murbhach.

He walked on, passing a pile of rubber tyres, following the drive out on to the promontory. He presently came to the MacCoinneach home, a large farmhouse built around a cobbled courtyard. It had been painted white once, but not for some years. Bright ferrous stains reached from the gutters to the ground. On one side there was a covered balcony on wooden piles leaning out over the cliffside that he remembered being hung with Chinese lanterns – though not now. He passed a row of wooden sheds and assorted rusting agricultural machinery.

At the bottom of the field that led to the sea was the precarious hulk of a windmill. Like many of the long-abandoned energy-saving devices that littered the estate, it had been cobbled together from salvage, and no one could remember it ever having worked. Light was visible through the holes in its riven timbers. As children they had laid siege to it and stormed up and down its rickety staircases.

He went through the stone archway into the courtyard. Weeds flourished between the cobblestones. There were various cars parked there, including Madelene's racing-green MG and a white Land-Rover Discovery. A rusting Land-Rover 110 sat on blocks, surrounded by older, less recognisable hulks of cars.

He crossed the courtyard, to the stable block, lifted the latch on a scuffed wooden door and let himself into a small kitchen with a stairway. A large husky with a dense white winter pelt raised its head from where it had been resting across the outline of a body in an army-green sleeping bag, and stared at him with its curious clear eyes.

'Kali,' he whispered, placatory. The dog settled back down beside the sleeping bag.

He climbed the stairs noiselessly, pushed aside the batik hanging and ducked his head as he passed through into the long, low attic above the stables. It was warm; there were still glowing embers in the fire and the rain seemed to have let up. A shaft of light came down through the skylight, illuminating all the floating motes of dust and the shards of mirror in the Rajasthani hangings, and lighting on Madelene des Esseintes's immanent face. He picked his way through the gloom of bottles and cans, silk cushions and beanbags, passing a low table constructed of salvaged timbers, each thicker than Cal's thigh. He remembered the difficulty they had had hauling them out of the sea. The table was three metres long and slightly over a metre wide, standing on a metal cradle welded out of old agricultural machinery. It retained the bleached, silvery patina of driftwood, and was covered in a dense mosaic of candle-drippings, wine stains, burn marks. It was crowded with food, garbage, bongs, Rizlas and smudged glasses with cigarettes unravelling in purplish wine dregs. There were opened and unopened cans of beer, and an unsheathed Gerber combat dagger. It was a time capsule; he didn't remember it any different.

He squatted down beside her just on the edge of the light.

The bedcovers had fallen away from her chest and he stared for a few seconds at her honey-coloured skin, her breasts small and high on her slim torso, and her tiny, puckered nipples so dark as to be almost purple. Then he leant forward in the light and touched her thick coppery-blond hair. She opened her eyes. She smiled. Tiny lines under her eyes crinkled.

'Calum,' she breathed.

'Damage,' he said, using the name he had given her when he came to understand the terrible things that Seb's half-sister could do to men. The part of her that turned against them – or herself. She shifted her arm out from under the sleeping body beside her and gathered the sheet round herself, folding it under her arms. She reached out her hands and he bent down to kiss her, lingered there.

She gently pushed him away. 'You're sodden.'

'It's been raining,' he explained.

'How was the sea?'

He shrugged, 'OK.'

'Calum,' she said and reached out to touch his face with her warm fingertips, tracing the scars. 'I'm sorry.'

He shook his head, dislodging her fingers. She laid her hands behind her head and studied him. He watched the shaven hollows of her armpits.

'What for?'

Her laughter was satisfying. 'Everything,' she said. 'I missed you.'

There wasn't a day in the previous two years when he hadn't thought of her.

'Seb's in Belfast,' she said.

'I know. I saw him a couple of days back, in London.'

'He told me. On the phone. I'm going to Donegal,' she said, 'when you're ready.'

Her eyes narrowed. It wasn't lost on him, this artful inclusion of him. He understood that it was her art, a facet of her art, the manipulation of men.

'Why Donegal?' he asked.

'Because I'm in demand there. There's a country estate on the coast that's been converted to recording studios.'

'I didn't know you were a musician?'

She wrinkled her nose. 'I'm not. Some Britpop band wants a contemporary artist on their record sleeve. Blur did Damien Hirst. I get some snotty Mancunians. I had Ed Crowe fix it. You know he's my agent?'

'So is that how he's laundering money now?'

She laughed. 'He's an impresario.'

'You can't fool me. He's a drug-dealer.'

'Who are you to talk?'

'Dealers adulterate and exploit,' Cal replied. 'Smuggling is an altogether more romantic and historical profession. You forget that I remember Ed from back when. I remember when he still had an Irish accent.'

There had been a time when Ed liked to encourage the impression that he was dangerously connected in the IRA – he claimed that it gave his drug-consuming clientele a certain vicarious thrill. In fact, he was a Protestant, and a nephew to one of the 'Shankill butchers', but apparently the loyalist paramilitaries didn't carry the same romantic association as the IRA. These days Ed was getting more sophisticated: his accent had taken on a certain mid-Atlantic blandness.

'You are an ass,' she said.

He grinned. 'Come on, tell me about Donegal?'

'The location is perfect for smuggling. Its own secluded cove. People come and go all the time. You know, music people. Nobody bats an eyelid.'

The body beside her shifted, and a nest of curly black hair emerged from under the cover. A pale hand reached up and parted the hair, revealing a stubbly face and bleary eyes. 'Awright, man.'

'Hi,' Cal said, softly.

'This is Graeme,' Madelene said. She pointed to Cal. 'That's Calum, my long-lost cousin back from the sea after years away.'

They shook hands over her.

'Graeme,' she said.

'Yeah?'

'Go and wake Organ up, and get him to make some coffee. I've got to talk to Calum.'

Graeme breathed out slowly and nodded. 'Sure thing,' he said, and eased himself out of bed and staggered to a chair where his clothes were balled. He pulled on a pair of torn jeans and padded across the loft to the doorway, his belt buckle flapping.

'Where did you find him?' Cal asked.

'Ayr. Hangar 13. I brought him home. The travellers have adopted him.'

'They're still here?'

'There're three caravans now, and some benders. A few more kids.'

'How does your dad feel about it?' he asked.

'He doesn't mind. They run the estate for him. How long will you stay?'

'Until after the wedding,' Cal replied.

'And then?'

'I don't know.'

'You should stay,' she told him. 'Seb needs you.'

'I don't think so.'

She smiled.

'Look away,' she said and pulled back the covers. He stared frankly after her as she brushed past him, and stepped across the room as if she could negotiate it in the dark, which, for all Cal knew, she could. Her hips were virtually without curve. She bent down to reach for her robe as if she was touching her toes, and he was almost overwhelmed by the force of his desire.

The robe seemed to shimmer as it draped her. She stood facing him and tied it at the waist, and smiled at him with all the knowing in the world. A friend had once said that she belonged to a vanished pre-AIDS era. The sixties, the seventies. She was only twenty-five.

'What will you do with your money?'

It was a strange question. He was unprepared for it. 'I don't know,' he said.

They both laughed.

At dusk they gathered on the burial mound, and sat with their backs to the green mottled stone of the Celtic cross, waiting for the sun to sink behind the exposed boss of dolerite at Cnoc Teindire. The crisp air was filled with the eerie, pulsing sound of the didgeridoo and their own clouds of icy breath. Madelene was on her hands and knees in front of him, the scarf loosened round her neck, her tongue out at him, a small square of blotting paper on its pointy tip. She was working her way round the base of the cross, dispensing pharmaceuticals. Laughing, he grabbed at the thick lapels of her suede coat and pulled her to him, crushed his lips against hers, and she deftly transferred the tab from her tongue to his. He released her and she tumbled backwards and fell into Organ's lap. The dog Kali, spooked, jumped clear of the huddled bodies, and started barking at them. Organ was grinning through his matted Charlie Manson beard. Cal remembered Seb telling him that Organ was a viscount, whatever that might mean. Organ owned a small plane, a Cessna, and together he and Kali meandered back and forth across the country, from airfield to airfield.

On the other side of Organ, Shuard was blowing into the painted eucalyptus tube, his bare feet cupping the end of it. Cal found himself staring at the scarring between Shuard's remaining toes. Shuard never wore shoes and he had lost three toes to frostbite on Ronaldsay a couple of years before.

On the far side of Shuard sat Andy MacDonald. Andy was half black, a sometime Rastafarian, and tall and skinny like Cal. Although he was born and bred in Dundee, Andy's mother was originally from Cual and had returned after her divorce; his father was Jamaican and had not been seen for years. Andy had shared a flat with Cal at university in Edinburgh.

'How old is this place?' Organ shouted, grabbing at Cal's shoulder, his wild appearance at odds with his plummy voice.

'Over a thousand years.' Cal called back.

'When they excavated here' – Madelene was leaning towards him, her eyes very bright in the dusklight – 'they found two mutilated skeletons.'

'The blood eagle,' Cal said.

She grinned and shouted, 'Spread-eagled! The Vikings had come and pinned them face down to the earth and cut their heart and lungs out from the back!' She popped a tab in Organ's mouth, and rolled out of his grasp and on to the next person.

'Wild,' Organ drawled.

Cal levered himself up against the rough stone and staggered down off the mound, through the darkening bracken and crusted icy bog. He made a wide circuit round the cross, watching the lengthening shadows. The weak winter sun flared briefly on the edge of the stone and then it was gone, leaving strips of fading pink light. Above him Madelene was rousing the huddled bodies, pushing them towards the travellers' camp.

They followed the fractured coastline, scrambling across the broken sills, dark crystals of augite and hornblende, while out in the Sound the surf crashed against the exposed spines of stone and beyond them the islands, Craobhach, Cromag, and Bhride, and another hundred rocks scattered like coaldust in the water.

They jumped from rock to rock across the Dilistry river, and joined the slope of the road, and climbed over the drystone wall and they were in the trees. Cal followed at some distance behind them, paralleling the trail through the woods and underbrush. The wind was wild in the tree-tops, and as it rushed down the aisles and corries of the hillside it made a sound like muffled drums. He moved deftly, though it was some years since he had been in these woods at night.

The trees were already beginning to elongate and shimmer as he worked his way through a stand of paper birch, and stepped out of the ring of shadow into the glade, and walked up to the crackling log fire and the travellers' camp. He circled behind the flatbed of a Mack truck, and a Bedford van up on bricks, and through the arc of canvas benders to the fireside. The Murbhach site.

He squatted down beside Graeme and accepted a mug of scalding herb tea from him, cupping it in his hands. The rushes were strong in him now, and the act of swallowing was exaggerated, and he could feel the fluid flushing through the whirls and loops of his intestines. He passed the mug to the person next to him. There were women here by the fire, and he listened to their relaxed and easy laughter, until Shuard came out of the darkness cradling a pile of logs and tipped them into the fire, causing an explosion of sparks that seemed to dance either side of Calum's head and then draw him down into the fire's shifting heart.

When the stars were falling out of the sky as sleet, he was dragged to his feet and a flare, a flaming branch wrapped in wax-dipped cloth, was thrust into his hand. He let all the air out of him in a great whoosh and staggered back and forth staring wildly around; already there were people moving like fireflies through the trees.

They ran down through the pine trees and beyond them the tangled, overgrown ornamental gardens, dripping orange flames through the sequoia and rhodies and monkey puzzle trees, to the charred ruin of the big house, Castle Murbhach.

The castle had burnt down when Cal was fifteen, the fire apparently started by a spark from an unattended fire – he remembered the controversy, the whispers that the MacCoinneachs had done it for the insurance; rumours that had abruptly ceased when it transpired that the house had not been insured and would never be rebuilt.

You could take your pick of other suspects. Seb. Madelene. They were both fascinated by fire. Seb might have done it to get at his father. Madelene didn't need a reason. There was a logical inevitability to the destruction she caused which led Cal to believe that it was in her nature.

The door at the top of the steps of Murbhach stood open, swollen and warped so it was impossible to close. The interior smelled heavily of mildew and rat droppings. They played hide and seek, clattering up and down the listing staircase, laughing and squealing, jumping across great rents in the charred flooring, and huddling in musty corners and high windows stained with budding yellow fungus.

Some time later, Cal stood in a downstairs doorway, looked first one way and then the other, and stole across the room, stepping between the chunks of broken plaster. He was making for the kitchens, and beyond them the dungeons. He paused briefly by a plaster-filled sink to confirm that no one was following.

On the far side of the kitchen, in a wood-panelled corridor that was still relatively intact, there was a low door, and beyond it a stone stairway leading down to a warren of stone-walled dungeons and foundation pillars. He held the flare out in front of him. There were fresh prints in the dust on the flagstones; they glistened with moisture in the flare light like slug-trail.

'Size five.' He smiled.

There had been a time, a crueller time, when a tenant-turned-poacher had been incarcerated here by one of Sebastian's ancestors and suffered five years in the same cold stone room, fed with the scraps of raw meat that fell from the butcher's block and were shared with the hunting dogs. The poacher was finally released on to the mainland after Lady MacCoinneach complained of the sound of his midnight howling, and it was said that for years afterward a beast preyed upon that region of Argyll, taking the young lambs and the odd unattended human child.

That wasn't the end of the story, because, like most stories that involved the MacCoinneachs, it ended in a curse. The man's wife, cleared off the land by the laird's men, foretold that one day the MacCoinneach family would own no more land than could be covered by the spread of her apron.

The Room of Beasts was at the end of a forty-foot wall of empty, dust-laden wine racks. There was a lozenge of flickering orange light in the space between the flags and the bottom of the iron-studded door.

She was seated cross-legged on the table – Madelene's Altar of Fucking – surrounded by candlelight, with curls of smoke drifting from her nose and mouth. He staggered on the broken flagstones. She reached out and took the thick curlicues of his hair in her hands. Behind her on the walls the painted Beasts shifted and drooled.

He imagined the timbre of their lust. For some reason they made him think of Seb, knife in hand, pursuing Byron across the hotel room, flicking his knife like a scalpel; his face acquiring a visibly harder skin. A terrible mask.

'Sometimes I think Seb is a true psychopath,' he said. His voice sounded strange, distorted.

Madelene was grinning at him.

She turned the joint over in her mouth so that the coal rested somewhere in the dark cave of her upper jaw and blew smoke into his mouth to steady him. He went to the nearest wall and laid his hands against the surface of the mural.

He could still smell the oil paint, and turpentine and boiled linseed oil. It was four years since she had started the Beasts, but still they were not finished. One wall was partially white and marked with the skeletons of charcoal that would be the final beasts. There were tubes of oil paint scattered and leaking on the flagstones. He reached to pick one up. Crimson Lake. It was bright as arterial blood on his fingers. Surprised, he dropped it.

Madelene was still grinning. There was ash on her face from the camp-fire.

He reached out and touched her face, left crimson fingerprints on her cheek. She closed her eyes and blew smoke at the ceiling, exposing her neck and clavicle, the vee of her loose cheesecloth blouse. He put his hands on her neck, leaving bright palm prints. His hands were in her unbuttoned coat, and at her blouse. He reached in and played with her hard, tiny nipples with his fingertips.

'Not here,' she whispered, and pushed him away.

'I want you,' he pleaded. He heard the echo of something ugly in his voice.

'Sssh . . .'

She rested her hand on his shoulder and hopped down off the table. She placed the joint in his mouth and took one of his hands.

'Outside,' she said.

She led him back down the passageway and up the stairwell to the kitchens. They climbed out of a broken window into the walled garden, and ran through the shattered greenhouses and the orchard, and went through a small wrought-iron gate and plunged into the mass of rhododendrons.

Within minutes they had dropped into a narrow defile between dynamite-scarred rock walls, and were moving through thigh-deep drifts of leaves, while above them arched the brittle fingers of the advancing tide of rhododendrons. Cal set the flare in a fissure in the rock and grabbed at Madelene's waist. She turned in his grip and set her mouth against his, and her tongue went into his mouth and darted at the hard plastic plate there.

She whispered, 'My wounded hero.'

He unbuttoned her velvet trousers and let them fall to her knees. She was naked beneath them, the flare light on her belly and the upward curve of her thighs. She surged against his cupped hand.

'I can't,' she breathed, breaking away from his mouth, with one hand stroking at the nape of his neck and the other reaching for the damage to his mouth that so intoxicated her, her gaze flicking from his mouth to his eyes and back again, 'refuse you.'

His free hand was on his belt buckle, pulling on the tongue of cracked leather, popping the buttons on his jeans. She dropped her hand from his neck and laid it against his belly. He turned her round, pushed up the tail of her coat and held one firm buttock in his palm. She lifted a leg, her velvet trousers stretched between her ankles, and he entered her.

They heaved against each other.

Dead leaves crackled, and their breath exhaled in clouds before them. She reached above her and grasped a rhododendron branch and it shattered and showered them with dried twigs. He ran his hand up under her clothes, tracing her vertebrae, and gripped her shoulder. She flung back her head and her teeth grazed his neck. He clenched his teeth and increased the tempo of his thrusting. She began to scream. Yesyesyesyesyes.

He gasped and came. She ground against him and shuddered and was still. She breathed and he breathed and their pumping hearts gradually slowed down, and she gave an exhalation that was somewhere between a laugh and a sigh, and eased herself away. She reached down for her trousers and pulled them up to her waist.

He did not move, merely rested his head against the cold rock beside him. 'I came back for you,' he said.

She ran her fingers through the tangled knot of her hair. 'You came back because your brother is getting married and because Seb told you to.'

'No. I couldn't stop thinking about you. All the time I was in Gaza, on the way back across the Med, in Holland – I was thinking about you.'

She shook her head contemptuously. 'That's lust.'

'No.'

'Yes.'

'I think I love you.'

'No,' she said. 'I think you're lying.'

Things went very still for a few seconds. It was an oppressive realisation, to know with sudden clarity that he did not love her. That what he felt for her was something else entirely: fascination.

'You got what you wanted,' she said.

He guessed that he'd never understand her and who she really was. She was alien and unsettling. The first time he saw her, a starved and half-naked stowaway on a Cal-Mac ferry, he had felt a frisson of fear and attraction; now, as before, in the aftermath of sex with her, he felt a mixture of triumph and revulsion.

'I love someone,' she announced.

He was taken aback. 'Who?'

'You couldn't handle it.' She smiled indulgently at him in the flare light and took his hand. 'Come on, let's go down to the sea.'

He followed her down through the defile, while the rock walls grew higher about them, and then they were through the rhododendrons and a slice of star-flecked sky was visible above them.

'Nearly there,' she said.

The defile opened out abruptly at a small cove with a stone wharf littered with coils of salt-damaged rope and a rectangular hut made from piled quartz. The crystals sparkled in the moonlight. They lifted their faces to the cold salt-spray.

'It's beautiful,' said Cal.

There were stars everywhere. It reminded him of the journey across the Mediterranean, the nights spent lying on the deck watching the sky unobscured by a city's sodium haze, the gentle lapping of the water against the pontoons. The feeling of being connected to a vast, incomprehensible universe.

'I don't understand,' he said.

'No,' she agreed. 'You don't understand anything.'

They went down on to the wharf, stepping carefully between the coiled ropes and pulled themselves on to the slab of black and purple rock beyond it, so that they could see the channel out through the rocks. He stood for a few seconds watching her as she crossed the broad plate to where it fractured into a series of sharp ridges and tidal pools. She was quick and sure-footed on the rocks.

He had his own reasons for being drawn out on to the broken spur, but he did not understand why Madelene should be similarly drawn. He wanted to call out and ask her. Then he heard her name being shouted and, looking back, he saw the silhouette of a figure on the cliffs above them.

'Madelene!'

She seemed frozen on the spot with her back to them. He got the feeling that she had been stopped on the brink of some grand and dramatic gesture. Had she been about to fling herself into the water?

She came back across the rocks to him. Her eyes shone with an unaccustomed intensity.

'It's Graeme,' she said. 'So I'll have to go back.' She stared into his face for a few seconds and then, abruptly, started back towards the entrance to the ravine.

He sensed that she was disappointed in him. She was right. He didn't understand. He leapt out on to a farther rock, and another beyond it that was drenched by the sea, following the broken spur out into the sound. When he had gone as far as he could, he lay down among the barnacles and kelp and clung to the rock and stared at the torn face of the water, and was stolen away into memory.

The desiccated adder husk swam amongst the watery debris of blackened leaves and mulch that filled the milk bottle, its smeary glass just visible, wedged in a fissure in the defile. It was a typical sombre June evening, chilly and damp. The rhododendrons were still dripping, and the rough, uneven stone of the defile was dark and wet from the rain that had not long stopped. Seb was only two days back from boarding school.

Crack.

The bottle shattered, destroying further evidence of the Campbell Dairy's protracted legal battle with Seb's father for the return of over a thousand used bottles. Seb, eleven years old and already striking, lifted the .22 rifle from his shoulder, his thin lips drawn away from his teeth, baring their sharp white points. There was charcoal daubed on his face, and lime plastered in his hair. Calum, ten but nearly eleven, squeezed past him and ran forward a short bound, dropped to his knee in the wet drifts of leaves and took aim at the next bottle. The live spider; it squatted among the husks of flies. He settled his breathing, closed one eye, and on the next exhalation fired.

Crack.

The bottle shattered. Cal was a better shot than Seb. It was a fact. An unstated fact. He lifted the rifle away.

Seb leapt over him howling, his black cadet-force boot scything past Cal's ear. 'Aaaaaooouuuu!'

The next corner. The Altar of Slaughtered Rabbits. Seb had jumped round the corner and was firing rapid shots. He spun back into cover. His colour was up, his cheeks bright red beneath the charcoal and lime. They were both breathing heavily.

'Bombs,' he gasped.

Cal had already shrugged the knapsack off his back and was pulling on the drawstring. He brought out the first of the pipe-bombs. Beside him Seb was reloading. The bombs were made of ammonium nitrate fertiliser and sugar ground in a coffee grinder. Cal reached into the pocket of his threadbare grey corduroy trousers and drew out a plastic lighter. He lit the fuse with the flame and inched up to the edge of the corner.

They both counted. One . . . Two . . . Three . . .

He risked a quick glance, saw the meshed lattice of barbed wire strung with dead rabbits and feathers, and brightly coloured strips of cloth, and slices of bared flesh torn from Seb's elder brother Rory's stock of porn mags, and ducked back, flinging the bomb round the corner at the altar-mesh.

Four . . . Five . . .

Seb held out Cal's reloaded rifle to him. He took it and they balled themselves tight against the wall.

Six . . .

Crump.

Twists of barbed wire and rags of fur slapped the facing wall and spun round the corner, followed by clouds of vaporised leaves and rock-dust. The sound beat at their heads. Seb was up almost instantly and dashed round the corner into the dust, Cal scooped up his rucksack and followed, with his mouth open wide and screaming, into the murk. He nearly tripped when his trousers caught in a tangle of barbed wire, and he grazed the side of his face on the rock wall; but he stumbled on, ripping a trouser-leg at the ankle, and went round the next corner without realising it until he ran slap into a crow. The big black hoodie was suspended from the rhododendrons by steel wire and it bounced off his forehead and swung away into the dust and came back to slap him again, knocking him to the ground. Other black shapes swam in the thick air behind it.

'Crows,' Cal squealed.

'Napalm!' Seb shouted, from somewhere behind him.

Cal, realising the danger he was in, scrambled back through the leaves and dust, desperate to find the corner. He caught a draft of sulphur from the burning fuse.

He knew what it was – the creosote bomb.

Counting . . .

His hand sliding along the fractured surface of the nearside wall. The deep leaves clutching at his calves like quicksand. The bomb sailed over his head, trailing the bright-red spark of its fuse. He found the corner and threw himself round it, landing on Seb, who was kneeling with his hands over his ears.

Crump.

The blast wave. The sound. Gobbets of burning tar striking the wall opposite them, two feet away. Seb winking at him, hefting his rifle. They both jumped round the corner. The defile was full of furiously burning crows.

Cal shouted, 'Go!'

They sprinted through the defile, dodging the dripping tar, and burst out into the cove and ran across the wharf and up on to the rocks and went as far out as they could in the fading dusk light and crouched against the wet stones. Seb tore off his jacket, which had a bright lump of smouldering tar attached to it, and plunged it in the water.

He shouted, 'Yesss!'

Cal stared curiously at the water. He reached slowly into his knapsack, digging past the last of the pipe-bombs and found his torch. He drew it out and switched it on, sweeping the torch beam across the silvered blanket of sea.

'There.'

A face floating beneath the surface of the water. A pale face with large oval eyes framed by thick lashes, surrounded by a mass of floating copper hair. A girl's adolescent chest, her tiny white breasts. A brief glimpse of something beyond understanding. She sank back into the darkness and the kelp closed over her pale upper body and the last thing they saw was the shiny black cone of blubber that was her tail.

Calum was nonplussed. Beside him on the rock, all the blood had drained from Sebastian's face. He seemed frozen, his hands still immersed in the water, his jacket twisting and sinking.

'What was that?' Calum whispered. He tugged at Seb's shoulder.

The MacCoinneach, Seb's father, had, on those rare occasions when he put in an appearance at Murbhach, regaled his children with an impressive collection of ghost stories from across the world and was therefore held to be an authority on the paranormal, so it was natural for Calum to turn to Seb for guidance.

Seb was in no mood for explanation. He shoved Cal aside and

went for his rifle, his arm looping through the sling, bringing it up to his right shoulder, hissing, 'The bomb.'

He fired five shots into the water, his face set and determined. 'The bomb!' he screamed. He threw down the rifle.

Cal handed him the bomb. Seb cursed him and fumbled with the lighter, sheltering the flame in his cupped hands. The fuse caught. He held the bomb aloft. One Two Three Four Five . . .

He dropped the bomb. It struck the water. Nothing happened. The fuse was extinguished.

'Shit!' Seb grabbed the sides of his head, as if in pain.

'What is it?' demanded Cal, his voice strident and fearful.

'Somebody's dead,' Seb told him. 'Really dead.'

'Who?'

'I don't know,' he shouted, the tears running down his face. 'Don't you see? I don't know!'

Later they sat among stacks of old furniture by the edge of the swimming pool while the last of the acid worked its way out of them. On the tiles beside Cal, Madelene was clearing out a chillum with a hairpin. Graeme leant against an old oak bureau, looking hurt and resentful. Opposite them sat Andy MacDonald, cradling a can of Export.

'D'ya mind the eel,' Andy said, scooping his locks out of his face. He had a seemingly endless ability to be surprised by other people's behaviour.

Cal held his hands against his forehead and groaned. 'Naw. Can we not overlook that particular episode?'

'No chance,' Madelene said. She smiled. 'It's a shocking tale.'

Andy spluttered and sprayed his beer mid-gulp.

'Ya great oaf,' Cal said.

'Let's hear it,' Organ urged them from the shadows where he was sprawled with his head resting on Kali's chest.

'Aw, it's a classic tale,' Andy told them, wiping the bright-white beer froth from his pitted mocha chin. 'There was this girl called Tania. A friend of Maddy's fae Brighton. Expressive arts, man!' – he put it in quotation marks with his fingers. 'She was totally off her heid, like.'

'No big surprise there,' Calum said.

'You weren't complaining,' Madelene said.

'This girl liked to shag in unusual places, among other things.

Well, she took a shine to young Calum here and dragged him down here for a bit of skinny dipping and some sub-aqua pro-creation. What they didn't know was that the pool wasnae un-occupied. Ye see, Maddy's old man was going through one of his energy-saving phases.' He paused and shook his head in bemusement. 'He'd bought hisself an electric eel.'

'Wait a minute,' Organ said. 'An electric eel?'

'Aye.'

Organ looked scornful. 'Rubbish.'

'Straight up, an eel. He bought it fae Brazil or Africa, some-where like that.'

'He got it from a tropical fish dealer in Miami,' Madelene informed them.

'Ay, whatever. He was going to run the house's electricity from this beast. He was getting it all rigged up, to a generator 'n' that. It was about three metres long and black as pitch, evil-looking. It used to just lie at the bottom of the pool and every now and then it would let oaf a huge shock. This particular night Calum and Tania, totally unaware of the eel, had jumped in the pool and were going at it. Then all of a sudden, mid-shafting, the eel lets off a shock. They were blown all the way out of the pool.'

'Get outa here.'

Cal was shaking his head back and forth.

'You're blushing,' Madelene chided him.

'Wouldn't you be? Naw, wrong person to ask.'

'Fuck you,' she said softly.

'They were knocked unconscious,' Andy said. 'I was out fer a walk and when I came back in I found them lying together on the tiles, completely out of it. Yer know what the funniest thing was?'

Organ said, 'What?'

'Yer know what she said when she came to?'

'Come on,' Organ groaned, 'what?'

'Wow!' He folded over, giggling. 'That's all she said. Wow!'

3

'There's a teuchter goes in a bar in Stornoway,' Moose said, 'and I kid you not, he's goat a heid aboot the size ov a satsuma. The barman sez, ken, waz the score wi' yir heid? The teuchter says – lissen tae this – he wiz sittin by the side ovay loch doin a bit a fishin, an awoah sudden thers this butefull mermaid comes swimmin up wi nae close on. She was fuckin majic, reid hot like, wi big tits and a great figger. He sat there fur a bit, stunned like, an she sed, ayl gie you three wishes. He coodnae bileev his gud luck an whan he gets his breth back he sez, fairnuf, doll, ayll have aw the trezure in Scotland, and sure enuf thers this huge pile of gold. The teuchter just aboot had a fit, soay did. So fer nummer two wish, he sez, ayll hav the hugest flock oaf blackface sheep in Scotland. Surenuf thers this huge flock of sheep, bleetin n baain. N fir yoor final wish? the mermaid sez. So he sez, hoos about you and me, doll, goin fir a shag? And the mermaid size an wipes a teer awae frae her cheek, an sez theres noway, its nawt possibul. The teuchter looks at her, an from the waist doon shes bilt like a fish. Poor lassy, he thinks, an he wiz totally scunnered fur a minit, an then he has an idea an he sez well, doll, howz aboot a litul heid?'

'Shu'up, ye bampot,' Seb drawled, and pitched a film-wrapped egg sandwich at him. He was careful tonight to project his customary laid-back persona.

They were together in the Operations Room. This was Fort White Rock ('Camp Jericho' to the 'RA): a cluster of cages, breezeblock-clad Portakabins and corrugated steel walls that squatted at the very limit of the city, on the slopes of the Black Mountain. Beneath it were the housing estates of nationalist West Belfast, Andersonstown, the Turf Lodge, Ballymurphy . . .

Only Seb was aware of the imminent incident – the first play in his master plan. The Freedom To Live.

He dropped his boot heels off the scratched plastic surface

of the desk, which was covered in a swathe of stiffening white bread sandwiches and catering-pack biscuits, and set *High Time* – a biography of the drug-smuggler Howard Marks – on its spine.

Moose, the quick-reaction force's commander, sprawled facing him across the low-ceilinged and windowless room, with his chin resting on the unzipped steel plate that stuck diagonally outward from his flak jacket and his legs straight out in front of him with his unlaced black Matterhorns at the end of them. He was grinning, between mouthfuls of the egg sandwich that Seb had flung at him. Beside him reams of cigarette smoke drifted through the hatch from the Intelligence Cell. Behind him, in a cabinet festooned with dusty cables, the air-cooling system of the UHF radio gave a fitful, strangled gasp.

There was a patrol out. A primary team and three four-man teams in close orbit working their way down through the Turf Lodge.

Dusty, the signaller, laid a finger on the transmit button. He was squat and bulky, with a bald head that gleamed under the dirty strip lights. His voice was soft but precise. 'TangoTwoTwo this is Zero. Send locstat. Over.'

The patrol commander's swift, terse response crackled out of the speakers. 'TwoTwo. My locstat Norfolk Way. Out to you.' There was a pause, then a change of tone as he addressed the Intelligence Cell. 'Hello, DeltaFourFour, gi' me a "personnel check" on a Mr P. Bear, first name Polar, down fae the Arctic circle.'

'Arrest on sight,' CW replied. CW was the duty corporal in the Int Cell. Moose mimed side-splitting laughter. CW gave him the finger through the hatch.

Dusty sighed with resigned tolerance and pressed the transmit button. He said, 'Watch your voice procedure.'

One by one the teams reported their location. Dusty reached up and, using a crayon-stained rag, erased part of the yellow line that marked the patrol's progress across the tribal map-board towards BravoAlpha, the Andersonstown police station.

'Red One oan the couch,' Moose observed, jovially, 'n nice n toasty.'

It was as if the patrol commander had heard him. 'Red One this is TangoTwoTwo. Ay'll see you in BravoAlpha in fifteen minutes. Out.'

Seb grinned maliciously.

'Ah ta fuck,' Moose muttered, and he dug under his chair among the crisp wrappers and clingfilm for his Kevlar helmet and rifle.

There was a long crackling as someone held down the stud on their fist mike. 'Check oot the size o' that heid!'

'Great patter,' Moose grumbled as he got up. He was six five and gangling, with a misshapen head and prominent teeth.

'Boss.' Gash, the medic, put down his cup of herbal tea and tapped the screen. 'Take a look at this.'

Casually, it was happening. There was no visible epiphany, or commotion. Just a voice in his head. So loud. It shouted, *Now!*

'Zoom in,' Seb instructed, and coasted over to Gash on his wheeled chair. He suppressed a nonsensical desire to start counting. If he started now there was no telling when it would end.

The man seemed to come from nowhere.

There was sleet in the wind, gusts of it, and it played across the screens like static. Gash was squinting and tapping at the screen, already directing the zoom at the jumbled blocks of concrete on the approach road. There was a sudden movement by the electronic bollards and then a shape, the form of a man with a slight but noticeable limp, struggling against the wind towards the Fort. The flash of something metal in his hand. Seb was conscious of Moose standing at his shoulder, just as he had hoped. It was up to Moose now to recognise the man, and after him CW. Vital for the unfolding plan. They got a short glimpse of the man's face lifted to the camera and then he was inside its range.

'Ootcha.' Moose frowned. 'Tell me thas noat who ay think it is . . . ?'

Seb clicked his fingers, the skin of his face taut against the bone, apparently struggling for the name. Secretly he was rejoicing.

'I'll get it . . .' he said. Then he stopped as if it had come to him suddenly. He looked at Moose, who was looking at him, his face guarded. Moose was thinking the same; neither of them wanted to say the name for fear of jinxing it.

'Mebbe,' Moose agreed, his upper teeth in his lower lip. Then he smiled. 'Mebbe it's his twin brother.'

'CW,' Seb called out. He put his hand on Gash's shoulder. 'Get us another angle.'

CW stuck his head through the hatch from the Int Cell and

tongues of bluish cigarette smoke drifted out past his head. Gash was searching with the camera mounted on the main comms mast, and then they had the man again, still coming on, with high walls of corrugated steel either side of him.

'Tell me that's not somebody you recognise, who's wantin a cup of tea n a bit ay a blether?' Moose said, pointing.

CW said, 'Oisin MaColl.' He added, 'I'd bet my life.'

The intercom crackled and spluttered into life. 'Ops Room, this is the gate sentry. Ah've goat a walk-in.'

Walk-in: unexpected visitor. The OC and the Ops Officer were at the Grosvenor Road police station at an RUC function. Seb was the senior officer in the fort, so it was his responsibility to talk to any unexpected visitors. It was on his shoulders. Everyone was looking at him.

He reached for the packet of Silk Cut by the row of phones. 'Who's on the gate?'

'That druth Macrae,' Moose replied. 'He was nae with us in ninety – he'll not ken who it is, suh.'

The intercom crackled again.

'Ops Room, this is the gate sentry, ken. There's a scrot here says he wants to speak to the boss man. He's on the swally like.'

'Did he tell you his name?' Seb enquired, tipping his head to one side.

'Aye. Mouse, he says. Michael Mouse.'

They looked at each other: CW smiling in the hatch, Moose easing himself out of his flak jacket.

'You could buy a forty-watt light bulb brighter than Macrae,' Moose explained.

Seb hit the button again. 'Keep him there. I'm on my way.' He lifted the palp of his thumb slowly off the machine.

'Get doon off the ceilin, boss,' Moose advised him sagely. He reached across with his Zippo and lit the cigarette poking out of Seb's mouth. 'Take a Condor moment.'

Anticipating Seb's order, Dusty issued instructions for the patrol to make its way to the Andersontown police station and await further orders.

'Moose, take the chair and don't log it in the book,' Seb told him.

'Jambo, boss.'

Seb stood up and took a long drag on the cigarette. He

ran his fingers through his hair and grinned. 'Wish me luck,' he said.

It was startlingly cold outside. He paused for a moment in the space between the door of the Portakabin and the surrounding blast-walls to draw the zip on his smock and finish the cigarette. Small preparations. He scanned the camp. The only visible light came from the red pin-lights on the unloading bays and the aircraft beacons on the radio masts.

He dropped the dout in a puddle and crossed the open space, up the grass bank and past the squat bulk of the guardroom encased in its steel mortar-cage, to the vehicle park. The dripping rows of Land-Rovers and Saxons. He stopped briefly by the armoured box-like shape of a Saxon and looked up at the Black Mountain through the squalls of sleet, its black, gorse-clad slopes rising west of the fort. He rubbed at his cold face.

Macrae, the gate sentry, was standing in the doorway, shifting from foot to foot to keep warm. He was bulky in his body armour, his face shadowed beneath his helmet. 'Yer man's inside,' he said.

'Go wait in the signals bunk and warm yourself up,' Seb instructed him. 'Don't speak to anyone.'

Macrae shrugged and ambled off.

Seb bowed his head as he entered the low-ceilinged room and stood for a moment allowing his eyes to acclimatise. The interior was spartan: bare breezeblock walls and a metal observation hatch. Black-and-white photos of known terrorists on the walls, the log book by the door. There was a man hunched over a wooden table, smoking a cigarette. He clutched a can of stout in his left hand.

Seb sat down in the chair opposite him.

Oisin MaColl lifted his head and studied him with violent brown eyes. He was a big man; he dwarfed the table; his hands were large and his fingers were long.

Seb reached into his pocket and took out a dictaphone, which he switched on and set on the table. 'It's 2333 hours, 7 January 1994. I'm 527138 Lieutenant MacCoinneach—'

'A Scotsman?'

'Yes.'

'You don't sound like a Scotsman.' His voice was slurred, his accent harsh Belfast.

'I'm in the gate sangar at Fort White Rock, with me I have—'

'No names,' he snapped.

'OK,' Seb said slowly.

'You know my name?'

'Yes,' Seb replied, 'but you haven't been seen around here for a while.'

'That's correct.'

Seb nodded slowly. 'You said you wanted to speak to someone in charge?'

'Yes,' MaColl said.

'I'm currently the senior officer in the fort.'

'Then we're stuck with each other.'

'You have something to say?'

'I have information.' His voice changed: there was a hint of cunning in it. 'Something big, something your masters will pay good money for.'

'What?'

'Not on tape.'

Seb stared at the dictaphone.

'And a gift,' MaColl said.

Seb looked up at him. 'A gift?'

MaColl reached inside his pocket and brought out his wallet, rummaged through the notes till he found what he was looking for, a creased twenty-dollar bill, which he laid with some care on the table.

'From across the Atlantic.'

'So I see.'

'Tell them I know the whereabouts of the rest of it. The other five million.'

'All right,' Seb said. 'I'll pass it on.'

'And something else. A condition.' He pointed across the table, the tip of his index finger inches from Seb's face. 'You. I'll only talk to you. No peelers, and no spooks. To you, and through you to them. I've no wish to be sucked into their double-dealing. Just you. Have you got that?'

Seb nodded.

MaColl reached forward very deliberately and dropped his cigarette butt in the aluminium can.

Seb smiled softly. He switched off the dictaphone. Everything had gone smoothly.

MaColl leant back in his chair and grinned.

Seb asked, 'How was Dundalk?'

'I still have my legs,' said MaColl, 'so I guess all is forgiven. The hardliners down there have a thirst for my genius. They feel left out, unloved. They want guns so bad you can smell it on their breath. I aim to please. Speaking of which, how is that sister of yours?'

'She's fine.'

'Still promiscuous I hope?' He helped himself to a cigarette from Seb's packet and lit it with Seb's bronze Zippo. The flame lit his face, his blunt nose and thick brown hair. He took a drag and pointed the lighted cigarette at Seb. 'Don't you worry about me.'

Seb studied him dispassionately. 'They'll try and split us up,' he told him. 'It's the way they operate. They'll want you to deal with one of their own.'

MaColl shrugged. 'There'll be some drama. It'll be fun.' He stood up, pocketing Seb's lighter. 'We'll speak soon.'

Seb gripped his head and pushed clockwise as if tightening a vice and stalked back and forth across the jetty with long streaks of charcoal on the smooth planes of his eleven-year-old face. 'I don't know! I don't know!'

The mermaid was gone; swallowed by the tide. It was a bad omen. Someone was dead.

'It doesn't matter,' Cal said quietly. He lowered his air rifle.

The rigidness went out of Seb suddenly. He stood staring at Cal, an expression of profound sadness under the warpaint. 'There's nothing we can do.'

Then he grinned. It was his saving grace, that grin. As fast or slow as a thought – it transformed everything. 'Let's go camping,' he said, using that tone, familiar to Cal, which implied that it would be an act of betrayal to deny him.

There followed an expectant pause.

Cal almost asked why, but then thought better of it. There didn't seem to be any point in antagonising Seb, and nobody in his family was going to miss him; after all, his mother and Auntie Mary were staying in Edinburgh.

'Awright,' he said.

'Good man,' Seb said, in imitation of his father's bluff manner.

He stepped away up the jetty, scooping up his rifle and bag, with a certain jauntiness in his stride, a message for all to see that he was looking forward – not back, never back – and striking out in new directions.

Cal followed.

They made sandwiches of white bread in the pantry at Castle Murbhach – this was before the Night of the Great Fire – and filled them with slates of corned beef and processed cheese, and shiny squares of gammon, and deflected Mrs Armstrong, the latest in a long line of short-lived housekeepers, with the sheer scope of their enthusiasm.

'It's a sudden thing,' Seb explained, striding back and forth for bread and butter, and mustard, and a five-pack of Blue Ribands. He pocketed a jar of jam. 'The river's full. We'll have to go down there and camp. By the river, I mean.' He assumed an aura of boyish sincerity. 'For the fish.' He subjected her to his most gleaming smile.

She faltered, 'I don't know. Your mother . . .'

'Always lets us camp down by the river. Come on, Cal.'

Cal went out of the kitchen and into the coppery musk of waxed jackets and waterproofs hunchbacked on pegs in the hallway. The floor was strewn with wellies and boots and big muddy prints.

Seb had stopped and was studying him critically. 'You'll do,' he said.

He dashed up the back stairway, past the nursery, and on up the steep carpeted stairway to his room in the attic.

'Watch your step.'

There were soldiers everywhere, plastic H0/06 figures pillaged from boxed sets with little deference for historical accuracy to recreate Wingate's campaign to liberate Ethiopia from the Italians in 1940. Wingate and MacCoinneach in ambush behind a stark escarpment of old sticklebricks and socks; Wingate in topee and shorts, with MacCoinneach beside him in a kilt brandishing a broadsword. They were flanked by an assortment of tribesmen with spears from an ancient Tarzan set, and, behind them, camels from the Lawrence of Arabia set. A column of dusty Italian tanks – the dust effect was created with a toothbrush and raw umber paint – and behind them weary footsoldiers advancing across the flat ochre-coloured desert while above them loomed the sheer face of a range of African mountains – a plumped-up duvet with a Star Wars cover inherited from Rory.

Cal was familiar with the handing down of used clothing, but not with having a wartime hero for a father. It seemed larger than life. He was secretly envious.

Seb tugged open a cupboard and things tumbled out – cricket bats, books, Action Men, clothes, a sleeping bag and tent. 'There,' he said, packing the sleeping bag into his rucksack, and strapping the tent to the outside of it with leather straps. 'Rory's got a maggot,' he said, and tiptoed back through the battlefield and down the low-ceilinged hall to Rory's room.

Rory's room was littered with copies of *2000 AD* and the walls were full of motorbikes: his coveted porn stash was under the mattress. His fusty sleeping bag was located beneath a pile of unwashed clothing in the corner. Rory wasn't back on the island yet. He had elected to stay with a friend in London at the end of term, and wasn't due for another couple of days. Cal stuffed Rory's sleeping bag into his rucksack.

'Ready?'

Cal nodded.

Seb looked thoughtful. 'We'll need more than sandwiches.'

A shadow fell across the doorway. A snuffling, nasal voice, redolent of a childhood's taunts, 'Mmmnn, Mmmnnn, Mmmnn. What you doing?'

Seb's eldest surviving brother, Torquil; the scarred combs of his upper lip the visible mark of a cleft palate.

Cal backed away fearfully. Torquil gave savage Chinese burns if he had a mind to.

Seb stood up to him. 'Fuck off, Torq.'

Torquil studied them, one after the other, his level, disorientating gaze coming to rest on Cal. 'What have you theen?'

Cal reddened.

'Tell me.'

Seb clutched Cal's shoulder and pulled him towards the doorway. 'Get out the way, Torq.'

His dark shining eyes narrowed suspiciously. 'You've theen her.'

Seb muttered, 'I don't know what you're talking about. Now get out the way.'

Torquil stood back from the doorway reluctantly and watched

them go down the hallway. 'You'll be thorry,' he called after them. To Cal it didn't sound so much like a threat as a prediction.

They knelt beside each other in the narrow defile and pulled the moss-covered stones away.

'Here.' Seb brushed the soil from the lid of the ammunition box and levered it open. 'See. Ration packs; cans, tea and coffee and matches. Enough for days.'

They filled their rucksacks.

'We'll take the sail-boat. Go to Garbh.'

They settled the stones and went back down the defile to the cove where the sailboat was tied to the wharf. Seb sprang on board and threw his pack down on the deck. Cal threw him his pack and then released the painter, while Seb hoisted the sail. Cal coiled the rope in loops through his fingers, threw it aboard and jumped after it.

Seb steered deftly through the channel, between cruel purple-and-black spurs of rock, and out into the roiling Sound where the water was compressed by the wrestling mass of the two islands. They tacked against the wind, zig-zagging back and forth as the current pushed them out towards open water, and they were lucky to make the other side.

Grotesque shadows flickered across the roof of the tent. North Atlantic breakers crashed violently on the beach. Seb was shadowy and bloodless beside him, a botch of black and white.

'You wouldn't let me down.' There was a plaintive, almost despairing, quality to his voice.

'No, Seb.' Cal sighed.

'Good man.'

There was a long pause.

'Why is it Rory?'

'It has to be,' Seb replied, with certainty. 'He's the only one left. Toby died two years ago.' Toby, Seb's eldest brother, an officer in the Queen's Own Highlanders, had been blown up by an IRA bomb at Warrenpoint in Northern Ireland.

'Torquil's alive, worse luck,' Seb continued. 'That leaves Rory.'

'I still don't understand why it has to be Rory.'

'The curse, you idiot.'

'What curse?'

'It doesn't matter.'

'It obviously matters to you,' observed Cal.

'You won't believe it,' replied Seb witheringly.

Cal was hurt. 'I might.'

'All right, then. When Dad was in Ethiopia he was cursed by a witch. She told him that he'd have four sons, one dim-witted, one buck-toothed, one hare-lipped and one purblind. She told him that he'd outlive them all.'

'I don't understand. I thought the curse was about an apron?'

'That's a different curse, stupid.'

'There are two curses?'

'That's pretty bloody clear.'

Seb had a habit of surprising him with dramatic news. Eventually Cal asked, 'Which one of you is dim-witted?'

Seb tutted in irritation. 'Toby, obviously. He was thick as pig-shit.'

'I thought he was an army officer.'

'So?'

Cal sighed and stared at the roof of the tent. After a while he said, 'What's purblind?'

'I can't see,' Seb muttered grudgingly.

'What?'

'When I sit at the back of the class I can't see the board, satisfied?'

Cal considered this carefully; it might explain why Seb wasn't shooting so well. 'Why don't you get some glasses?'

'Good plan!' he sneered dismissively.

Cal protested, 'You could sit nearer the front of the class.'

He should have anticipated the response. The full thrust of Seb's sarcasm was aimed at him. 'I rule the fucking back row.'

He shifted round in his sleeping bag so that his back was to Cal, signalling that the conversation was at an end. They lay that way, neither of them sleeping, while the wind brought the waves further up the beach.

Cal was collecting bracken to put on the fire to keep the midges off when he saw Rory came over the brow of a hill. Rory was following a sheep's trail through the heather with the spine of Kintyre behind him on the horizon. Cal ducked down beneath a granite outcrop and followed the sandy trail down the cliff face to the beach, leaving a pile of bracken behind him. He ran between beachcombings and matted lumps of seaweed, along the curve of the bay to where they were camped in the shadow of an overhanging rock at the mouth of a cave. He unzipped the tent. Seb sat up in his sleeping bag and shook his head.

'It's Rory,' Cal said breathlessly. 'Coming this way.'

Seb stared at him hollow-eyed.

They waited twenty minutes. Cal carried firewood from the pile they had drying at the back of the cave, and for the first time lit a fire out in the open on the sand and set a pan of water on it for tea; Seb remained seated in his sleeping bag, staring at the breakers out on the headland.

Rory came up the beach, at first a black, sticklike figure on the shoreline, and then gradually his features became visible, his clear, unblemished face and windswept hair. He stopped short of them and squatted down as if waiting for permission and when Cal realised that Seb wasn't going to make any gesture he waved him over. Rory nodded in quiet gratitude, and sat down in front of the fire. He took his pack off his back and set it beside him. He looked desperately sad.

Cal passed him tea in an enamel mug.

'Thanks,' he said, cupping it between his slender pink fingers.

'I borrowed your sleeping bag,' Cal said. 'I hope you don't mind.'

'It's all right,' Rory said, revealing the grid of orthodontic metalwork encasing his teeth.

Cal asked, 'Have we caused a lot of trouble?' Twice now they had hidden from RAF Search/Rescue helicopters.

'I think we should go back now,' Rory said. 'Let them know they can call off the search.'

'Who knows we're here?' Seb spoke out clearly, an angry edge to his voice.

Rory shook his head. 'Torquil found you yesterday; he just didn't tell anyone. I got it out of him this morning. It cost me an Escort—'

'Who's dead?' Seb interrupted, the irritation clear in his voice.

Rory swallowed. 'Let's go back. We can be back by lunchtime.'

'You heard me.'

Rory ducked his head. 'Dad's coming back from the Middle East. He's on a plane.'

THE LONG-HAIRED ACHAEANS

53

'Dad's alive?'

Rory nodded, and then something seemed to well up in him, and he sobbed silently.

Seb screamed, 'Who's dead?'

'Mum,' Rory said, softly.

Cal frowned. The world seemed to have pivoted suddenly to an unfamiliar angle. He gripped the end of a branch in the fire.

Rory regarded him through clear, liquid eyes. 'Yours too. Mum and Auntie Ann. Both of them dead. A car accident. I'm sorry.'

The two sisters, Mary MacCoinneach and Ann Bean had been returning to Cual on the Glasgow road in Mary's red mini, when they were hit by a construction lorry that jacknifed across the road, tipping its cargo of hot roadbed asphalt over the car. The two sisters were buried alive and subsequently burned to death.

Seb was already striding down the beach, a strobe-like flickering behind his eyes, a red splash of fury.

4

Seb was relieved at 0700 hours and walked across to the officers' mess. It was still dark, although it was no longer sleeting. He passed beneath the dripping branches of two etiolated saplings – the only adornment in a featureless sea of grey tarmac – and entered the concrete chicane that protected the doorway to the main kitchen block.

The mess comprised two small rooms with the windows bricked up: a recreation room with a television and army-issue sofas covered in polyester fabric that rustled with static; and a dining room with a table and eight army-issue chairs. Owing to the constant cycle of patrols and duties, there were rarely more than four officers present at any one time. The white breezeblock walls were adorned with nineteenth-century cartoons brought over from the mess in Germany, and there were a few pieces of silver, salt and pepper pots from the Afghan wars. He helped himself to a bowl of Weetabix and sat in front of *The Big Breakfast* for an hour. The multiple commander coming off night patrols joined him for a while, ate two bowls of cereal, and leafed through the mess copy of *Club*. He was new to Belfast, a second lieutenant. They did not speak. Seb knew that, behind his back, the young officers called him Wondersulk. They wouldn't do it to his face.

When he felt his head dropping forward, he shook himself and got up. He went across to the accommodation block, to the small room that he shared with the company Admin Officer, a rather ineffectual but well-connected captain who had just received a compulsory redundancy notice, and had flown back to the mainland to pull some strings.

Seb kicked off his boots and lay face down on his bed, still in his uniform. His mind was restless. He worked through his meeting with Oisin MaColl over and over again. He was satisfied that everything had gone as rehearsed. A flick of the wrist; a sleight of hand. The bait cast.

Now it was up to them to bite.

He was confident that it would not take them long to trace the numbers on the twenty-dollar bill. Then the questions would start. He was ready.

It felt as if he had been preparing for this moment all his life, channelling a headful of rage towards this objective.

The Commanding Officer came for him at 1300 hours, Seb was dimly aware of the door being opened and the light coming on. He squinted, raising his hand against the harsh glare. He had not removed his contact lenses before falling asleep, and now it felt as though boulders of grit were grinding against each other in his eyes.

'Sebastian.'

'Colonel.' He groaned.

He swung his legs off the bed and shook his head back and forth. Colonel Hector had sauntered across the room and was standing holding the doors of Seb's cupboard open and was sucking on his dentures while studying the clothing on the rack. No one in the battalion was brave enough to have asked the Colonel how he had lost his teeth, though there were various underground rumours. Despite the weather he was in shirt-sleeve order and his tanned forearms bulged as he gripped the cupboard doors.

The young subalterns treated him with awed respect and told each other impressive, probably truthful, stories about his feats. Seb's relationship with him was less definite.

The Colonel growled quietly to himself, slid Seb's Meyer & Mortimer tweed suit to one side on the rack and reached beyond it into the darkened pile at the rear, pulling out Seb's worn Barbour jacket with the holes at the elbows, then a woollen jumper from Mactaggart's store at Droch that Madelene had given him. It smelled of lanolin and peat. A pair of unwashed jeans and a T-shirt. His cowboy boots.

'Put these on,' he said. 'First wake yourself up; take a shower. Don't shave.'

Seb scratched at his stubble and started to undress.

'I'll be in the mess,' the Colonel said. 'You've got fifteen minutes.'

Fourteen minutes later Seb knocked on the door. He received the command 'Enter.'

Colonel Hector Macleod, OBE, MC, was slouched in one of the chairs with his legs crossed at the ankles and his jungle boots pointed directly at Seb. Beside him, and sunk even further into a chair, was Seb's pale-faced and insomniac company commander, Major Hugh Lennox. He viewed Seb with baleful red-rimmed eyes. This was entirely due, Seb supposed, to the fact that he had passed the information concerning MaColl's walk-in and offer to turn informant directly to the Colonel at battalion headquarters, bypassing the usual chain of command. Lennox would regard this as tantamount to treason.

Seb smiled at the Colonel. 'Sir?'

'Sit down, Sebastian.'

Seb settled into the nearest seat and leant forward expectantly, resting his forearms on his knees. He'd cleaned his lenses and his eyes felt clear and fresh.

The Colonel studied him without expression. 'You did well to keep a lid on it.'

Beside him, Hugh seethed silently.

Seb shrugged. 'I thought that the fewer people who knew about it the better.'

The Colonel nodded. 'I'm moving Macrae up to the Mill, where the RSM can keep a close eye on him, and I've asked Hugh to speak to the others. I understand that MaColl has a history of walking into security forces bases and being abusive. We will treat it as being no different from any other time.'

'Yes, sir.'

'You've come across MaColl before, haven't you?'

'Yes, sir, but I don't think he recognised me. It was five years ago, on my first tour. We found him in a ditch on the Upper Springfield Road. He'd been kneecapped.'

The Colonel nodded again, as if satisfied by the explanation. 'You will not speak to any of your fellow officers about what has occurred. I will be the only exception to that rule. Is that clear?'

'Sir.'

'Hugh?' the Colonel demanded.

'Yes, Colonel,' Hugh agreed, through gritted teeth. Seb smiled at him.

*   *   *

THE LONG-HAIRED ACHAEANS

As they were mounting the steps to the vehicle park, the Colonel turned to him and said, 'How's Hugh?'

Seb chose his words carefully. 'I don't think he gets that much sleep.'

The Colonel stared at him strangely. 'No, I meant your father.'

Seb was taken aback. It was not typical of the Colonel to encourage such intimacies. 'There's no sign of improvement,' he said, after a pause.

The Colonel laughed. It was a dry mirthless laugh. 'More kids?'

'Another one last year, Colonel. A girl.'

'How old is he?'

'Seventy-five.'

'Jesus,' said the Colonel, 'I've never known a man with such potent sacs.'

'Aye, sir.'

'No more boys?' The substance of the MacCoinneach curse was well known in the regiment.

'No more boys,' Seb replied.

The Colonel nodded. 'What was her name? The Filipina?'

'Breeze,' Seb replied stiffly.

'So who's going to get the money?'

Seb shrugged, 'I don't know that there's that much left. Breeze, probably. I don't think Torquil is that interested.'

The Colonel said, 'I went back to Hereford last week.' He added, 'I saw him.' He looked suddenly thoughtful, the shadow of some misgiving crossing his hollowed-out face.

Torquil MacCoinneach had made his home at Stirling lines in Hereford, the home of the SAS. There he found companionship, free of the excruciating shyness that had characterised his youth. He appeared irregularly at Murbhach, and when he did he stayed in a bothy out on the moor that he had converted for his use. He rarely spoke to the members of his family.

'Sir?'

The Colonel shook his head, and smiled opaquely. 'You should speak to your father,' he said. They stared at each other.

Seb broke the silence. 'Correct me if I'm wrong, but didn't he steal my girl?'

'I'm not taking your father's side, Sebastian; I'm saying don't overestimate its importance.'

'She was mine.'

The conversation over, they reached the top of the steps. The Colonel gestured to his armoured Land-Rover, 'Get in.'

The Regimental Sergeant-Major was standing beside the driver's door of his vehicle. He pursed his lips at the sight of Seb's unshaven chin and generally dishevelled appearance. Seb let his face slacken out into his most fuck-you grin. He climbed into the rear of the Land-Rover between the legs of the two standing riflemen who were leaning out the open hatch in the roof, and curled up next to the radio sets.

The Colonel got into the passenger seat and picked up the radio handset. 'Drop bollards. Two vehicles to MPH.'

The two Land-Rovers swept out of the fort, through the narrow steel-sided channel and over the pits containing the electronic bollards, and out on to the Monagh bypass. They fed through the traffic on the Glen Road roundabout and headed down the Upper and Lower Kennedy Way, past the permanent vehicle checkpoint on the Stockmans roundabout, and crossed into the comparative safety of Protestant East Belfast. They turned off the Stockman's Lane into the Musgrave Park hospital complex.

Tucked away at the back of the complex was another security forces base; the usual mishmash of Portakabins encased in concrete blast-walls, ringed by a corrugated-steel fence and brick sangars. It housed the doctors and nurses of the military wing of the hospital and the echelon support elements required to maintain the Belfast Roulement Battalion.

They parked by the entrance to the Ops Room and Seb climbed out the back and joined the Colonel, who was standing by the bonnet. He pointed to a vehicle parked against the far wall by the helipad. It was a beaten-looking brown Ford Orion with Belfast plates. The windscreen was smeared with grime, though Seb could make out the silhouettes of the driver and one passenger.

'Go and get in that car.'

Seb pulled up the zip of his jacket and stuck his fists in his pockets. He crossed the tarmac forecourt to the car and got into the back seat next to a pile of unmarked cardboard boxes. The car smelt strongly of stale sweat and cigarettes and the floor was littered with plastic cups and shreds of chocolate wrappers.

The driver had unwashed shoulder-length brown hair, and dark-skinned Romany features, a spectacular hooked nose. He regarded Seb in the rear-view mirror with dead-level brown eyes. He was chewing peanuts and his voice was full of the sound of eating.

'I'm Bravo,' he said, 'and this is Alpha. You can call us Bob and Angie if you want.'

The passenger twisted in her seat and studied him in silence. She had a dark and tatty perm, and dark eyes made mournful with kohl pencil.

Seb said, 'Hello, Angie and Bob.'

'There is a radio in the glove compartment of the car.' Bob spoke slowly and clearly, his eyes still in the rear-view mirror. 'Our callsign is RomeoFour. We are both carrying SIG 226 9mm pistols. There is a Heckler & Koch MP5K wrapped in a newspaper between Angie's feet. In the boot is a bag containing a Heckler & Koch G3K rifle and spare magazines, also a handheld radio on the correct channel. Do not speak unless you are asked a direct question. Ready?'

'Yes.'

The sentry dragged the gates open, and they drove out of the base and into the hospital complex, Sebastian resting his head against a cardboard box and yawning, while in front of him in the passenger seat the woman spoke quietly but continuously, describing the car's current location and direction for the benefit of a hidden microphone.

On the Stockman's roundabout they mounted the ramp on to the M1 and drove south-west out of the city to Lisburn, where they followed the signs for Glenavy, climbing the mountain towards Lough Neagh, and then doubling back and re-entering Belfast on the Upper Springfield Road, driving swiftly past the farms, quarries and outlying cottages on the slopes of the Black Mountain.

They dropped down on to the Glen Road and they were back in familiar territory, skirting the northern edge of the Lenadoons, the steel railings and littered grass banks, the two-storey houses and, looming above them, the three boarded-up concrete monsters, the Glenveagh apartment blocks, daubed with dire warnings from the Provisionals: TAKE HEED NOT SPEED.

It was an affront; more than a challenge, it was an invitation. An embargo just waiting to be broken. Justification enough, thought Seb, for bringing drugs into the city.

Beyond the junction with the Shaws Road they slowed and Bob indicated left by the access road that led up to the gypsy camp. He started whistling the theme tune of *The Twilight Zone*.

They drove between steep banks of littered rock, swerving to avoid the larger pieces of scrap, crossing the stretch of wasteland that isolated the camp from the housing estates beneath it. This modern no man's land was strewn with garbage and the rusting hulks of cars; it fulfilled the same function as the 'Peace Wall' that separated the Catholic and Protestant populations of West Belfast.

'You stay in the car,' Bob instructed.

The camp was two car-parks, one with trailer hook-ups, the other dotted with small white-painted huts, a kitchen and a lounge, round which caravans clustered. Many of the huts were burnt and boarded up. There were children and adults everywhere. They watched the car cross the tarmac without interest. Bob parked next to a battered Nissan pick-up beside a caravan standing on bricks. He left the engine running.

A man regarded them from the window of the caravan, his hand resting on the curtain and his lips moving as if he was speaking to someone unseen. He was grey-haired and ravaged and in his fifties, with dark, stained lips and puffy eyes.

'That's Big Anthony,' Bob told Angie. 'Anthony's the man. The Maan. You want it, Anthony's got it. You want to move it, Anthony will move it.'

He waved cheerily to Anthony, who shook his head and tugged the curtain closed.

'They moved him up here from down by the border.'

'Why'd they do that?' Angie asked.

'He was selling hash to the squaddies and they were going out on patrol and selling it door to door.'

'No,' she protested.

'Straight up. Door to door, like milk. The paramilitaries weren't best pleased. Caused a bleeding turf war, didn't it? It all got hushed up, of course. Northern Ireland Office towed his caravan up here, gave him some stern words.'

'I don't believe it.'

'It doesn't matter what you believe,' Bob said. He got out of the car, and went and lounged on the bonnet and smoked a cigarette. Five minutes passed. Seb contemplated the litter on the floor of the car.

Angie raised her head slightly. Seb realised she was listening to a voice from the receiver in her ear.

She rapped on the windscreen with her knuckles and Bob came round and got in the car.

'He's just left the White Fort Inn and is heading west on the Andersonstown Road.'

'I heard,' he said.

They left the gypsy camp, turning right on to the Glen Road and drove back to the junction, where they headed south on the Shaws Road past the Ramoans and Rosnareens. It was as they were passing the St Agnes church on the Andersonstown Road that Seb spotted Oisin MaColl at the sharp end of a phalanx of Belfast's teenage drug-dealers. He was walking with his shoulders hunched forward against the wind and his hands thrust deep in the pockets of his tatty brown leather jacket. Six gangling youths flanked him, some of them limping – a sure sign of earlier brushes with the IRA – expressions of resolute bravado on their fearful faces.

Bob's head never moved. The car didn't slow.

'Confirm that's the man,' he said so softly that Seb did not hear him the first time and he had to repeat the question.

'Yes,' Seb replied, his spirits soaring. Counting.

Behind him, Oisin MaColl reached the Sinn Féin office at Clonnelly House. Standing outside the iron gates, he pointed a blunt and accusatory finger at the video eye above the door and announced a fast in protest at ninety punishment beatings since the ceasefire.

Cal brushed his fingertips across the matt surface of the glass, lifting an oily film of dust, revealing Seb smiling complacently at the camera, his lank and sinewy form sprawled on the turret of his Warrior armoured personnel carrier. He had his goggles high on his forehead in the peak of his wild black hair, a grey-green *shemagh* draped round his shoulders, and his boots resting on bins that were filled with ragged bundles of camouflage netting, sleeping bags in compression sacs and black jerry cans. Beside him, standing in the gunner's hatch, with only his chest and head visible, was Moose, the gunner. He scowled at the camera as if uncomfortable with its intrusion. The driver, Jimmy the Bus, squatted on the sand in front of the track-wheels, shielding a hexamine stove from the desert wind. The sky behind the vehicle was overcast and grey. The sand was hard and rutted and stretched away to the horizon.

He wiped the caption clear: 'Recce Platoon, Operation Granby, 1991' – Granby being the typically unassuming British codename for what the Americans called Desert Storm. Madelene called it 'Seb goes to War'.

There were others, all coated in peat-dust, framed on the gable-end wall. Cal stood naked in front of them, before the dull-red sods of peat in the grate. Rows of young men seated and standing, staring fiercely into the camera above tribal captions: Rowallan, Sandhurst, Warminster. Seb looking younger, his neck thinner, less broad-shouldered. There was even a photo of Seb and Organ at Eton, on a neatly trimmed grass square in their outlandish school uniform with sixth-form hair-to-the-collar.

Beneath them, more recent photos: 'The Officers of the 1st Battalion', serried ranks of kilted officers in front of the German mess, wearing their service dress jackets and bull-polished sam brownes, kid-gloved hands crossed on the pommels of their swords; 'Belfast 1990 – The Clan MacDelta', tiers of soldiers in combat smocks clutching their SA80 rifles, flanked by two Pigs, long-snouted armoured vehicles, and behind them the green and gorse-clad slopes of the Black Mountain; 'UNIKOM 1992', the United Nations Iraq–Kuwait Observer Mission, eight soldiers from eight different nations wearing the blue beret of the UN, standing round a white-painted Toyota Landcruiser in the Iraqi demilitarised zone. Seb called it 'the Zone' – an expression that reflected a state of mind as much as a place: where everything was a commodity, and all was permitted.

Seb hadn't been back on the island for years. Not since he had fallen out with his father. It was Madelene who was the archivist of Seb's army career, framing the photos that he sent her; preserving his room as a shrine to what he called his 'other life'.

Cal turned in front of the fire, on a haphazard pile of *dhouris*, letting the heat lick at his calves. Madelene lay on her stomach, with her hair on the pillow, softly breathing. The quilt was rucked in the corner, and Seb's Seaforth tartan rug divided her body, its tasselled edge on the cord of her spine, and between her slightly parted legs.

He gently massaged his penis and raised his hand to his nose to catch the malty tang that lingered there. Her sign, there for anyone to read.

Does she really control me so easily? he wondered.

He dropped into the leather-backed seat in front of the mahogany desk and laid his bare feet on the window-sill. He laid the palms of his hands against his face and rubbed vigorously in a circular motion until his head felt raw. He stared blearily at the surface of the desk and tried to focus his mind.

The desk was littered with mementos, papers and an American bayonet inscribed 'The Big Red One'; a clay chillum and a lump of the Berlin Wall; some welded steel candlesticks he had made one Christmas for Seb from plumbing-joins and part of an old jack, which were dripping with cold threads of beeswax. Under the desk was a cardboard box full of old Action Men, their naked and sexless bodies contorted in strange configurations, and beside it Seb's skydiving harness and chute, in bright red and black.

Above the desk were twin framed prints of Seb's mother and father: his mother – Cal's aunt – in three-quarter profile as Mary Campbell when she was courting the dashing young spy Hugh MacCoinneach; the one of his father in shorts and puttees, standing with Orde Wingate in the Ethiopian desert in 1940.

Cal knew that the main house was also filled with photographs and portraits, the walls full of martial ancestors, and more recent soldiers, namely Seb and his brothers, in the desert and the jungle, in Belfast and bandit country. The eldest, Toby Chisholm MacCoinneach, who died at Warrenpoint, and Torquil Gairloch MacCoinneach, now serving with the SAS. The middle brother, Rory Grant MacCoinneach, the only one not to join the army, standing beside the racing car that he had driven for the McLaren team until he too died.

Calum regarded it as a peculiar MacCoinneach trait, this need to chronicle themselves in action and in recreation. In his house photographs were stacked in their paper sleeves in the drawers of the kitchen table. He only had one photograph of his mother, and he kept it out of sight and rarely consulted it. He didn't know whether to regard this MacCoinneach trait as vanity or some inescapable requirement of history.

'Are you jealous?'

He looked up, surprised. Madelene was watching him, propped on one elbow, with her tousled hair falling across the tips of her breasts, curving past her throat. She had pushed the rug aside and she was naked. The spartan slopes of her body were offered to him: the puckered eyelid of her navel, her smooth, fatless thighs.

'Of Seb?' Cal wondered. 'Or of the fact that you frame his photos?'

'Either.'

Cal shrugged. 'He's your brother.'

'My half-brother,' she corrected him, as if it made a difference.

He stared out the attic window at the cobbled courtyard. 'Seb's really going to do it, isn't he?'

She knew exactly what he was talking about. The Freedom To Live.

'Yes,' she said.

'Why do I think that you're making him do it?'

'It was his idea,' she replied. 'Or maybe it was your idea.'

'You could stop him,' Cal said.

'Why should I?'

'Why do it?' Cal pressed her.

She laughed at that. 'Why not?'

He knew he wouldn't get an answer out of her.

Beneath him he heard the door to the stable block open and Hugh Humberstone MacCoinneach, known to the inhabitants of Cual as simply The MacCoinneach, emerged holding a pair of red boxing-gloves. Steam rose in clouds off his compactly muscled torso and patrician head with its shock of silver hair. He was naked to the waist, wearing only a pair of grey jogging pants stained with a deep vee of sweat, and unlaced black combat boots. The grizzled grey hairs on his broad chest stood out in the cold January air. He strode diagonally across the courtyard towards the front door of the main house with a couple of deerhounds at his heels. Just before he reached the door it was opened for him, and Cal caught a brief glimpse of a willowy Asian woman clutching a baby in the doorway. Breeze.

It came to him then, unbidden, a vision of the legacy of The MacCoinneach's profligate sperm: the lacework of relations and those he could not turn away; his children, legitimate and illegitimate, with their violent and often self-destructive nature; his succession of lovers and partners, garnered and stolen.

Seb had brought Breeze back from Hong Kong after the Gulf War. After his return from the desert Seb had taken a month's leave, and hopped on an eastbound RAF flight. He'd met Breeze at the jockey club and within a week had asked her to come back with him to Cual. It was the first time anybody had seen Seb with a regular girlfriend. He was an acknowledged veteran of one night stands. She was, by all accounts, extravagant and wild – and she knew her own mind. Cal hadn't been on the island at the time, so he'd received the story second-hand, in fragments and mostly from Madelene – Seb never spoke about it.

It was a misconception that Breeze was from the Philippines; she was Taiwanese, the daughter of an aged general of Chiang Kai Shek's Chinese Nationalist Army. Educated in the United States, she had a degree in biochemistry from the Massachusetts Institute of Technology.

After a week on Cual, sharing Seb's bed, Breeze had made the transition from above the stableblock into the main house. Into the bed of the father.

Seb left the island on the first available flight, and hadn't yet returned. General Ly, Breeze's father, had arrived on the island some months later in search of his wilful daughter. She was married and pregnant by then, expecting The MacCoinneach's child. The two old military men had shut themselves up in the main house and by morning they had reached an accommodation, which was widely believed to include the disinheritance of all previous MacCoinneach children.

'She'll sell won't she?'

Madelene shrugged.

'Does he know?' Cal asked.

'Who can say?' she said.

'What will you do?'

She didn't reply. It was difficult for him to understand her lack of interest; he had always associated her with a certain fierce loyalty to the estate. She had been a latecomer to the Murbhach, but she had made it her home. Was she now preparing to leave? It made him want to growl in frustration. He reached under the chair for his boxer shorts.

She continued watching him. 'Why don't you come back to bed?'

'I guess I don't want to,' he replied.

She sighed and stared up at the ceiling.

'I'm going for a walk.'

He dressed quickly, retrieving his crumpled two-day-old socks and Doc Martens from under the bed, while Madelene continued to stare at the ceiling without speaking.

'I'll see you later,' he said, embarrassed suddenly, and quickly ducked out of the room through the yellow hangings printed with images of Ganesh, the elephant-headed god of wisdom and new beginnings.

Calum dropped down into the defile, under the overhanging rhododendrons, and followed it down to the stone jetty. From there he scrambled across the grey-slick rocks along the coastline until he located another deep trench blasted in the rock that led back into the interior. The whole point was a warren of tunnels and trenches which had been used by the whisky-smugglers.

He squeezed between the two fallen boulders that seemed to guard the entrance to the trench, and masked it from any but the closest observer, and dropped down into a small drift of windblown leaves. It was like entering a different world. The walls and the rocks on the trench-floor were covered in a deep carpet of dripping vermilion mosses, zebra-striped with shadow. After twenty metres, he had to ease himself through rusted strands of barbed wire that had been strung between bolts sunk deep in the rock on either side. Beyond, he found a few rusted tin cans. An old encampment. He continued, treading carefully between the broken rocks, until he came to a spot marked by three parallel scars gouged deep in the rock. They were newish, and the moss was only just getting into the fractured granite. He looked behind him. The thick walls of green had closed upon his route.

He was alone.

He squatted down in front of a broad flat stone, traced its outline with his fingernails, got a firm grip on it and heaved it to one side. There was an old dark-green ammunition box buried to the lid in the moist black earth. He untwisted the steel loop threaded through the catch and lifted the lid. At the top lay a rolled-up waterproof bag. He unrolled it, held it up to the light, and then opened it. There was a loaded handgun – the IMI 'Desert Eagle' .44 Magnum that Seb had brought back from the Gulf War – a loaded spare magazine, and a bundle of notes held together with a rubber band. He removed the money and counted it. He replaced the money, folded up the bag and looked down into the bottom of the box. There were eight paper-wrapped tubes of vanilla-coloured plastic explosive, a spool of white detonator cord that resembled washing line, and a polystyrene box containing military detonators. He squatted back on his haunches and whistled, and it was with him again, the almost sublime expression on Seb's face as he danced across the hotel room after Byron.

Sometimes it frightened him to think what Seb was capable of doing.

He had his hands on the rock and was about to lower it over the ammunition box when he was stopped by a voice hissing at him, 'What are you doing?'

He froze. A couple of small pebbles rattled down the side of the trench.

There was no mistaking that voice, the cleft palette. 'Torq?' He could feel Torquil's eyes watching him intently.

'I was just checking some things, Torquil,' he explained sooth-ingly, deliberately calling him by his name. Torquil could be unpredictable, violent. 'Seb asked me to, to make sure they were safe.'

'Whath he up to?' Torquil demanded.

'I don't know, Torq.'

'Explosives. Guns. Cash. Big boys' games.'

'He hasn't been on the island in two years.'

'Hathn't he?'

A shadow loomed over the top of the trench, Torquil stood astride it, one mud-caked booted foot either side, and looked down at Calum. They studied each other in silence. Torquil had changed. His hair was long and matted, and he was wearing a straggly beard that reached his chest. The scarring on his upper lip stood out among the patches of russet hair. He looked like a tramp, or a crazed cult leader.

'I think he'th been here,' Torquil said.

'I'm going to put the rock down,' Calum informed him eventu-ally, because his arms were hurting. There was no reaction. He gently lowered the stone and stood away from it, keeping his hands where they could be seen.

'You tell him to watch out.'

'I will,' Cal assured him.

'Lithen,' Torquil said suddenly, 'Ssh.'

They stayed very still while Cal strained to hear something, but all he could hear was the rustling of the wind in the beech trees above him.

'I thought I heard her thinging.' His eyes were shining brightly, his voice keening. 'Nobody cares. A mermaid. It dothn't matter, does it?'

His shadow passed over Cal, and he was gone.

Cal waited, and after a suitable pause continued down the trench. It ended abruptly, and Calum climbed the rubble slope to emerge among closely packed and ghostly grey beech trees, on a crest above the sea. He followed a sheep trail leading down to the cliff's edge, intending merely to sit and watch the sea, as he had done in the past when he wanted to be alone with his thoughts. Instead, as he eased himself down on the beech leaves he saw that Torquil was standing on the beach below him.

He was fishing, playing a weighted line between his fingers. He appeared relaxed and oblivious, in contrast to the threatening figure of just a few minutes before. Still, he was not a man to spy on. Calum got up carefully, and backed away from the edge to avoid being detected. He went back over the hill through the beech wood, and down into the sheep pasture beyond it.

Madelene was in her workshop when he returned, sitting in a wickerwork chair in a black dress with a cashmere scarf wrapped tightly round her neck and long leather boots that were resting on an anvil. She looked cold and thoughtful. Cal stood at the stable door waiting for her to notice him.

'Damien Hirst's asked me to put it in an exhibition. What d'ya think?' she asked him.

On the large wooden workbench made from old railway sleepers stood one of her constructions. Cal recognised it: he had made the steel bracket for the three glass jars. Madelene had called it *Things I Carried and Discarded.*

They stood beside each other, in their steel frame, three beautifully hand-blown glass pickling-jars, each one about a foot high and sealed to the air. They contained, respectively, pubic hair, toenail clippings, and used tampons. The glass was greenish, and the dried blood on the tampons appeared very black.

There had been times when Calum had contributed by trimming Madelene's pubic hair for her, though it was not, he imagined, an exclusive job. She'd been collecting cuttings for years. He remembered other works in a similar vein. Vacuum-packed excrement. *The Real Hair Shirt.* Whereas Hirst used the bodies of dead animals, Madelene's preoccupation had always been with the products of the human body. Her body. The islanders treated her with the awed fear that he presumed had in the past been reserved for witches. In the seventeenth century, they would probably have burnt her.

She came from a formidable line of women who had exhibited precocious talent. Her grandmother, Leonor des Esseintes, had been a surrealist painter and one-time lover of Max Ernst. Some years before, Cal had spent a long winter afternoon with Max Ernst's diaries in the reading room of the National Library in Edinburgh. Ernst had described Leonor as exuding 'Italian fury, scandalous elegance, caprice and passion', a description which, it seemed to Cal, fitted her grand-daughter just as well.

'Where?' he asked.

'At the Serpentine,' she replied. 'Darien's calling it "Some Went Mad, Some Ran Away".'

'Do you want to?'

'I don't know,' she said indifferently. 'I suppose so. Ed Crowe says I should.'

She must have sensed his annoyance. 'Do I make you rage?'

'No,' he lied.

She laughed knowingly.

'I saw Torquil,' he said finally. 'He was fishing.'

She looked at him. The tip of her nose was red from the cold, and a drop of moisture lingered there. 'Are you sure?'

'He looks different, but I'm sure it was him.'

She turned her attention back to the construction on the table.

'I didn't know he was here,' she said. She shuddered and wiped her nose with the back of her hand.

'He thinks Seb has been back to the island recently.'

She laughed. 'You're so obsessed.'

Calum frowned. 'What d'you mean?'

'You hang about Seb's ankles like a child.'

They stared at each other until he said, 'You should exhibit it.'

'You'd get a credit,' she added, brusque now, 'and a cut of a sale.'

'Everybody is offering me money all of a sudden.'

'Then you should take it,' she said, and shook her head almost imperceptibly, as if she was irritated or trying to shake off a nasty thought.

'I'm going,' he told her.

'I'll give you a lift,' she said tersely.

They drove in silence. Madelene didn't seem eager to talk. She was intent at the wheel of the small racing-green MG, downshifting through the curves in water-spray, and opening her out to a hundred on the Deochmore road. Sheep scattered in front of them like chaff. Calum rested his cheek on the doorframe and let the wind, with its needlepoints of moisture, break across his face. He felt lousy, down in the retribution of his hangover, confused in his feelings for both Seb and Madelene.

She lost it for a second on one of the long open bends into Deochmore – the same bend that had claimed the licence and career of her half-brother Rory – the tail of the car sliding out from under her as she fought the curve through a fan of grey-white sludge, passing within inches of a council-yellow JCB parked beside a mound of earth on the far side of the road. Calum closed his eyes and gritted his teeth. Madelene leant with the movement, regained control, and accelerated cleanly away.

Afterwards she raised her chin, exposing her throat, and shouted, 'Yessss!'

Watching her, he wondered if a general indifference about death was a necessary characteristic of Seb's new venture. Or any MacCoinneach venture. Looking back over his shoulder, he saw the rusted upturned hulk of Rory's Aston Martin DB5 in the field beyond. Rory had crawled out of the wreckage with no worse than a broken leg, but he'd been so abusive to the police that they had reluctantly breathalysed him. He'd lost his licence and his job with the McLaren team. Two months later he was dead.

They drove through Droch, past the burnt-out wreck of the Mermaid fish bar, and turned up the road that led to the distillery at Burgaid.

She accelerated into the farmyard at Skurryvaig, past all the rusting heaps of machinery, and slammed on the brakes just in front of the farmhouse door. The Collie With No Name charged viciously at them, yo-yoing on the end of its chain.

He looked up at the face of the building; it didn't look any different.

She spoke to him. 'When are you going to learn to drive?'

It was a strange question. He'd had his licence for years.

'You're fast enough for me,' he replied.

She regarded him coldly. He got out of the car, and went into the darkened farmhouse, and didn't look back until he'd picked his way gingerly through the Massey-Ferguson engine that was spread in all its constituent parts across the kitchen floor. He went to the window, pulled back the curtain, and swept away the covering of dust on the glass. He watched Madelene reverse out of the farmyard in a flurry of mud and drive away.

5

It was a foul December day, bleak, full of drizzle and mist. Beads of water clung to their hair and ran down the back of their necks beneath their flak jackets to the steamy, sweat-soaked T-shirts beneath. The skin of their inner thighs was chapped and sore from their sodden trousers. They had not been dry since the first patrol that morning.

Seb led them up out of Andersonstown, through the bottleneck, and into the grounds of the St Patrick's boys' school. It was already dark and he wanted to get them off the street and back to the fort, and quickly hand over to the night patrol. It was giro day, the fortnightly social security payout to the unemployed of the housing estates, and the primary team had spent four hours static outside the post office while his other teams satellited slowly round him. They had stopped a number of 'players' as they approached the post office to collect their cheques. It was the only relief in a morning of tedious predictability. The soldiers were bored and irritated.

After lunch they made a foray into the Falls Park and had rocks thrown at them by a desultory group of teenagers from Fianna Eireann, the IRA youth movement.

Beside him on the wet grass, Moose lifted his riot gun to his shoulder.

'I suppose,' Seb observed, 'that this is what Danny Morrison would call an unarmed strategy of civil disobedience?' Danny Morrison was Sinn Féin's publicity manager.

Moose was unimpressed. 'N ay thought they wee cunts were flingin rocks. Youse want me to gie them a rubber enema?'

'Yes.'

'Sure?'

'No. It'll just cause trouble.'

'This is shite,' Moose exclaimed.

'You're not wrong,' Seb told him.

They retreated back into the Andersonstown police station and Moose and the rest of the platoon slumped in front of MTV. Seb played the fruit machines till it was time to give orders for the final patrol of the day, which would take them back through the Bingnians and Bearnaghs.

He could draw a route blindfold, he could guess and second-guess PIRA, but there were only so many routes, and he knew that they were still being targeted, though no one actually pulled the trigger, or set the timer, or pressed the button, or put any actual Semtex in the bottles full of nails that they still threw and that made him wince as they shattered on the road. Not while the ceasefire held. It was gruelling and tedious, and required the muscle of his resolve to motivate his soldiers, even though many of them had been through thick and thin with him. It was a pretence, and he had to fight hard to maintain it.

He pressed his fingernails into the raw meat of his palms, sloshing though the sodden field towards the bypass. His rifle rode in its sling on his chest. This was the most dangerous time, as they closed in on the Fort, shift-change. His forward left team was on the Black Mountain, above the gypsy camp on the corner, his forward right up by the Holy Trinity school on the bypass. The rest of his team ranged across the field around him and the Peeler beside him. One of the soldiers tumbled over the barbed wire into the field, ripping his trousers from crotch to knee. They'll all be sewing tonight. Seb tried hard to concentrate. This was the most dangerous time. He said it over to himself, but he did not believe it. His palms were covered in thin red welts. They climbed on to the bypass, stumbling between the passing cars, and followed the central reservation up the hill past the Turf Lodge, and when they saw the Fort they broke into a sprint that carried them in through the gate to the loading bays where they slumped on the dripping concrete and smoked damp cigarettes with the filters torn off and waited for all the teams to be in and safe.

When they were all in, Moose supervised the unloading and Seb wandered across the tarmac forecourt to the Med Centre and stuck his head inside the door.

Farooq, the doctor, looked up from *Star Trek: The Next Generation*. 'How is it out there, Mr Sebastian?'

'The Romulans were throwing rocks in the Falls Park again.'

'Ah, bless the ceasefire, it is indeed a strange new world. Shall we retire to my office for a festive drink?'

'Yes we shall,' Seb replied, the effort of his smile leaving deep lines in his face. 'But first I must hold a debrief and find warm dry clothing.'

Seb lay flat on his back on the hot plastic surface of the examining table with a half-empty glass of whisky within reach of his right hand. He stared at the polystyrene ceiling, feeling tired and hungry and lightheaded from the drink. Farooq was perched on a cabinet opposite, watching him. He also had a drink beside him.

'There've been some guys from Special Investigation Branch here. Talking to Hugh in his office,' Farooq told him.

'Mmm . . .' Seb murmured.

'You'll never guess. They found another sandwich in the Milltown Cemetery, on Bobby Sands's grave.'

'Really,' Seb said, and sighed as if he was bored. 'What flavour this time?'

'Chicken tikka.'

'That's your kind of food.'

Farooq said, 'Somebody has a rich sense of humour, leaving sandwiches on a hunger striker's grave.'

'I think so,' Seb agreed.

'How do you do it?' Farooq asked him. 'I mean I wonder who buys the sandwiches for you?'

'Can't imagine what,' Seb drawled, 'you're talking about.'

'Duty rumour is that the military police have found a usable print on the cellophane. They want to fingerprint the whole platoon.'

Seb shook his head slowly. One of the polystyrene tiles on the ceiling had been kicked in, the outline of the toecap clearly visible. He realised that somebody must have climbed up a ladder to achieve the effect. Boredom bred strange activity in the Fort.

'Don't they have anything better to do?'

'Third time this month,' Farooq told him. 'The Republicans are getting upset.'

'Fuck the Republicans.'

'It's smart not leaving army sandwiches.'

'Maybe it's not the army.'

'Maybe,' Farooq conceded, 'but seriously, do they have a fingerprint?'

'No.'

'Good. Do you want any more specimen gloves?'

'No.'

'Moving on to greater things?'

''Ooq, I came here for an illicit drink, not to get the third degree.'

'Can I ask you a question?'

'Now you ask,' Seb exclaimed.

'What are you doing here?'

'I don't know what you mean,' Seb replied.

'Why come back to Belfast? You must be the most over-qualified platoon commander here. You weren't supposed to come. You're clearly bored.'

'If you remember, Patrick was due to come out and then he broke both his ankles. I replaced him.'

'I was there. I was sober. You know, there are some people who think you engineered the accident.'

'For God's sake, 'Ooq, the guy tried to climb round the outside of a three-storey building. He fell off. So what, that's my fault? Come on, he didn't have to do it.'

'I think he did, especially since you had just done the very same thing.'

'I didn't fall off,' Seb countered.

'I don't think you were as drunk as you made out,' Farooq said. 'I think he was a young second lieutenant who was due to take your platoon on a Northern Ireland tour. I think he was trying to prove himself to you.'

'Bollocks.'

'Of course he was, and you know it.'

'I'll need more whisky if this is going to continue.'

'Here.' Farooq brandished the bottle of Lagavulin. Seb still hadn't worked out how a Punjabi from Henley had developed such fine taste in whisky.

'You know, you still haven't answered my question,' Farooq chided him.

'What am I doing here?'

'Exactly.'

'The same old shit,' Seb told him. 'Except they throw rocks at us now instead of worse.'

'Why do it?'

'I was hanging around kicking my heels. Patrick broke his ankles. So I stepped in at the last minute.'

'They could have got someone else. The Gordons would have sent someone. So, what are you doing here?'

What indeed? He smiled.

Creating a smokescreen, he was tempted to say. Working down the check-list of my master-plan. Assembling the character of an oafish, impetuous and not-so-very-bright army officer, with a hateful father-figure and a mammoth chip on my shoulder. Why? Because I want Them wary of me, and most of all I want Them to think I'm incapable of premeditated action.

'The bottom line is it's my platoon,' he said. 'I wasn't going to let them come out here with any old cunt. That's what I said to the CO, and it's what I'm saying to you. Anyway, who the fuck are you to talk? What are you doing here?'

'Good question,' Farooq conceded.

'You're a Muslim,' Seb observed affably. 'A rag-head.'

'A British citizen.'

'You shouldn't even be drinking.'

'Neither should you,' Farooq retorted.

'I'm not. Give me an Extra Strong Mint. I gotta go see the Grim Reaper.' Seb lifted himself up on to an elbow and prepared to swing his legs off the table.

'How is Major Lennox?'

'Same old nuts, paranoid, whatever you want to call it.'

The mental health of their company commander was a favourite topic of discussion among the occupants of the Fort. That and grumbling about the battery-hen-like living conditions.

Seb said, 'You hear about the cats?'

'I signed for them. I've got the receipt somewhere.'

Seb grinned. 'You may have trouble handing them back in.'

'Really?' Farooq frowned. 'Why?'

'He's shot two of them already. Target practice on the pipe range. Seems he prefers the rats.'

Farooq looked outraged. 'You know, I could jolly well have him relieved of his command.'

'I wish you would. No, I don't mean that. At least he's

predictable in his insanity. I couldn't bear the thought of our arsehole-graduate Ops Officer in charge, however temporarily. The humiliation. Look at me, I'm still just a platoon commander.'

'You didn't have to come.'

'Don't start.' He sprang off the table and landed on his two feet, rolled his shoulders and ran his fingers through his dishevelled hair. 'Ready for anything,' he said.

'OK,' Farooq said. 'One last question.'

Seb lifted his eyes heavenward. 'What?'

'Who gets you the sandwiches? The RUC?'

'No.'

'Who, then?'

'The Paki barber. He buys them at Boots in Lisburn in the morning and brings them up with him. Bobby gets his gift after the barber's been. It's so simple it's beautiful.'

'Seb,' Farooq said quietly.

'Yeah?'

'Don't use that word. Paki.'

'Sorry 'Ooq.'

'Come back soon.'

'I'm not going anywhere far.' Far? He was in orbit. He was beyond the point of no return.

He found Hugh Lennox playing snooker with the Int Sergeant in the NAAFI room. He was shuffling round the table with the diffident gait of a man uncomfortable with his height – he was six foot six – and with his head lolling below his shoulders like a hunchback. He glowered with insomniac eyes at Seb as he entered and immediately missed a shot, sending the white ball into a pocket.

'Bugger.'

'Nae luck, sir.' Sergeant 'Chunnel' Swinhe grinned and began stroking his moustache as he prepared to take his shot. Swinhe had earned his nickname for being the greatest bore in Europe. He was never going to make the rank of warrant officer.

Hugh thrust his chin out at Seb so that his pointed nose was only a matter of inches from Seb's forehead.

'Colonel Hector wants to see you,' he sneered.

'When?' Seb enquired, ingenuously.

Hugh did a double-take. 'What do you mean?'

'I mean when does he want to see me?'

Hugh regarded him suspiciously. 'Now,' he said slowly.

The start of Hugh's decline could be traced to the previous year when his wife had left him, taking their three children, although some maintained that he hadn't been the same since he was hit by lightning in the Falklands during the post-war clean-up campaign in 1983.

'Where?'

'At the Mill,' Hugh replied.

Battalion headquarters was located in a squat five-storey red-brick building, a nineteenth-century mill with all the windows bricked up, which sat astride the peace line between Catholic West Belfast and the Protestant Shankill to the north.

'Do you know why?'

'No,' Hugh snapped.

Hugh was all bark, particularly since Seb had found him one night, in the months after his wife walked out, lying on the floor of his cottage in Carlops on the outskirts of Edinburgh, surrounded by piles of German hard-core transvestite magazines, and wearing some of his wife's discarded clothing. Hugh's secret was safe with Seb, on the unspoken understanding that Hugh allowed him to do whatever he wanted. Any protest by Hugh was purely saving face.

'I'll take your Rover group,' Seb informed him.

'Can't you take the Reds?'

'No, they're in the middle of changeover.'

Swinhe potted the black. 'Best ov three, suh?'

The Regimental Sergeant-Major straightened his back, tucked his paystick under his arm and cocked his hand on the shaft so that the swallow between his thumb and index finger stood out crisply blue.

'Ay'll open the door. You, suh, should march in and salute.'

Seb pulled on his combat smock in a vain attempt to pull out some of the creases. 'Thank you, RSM.' He nodded.

The RSM rapped on the door.

'Come.'

The RSM bent slightly at the waist and opened the door. Seb marched into the room and came to a halt in front of the desk. He threw up a salute and remained at attention, staring straight ahead of him at the aerial photographs pinned to the wall above the desk. He waited. He sneaked a glance. He found himself looking down at the Colonel's closely shaven pate and the razor line just above the collar of his green shirt. He seemed to be reading a dossier on the desk in front of him.

As he waited Seb became aware peripherally that they were not alone, that there was a small, bespectacled man standing, with his hands folded across his belly as if he was a mourner at a funeral, staring at a tribal map on one of the walls. He was about five feet from Seb, and had not moved since he entered.

A spook. *They* were testing the water. His spirits soared.

The Colonel looked up at him, his eyes narrowed. 'I should throw you out of the province.'

'Sir.'

'I've had three complaints against the military that are directly attributable to your actions.'

'Sir.'

'Sandwiches,' the Colonel growled. 'What the fuck do you think you're playing at?'

'Sir?'

'The RUC want to press charges. The Military Police want to crucify you.'

'Sir.'

'It reflects badly on the soldiers you command and on the regiment to which you belong. I might expect it of a junior officer. I do not expect it of someone of your experience. Be under no illusion, your commission is in jeopardy.'

'Sir.'

'I brought you to Belfast against my better judgment. I did it because you pleaded with me to come and because you have been away from the battalion for a long time and I wanted you to command soldiers again. Obviously I made a bad decision.'

'Sir.'

'I'm taking you off the streets.'

'Sir.' He would not protest in the presence of someone outside the regiment.

'And one other thing. You fucking look at me while I'm talking to you.'

'Sir.'

Seb stared into the Colonel's dark-brown eyes, his skull face, and saw there the same cold determination that he had seen on the street in the terrorists' eyes.

'I knew Julian Ball, I worked with him. He was a good soldier but he was a lousy judge of character. He should never have taken on Robert Nairac. I told him that.'

'Yes, sir?'

The Colonel rarely addressed his junior officers and when he did so they were expected to treat the information imparted, however opaque, with reverence.

'Nairac thought he could dance with the devil. He was a bloody fool. He thought he was invincible, that PIRA wouldn't touch him. They killed him. We never even found his body.'

'Sir.'

'You remember that, Sebastian. Don't be a bloody fool.'

'Yes, sir,' he said with emphasis.

'Right. At ease. Sit down.'

Seb obeyed. He sat on a metal and plastic chair that was against the wall, and at a right angle to the desk. He put his hands on his knees.

'He's all yours,' the Colonel said.

The small, bespectacled man nodded slowly. He was wearing a rather old Burberry mackintosh over a grey worsted suit with a thin chalk stripe. His shoes were leather, but scuffed. He had an air of genteel shabbiness about him.

'Thank you Hector,' he said. His voice was soft and unassuming.

Colonel Hector stood up and rolled his shaven bullet-head on his thick neck in a manner that was distinctive to those who knew him. 'Tea? Coffee?'

The small man seemed to take his time in answering as if mulling over the question. He had his chin resting on his chest. Seb saw a flicker of irritation cross the Colonel's face.

'Thank you,' the man said. 'A cup of tea would be nice.'

'Nato?'

'I beg your pardon?' he looked up. His prescription was obviously strong. His watery eyes seemed almost disembodied behind the thick lenses.

'Milk and sugar?'

'Oh yes, of course. I'd forgotten. Nato standard. Yes, three sugars please.'

The Colonel pointed across the table with his whole hand, as if brandishing a spade. 'Sebastian?'

'No, thank you, sir.'

'Whisky?'

'Sir?'

The Colonel leant over his desk and yanked open one of the drawers of his desk. He produced a bottle of Talisker and a tumbler and poured Sebastian a measure. It was unexpected. Seb had never seen the Colonel offer anyone a drink. It amused him to think that they were trying to loosen his tongue.

'You'll only get one.' the Colonel growled and stood up. 'You'll excuse me. Take as long as you want.'

The small man said, 'Thank you,'

The Colonel stalked out of the room, leaving by the doorway behind his desk that connected with the Adjutant's office.

The man picked up the briefcase that stood by his right leg and carried it across to a small grey settee opposite Seb's chair. He sat down and opened the briefcase on his lap, removing a pad of legal paper and a Parker ballpoint.

'You don't mind if I doodle while we talk, do you?' the man asked him.

'No, sir.'

'Please don't call me sir. Call me Holdfast.'

'Holdfast.'

'That's better. You see,' Holdfast said, 'I'm not a military man. National Service of course, but nothing muscular.' He smiled in a self-deprecating manner.

There was a knock on the door and Lance-Corporal McEnroy, the battalion movements clerk, ducked his head inside. 'Tea, suh.'

'Ah yes,' Holdfast said. 'That was quick.'

'The kettle wuz boiled, suh.'

McEnroy smiled conspiratorially at Seb as he crossed the room and set the white china cup on the small teak-varnish table next to the settee.

'Awright, suh?'

'Aye, Corporal Mac.'

After he left they sat in silence. Holdfast seemed to have the gift of quiet. He sat, apparently contentedly, sipping his tea. Seb drank his scotch.

Holdfast smiled at him over the rim of the teacup. His teeth were bad. 'Good whisky?'

'Yes, from Skye,' Seb replied.

'Hector says you live on one of the islands.'

'Yes.'

He returned the teacup gently to the table. 'I'd forgotten,' he said, 'just how dire army tea-bags can be.'

Seb nodded. He shifted on the chair. It was hard and uncomfortable.

Holdfast shook his head, as if reminiscing. 'I remember Captain Nairac when he was based in Crossmaglen. He used to go in the pubs. Short's. The Three Steps Inn. They wouldn't serve him but I rather think they tolerated him, particularly because he had a fine singing voice. He knew all the songs of the IRA, 'The Soldier's Song', 'Danny Boy', 'The Broad Black Brimmer'. He knew the words in Irish, too.

'When local people were taken in for questioning, he would often turn up at the base and demand that they be released. He was very involved in his job, perhaps too sympathetic. I believe they became genuinely fond of him in Crossmaglen. Of course, it didn't stop them killing him. He was, after all, a spy.' He sighed. 'Hector says that you have not been well used?'

'I'm not sure what you mean.' Seb said, carefully.

'I've been reading your file. It makes for impressive reading. This is your second tour in Ireland. The UN in Kuwait. You were put forward for the Military Cross in the Gulf. You didn't get it?'

'No.'

'Bitter?'

'No.'

'You've done a lot of courses.'

'I've had a lot of time on my hands,' Seb explained.

'Yes. The jungle warfare instructors' course in Brunei, the combat survival course in Germany; ah yes, the interrogation course at the Joint Services Intelligence School in Kent; enjoy that one, did you?'

'It wasn't easy.'

'But you did well. In fact, you've done well on all your courses. With one exception: the army's Northern Ireland surveillance and intelligence-gathering unit, 14 Intelligence Company. Under-cover work here in Ulster. I understand that 14 Company turned you down?'

'I completed the course. I wasn't kept on.'

'Why not?'

'I made disparaging remarks about the Parachute Regiment.'

Holdfast raised his eyebrows. He'd started to write or draw on the pad – it was unclear which. 'What sort of remarks?'

'I said they shouldn't be in Northern Ireland.'

'I expect there are lots of people who would agree with that.'

Seb shrugged. 'The directing staff were predominantly Paras. They considered me arrogant and insubordinate.'

'Are you?'

'Sometimes.'

Holdfast nodded in apparent sympathy. He was intent on his legal pad. He spoke as if he was chewing his lip. 'I spoke to the officer commanding 14 Company, and he said they had decided you were too wayward for Special Forces work. His words, not mine. He said you were a gamble they weren't prepared to take. Not level-headed.'

'What can I say?'

'Hector speaks very highly of you.'

'I have great respect for Colonel Hector,' Seb replied, without hesitation.

'So do we all. He says you have potential.'

'He hasn't mentioned it to me.'

'I don't suppose he would; he doesn't strike me as being the type who goes in for praising people. Not his way. He said something else. That you would rise to the occasion, that was the type of chap you are.'

'I don't know what you mean.'

Holdfast pushed his glasses back up on to the bridge of his nose. His pen was travelling up and down the page like the trace on a lie detector. 'He meant that given a demanding job you'd show enthusiasm and commitment. Do you think I should believe him?'

Seb stared at his creased grey forehead, willing him to meet his eyes.

'Sandwiches on Bobby Sands's grave. It's not very mature, is it?'

'There's no proof it was me.'

'Then I suppose we must consider you innocent,' Holdfast observed sceptically. 'Let's return to this comment about the Paras. You were in the Paras? As a private soldier if I'm correct?'

'Yes,' Seb replied.

'Why did you choose to do that? Serve as a private soldier? Surely that's not a common occurrence?'

Seb shrugged.

Holdfast continued, 'Now, correct me if I'm wrong, but your brother Torquil is in the Parachute Regiment.'

'He's different,' Seb countered.

'He's serving with the SAS now, isn't he?'

'That's correct.'

'Were you never tempted down that path?'

'I wouldn't pass the medical.'

Holdfast blinked. 'Really? Why not?'

'My eyesight,' Seb told him. 'I wear contact lenses.'

'And that would disqualify you. That doesn't seem very fair. I mean, are you hindered in any way by wearing contact lenses?'

'No. I wear high-water-content lenses. I can leave them in for days at a time. I'm a good shot.' The indignation came unbidden to his voice.

Holdfast smiled. 'You must feel rather hard done by?'

'Sometimes I do,' Seb said carefully, annoyed at himself for the outburst. He reminded himself that he must be on guard against this man. 'Sometimes I don't.'

'You're not a graduate, are you?'

'I dropped out of university in my first year.'

'Yes. It makes it difficult, doesn't it? For promotion, I mean. The graduates get all the best jobs. Your brother is a graduate, isn't he?'

'Yes.'

'Oxford,' Holdfast said.

'Oxford Poly,' Seb corrected him.

'And you were at Edinburgh, at the university?'

'Briefly.'

'What were you studying?'

'Classics.'

'I see. And what about your father? He worked for the Secret Service?'

'He'd deny it.'

Holdfast seemed to mull this over. Then he looked up from the legal pad, though only for the briefest time. 'I expect you would like a proper job.'

'I beg your pardon?'

'A proper job. Something demanding. In the family vein. A chance to prove yourself.'

'Yes,' Seb said.

'You can go now.' Holdfast said. He clicked the top of his pen to retract the nib and returned it to his inside pocket. 'That's all.' He smiled myopically.

All the whisky tumblers in Cal's pockets clinked as he staggered and slipped on the beer-soaked linoleum, catching himself against the edge of the pool table. Dugald, his eldest brother, had one huge hairy forearm slung round his neck and was staggering with him.

'I wansha to be my best man,' Dugald told him, and his forehead struck the felt surface of the table, scattering balls.

'What about Aulay?' Cal protested, attempting to drag him off the table.

'He's nae said more than three wurdz in his life, is that not right?'

'Aye.' Aulay was rocking slowly back and forth on his feet, and shaking his head slowly as if struggling for the other two, 'Iss true . . .'

'What about Nially?'

Nially was still talking, sliding along the bar-rail, and rattling on like a radio that couldn't be switched off. Dugald straightened up, and released his grasp on Cal. He staggered backwards for a few steps before he found a precarious balance. There was an expression of drunken affront on his face.

'Aye, you can hear him, but ya wouldnae care to listen to him.'

He broke into wild laughter. Nially fell off the bar-rail.

'Ah yes, Calum, yer the only wun.'

Calum had a moment of sudden clarity, and found himself staring into the open, beatific smile of the Cradden. He was in his usual place, in the corner by the window, sitting on the back of a chair with his accordion in his hands. It was said that he had the second sight. Tonight he was being accompanied on guitar by the hippy Dylan, who nurtured a rust-red Afro and worked at the abattoir. They were both nodding and grinning, oblivious.

'I cannae,' Cal protested.

'Ay've tolt the auld man,' Dugald leant over him and spoke in a deafening stage-whisper in his ear. 'An the priest wants to see you.'

'No,' Cal groaned.

'Aye.' Dugald grinned, a familiar expression of childish mischief written across his face. 'Iss all fixed. Yir the man.' He raised an arm, and waved it so that Cal was forced to duck to avoid being hit. 'A sweetie fir the best man.'

He yelled to the barman, 'Jamesy, more drams! An one fir yersel. A dram, Nially.' He grabbed Nially under the armpits and tried to drag him to his feet.

The Cradden had ceased struggling with his accordion and emerged from the corner, in search of whisky. Dugald saw him and abruptly dropped Nially. The Cradden nearly made it, his small, delicate hand darting out to grasp the whisky glass. Dugald grabbed him, and lifted him up into the air.

'Put ays doon,' the Cradden squealed. He looked terrified. It was hardly surprising: Dugald's fist was larger than his head. Dugald had the largest hands Calum had ever seen.

'Hav ye bin lyin' wi the goats up oan the Og again?' demanded Dugald. 'Yir no tryin tae tell ays that it's natural, tae huv sex wi goats?'

He looked round the bar, at each of them in turn, before returning his attention to the Cradden. 'In sight ov Ma's ghost,' Dugald growled. 'Huv ye seen her?'

'Noo, ah naevir,' the Cradden said.

'Aye, ye huv.'

Released, the Cradden fell in a heap on the floor. 'Aye, ay haav,' he said slyly. 'She wuz oagin wi maids.'

Dugald scratched his forehead. 'Maids?'

'Maggots,' Cal translated.

The Cradden scuttled away.

'Ya wee cunt!' Dugald snarled, and followed him with his small dangerous eyes all the way back to his corner. 'And dinnae forget my brother Calum, wat ay sais to ya!'

'What did you say to him?' Cal wondered.

'Ay tolt him to git the faeries to find ya a wummin.'

'Ay toalt you,' shouted the Cradden from his corner. 'The new vet.'

'The vet,' Dugald exclaimed, and spun round to face the bar. 'Jamesy!'

'I'm nae deaf.'

'The new vet!'

'Ay,' James the Barman said, 'She lives next to us, up at Carndonald. She's not seeing anyone, I don't think.'

Dugald was triumphant. 'Exactly!' He took up his whisky and pressed one into Cal's hand, and slung his arm around Cal's shoulders and said, 'I love you, Calum.' Then he giggled insanely. 'No tongues, though.'

'I'd be proud to be your best man,' Calum told him. All the bottles behind the bar were spinning, and his reflection behind them didn't make any sense. It felt like he was in over his head in a Cubist nightmare. He wondered if he was going to be sick.

Dugald pushed another empty glass into Cal's pocket.

Cal protested, 'Why d'ya keep doing that?'

'Shhh,' Dugald hushed him, in another deafening whisper. He winked. 'Fir the reception.' Cal looked at James. James shrugged and went off through the curtain to the lounge bar.

Cal said, 'Shud you not just hire them?'

'No no no,' Dugald cried. 'Don't be daft!'

Cal fell over. Miraculously, none of the glasses broke.

'Wat are ya doin?' Dugald asked him, with a genuine look of puzzlement on his face.

'I cannae feel my legs,' Cal groaned.

'Dinnae worry about that,' Dugald said, and handed him down one of the many half-finished whiskies that littered the bar top. 'Get this down yir neck.'

Calum knocked back the contents of the glass, pulled himself up on the bar-rail, took two fragile steps and fell over Nially. He drifted away into oblivion surrounded by shattered glass.

It was pitch black. The course was a dark and terrifying distance stretched out ahead of them.

'No the kitshun,' Cal protested. There had been a time when any one of them could make it from the kitchen to the bedrooms without recourse to a light switch. Then Aulay had started rebuilding cars in the kitchen, and what had been a simple drunken ritual had become a matter of survival. Somewhere in front him lurked dangerous and life-threatening obstacles.

There was a chorus of chicken noises. A huge body leaned heavily against him. It could only be Dugald.

'Are ye a maan, ur a muus?'

Aulay giggled from somewhere. 'Durs a safe route,' he insisted. 'I'm pointing.'

'Cheers,' Cal said. He heard what sounded like Aulay tumbling back through the doorway into the yard and the Collie With No Name lunging at the end of its chain in a paroxysm of rage. There was no moon and the sky was obscured by heavy cloud. It was as dark outside as it was inside.

'Somebody shut that dug up,' Cal groaned.

'Ish jus been frendly,' Dugald told him.

The door was dragged closed.

'Sshtil there?' Dugald asked.

Cal said, 'Aye.' Then, 'Where's Aulay?'

Silence.

'Dishqualified,' Dugald pronounced. 'Are you ready?'

Cal swayed back and forth, trying to concentrate. After the kitchen it was the stairs; each stair was a different height and he could not remember them all. The trick was to let yourself be carried forward by instinct. He closed his eyes and a field of red dots drifted downwards across the inside of his eyelids.

'I can see,' he said triumphantly. 'I'm weightlesh and invulnerable.'

He was nudged awake by a slippered foot. He passed his hand tentatively across the front of his face, and was relieved to discover that he could see. He was halfway up the stairs.

'Yer the winner,' his father said.

He looked up at his father. Angus Bean was the same nacreous colour that he remembered.

'Hi, Dad.'

'You better see to Dugald,' his father muttered.

Cal slid carefully down the stairs and staggered into the kitchen.

'Ay've broakin my leg,' protested Dugald, from beneath an engine block. 'She'll kill me fir sure.'

The leg didn't look good. They were all likely to be in danger when Dugald's fiancée found out.

'I'm oaf to my room,' said their father.

Aulay crawled in out of the yard. 'Who won?'

Dugald brandished an accusatory finger. 'That bashturt.'

Cal just about managed a bow. Together with Aulay, he lifted the block off Dugald and half dragged and half carried him out to the pick-up. They drove out to the cottage hospital, where they encased Dugald's leg in a cast and gave him a set of crutches. Then they drove over to the LochIntake Hotel to pay for all the broken glass, and were told they were banned until after the wedding. It would have been a permanent ban, James told them, but the owner recognised that it was the only bar on the island that hadn't already banned Dugald for life, and that to deprive him of a place to drink with his friends would be torture. They thanked James for interceding on their behalf and went back across Main Street, Dugald brandishing his crutches at any onlookers.

'Away wi'ye!' he shouted.

After lunch, Cal packed a thermos of fresh-brewed coffee in his daysack and set off walking north-westwards, past the old Viking settlement that had given the farm its name. As he climbed the last of the drystone walls that marked the boundary of the farm, and struck out on the open moor, he felt the full force of wind on his face and the last painful bands of his hangover fall away.

He forded deep, peaty streams by jumping from rock to rock, and sloshed through swamps of marsh-grass that were too large to bypass, and scrambled over rock outcrops. He walked for two hours and then sat down with his back resting against a standing stone. He drank his coffee, and considered Seb's proposition.

He waited for some feeling to seize him. He felt no moral qualms. It was only the old and the ill-informed, and the reactionaries who whipped them up for their vote, who believed cannabis was evil. He'd got over that particular hurdle years before. It was not in his nature, but it seemed best to think about it logically. The money would be useful. Eventually, when the money was laundered, he would be able to buy the farm. It would help his brother and his new family. The Freedom To Live. He said it over to himself, savouring the words, the idea.

Greed wasn't his motivation, but then if it wasn't what was?

Deep down – and he wasn't sure that he had a deep – what did he want?

He was bored with working on the rigs and equally bored with the constant failure of environmental protest. He was uninspired by the jottings in his notebooks. He didn't seem to be able to sustain a relationship with a woman, and he suspected that he had no insight into the relations between men and women beyond the act of sex itself. He felt stunted.

He was conscious of his hand going up to his face, feeling the outline of hard plastic in his jaw through the flesh of his upper lip, and tracing the knife scar in the gristle of his nose and on his right cheek. The visible marks of the beating that he had taken. If truth be told, he had a fierce desire, something like lust, to prove himself – to show that he was not without courage. In a dark stairwell in Leith he had been savagely beaten by two men. They had told him to leave Edinburgh and he had responded in the only way he could: he had left. Now he wanted to go back to that dark place and fight for his life and survive on his own terms.

So he began to think, to make preparations of his own, because he knew that once he was caught up in the irrepressible dynamic of Seb's 'Just Cause' there would be no turning back. It was Seb who worried him, his explosive and unpredictable nature.

He thought and achieved no resolution and after an hour he picked himself up and packed his daysack and set off on a round-about route back to the farm, walking with fresh determination eastwards in the direction of the three conical mountains, the Paps of Garbh.

He skirted the edge of a loch, and entered the woods that clung to the edge of the cliffs above the Sound of Cual, the narrow channel between Cual and Garbh.

There was a ferry from Kennaicraig unloading on the pier at Port Siobhag far below him, and from where he stood in the dense foliage he could see down between the trunks of trees and beyond all the switchbacks in the road, to where Aulay and all the other part-timers who supplemented their income by working for Cal-Mac were directing the lorries and other traffic off the boat.

There had been a time in his youth when he had always come here to watch the ferry arrive. When his mind had been filled with fanciful dreams of what the boat might carry across the water to him. He sat on an old rotting oak log and watched the people on the gangplank, and he remembered the day the boat brought him Madelene.

Damage. She'd caused damage that day.

It was two days before the funeral, and two days after he had seen a mermaid and learnt that his mother and his aunt were dead in a car-crash on the mainland. It was his vantage point. It got him away from all the cloying relatives and their unwanted concern and sympathy and their 'keeping a close eye on him'.

On that particular day he'd seen a wild-haired and half-starved young stowaway break free of the grasp of the steward, rush down the gangplank, drop the harbourmaster with a solid kick to the balls, sprint across the car-park between the astonished tourists and scramble up the hill through the trees while fat, sweating seamen fell far behind. She'd hardly eaten during the week it had taken her to get to the island, but she could still outrun any man on the island. He remembered her stopping to catch her breath on the crest of the hill, just a few feet away from where he was sitting. Her clothes were torn and thick with burrs. Her face was dirty and beautiful – her coppery-blond hair like a mane. She had cast one defiant, imperious glance in his direction; and, for one breathless moment, he had thought she was the mermaid, come to him out of the water. Then she was off again, out on the moor. Sprinting.

That Major (retd) Hugh Humberstone MacCoinneach, one-time soldier, gentleman-spy and managing director of numberless fraudulent offshore companies, was, among other things, an adulterer, was not information that he had shared with any of the islanders. Certainly Mary, the now-dead mother of his four sons, had not been privy to the secret. It had all come out at the funeral. In driving rain The MacCoinneach had appeared at the graveside flanked by not only his stone-faced sons but also, with her hand resting lightly on his right forearm, his newly washed and scrubbed and utterly breathtaking daughter, Madelene.

Madelene des Esseintes was of mixed Argentine, Spanish, Slavic and Scottish blood. She was born in Buenos Aires, where her mother, a noted beauty, conducted a brief but passionate affair with Hugh MacCoinneach. She grew up in a succession of cities across the globe, including Trieste, New York, Beirut and

Barcelona. Her education was, despite considerable expense, fragmentary. She read five languages but she could hardly count. Her vocabulary displayed a wilful, and sometimes startling, mixture of the demotic and the sublime. She claimed to know more swear words, in more languages, than anyone else on the island.

The island, in turn, was utterly scandalised. At the funeral, Cal's father, fortified with a bottle of whisky, had assumed the unaccustomed mantle of outraged family member and thrown a punch which The MacCoinneach, despite having sedated himself with a wartime stock of morphine, had easily side-stepped. Unbalanced, Angus Bean toppled over and slewed away in a flurry of gelatinous mud that carried him down into his wife's grave. He struck the coffin with a hollow crump and started snoring loudly.

The sons fell upon one another; the three remaining MacCoinneachs and the three Beans. Despite their father's military background and his enthusiasm for boxing, the MacCoinneachs did not emerge victorious. Dugald Bean's size more than made up for any imagined disadvantage of history. The families fought themselves to a stand-still. At the end of it all their corner of the graveyard resembled the aftermath of the Somme, unrecognisable shell-shocked figures stumbling in a morass of mud.

The sons were friends again within a week, their shared grief binding them. The widowed fathers were never reconciled. Angus Bean gave up fishing for a living and retired to his armchair in the kitchen of the farmhouse at Skurryvaig, and The MacCoinneach remained on the estate at Murbhach and continued to come and go from the island on mysterious business trips to the Middle and Far East. That he was ostracised by his fellow islanders did not seem to bother him. He was no stranger to controversy. His dabblings in the occult and his unusual methods of land-management were already widely publicised. Now sexual rapacity was added to his list of activities.

So when, over a decade later, he stole his son's lover and proceeded to sire a new family, there was much gossip but little real surprise. Similarly, there was little surprise in the aftermath of the Gulf War when a former Conservative minister now languishing on the backbenches stood up and named him on the floor of the House of Commons as a former member of MI6.

*   *   *

Cal went out of the woods, following a path away from the edge of the cliffs and dropped down on to the road that led back to the farm, walking between steep banks of black-green winter grass. The ferry traffic passed him heading for Deochmore. He crossed a stone bridge over a gushing peat-coloured brook. The wind was getting up now, and there was dampness in it, the moisture clinging to the exposed flesh of his face. The Paps of Garbh, across the water to the east, had turned blue with rain.

When he got back he had a bowl of stew from the stove, and made a few half-hearted attempts at conversation with his father. When he'd finished the food he went up to his room and climbed under the covers where it was warm.

He was woken in the middle of the night by the rubber tip of a crutch, thickly coated with fresh green cow-shit, being wafted under his nose. The room flooded with light. He groaned savagely.

'Up wi'ye! Up wi'ye!' Dugald yelled at him.

Cal squinted and strove to comprehend. Dugald had found a cow up the top field at eleven with her waterbag out, and he'd brought her in and put her in the byre and now he thought she was with twins and he wanted an opinion.

Cal had no wish to get out of bed. He said, 'My opinion is that she has twins.'

Dugald dragged the blankets off the bed, lost his balance, fell on the bed and eventually, predictably, grabbed Cal by the balls. Not so predictably that Cal thought to take any evasive action, but then he had been away for a long time.

He screamed. Dugald grinned.

'Jesus,' Cal groaned. 'I'm coming, I'm coming.'

He rummaged among the piles on the floor for some clothes while Dugald clacked and hopped his way down the stairs.

Outside, it was lashing with rain. He put his head down and stumbled across the yard past the Collie With No Name and into the low entrance of the stone shed. He squelched across the slick grey-brown concrete floor, while other, less aggressive collies eyed him suspiciously, rolling up his sleeve as he went, and holding out his arm like a blind man. Dugald took him by the elbow and hopped him towards the end stall, and within seconds his arm was enfolded in the warm, wet vagina, his hand in the uterus, his fingers sliding across the smooth, waxy surface of a calf's hoof. He felt his way up the leg, testing the joints. The first two joints bent in the same direction as he manipulated them. Front leg. Exploring further, he located what he thought were three front legs.

'Definitely twins,' he said.

'Can ye tell which legs belong to which calf?'

'Aye, mebbe,' he said, pushing the cow's feathery tail out of his face.

Dugald held out the calving ropes. 'Well, go to it then, Tonto.'

Cal hooked the knotted rich-smelling ropes around two of the hooves and for five minutes they heaved on them, bracing their feet against the side of a drainage channel. The cow let out a series of awesome bass groans and milk started pouring from her udder on to the concrete.

They looked at each other.

'Ay'll call the vet,' Dugald suggested, and went out into the rain. He called out, 'Get some calcium into her.'

There was a dark brown bottle marked 'Calcium' sitting in a bucket with a flutter valve and some needles in plastic envelopes. Cal ripped them open and slapped a needle under the skin behind the cow's shoulder. He attached the valve and the bottle and held it up above his head, allowing gravity to carry the calcium down and into the cow. He waited for the bottle to empty, and then used it to mash the lump of fluid that had accumulated under the skin, pushing it back and forth across the surface like a rolling pin.

The cow continued to groan. Dugald returned. He stood propped on his crutches, patting her neck and muttering words of encouragement.

'At least it's stopped raining,' he said.

Eventually, they heard a car pull into the courtyard and brake in a flurry of gravel chips that struck the door of the shed, the beams of the headlights sweeping across the corrugated-iron roof.

Dugald went off to fetch the vet. Cal rested his head against the cow's swollen belly and listened to the sounds of movement there. He felt fully awake now, and his spirits soared as if the effort of pulling at the calf had dislodged the black mood that had weighed on him since the rig went down.

The door was tugged open and the vet strode in with Dugald at her shoulder, struggling to keep up.

'Hello, Calum,' she called out. Her voice was loud and deep. Irish. The light caught her eyes, and they sparkled as if with wry amusement. She was wearing wellies, bulky green waterproof trousers that were elasticated at the waist, and a sleeveless black T-shirt. The veins stood out crisply on her compactly muscled arms. Her breasts were unsupported and swayed as she moved, the nipples tiny sharp points.

'Hello, Oonagh,' he said, stunned.

She brushed past him, all crackling green plastic, and set her bucket down by the cow. Her hair was longer and thicker, red and chestnut, with the texture of hay, and gathered in a simple pony-tail secured with a leather bootlace. She covered her freckled arm in thick gelatinous Lubrol from a squeezy bottle.

'Are you having difficulties?' she asked, as she slipped her arm into the cow.

'Believing my eyes,' he answered. She looked great: lithe and hard.

'I was wondering when you'd come home,' she said.

'You two know each other?' Dugald said, his head going back and forth between them.

'It's a long story,' Cal explained.

She started laughing – he remembered that laugh, the reck-lessness of it. 'Don't be so pompous,' she said.

Dugald's large, weatherbeaten face broke into a broad, toothy grin.

'I like this,' he said. 'Oh yes, yes, yes.'

'Who put these ropes on?' she demanded.

Cal winced, raised a finger like an errant schoolboy. 'Me.'

'You've got them on a back leg and a front leg. There's only one calf in here.'

Dugald cuffed him affectionately round the head. 'Ay told him,' he said smugly.

'You did not,' Cal protested, rubbing at his head.

'Did too!' Dugald whooped.

'I'll get the calving jack,' she said, 'while you two decide who's the bigger fool.'

'I'm the biggest,' Dugald called after her, 'he's the most foolish.' He rounded on Cal and wagged a finger at him. 'So the Cradden was right.'

'Away an shite,' Cal muttered.

Oonagh returned with the jack laid across her shoulder.

'Has the prospect of marriage robbed you of your intelligence as well as your feet?' she said to Dugald, whose grin was getting wider and wider. 'You're no use in that state. Come on, Calum, give me a hand.'

They attempted to ratchet the calf out, planting the heel of the jack against the cow's hindquarters.

'It's big,' Cal groaned, straining at the handle.

'Away wi'ye,' Dugald scoffed.

Slowly, the feet emerged.

'Hold it steady,' she instructed them, 'while I feel what the head is doing.'

She squeezed a dollop of fresh Lubrol on her hands and reached in, searching for the nostrils and the dome of the head. 'It's a big bugger,' she said.

'You're not wrong,' Cal agreed.

'Try another couple of notches,' she told him

He breathed out hard and strained at the handle.

'Jesus!' he gasped.

'No,' she said.

'No?' Dugald asked.

'It won't come through the pelvis,' she said.

'It won't come through the pelvis?'

'Is there an echo in here?'

'No,' Cal said, turning his thigh to ward off a possible assault. 'Unfortunately it's my brother.'

Dugald waved the tip of a crutch at him threateningly.

'It'll have to come out the side,' Oonagh told them.

'The side? Are you sure?'

'Certain.'

'I don't know . . .' Dugald grinned.

'We need to do it now,' she said.

Cal remembered her as being confident, arrogant even. Now she was self-assured. She was watching his face, a half-smile on her face. She raised an eyebrow.

'All right,' Dugald conceded, 'I'm convinced.' He hopped away in search of hot water.

'Come on,' she said, tilting her head at Calum, and he followed her out into the wind and watched her by the car's roof-light as she rooted about in the boot of the Subaru, among the palettes of drugs and piles of tools. She thrust a steel box into his hand.

'You seem so . . . different,' he called out, raising his voice against the wind.

'I was a student then,' she shouted over her shoulder. 'Now I'm a vet. It was years ago.'

'You look great,' he said.

'What?'

'You look great!'

She thrust a large green bucket into his other hand and held the door open for him. 'Come on.'

'I said you look great,' he repeated, out of the wind now.

'You look the same,' she said.

'No different?' He paced her down the shed.

'Older maybe,' she replied swiftly.

'That's it?'

She stopped and eyed him speculatively. 'Are you all right?'

'Ach dinnae take any notice of him,' Dugald put in, recklessly swinging a bucket of hot water. 'He's sufferin an existential crisis. A good shag wull see him right.'

'Shagging anyone?' she asked archly.

'No,' he said quickly, meaning it to be true.

'He's available,' Dugald agreed.

'The cow,' Oonagh said firmly.

First, she sedated it and then she soaped its flank with Pevidene antiseptic. When she was done she shaved the hide, deftly wielding a razor blade with her long fingers, scooping it through the nicotine-coloured soapy gloop. Then she anaesthetised the cow, working down an imaginary line with a needle and syringe, injecting the local into the skin and the muscle layers. She was moving quickly, the sparse planes of her face taut with concentration.

She scrubbed herself with Pevidene, going vigorously at her bare arms with the brush, and then she took up a scalpel and, without hesitation, made an incision in the skin, opening the fat. She went back into the wound with the blade and cut at it repeatedly, and blood poured from it on to the concrete as if from a tap. The cow was groaning and heaving.

There was a loud sucking noise as she cut through the lining of the abdomen and the air rushed in. She went into the abdomen with her hands and heaved at the pink sac of the uterus, searching for the outline of a calf's leg. Finding one, she made an incision in the uterus and went in and got hold of the leg.

'Get those ropes off,' she commanded, her brows tightly knit. Dugald reached in from the other side and unhooked them.

She squatted against the cow's flank and the muscles under the pale and freckled skin of her neck and shoulders tensed, and she heaved upwards with her full strength and the calf came up out of the uterus and spilled on the floor.

'I was right,' she said. 'It's a big bugger.'

Cal was immediately astride the calf, his fingers in the clogged tubes of its nostrils, scooping out the fluid and squeezing at the flesh. The calf snorted and started breathing. 'Welcome to the world,' he said.

Grey whorls of afterbirth were tumbling out of the wound, and Oonagh severed them with scissors and began suturing the uterus with catgut, stitching it and pushing back the remaining afterbirth at the same time. Over her shoulder, she asked, 'What is it?'

'A bull,' Dugald answered.

'Happy, then?'

'Aye.'

Cal saw that the tension was out of her neck now; she was relaxed, stitching with apparent ease, pausing every few minutes only to run her forearm across her brow. Her head was steaming. There were damp patches in the dark material below her shaven armpits. The heat and smell in the shed were a powerful stimulus.

It took her half an hour to finish the stitching and then, while Dugald was coaxing the calf on to the cow's teat, she injected the cow with an antibiotic and began to pack up her instruments.

'Are you hungry?' Cal blurted out.

'Not at all,' she said, smiling at him.

'How about a drink? A whisky?'

'I've to get back,' she said, gathering her buckets and boxes. He took a bucket out of her hand, and followed her out to the car.

'Will I see you again?' he asked.

'I expect so,' she said, pausing by the car and looking at him.

'When?'

She laughed at him, that wild chaotic laugh. 'At the wedding, of course.'

6

Seb spent five excruciating days loafing in the bland, characterless officers mess at 39 Brigade in Lisburn, while in his imagination the water churned, and then, on the afternoon of the fifth day, *They* came for him. They sent him an acquaintance, a one-time Royal Scot named Richard Brannon, who was now serving with the SAS.

He threw himself down on to the sofa next to Seb and stuck his Timberland boots up on the coffee table. He ran his fingers through his fine sandy hair, and lit a cigarette. Seb switched off his Walkman and removed the earphones.

Brannon said, 'How the devil are you?'

They knew each other, though not well, Brannon had been a couple of years before him at Sandhurst. Now he was a captain. They had met at the occasional Scots Division function.

'Bored shitless,' Seb replied.

Brannon took in the litter of coffee cups, Rich Tea biscuits and rinds of toast, and the pile of ancient magazines on the table, *Field and Stream, Sporting Life.* The first showing of *Neighbours* on the television. These carefully cultivated signs. With the exception of dinner time, when the three other 'living-in' members put in an appearance, Seb had been left almost entirely alone in the mess. Each morning the cleaners had hoovered around him as he lay in bed. He got up at coffee time and spent the day slumped in front of the television. His dining companions were the Catholic padre, the doctor and a recently divorced staff major. He had treated them with oafish disdain and when, on the second day, he asked to have his meals in the TV room no one had objected.

'*Neighbours,*' Brannon beamed. 'Wicked.'

He sank further down on to the sofa and gave the television his undivided attention. Brannon was big and slightly knock-kneed and his thighs rubbed together as he walked. There was a coin-shaped scar under his right eye, received after a drunken prank that involved jumping from a moving train. He was not, to Seb's mind, very bright, and therefore perfect.

When the soap finished Brannon immediately lit another cigarette.

'There's lots of interest in you back at the Kremlin,' he said. He meant SAS regimental headquarters in Hereford.

'I'm honoured,' Seb replied dryly. 'What are you doing here?'

'I've been seconded to 14 Company from the Training Wing at Hereford. Not just me. Everyone's been flown in for this one. Hauled out of retirement and dusted off. No local talent, you see, not since the Chinook crash took out the big spooks. They're all running around like headless chickens. Anyway, you're my baby. Want to come play?'

'Certainly,' Seb replied.

'Well then, let's get you in some casual clothing.'

The meeting was held in a Portakabin tucked away at the back of a hangar in the military section of Aldergrove airport. The woman from MI5 arrived by helicopter as Seb was crossing the tarmac in the company of Brannon. The army Gazelle touched down on a patch of icy grass not fifty metres from the hangar. They paused mid-stride and watched her leap out of the helicopter and come running towards them with her head down against the still-spinning rotor blades. When she straightened up Seb saw that she was not tall, about five foot six he estimated, late twenties with glossy dark-brown hair to her shoulders, a slightly long face with a thin nose supporting wire-framed glasses. She was wearing practical clothes; black Levi's, a purple fibre-pile jacket and leather walking boots. She nodded curtly at them and they followed on as she strode towards a small grey door to the hangar.

The man who opened the door wore pressed tropical combats with the sleeves rolled to the elbow despite the weather. He simply smiled, revealing a gap between his crooked front teeth, and nodded to them to enter.

'Hello, Bob,' Seb said, recognising him.

The woman went through first and Seb and Brannon followed, dipping their heads under the low doorframe. The first thing Seb saw was a blue Ford Sierra. Riding low on its armoured chassis, it was obviously Special Branch. It was parked at the centre of a clear area of tarmac that was surrounded by apparently haphazard stacks of wooden packing cases and pallets. The spaces between these looming masses were passageways in a darkened maze. There was no central light source, and what light there was came from occasional caged bulbs, strung from overhead conduits that followed passageways through the hangar.

The woman from MI5 stopped by the car door.

'Wait here,' she said. She turned her back and walked down one of the narrow passageways between piles of crates. Seb lost sight of her at the first turn. He listened to the echo of her footsteps in the cavernous space.

Brannon rolled his eyes and reached for his cigarettes. 'Snout?'

They leant against the bodywork of the car and smoked in silence.

Gradually Seb's eyes became accustomed to all the rectangular shadows. He realised that the hangar was a sort of temporary shelter, with the character of a refugee camp: many of the larger packing crates lay on their side with blankets pinned across the open end for privacy. There were several washing lines strung between crates. The hangar might be full of people; it was impossible to tell. The occasional cough hinted at a presence.

Grinding the dout beneath his heel, Brannon hawked and spat, then climbed into the back of the car, stretched out on the seat, and promptly went to sleep.

Seb slowly circled the car. As he was coming around the bonnet, he heard the strike and flare of a match off to his right. He looked up quickly, and saw somebody bending over a stove about twenty metres away, the hunched bulk of his shadow thrown against the interior of a crate, then the hexamine bricks catching and casting wild and dazzling flames around a rectangular mess-tin, the flames lighting his bearded messianic face and clots of hair, the deep shadows under his all-too-familiar eyes, the cruel beak of his MacCoinneach nose. He looked straight at Seb.

'Christ,' breathed Seb. He took a few steps forward. The last time he'd seen Torquil had been in the immediate aftermath of the Gulf War, on the Mutla Ridge. Some radical transformation had clearly taken place since then.

Torquil immediately tipped the water in the canteen over the fire. There was a loud hissing, then blackness.

Seb was blinded, his vision filled with geometric lights. He took a few more steps but he was disorientated. Torquil was gone.

As he stood waiting for his eyesight to return, he heard the staccato sound of steel segs approaching across the tarmac. And a voice, its harsh East Belfast brogue travelling ahead of its owner, as loud as his footsteps.

'Hail thar, young Sebastian MacCoinneach, our latest alchemist amok in this garrison of spies and shock-troopers.'

Seb turned towards the sound of the voice. A heavily built man was striding towards him, from beneath a string of swinging light-bulbs, the light catching the worn shiny patches on his suit. His suit jacket was hitched up, revealing the swollen barrel of his belly.

'What shit will you turn to gold this Christmas, I wonder?'

'Shut the fuck up!' somebody called from the darkened depths of the hangar.

'Ah fuck ya, ya carpetbaggin' Brit bastard,' the Irishman called out, jabbing his finger away into the depths as if he could see what he was pointing at. He slammed to a metallic halt in front of Seb and squared up to him as if to fight him. Seb studied him. He had a raw, blunt face, with a broad forehead and a shock of grey hair, a thick salt-and-pepper moustache and a purplish nose split with veins.

'Whatya lookin at?' he sneered. 'Yes, I'm a bruiser. What are you? The last gasp of MI5? Go home. Take your fiction with you.' He reached past Seb and rapped his knuckles on the car window.

'Hey, you, young pup, git the fuck outta my car. I earned the right to sleep in that car. I work for a living.'

'Hello, Bertie.' Brannon clambered out of the car. 'Sebastian MacCoinneach, this is Bertie Nugent, Special Branch.'

The Irishman's hot breath on Seb's face. 'Never mind that. I know MaColl. He was in the Long Kesh on the 'blanket', and after that on the 'dirty'. He knows the smell of his own shit. And he never believed in any of it. He knows shit, and he knows how to peddle it as information. You tell her that. In her arrogance she'll not listen to me.'

'I'll tell her,' Seb said, softly.

'You do that.' He opened the driver's door. 'And another thing. Don't come crying to me when it blows up in all your faces. I know when I've been snubbed. I don't forget.' And to Brannon: 'She's a great gal, but get her out of here. They'll crucify her.'

She looked up at Sebastian with the frank and fearless look of a woman who knew her mind and would not be deterred. Her eyes were the colour of polished walnut.

'I'll tell you this, in absolute honesty,' she informed him. 'You screw this up and you're finished. You'll get one chance. We put you in the car, you find out what Oisin MaColl knows about the Brink's Depository robbery.'

The Portakabin was roasting hot. There was condensation dripping down the panes of glass in the windows and across his forehead and down the back of his neck. She sat on the far side of the hut, with her hands crossed on the table in front of her. Seb stood, with Brannon lounging against a wall behind him.

'What robbery?' he heard himself say.

'The robbery that took place on January fifth of last year,' she told him. 'At the Brink's cash depository in Rochester, New Jersey. That's in the USA, in case you haven't been paying attention. Seven million dollars stolen, and five million of it still missing. The FBI has the number of each and every note. Twenty dollars of it showed up last week here in Belfast, in Oisin MaColl's grubby fist.'

Beyond her there was a bureau with a coffee percolator, a carton of milk, bowl of sugar, four plastic spoons and a collection of mugs. He found himself staring intently at them.

She said, 'You ask him where the rest of it is.'

'Fair enough,' Seb answered.

She turned to Brannon, her tone brusque and commanding. 'Get your people together and give your orders. MaColl spent two days on Inishmore. That's an island off the west coast of the Republic. Since then he's been going back and forth between Belfast and Dundalk. He's being careful, varying his route. He has access to a couple of cars. The numbers have been released on Vengeful. The analysts tell us an accumulation of indicators suggests that next time he'll be coming back through Aughnacloy.'

Brannon rolled his eyes. 'Computers.'

She ignored him. 'I've got a map of Aughnacloy here for you. JSG have lent us their shed.'

JSG was the latest in a series of bland acronyms, really code-words, that identified the human source handling group of Military Intelligence. They ran a network of informants, known as 'touts', across the province.

'I'm told there's parking space for five cars,' she said. She fished a sheaf of papers from a buff folder and handed them across the table to Brannon. 'The Armagh Roulement Battalion have been tasked to provide their close-observation platoon as a quick-reaction force. They'll be on airborne standby at Bessbrook. I'll say it now so I don't get an earful from you later, Richard. There's no telling how long we'll be waiting.'

'We can't approach him in Belfast?'

'No way,' she snapped. 'Not if we want to keep it secure. Anyway, he's too wily – he won't stay still for long enough.'

'You've been watching him?' Brannon asked.

'Trying to. He hasn't slept in the same bed twice.'

'He's on the run?'

'We don't know. We think so. He hasn't been seen on the streets since he pulled that stunt walking down the Andersonstown Road with his drug-dealer friends. We can only assume that PIRA are after his blood; we can't risk him by asking our sources.' She paused. 'I wouldn't piss on a tout from Belfast if he was burning.'

She looked defiantly at Seb. He let his face relax into an amused smile.

'Wankers,' Brannon added, good-humouredly.

'You should be aware that an attempt to make contact with him was undertaken at the crossing-point at RomeoEight four days ago,' she told Seb. 'It was unsuccessful. Since then he has not used that border crossing. That's right, we went ahead and did it without you. And he wouldn't talk to us. Now's your turn. Find out what he wants.'

Seb nodded in assent. Afterwards on the steps Brannon laid his hand on Seb's shoulder and said, 'Don't worry. She just hates toffs. Thinks she's an outsider. Not public school. As if we gave a damn.' He laughed out loud. 'If you pull this off, everyone will want to know your name. They'll all want to touch you in the hope that a bit of luck will rub off. That's what they're like. Not her, though.

She's a cold fish. Good, though. Doesn't spare herself. The boys say she's a dyke.'

Seb wasn't really listening. He should feel happy, elated even; everything had gone smoothly, the twenty-dollar bill had caused sufficient excitement amongst the spooks, but Torquil's unexpected appearance caused him some disquiet. Torquil could jeopardise everything. He knew what Seb was capable of.

As they negotiated their way between stacks of crates he asked, 'Do you know what my brother's doing here?'

Brannon shook his head. 'Need-to-know basis, mate,' he explained.

'Not this operation, then?'

'Different caper. Different agencies and different intelligence. By the look of him, and it's just a guess, I'd say some kind of deep-cover surveillance.'

So it was just a coincidence, nothing more. They walked together out into the early evening.

'What now?' Seb asked.

'Orders. Insertion. Then the wait.'

It rained, the raindrops drumming on the metal roof of the JSG shed at Aughnacloy. They had brought him in at 03.00 hrs in the boot of a car, while Brannon sat in the front seat talking him through their surroundings: the twin housing estates, Catholic and Protestant; the triangle made by the RUC station, the army camp and the permanent checkpoint astride the border; the approach to the checkpoint, the road signs and the traffic lights.

Seb had felt them slowing for the sangar and listened for a soldier in the rain. Brannon described the control tower and beyond it the raised concrete black-and-yellow-striped barrier, which was packed with explosives in case it became necessary to block the border.

'Red light, then green,' Brannon said. 'We're into the chicane.'

Bollards steered them out of the main lane, and before them the metal shutter rolled up on the JSG shed and they were in. It rolled down behind them and the wait began.

The shed was spartan: oil-streaked concrete floors and unadorned breezeblock walls, a Portakabin, a vehicle-inspection pit and beside it a plastic table and four chairs. It was cold and draughty.

They lived in the Portakabin. He had slipped, apparently effort-lessly, into a secret world of small enclosed spaces, of Portakabins and car boots. Another facet to add to his many deceptions.

He observed her closely. To his surprise he did not become bored. Her name was Claire, he knew that much. She was hard. Even in sleep, curled fully clothed in her 'maggot' – her army-green sleeping bag – her face was closed to him. He studied it. There were the small red marks on the bridge of her nose where her glasses rested. Now they were snug in a leather sleeve in her left breast-pocket. There was a tiny scar just short of the hairline on her right temple. Her thick brown hair. She was lying only a few feet away and it would be possible to reach across and touch her if he wanted. He shut his eyes and attempted to breathe in the smell of her, but there were too many other distracting smells.

He was the real outsider. They made him aware of it. They surrounded him, sprawled in their sleeping bags, as if they were guarding him with their snoring and heaving bulk.

His watchers. Sometimes, when they thought he wasn't alert, he felt their eyes on him.

The interior walls flickered with blue light from the television pornography that occupied the late shift when the women watch-ers slept. Two hard men sat with their backs to him, watching the screen with the sound turned down, with half an ear always on the Motorola. Against the wall were a row of telephones – panic lines – with a name printed on magnetic tape above each one; the name of the tout at the other end of it.

The Portakabin was white-walled and windowless. It stank of two days' occupation, of fried food, cigarette ash and human sweat. Their clothes were warm and sticky. His eyes were dry as dust. There was no respite. He felt as if someone had their hand on a key in his back and was slowly winding, coiling him up inside. Nobody spoke to him. It was a rite of initiation. He maintained an equal silence.

Twice now she had gone out with Brannon to one of the cars parked behind the Portakabin, and he did not know what they had discussed. Brannon was the only one she spoke to in other than a cursory manner. She ignored Seb. The others joked and moaned, and moved around him as if he was a blind spot, and did not share their cigarettes with him. Even Brannon wasn't speaking to him.

He shifted in the sleeping bag to make himself more comfortable, and opened the sleeve of MaColl's file to read it again, to reacquaint himself with the facts. The fatherless youth in Fermanagh, his mother struggling to survive on a ten-acre holding, inevitably selling up and then the move to Twinbrook in West Belfast on the advice of the Housing Executive – find an empty house and move right on in; an early failed marriage, a similarly failed apprenticeship, followed by membership of the newly formed Twinbrook active service unit of the IRA, commanded in its infancy by Bobby Sands; they served their first five-year sentence together as special-category prisoners in Cage 11 – Cage 11 had a reputation among the other more conservative Republican prisoners as a bunch of renegades.

Someone had gone to the effort of keeping track of his reading habits in the Cages; Fanon, Torres, Guevara. Seb found it distasteful, and he wondered what the watchers would make of his own reading habits. What would they make of Bakunin, Proudhon, Nietzsche, Schopenhauer . . . ? Scare the shit out of them.

On release, MaColl returned to Twinbrook and became involved in selling forged tax-exemption certificates to raise cash for the IRA – he had the gift of making money. Meanwhile, he continued his involvement in the active-service unit and was suspected of involvement in the attack on the Balmoral Furnishing Company. He was finally convicted for his part in the bombing of the Protestant Bayardo bar, a UVF haunt, in Belfast's Shankill district. Five people died in the blast, which made Oisin a sectarian mass murderer. Vicious. Then the H Blocks 1977 to 1981, on the blanket and the dirty protest. Smearing his own shit on the walls of his cell every day, he ended up under psychiatric observation and in the aftermath of his release set out on an alcohol and drug binge that finally ran him foul of the IRA. Seb knew the rest by heart, better than the file which had obviously been doctored – sections were missing.

He skimmed the remaining pages. At the back of the file he found a copy of the FBI report on the armed robbery at the Brink's depository, including details of the missing money and the suspicion that an insider might have been involved. The subsequent issue of warrants for the arrest of various persons connected with the Irish-American community, and specifically Noraid, including missing Brink's employee Oisin MaColl.

Then one dark and foggy night, Oisin MaColl staggers into Fort White Rock and into the life of Sebastian MacCoinneach, with a can of stout in his hand and a red-hot twenty-dollar bill in his back pocket. So the story goes . . . It was a nice touch, the twenty-dollar bill. He was proud of it.

Days had passed. He had not been outside. He dragged his fingers through his shock of hair and sniffed his fingertips and his armpits. A searing heat seemed to come off them. He rubbed at his eyes. He had the determination in him to see it through to the end.

Seb turned up his collar and put his head down against the bitter cold. He went down the steps from the Portakabin and strode across the tarmac towards the car astride the vehicle inspection pit, while behind him they loaded their weapons and scrambled for their cars. A head dipped down into the pit beneath the car. MaColl studied him without expression from the driver's seat. Seb walked around the car to its rear, sprang the lock on the boot, climbed in and curled up tightly. The boot-hatch was slammed shut above him.

MaColl started the engine. Seb heard the sound of the metal shutter rolling up, and the car started to move and they filtered out into the chicane. Then they were out of it and on the open road and accelerating.

'You're clear of the checkpoint,' said a voice in the button in Seb's ear. He pressed the nipple at the tip of the pen in his pocket, one pulse for Yes to acknowledge.

He listened to the indicators as the car accelerated to overtake on the straight road. After ten minutes a voice said that he was clear to climb through into the car. He acknowledged, popped the catches on the back seat and climbed through. He squeezed between the front seats and dropped into the passenger seat.

MaColl said, 'You reek.'

Glancing in the rear-view mirror, Seb saw the first of the watchers' cars.

'Are you wired?'

'No,' Seb replied.

MaColl glanced across at him. 'I'll check.'

'Go ahead.'

'I'll bet they've been in my fucking car.'

'Probably,' Seb told him. 'Can I have a cigarette?' Three days of torture, while he'd suffered for his pride. 'I'm gasping.'

'Sure, there's a fresh packet in the glove compartment.'

A packet of Dunhill. Seb split the cellophane with his thumbnail, ripped out the foil, and removed a cigarette. He lit it from the car lighter and sat back in the seat, blowing smoke out in front of his face.

'That's good,' he said, and looked at MaColl. 'So what about the Brink's Depository robbery?'

'Smoke your cigarette,' Macoll snapped.

'Where's the money?'

'Will you smoke your friggin cigarette!' He slammed his open palm down on the steering wheel. 'Jesus. Did they not teach you anything? Turning tout is still a fuckin death sentence hereabouts. They might have stopped shooting at you lot, but it won't stop them shitting in their own back yard. I expect a little sensitivity, a little subtlety.' MaColl was grinning. No hint of it in his voice.

Seb said, 'I'm sorry.'

'Too right.'

Seb looked out of the window at the passing fields. 'Where are we going?'

'Sightseeing. Somewhere out of the rain. Be quiet.'

Seb settled back in his seat and watched the windscreen wipers sluicing back and forth, while the button in his ear maintained a continuous commentary. They drove south-west on the A4 through Tyrone towards Enniskillen in County Fermanagh.

MaColl said, 'A blue Escort, a white Granada, a gold Nissan. Tell me I'm wrong.'

'You're wrong.'

'Sure I am.' He laughed.

A helicopter flew overhead. MaColl leant forward over the wheel, craning his head to look at it. 'Jesus,' he said. 'You must be valuable. Is your father somebody important?'

'I don't think they had a ramble through Ulster in mind,' Seb replied.

They drove through Enniskillen and took the main road to Florencecourt, turning off at the signs for the Marble Arch Caves.

The car-park was empty, the caves closed. MaColl parked

diagonally across two parking-spaces and switched off the engine. Diagonal parking was clearly a trait they shared.

'I'm going to make a phone call,' MaColl said, 'get the place opened for us. You stay here.' He winked. 'Don't worry, the car won't go boom.'

He struggled against the rain across the tarmac to the telephone booth, favouring one leg slightly.

Seb spoke the time and his location loudly to the car. He smoked another cigarette. MaColl returned, scanning the surrounding countryside as he came, and climbed into the car.

Once the door was closed Seb asked, 'Why did they kneecap you?'

'Christ,' MaColl swore good humouredly. 'All right, I'll tell you. I got sidetracked from the cause of freedom by the allure of drug money.'

'You were selling drugs?'

'Don't sound so fucking outraged. A bit of speed, some eccy. Nothing that wasn't freely available in London, and that the good people of Poleglass weren't entitled too.'

'I'm not here to judge you,' Seb said slowly, fighting not to grin.

'You're not,' MaColl cut in, suddenly serious. 'Where are your friends?'

Going ballistic in my ear, he was tempted to say. Instead he shrugged. He'd stopped listening.

After ten minutes a Land-Rover turned off the road and circled the car-park, following the traffic signs painted on the tarmac, and pulled up next to them. It had 'Fermanagh Cave Rescue' written on its side in large white letters. The driver leant out of the window and regarded them suspiciously.

Winding down the window, MaColl called out, 'I've a special friend who wishes to have a private word.'

'The water is high in there,' the driver protested. 'It's not safe.'

'Do what you're fucking told,' MaColl advised him pleasantly.

'All right, all right,' the man grumbled. 'Give me five minutes. I'll put the lights on and get the boat ready.'

They were led down to where the rock was slimy, and the air was damp and cold, and MaColl instructed him to remove his clothing, and while he stood naked MaColl searched him methodically, using a small torch. Finding the small plastic button in Seb's ear he removed it – there was a snatch of whispering and crackling – and flung it behind him. It struck the black, shimmering surface of the water with a soft plop and disappeared. He was given a boiler-suit and a pair of trainers to wear; they were a couple of sizes too large, and there were no laces. He climbed into the boat.

They were carried across the underground lake, which was swollen with the rain and had flooded the cavern, through a forest of glistening stalactites that plunged down and were swallowed by the still water around them. As they travelled they were forced to lie low in the boat as the sharpened ridges of rock swept over their heads. Many of the halogen lights were submerged, creating weird luminescent-green smudges in the black water, and when Seb leant out over the water to look more closely he saw an albino trout in the water, its sickly white body shining in the unearthly light.

MaColl said to the boatman, 'You have my package?'

The man reached inside his overalls and drew out an A5 envelope. He handed it to MaColl, who put it inside his jacket.

'Well done,' MaColl told him.

The man beached the boat on a steep shingle beach. 'There's not long,' he said.

'Don't you go anywhere,' MaColl ordered him. The man turned in the boat, so that he faced out across the river, and lit a hand-rolled cigarette from a tin.

MaColl looked at Seb and grinned. 'Well, shall we go for a walk, Sebastian?'

He nodded.

They sank and slid with the shingle as they crossed it, and then scrambled across a molten-looking shelf of rock, into what seemed like a field of huge, dripping fungi.

MaColl produced Seb's Zippo from his pocket, and lit their cigarettes, the flame illuminating their faces grotesquely. Then he pulled out a half-bottle of Bushmills from the poacher's pocket of his tatty waxed-cotton jacket. He took a long pull on the bottle and handed it to Seb.

He smirked. 'They'll not be listening here, I think.'

'They'll be furious,' observed Seb sipping from the bottle.

'I'm fucking furious.' He produced the A5 envelope from

the same pocket and slapped it against Seb's chest. 'There you go. Your Moscow holiday snaps. That'll set the cat among the pigeons.'

Another clue for the watchers. It had been a deliberate strategic decision, with each meeting a physical clue. A twenty-dollar bill. A photograph. Pieces of a jigsaw. Give them a little bit, and let them grow fat on conjecture.

MaColl clearly had his doubts. 'Are you sure about this?'

'About the photo?'

'Sure. You don't think we're maybe giving away a little too much?'

Seb smiled. 'The most convincing lies are hidden between truths. Don't you worry.'

'I am worried,' MaColl retorted. 'Scared shitless, in fact. I'm on every IRA wanted list. That fast didn't go down so well in Belfast.'

'It was a necessary part of the strategy,' Seb countered. 'To muddy the water.'

'That's all right for you to say; they're not your kneecaps. Once was enough. Besides which, I practically starved. What took you so long?'

'I told you they'd try and do it their own way first.'

'It was a fucking joke. Some eedjit at the checkpoint on the Dublin Road outside Newry asking me if I want a cup of tea and a chat.' He tapped Seb's chest with a stubby finger. 'You've got your dirty snaps. What now?'

'Sit down,' Seb commanded. MaColl sat. 'First smokescreen, then logistics. Give me a progress report.'

MaColl drank thirstily from the bottle. 'All right. I spent a couple of days on Inishmore like you said. I stared expectantly out to sea. I acted suspicious. The island's quiet this time of year; if they were watching, they kept their distance.'

Seb nodded. 'They'll be keeping a low profile if they're in the Republic.'

MaColl laughed. 'After they've seen your photo they'll be kicking themselves.'

'They'll be watching you like a hawk,' Seb agreed. 'How about Dundalk?'

'Coming along swimmingly,' MaColl replied. 'The pitbulls are straining at the leash. Salivating at the very thought of getting their ugly paws on my cut-price consignment of Russian guns. They want to immolate the province. Kill all the traitorous peacemakers. They're talking about popping Gerry Adams. And that's just a starter.'

'Excellent,' Seb said.

'I tell you, everyone's going for it. Hook, line and fuckin sinker. Just you wait, word will get out. The touts will start screaming, and your people will get the confirmation they're looking for.'

It was all unfolding smoothly. Within days the Security Service would be so preoccupied with the prospect of a shipload of Russian guns getting into the hands of a hardline Republican splinter group that they'd be blind to the scam going on beneath their noses.

'I'm a genius,' Seb declared.

'I'll give you that,' MaColl said.

'Right,' Seb said, businesslike. 'Let's talk logistics. Let's talk check-list.'

The to and fro continued for some minutes. They talked players and security, timings and equipment, venues and modes of transport. They went back over all the work done in London months before. The tactical minutiae.

Claire was standing on the shoreline, beside Seb's pile of discarded clothing, her fists balled at her sides, pale with rage. MaColl hopped out of the boat and limped up to her so that his cold breath was on her face.

'Go wait outside,' he said to the boatman. Then to Seb, when the boatman was out of earshot, 'This is what they sent?'

Seb shrugged.

'A woman,' MaColl snorted and stared into her face. 'I've no time for this stupidity.'

'Your time, Oisin MaColl,' she spat through gritted teeth, 'is nearly up.'

He was taken aback, and stood silently for a few moments watching her, then he grinned. 'I like her,' he said. 'Give her the photo.'

Seb offered her the envelope.

'Another gift,' Seb explained. 'Like the twenty-dollar bill. Another piece in the jigsaw, at least that's what he says. Apparently there's a photograph of a couple of Russians in the envelope. He's interested to know how quickly the powers that be will work out where it was taken.'

'Couldn't have put it better myself,' MaColl said. 'I just hope you work this one out quicker than you did the last one. Remember, my life's on the line.'

'What do you want?' she demanded.

MaColl reached out and grabbed Seb's shoulder. 'Tell her.'

Seb said, 'He wants a new identity, a passport and a job. And he wants money. Fifty thousand pounds, up front.'

'Cash,' MaColl added.

'We don't have that kind of money,' she said.

'No? I'll give her a cache full of Russian weapons and a nasty little Republican splinter group with a whole agenda of deadly surprises. A mortal threat to the ceasefire. A plot to kill Adams. Tell her that.'

'You want me to repeat it?' Seb asked.

'No,' she snapped.

MaColl said, 'Get me the money.'

He took his hand off Seb's shoulder, pushed him to one side, and set off up the rock-slope towards the exit, favouring his damaged leg.

About halfway up he stopped and looked back. 'You keep that bottle, young Sebastian.'

'You keep my Zippo,' Seb called after him.

As soon as MaColl was out of sight Seb turned to Claire and subjected her to his most winning boy-hero smile, as if to say, 'I've been down into the depths of the earth, fought with demons and emerged unscathed.'

She slapped his face.

The heaving mass parted suddenly and she was standing in front of him, the top of her head level with the bridge of his nose in her heels, smiling at him. He'd been looking out for her all day.

'Where have you been?' Cal shouted over the din.

There were faint lines of kohl round her eyes, and her thick chestnut hair was loose and tousled. She was wearing a simple black dress with a man's double-breasted dinner jacket over it.

'I was called out to a cleansing,' Oonagh replied, resting her hand on his chest and speaking into his ear. 'I had to have the longest bath.'

THE LONG-HAIRED ACHAEANS

'Are you on call?'

'No. That's it. I'm off-duty.'

'Would you like to dance?'

The old folks had given up dancing long before. Dugald had already split his cast from top to bottom.

'No,' she replied.

'A drink?'

'Are you serious?'

There were at least two hundred and fifty people between him and the bar, most of them relatives. He grimaced ruefully.

'Don't worry,' she said, her breath on the flesh of his neck, 'I've a bottle of whisky in my pocket. Come on, let's go outside.'

He put his arm round her shoulder protectively and they surged forward across the hall through the crowd, were involved briefly in the Gay Gordons, and forced to make introductions to numerous aunties sitting against the walls, who clucked over Oonagh as if she too was an addition to the family. Out of the corner of his eye he caught sight of his father, looking lost and confused this far from his armchair.

Then they bumped into Sile, Oonagh's daughter. She was holding hands with one of the travellers from the Murbhach site, a nine-year-old with a wooden totem around his neck and an already impressive set of dreadlocks.

Sile took in Cal's locks, and then rewarded her mother with a knowing look. 'Snap,' she said.

'Please!' Oonagh groaned.

'Hello, Cal,' Sile said.

'Ten minutes,' Oonagh instructed her.

'OK,' Sile called, and she dodged away through the crowd with her friend. 'Bye, Cal.'

'I can't believe it,' he said when they finally got out into the open air. 'She's . . . I mean, shit, she's big.'

'You haven't seen her for years.'

'I guess,' said Calum. 'Come on, let's go sit on the bridge.'

She put her arm through his and together they walked across the gravel park between the cars, to the stone bridge by the telephone box. They sat on the cold, dry stones and looked out across the marsh at the lighthouse on the island of Carna. She produced a half-bottle of Grouse from her pocket, took a long pull on it and handed it across to him.

'You can see Ireland from Carna on a night like this,' she said.

The whisky was sharp in his mouth. He shifted closer to her on the stone.

He asked her the question that he'd been thinking on since the night in the shed: 'Why are you here?'

'I wanted to work with cattle,' she replied. 'Somewhere where they'll accept a woman vet. The women are strong on this island. The men respect women here.'

'The men are terrified of women here.'

She laughed, and it made him happy to hear her laugh. Their shoulders touched.

'And so they should be,' she said. Then she became serious. 'I wasn't going back to Ireland.'

He passed her the bottle, and their cold fingers brushed. He wanted to put his arm round her. Instead he stared at his feet. Seeing Sile had really knocked him off his feet. He asked the question, to get it out of the way early. 'Where is he?' He meant Sile's father.

'In Whitemoor prison, down in England,' she explained. 'It's not him – he can't touch me – it's the whole Troubles. I don't put much faith in the ceasefire.' She turned to him and laid her cold hand against the side of his face. 'I'm sorry about what happened to you.'

He shrugged. 'I had the shit kicked out of me. I learnt a valuable lesson. Not to mix with dangerous women.'

'I don't believe that,' she said. 'You were always surrounded by dangerous women. What about your cousin Madelene?'

'She didn't have a convicted terrorist for a boyfriend.'

A flicker of anger crossed her face. 'He wasn't my boyfriend.'

'He was the father of your child,' Cal pointed out, trying to be reasonable.

'They had no right to do what they did to you.'

'It's all right.' Cal rolled his eyes 'It was only a few teeth.'

She chuckled. 'I'm sorry. It's the way you said it.'

He took a swig from the bottle. He'd meant to turn it to humour. But now he couldn't help looking down into the memory, his beating and subsequent flight.

'They don't know I'm here,' she said.

He considered this information. It made him suddenly optimistic. 'You knew I lived here,' he said.

'The job was available. It suited me.' She paused. 'Then there was you. Of course, I didn't know then that you'd disappeared off the face of the earth.'

He looked up sharply. She was staring into his face.

'Where did you go? What have you been doing for the last two years?'

Cal shrugged lightheartedly. 'I drifted, I guess. I careered between careers.'

'Tell me,' she insisted.

He sighed. 'I worked on the fishing boats down in Cornwall. After that I worked on a drilling rig, welding mostly – doing investigations for large-scale developments. At the same time, I got involved in some of the anti-road protests, some environmental stuff. I worked for both sides, I guess. If there's a lesson there somewhere, I'm damned if I can see it.'

She kidded him, 'You're a lost soul.'

He didn't have the words to answer her. The truth was that fear had set him careering like a pinball, without any idea of what he was doing or where he was going.

'I remember you wrote a play,' she said.

'Yes,' he replied, relieved to have something else to consider. It was true. He had written a play that had won at a student festival in Edinburgh and been transferred for a short run to London. He had been told that he had great potential.

'It was a good play,' she said.

'Thank you.'

'Did you write any more?'

'No.'

There was a pause. Cal stared at the lighthouse.

'I liked you as you were,' she said. 'Have you changed?'

'I've definitely become bitter.'

'Better?' She laughed. 'I doubt it. Stop hogging the bottle.'

'I liked you,' he said, realising how true it was, watching her drink, her gulping throat.

She looked at him sideways, the mouth of the bottle inches from her lips. 'We could give it a whirl,' she said, and drank again.

He was suddenly serious, more serious than he had ever been. 'Do you mean that?'

'I don't know. Do people get a second chance?'

'If there's any justice.' He felt passionately about that. He thought of his own words, the Freedom To Live. Seb had reminded him. It was all the same thing. It was what he was after, another chance.

'We'd have to take it slow.' She stood up. 'I must go.'

Quickly he got to his feet, and blocked her way. 'You've only just arrived.'

'I'm working in the morning. I'm going home.'

He felt impulsive, suddenly elated. Brave. 'I could come with you.'

'I don't think so,' she said, and handed him the almost empty bottle. He shifted it from one hand to the other, and swiftly gathered her in his arms, and held her there, looking at her.

She was smiling. 'Unhand me,' she said, and put her fists on his chest.

Reluctantly he let go of her. She backed away, watching him with her head tilted to one side and then spun round, her hair and her dress sashaying after her. She called over her shoulder, 'Besides, I'm bleeding like a stuck pig.'

'That never stopped you in the past,' he said.

She did a double-take, and looked back at him. 'You remember the strangest things.'

'I remember everything,' he said. 'It's my curse.'

She laughed out loud. 'Don't be so pretentious. Come and see me soon.'

Sile had appeared from somewhere in the car-park behind them, and he wondered briefly if she had been listening to their conversation. He took it as a reminder that he should not play lightly with Oonagh's emotions. He stood in the middle of the road with the last of the whisky, and watched them walk to her car, and he willed her to look back, which she did briefly as she paused with her hand on the car door. He raised his hand and toasted her with the empty bottle. He felt self-conscious; he could see the white of her teeth, as she laughed at him. She climbed into the car. The engine caught on the second beat, and she reversed across the rutted car-park, with her head out one window, and Sile's out the other.

He listened to the sound of her changing gears, and watched the tail-lights of the car as it drove away across the Rhinns, as if by concentrating he could will everything to work for the best.

Moments later, as he crossed the car-park, heading back to the hall, he saw that Madelene was standing just outside the entrance, half cast in shadow.

'Spreading yourself a bit thin?' she asked him.

She was wearing a vellum mini-dress, fine as parchment and the colour of red earth, and black leather boots that reached above her knees.

He didn't trust himself to speak to her. He brushed past her and went into the hall.

7

He survived on sheer bloody-minded willpower. They debriefed him for two straight days, but he seemed to feed on it. They went over every nuance, every expression on MaColl's face, and each and every word that he was reported to have said in the cave. But they had nothing to check Seb against, except his own word. The constant mind-numbing rehearsals paid off. He used the exhaustion and emotion to become a still more extravagant and outspoken version of himself. He could answer any question.

Then on the third day they changed tack, and the questions became more personal. The interrogation took place in the billiards room of a County Down golf club in the shadow of the Mourne mountains. They drove him down from Belfast for the occasion. The billiards table had been hastily removed, and a row of chairs behind a table laid out on the polished wooden floor facing a single chair in a pool of downlight at the centre of the room. Seb was obliged to sit facing his interrogators. To the left sat Holdfast of MI5, with his hair combed and his tie set straight. To the right sat a Northern Ireland Office mandarin, who was not given a name. He was crumpled, and overweight and his hair was thinning. Between them, tugging at his pink-striped cuffs, sat the representative of MI6. He was sharp-suited, in a Sackville Street pinstripe and Brooks Brothers leather shoes, a Household Division tie. His jaw was firm, and his hair was sleek and expensively groomed. But there were bags under his eyes, and his skin had the bleached pallor of someone who'd been spending too many hours recently on aeroplanes.

Been to Moscow? Seb thought. Enjoyed my holiday snaps?

'My name's Fisher-King,' he said with the clipped vowels of power and privilege. 'You are welcome here. I knew your father some years ago.'

And beside him, behind a sheaf of papers, sat Claire. She was wearing a smart grey skirt and had her legs crossed under the table. She wasn't wearing her glasses. It pleased him to think that she was being evaluated – if so, it gave him an edge. Her eyes seemed shackled to the sheaf of papers before her. She was clearly on edge.

'Are you or have you ever been a practising homosexual?' She spoke softly, so that they had to remain still to hear her.

Holdfast's head was lowered and his mouth hung slackly open. Only the slow movement of his pen, describing spirals across the single sheet of paper in front of him, suggested that he was awake and listening. Fisher-King was frowning slightly, his attention fixed on the broad window behind Seb, the golfers teeing off on the light dusting of snow outside the clubhouse. The mandarin looked on coldly.

Seb contemplated the question without expression. Finally, after a long silence, he asked quietly, 'Does Eton count?'

'Answer the question,' Claire said, without lifting her eyes from the papers in front of her.

Seb's eyes narrowed. 'You first.'

There was not even a flicker of interest. 'My sex life is not the issue here. Yours is. Why were you expelled from Eton?'

'Not for buggery,' Seb said reasonably.

'Are you a practising homosexual?'

He shrugged. 'I'd rather make love to you.'

Fisher-King almost sniggered.

'Answer the question,' she snapped, the colour rising in her cheeks.

'No, I'm not a homosexual.'

She looked up at him; he met her gaze and lifted an eyebrow. She returned her attention to the papers in front of her. 'Why were you expelled from Eton?'

'I broke my Greek teacher's jaw.'

One blow. The old bastard toppling. Two days after the last time he saw his brother Rory alive. A sense of satisfaction, a dramatic release of tension. He smiled.

She asked, 'Why?'

Seb paused. 'He tried to humiliate me.'

Holdfast interrupted, his ballpoint pen momentarily suspended above the sheet of paper. 'Do you think the expulsion was fair?'

Seb considered this. He offered his opinion. 'I think the aristocracy are terrified of violence.'

Holdfast seemed to be confused by the reply: he was slow in responding to it. 'Why?'

Seb shrugged. 'It's obvious. They have the most to lose.'

'I'd have thought with your background you'd have identified with the upper class?'

'I'm an upstart. My father is a conman.'

Fisher-King raised his eyebrows.

Claire resumed. 'You were subsequently expelled from Rannoch school?'

'Yes. I wasn't there long. A couple of months.'

'Why?'

He smiled. 'I was caught smoking dope.'

'Dope?'

'Cannabis.'

Fisher-King got up, his chair screeching on the floorboards, went to the sideboard, and poured himself a cup of coffee. Claire sat waiting for him. She appeared impatient, her lips pursed. Seb cocked his head, and after a few seconds she became aware that he was staring at her legs under the table. Impulsively her hands went under the table and smoothed her skirt over her knees. He slouched in his seat and leered at her. She looked furious.

As soon as Fisher-King was seated she continued.

'The colonel who interviewed you for the Regular Commissions Board noted that you were expelled from Rannoch for fighting.'

'I lied. They didn't check,' replied Seb with apparent indifference. He looked around the room, affecting boredom.

Her voice was strident. 'Do you lie regularly?'

He shrugged. 'Only if I think I can get away with it.'

'What made you think you could get away with it?'

'The army expect you to fit in. If your face fits and you come from the right background, and you make the right sounds, it's easy to con them,' Seb replied, after reflection. He added, 'My father conned the establishment for years.'

'Have you lied to us?'

'I wouldn't get away with it.'

'Are you being blackmailed by Oisin MaColl?'

'No.'

Holdfast asked, apparently surprised, 'Do you resent your father?'

Seb said, 'I pity him.'

Claire continued remorselessly. 'Do you still take drugs?'

'No.'

'Why not?'

He paused as if unsure how to answer. 'I like to be in control of myself.'

'Will you consent to a urine test?'

'No.'

'Why?'

'You can go fuck yourself,' he said, matter-of-factly.

'A refusal to take a urine test will be considered an admission of guilt.'

'I don't care,' Seb sighed. 'I didn't ask to work for you. You can send me back to my battalion.'

The pen halted again, the nib lifting off the paper. Holdfast raised his head and his watery eyes focused on Seb from behind the thick lenses of his glasses. 'You understand why we are asking you to take a urine test?'

'Sure. You think MaColl is exerting some kind of control over me.'

Claire interrupted. 'Is he?'

Seb smiled pityingly and shook his head. 'No.'

Holdfast said, 'We could ask you to take a polygraph test.'

'I know how to beat a polygraph.'

'Yes. Your interrogation course.'

Seb smiled. 'I haven't slept for two days. I've drunk gallons of coffee. You couldn't get a reliable reading if you tried.'

'He's right,' Fisher-King conceded.

Claire said, 'Tell us about your brother.'

'I don't have anything to confess, and I don't carry the burden of a guilty conscience.'

'Tell us about your brother,' she repeated.

'Which one?'

'Which one do you think?'

'Rory, of course.'

She said, 'Tell us about Rory.'

'He was a racing driver, a successful one. He was also a drug addict. He died of an overdose of heroin.' Think you've got me now, do you?

'He killed himself?'

Seb said, 'It's not that simple. He was on a binge.'

'Why?'

'This is a little obvious, isn't it?'

'Answer the question,' she demanded.

'He'd lost his driving licence.'

'Why?'

'I said he was on a binge,' Seb replied.

'Answer the question.'

'Ask me a decent question, Claire.' He said her name loudly, challenging her to meet his level stare.

'Answer the question,' she demanded again.

'You know, contact lenses suit you,' he said. 'They bring out the best features in your face. Are you flirting with me?'

'Answer the question.'

'He was being blackmailed.' He smiled witheringly. 'Does that satisfy you? One of the team mechanics was threatening to expose his drug-taking. The team would have been forced to drop him, the press would have crucified him. He lived for his job. He reacted in the only way he could. He went on a binge. He trashed a couple of cars, so he lost his licence. He went on a bigger and terminal binge.'

Holdfast asked, 'What did you feel?'

'I felt like going on a binge.'

The pen nib tapped up and down on the paper a few times. Holdfast had stuck out his lower lip. 'Would you say that there is a self-destructive streak in your family?'

Seb said, 'I'm not a psychiatrist.'

Claire pressed him. 'Are you being blackmailed?'

'No.'

'Do you take drugs?'

'No.'

'Describe your relationship with Oisin MaColl?'

He laughed at that. 'We're just a couple of queers.'

'When did you first meet him?'

'We were never formally introduced. Not my social class, you see.'

'I thought you considered yourself classless?'

'I was joking.'

'When did you first set eyes on MaColl?'

'I was in command of a patrol that found MaColl after he'd been kneecapped. He'd lost a fair amount of blood. It's unusual to find someone like that. Normally the IRA call an ambulance for the victim after they've shot them.' Seb smiled. 'They're nice like that.'

'In the car you asked him why he had been kneecapped?'

'Yes,' he replied.

'Why?'

'I'd been told to find out his motivation and I wanted to know if he recognised me.'

'What did you conclude?'

'He described the kneecapping as if it was a matter of course. As if he'd broken a law and been caught, and accepted the penalty.'

'Do you think he recognised you?'

'No, I don't think so. On the night we found him I was wearing a helmet, it was dark and, like I said, he was in a lot of pain. We called an ambulance and it came quickly. That's it.'

'Do you not find it odd,' Claire said, 'that you save a man's life and then, five years later, he walks into a security forces base and by a remarkable coincidence you happen to be on duty?'

He shrugged. 'No. My regiment is regularly posted to Belfast. It's a small patch.'

'My master has a phobia about scandal,' the mandarin announced.

'Let's break for lunch,' Fisher-King said.

Claire and Seb ate in the empty lounge bar of the club, surrounded by tables stacked with chairs. They dined on luke-warm plates piled with scampi and chips that were served to them by a middle-aged woman in a white blouse who hummed as she arranged their knives and forks. The others ate else-where.

'Fattening me up for the kill,' he said midway through the meal, to break the silence. He dipped a piece of scampi in some dubious-looking tartare sauce. 'At least I won't die hungry.'

'Are you ever serious?' she demanded.

'Yes,' he told her. 'I was serious about wanting to make love to you.'

She put down her knife and fork either side of her plate and stood up.

'You're not going to slap me again are you?'

She turned her back on him and walked away.

'Wait.'

She didn't falter.

'Please.'

She stopped.

'My brother Rory was a fool. I'm not that kind of fool. I don't do anything I don't want to, and I don't say things I don't mean. I've spent time with you over the last few days. I've watched you. You're strong. You're a loner. We have more in common than you think. I find you very attractive. I'm just saying it. So that you know I meant it. That's all.'

When he finished speaking there was a slight pause; she remained with her back to him. He willed her to turn round, but she walked out of the lounge bar, the double doors swinging back and forth in her wake. He grinned sheepishly at the waitress who brought him a cup of coffee.

'Don't you worry, love,' the waitress told him. 'She'll come round.'

He sat in silence contemplating his coffee. After five minutes Colonel Hector strode in through the doors towards him.

Seb climbed quickly to his feet. 'Afternoon, sir.'

The Colonel stopped three paces short of him and looked around. He was in his usual uniform, green lightweights bleached from years of ironing and with all the belt loops torn off. A short-sleeved shirt, jungle boots without any socks.

His hard black eyes studied Seb inscrutably. 'Take a urine test,' he said, after a pause.

'Yes, sir.'

'Good.'

There was a silence between them.

Seb asked, 'How's my platoon, sir?'

'Good.'

'And my replacement?'

The Colonel paused. 'There is no replacement. We have ceased all patrols. The Mill has closed.'

Seb considered this news. 'It's really over, isn't it?'

'We'll see. Don't play games with these people, Sebastian.'

'Sir.'

The Colonel nodded to him in dismissal, and turned around and strode out of the room. Warrant Officer Pender and Staff Sergeant Mavery of the Special Investigation Branch of the Royal Military Police entered a few seconds after he left.

Seb unzipped his trousers and took out his penis. Gripping it in his right fist, he pointed it at them.

'Where do you want me to put it?'

Pender looked at Mavery, who rolled his eyes and asked, 'Where do you find baby soldiers?'

'In the infantry,' Pender replied cheerfully. He went across to the table and laid his steel briefcase down on it. He popped the catches, allowing the lid to spring open, and brought out a plastic vial, which he offered to Seb. 'In there, please, sir.'

'Did you know that "weapon" is the Anglo-Saxon for cock?'

'Really sir?' Mavery said. 'You learn something new every day. I'll tell that to my wife.'

'If she ever comes back,' Pender added. 'Now, sir, if you'd care to unload your weapon.'

Holdfast came for him after an hour and escorted him back to the billiards room. Claire's chair was now occupied by Bertie Nugent, the man from Special Branch. Seb remembered him from the hangar at Aldergrove. Nugent had his feet stuck out in front of him, and his chin resting on two upright fingers.

The atmosphere had lightened. Fisher-King met Seb at the entrance, grasped him by the arm and whisked him across the floor to the upholstered chair that had replaced the plastic one at the centre of the room.

'Part two,' he said in mock-confidence, tapping the side of his nose. He retreated to the edge of the downlight, by a large bay window that looked out over the golf course.

Nugent growled, and shifted noisily in his seat as a prelude to his first question. 'When and where are you next meeting MaColl?'

'Two days' time at Caldragh Cemetery on Boa island,' Seb replied.

'He suggested that?'

'Yes.'

'That's sidesplitting,' Nugent said. 'There's a pre-Christian sculpture in the cemetery, a Janus-headed figure – that's double-faced to you. Looks both ways, you see. A double-edged sword. Is that referring to you?'

'Maybe MaColl wants you to think that.'

'You're bright as a button, you are!' he exclaimed. 'How much does he want again?'

'Fifty thousand.'

'Is that sterling?'

'I assume so.'

'Have you noticed that they never want paying in the currency of the Republic? You can understand it. I wouldn't want fish on my thirty coins. It's slimy. You know where you are with the Queen. Not like this lot.' He nodded in Fisher-King's direction. 'Aristocrats, communists and homosexuals to a man.' His eyes flicked back in Seb's direction. 'Like you?'

'Not me, old chap,' Seb replied, lounging in newfound comfort.

'Have you finished playing the buffoon?' Fisher-King enquired.

'Never,' Nugent retorted, grinning broadly.

'Never. I hear that a lot from Protestants,' Seb said. 'No. Never. Not. Nowhere.'

'I forgot,' Nugent said, 'You're a taig aren't you?'

'I'm an atheist.' Seb crossed his arms.

'A Catholic atheist. Everything is permitted, right?'

'Not everything,' Seb said evenly.

Nugent laughed. 'You know, I think you'd be anything to anyone. A toff, a taig, a thug, a lover. Let me ask you a serious question. Do you think these weapons really exist? I mean, other than in the imagination of this roomful of spies?'

Seb lifted his chin and spoke very clearly. 'No.'

'You knew I wanted you to say that! Come on, why not?'

'He's a conman.'

'That's right, and you'd recognise one. I listened to the tape. Your father's a conman. I've listened to all the tapes. It's so neat. Do you want a cigarette?'

'Yes.'

Nugent dug in the pocket of his cheap suit and produced a packet of Regal, still in its cellophane, which he lobbed across the room. Seb caught it deftly in his right hand. They all watched him as he lit the cigarette with the plastic lighter he had bought to replace his Zippo. He inhaled with pleasure.

'Do you always carry a lighter with you?'

'You never know when you might get lucky,' Seb replied.

'I have a theory. You see, I think I know Oisin MaColl. He's a drug-dealer. But Ireland is not ready yet for drug-dealers – it's hardly ready for ordinary, decent criminals. He was lucky early on, and did the Kesh, which means he's got some cachet with the hardmen. That's why they haven't killed him before now. Just played around with his joints. A little bit of Meccano. Now he thinks he's a supergrass. Why? My guess is he's trying to move drugs across the border. He can't ask the IRA to do it – according to them he's still banished – so he's trying out the spooks. He's an opportunist. He watched Stella Rimington's lecture on the telly, so he knows that most of MI5's resources are now dedicated to the war against the IRA. Peace is going to put them all out of a job. So along comes Oisin MaColl, larger than life, promising the earth. They'll drink it up like champagne.'

'Intriguing theory,' Fisher-King said. 'What do you say, Holdfast?'

Holdfast nodded, his mouth agape, a fleck of spittle brightening his lower lip.

'I'm not finished,' Nugent said. 'You see, I think Oisin knows that Sebastian here is a soft touch, a bit of a smoker of cannabis. But how does he know? Maybe it's just one of those things – you can just tell. Is that right?'

'I don't think he wants you to trust me.'

'I don't trust you!' Nugent slammed his hand down on the table.

'Then he's succeeded,' Seb told him.

There was a loud knock on the door. Holdfast got up slowly and went over to the door. He opened it a fraction, had a quiet conversation with someone unseen and then returned to his chair.

'The test was negative,' he announced.

'You're a fucking star!' Nugent told Seb. 'I like your style. No further questions.'

The Northern Ireland Office mandarin stood up. 'That was the green light my master required. Now, if you gentlemen will excuse me, I have no wish to learn any more.' He went out of the room.

Fisher-King levered himself free of the sideboard with his long fingers, and strode across the wooden floor, walking in front of the table and scooping up a rigid manilla envelope. 'Thank you, Bertie,' he said.

'State secrets time, is it?'

'I'm afraid so.'

'I wouldn't trust me either.'

Fisher-King sighed. 'It's nothing personal.'

Nugent stood up abruptly. 'This pesky Irishman knows his place,' he said. 'I'll be going, then. Somewhere I can get a good wash. You can pick up germs in company like this. Well, top of the morning to you.' Pointing at Seb, 'You keep them cigarettes.'

'Tickety-boo,' Seb replied.

'Sorry about that,' Fisher-King apologised, after Nugent had left. 'Holdfast?'

Holdfast removed his glasses and started cleaning them with a handkerchief he produced from his breast pocket. He kept his eyes closed and his nose raised while he was speaking, as if he was sniffing the air for scent.

'The Provisional IRA's "totally unarmed strategy" is coming apart at the seams. Now that Albert Reynolds has gone, they can no longer count on a sympathetic ear in the Republic. Their support in the USA is largely cosmetic, and is not being translated into cash donations. Their support in Europe died with Mitterrand; Chirac is no friend to the IRA. The issue of decommissioning weapons is likely to prove intractable, for the simple reason that there is no historical precedent. Weapons buried after the Easter rising are still rusting in their hides. Already there are signs of deep divisions within the Republican movement; between the peacemakers in Derry and Belfast, and the hardliners opposed to the ceasefire in South Armagh and Lough. The recent robbery in Newry was only the first sign of that rift. An embryonic splinter group, the INRA, based in Dundalk in the Republic, are becoming increasingly active. It is only because they are small and disorganised and relatively poorly armed that they have proved unable to disrupt the peace process. For instance, they don't have access to Libyan-supplied weaponry.'

'And they don't have access to the American fund-raisers,' Fisher-King added. 'The leadership of Noraid is implacably opposed to the ceasefire. Last year Michael Flannery said, and I quote, "There will always be an IRA. If one gives up then there will be another IRA. This fight is not going to stop."' There followed a pregnant pause, then, 'MaColl has access to Noraid.'

'After he was first expelled from Ulster by the IRA, he went to the USA,' Holdfast said.

Fisher-King took up the story. 'Which is where, from my perspective, he becomes interesting. MaColl spent a year working for a circus travelling up and down the eastern seaboard, Boston, New York, et cetera. During this time he was involved in fund-raising activities for Noraid, speaking of his experience in prison. They liked him. Subsequently he worked as a mule for Noraid, carrying money across to the Republic and other destinations. Throughout the eighties he travelled internationally – Europe, Libya, Bulgaria, the Lebanon. He met officials in Soviet Intelligence – I'll return to that later.'

Holdfast, who'd been scribbling, laid his pen down and looked up. 'MaColl's work paid off in 1990, when the army council of the IRA agreed to revoke the expulsion order on him. He returned to Ulster. We understand that the IRA let him come back on condition that he kept a low profile. So much for that. The next time we encounter him he had taken up with members of IPLO (the Irish People's Liberation Organisation), using them as the footsoldiers in a major network for the distribution of Ecstasy. Ecstasy had been present in Belfast since 1987, but mostly in small amounts, and mostly confined to Loyalist areas. Until then PIRA had been content to turn a blind eye to IPLO's small-time drugdealing activities, but the bad publicity associated with Ecstasy apparently caused them to move against IPLO. A number of members of that organisation were murdered. As you are aware, MaColl was kneecapped. After his release from hospital he left the country.'

'And nobody,' Fisher-King observed, tapping his carefully scrubbed fingers on the manilla envelope, 'thought to keep an eye out for him.'

Holdfast shrugged. 'Not of sufficient interest. We thought he was finished.'

'Until he pitches up back in Belfast offering us tantalising morsels of information,' Fisher-King countered. 'We believe that Noraid are perfectly capable of organising a robbery to finance an arms deal if they believe it might deliver a death-blow to the ceasefire – and every indication is that they masterminded the Brink's Depository robbery.'

'MaColl is the link,' Seb added thoughtfully. 'He knows the hardmen in South Armagh and he knows the hardmen in New York and Boston.'

'That's right. And now he's ours. You've struck gold, Sebastian. I like MaColl. We all like MaColl. He'll sell anything for gold. You know where you are with a fellow like that.'

With his long fingers Fisher-King teased a photograph out of the envelope. 'This is an enlargement of the photograph in the envelope MaColl handed to you in the Marble Arch Caves. I can tell you, it caused quite a stir. You haven't seen it, have you?'

'The envelope was sealed,' Seb said.

Fisher-King smiled. 'Yes, I understand all that has been exhaustively covered in previous interviews. Now, Sebastian, I want you to have a look at it. The quality is not great.'

A token of trust, the photograph passed from Fisher-King's hand to Seb's. The significance of the gesture was not lost on Seb: he had been admitted to the charmed circle. He contemplated the photograph as if it was a mystery and a challenge to him; as if he was unaware that the photographer, a Moscow journalist, had received a bullet in the back of the head for his curiosity. It was a simple photograph, of two men emerging from a low brick building with Cyrillic writing above the door. There were watch-towers and high walls in the background. Enough clues.

'Somewhere in Russia?' Seb suggested.

'We've had a team of analysts working day and night to pinpoint the location,' Fisher-King said, 'but I shan't keep you in suspense. It was taken in the Saratov region of Russia, some five hundred miles south-east of Moscow on the River Volga. It's a forced-labour camp, Establishment III 391/36, maker and purveyor of barbed wire by appointment to the Gulag. The man on the right is the director of the camp, and with him, on the left, is a man named Dzukhokar Imayev.' He paused for effect. 'Predators from all across the globe are descending on us here in Ireland, Sebastian. Imayev is a deserter from the Soviet armed forces, now believed to be a godfather in the Chechen mafia. Through the efforts of Imayev and others like him, the so-called Independent Republic of Chechnya has been turned into the main base for criminals in the north Caucasus and beyond. The Chechens are behind one of the most powerful mafia groups in the former Soviet Union. Their command structure is dominated by veterans of the Afghan war.

'Until his desertion, Imayev was a lieutenant-colonel in the Glavnoye Razvedyvatelnoye Upravleniye, better known as the GRU, the Central Intelligence Directorate of the Soviet armed forces. In Afghanistan he was in charge of a special designation brigade, a unit of GRU commandos, mostly Chechens and other ethnic Muslim groups, that operated in the Kandahar region. There are reports that they used pseudo-gang tactics similar to those used by the SAS in Malaya and the Selous Scouts in Rhodesia. They dressed themselves as Mujahedeen and attacked villages and other armed groups, spreading fear and inter-group tension.

'More recently he commanded the GRU cell at Vilnius in Lithuania. He was responsible for monitoring arms-control measures in Lithuania. He had access to munitions dumps and armouries throughout that country.'

'He had access to guns,' Seb said.

'Huge quantities of them,' Fisher-King agreed.

Seb reacquainted himself with the men in the photograph, the barbed-wire man and the soldier-mafioso. He struggled for a second for the barbed-wire man's name. Ivanov. A petty bureaucrat out of his depth. Beside him, the Chechen mafioso Dzukhokar Imayev, his features sharp and weathered in comparison with Ivanov's lardy complexion.

'The Chechens specialise in forgery, protection rackets and gun-running. Yeltsin's invasion of Chechnya was partly motivated by a desire to break the back of the mafia,' Fisher-King said.

'So what's the connection with barbed wire?' Seb asked.

'The camp is now a private enterprise – same product, but now they have to go out and look for customers. The order book has been understandably lean since the collapse of the evil empire. Mr Ivanov's future was, until recently, looking rather bleak. That is, until he secured a hundred-ton order to supply barbed wire to an American-owned company in the Republic of Ireland.'

'Bingo,' Seb said.

'Exactly,' Fisher-King said.

'A four-thousand-ton general cargo ship, registered in Panama, offloaded a hundred tons of barbed wire at Limerick harbour over a month ago,' Holdfast said.

'We have gained access to coastguard and customs authorities records in the Republic. As far as we can tell, police, harbour authorities and customs were thorough in their examination of the ship. We are inclined to believe that any smuggled cargo went overboard, probably with a buoy attached, before the ship docked. Coastguard records indicate that there was a small change in the relative speed of the ship on their radar as it passed close to the island of Inishmore off the west coast of Ireland. MaColl was on Inishmore last week.'

'The guns have landed, Sebastian,' Fisher-King told him. He whisked Seb out of his chair and over to the window. 'We've taken a shine to you, Sebastian, for all your faults. That doesn't always happen. We want you to go all the way. You deliver us MaColl, and his nasty Russian guns and his murderous splinter group and we'll make you a fully fledged spy. We'll give you a pearl-handled Beretta. You go back to MaColl and tell him we want the lot.'

Cal rose late on the day after the wedding. Despite the pounding of his head, he felt quietly satisfied. He practically had the house to himself, now that Dugald had left on his honeymoon; Aulay surfaced briefly at lunchtime but soon returned to his bed, muttering woefully. His father didn't surface at all. Calum lay on the sofa with a pint glass of orange juice and squinted at the *Cualach*, the local paper, when he felt able. After a bacon sandwich he went out into the cold and felt much better. He welded a sheet of steel across the rusted hole in the floor of the tractor cab, and all the time he was thinking about Oonagh.

It had taken him over three years to establish a relationship with her, and it had been short-lived – six months only – but intense for all that. As powerful as, but the exact opposite of, his relationship with Madelene. He had genuine respect for Oonagh: she had a hard-won integrity and an independence of mind that he envied. She was nobody's fool and she wore her achievements with an easy grace. If he was honest, like Madelene she intimidated him.

When he had finished welding, he decided he needed a larger and more significant space in which to think, so he hiked across the moor to the broad bay known as the Big Strand. The beach stretched from the mist-shrouded granite outline of the Og at the southernmost end of the island, to the lighthouse at Carraig Fhada at the north end. He went down through the rabbit breeding-grounds on to the sand, walking towards the surf with his head down, to keep the blown grains from his eyes. For a while, he watched the Atlantic waves breaking on the shore. They seemed to dwarf all other considerations – he remembered, years before in Edinburgh, describing the Big Strand to her as a vast and hallowed space. The Atlantic, as far as the eye could see. A place for taking a hard look at yourself.

To warm himself, he started collecting stones and skimming them across the waves.

It was about mastering fear. He had run, and he was only now beginning to believe he had stopped running – and now, by luck or providence, it seemed as if he had run full circle. That he was back at the beginning, with Oonagh again, and with the opportunity to try again.

A second chance. It came back to bravery.

She was waiting for him when he got back; when he saw her Subaru parked outside the farmhouse he took it as a sign, another act of providence. Even the Collie With No Name seemed subdued.

'Aye aye,' his father shouted after him.

She was sitting on his desk. When he entered the room she stood up and kissed him.

'Thank you,' he said into her ear.

'For what?' She cupped her hands round her mouth. 'Why are we whispering?'

He put a finger to his lips, moved over to the door and closed it. 'There,' he said. 'Let the old bastard think we're talking about him. Have you been waiting long?'

'Long enough to hear your life story,' she replied, sitting back on the desk.

He smiled. 'Not long, then.'

'An interesting perspective, your father has.'

'That's one way of putting it.'

She coiled her hair in hands, lifting it off the back of her neck. 'I've been going through your stuff,' she said. 'There's not much to steal, that's for sure.' She pointed to the piles of tapes on his desk. 'You still listening to Leonard Cohen every night?'

'Without fail.'

'It's no wonder you're so introspective.'

She opened one of the drawers in the desk and took out the framed photograph. 'That's your mother, isn't it?'

'Yes.'

'She's pretty.'

He nodded.

'Am I annoying you?' she asked.

'Not at all.'

'Are you stoned?'

'No,' he replied.

'It's difficult to tell with you. You seem to glide. Where have you been walking?'

'On the beach. Out towards the Og.'

'That's where she's buried, isn't it?' She handed him the photograph. He put it down on his bed.

'I've been walking up there with the dog,' she said. 'I saw the goats.'

Wild goats lived in caves on the cliffs.

'I know it's called the Og, but what does it mean?' she asked.

'Some say it comes from the Old Norse "Oy", which means island,' he told her, 'but there's another meaning, one that points to its function. "Oag", to wriggle or crawl, as in "oagin like a worm".'

Her brow furrowed. 'Why do you know things like that?'

There was no way for him to answer.

'The wedding's over,' she said suddenly. 'You're still here. Why's that?'

He shook his head. 'What do you want me to say?'

She laughed, but her eyes were troubled. 'What was the biggest, most awful lie you told a girl to make her sleep with you?'

He thought about it. Not for long. 'I told an Irish girl once that I'd read the whole of *Ulysses*. It was a terrible lie. I'm sorry.'

'I forgive you,' she said. 'Now tell me why you're here?'

'I'm involved in something,' he admitted.

'Something?'

'Well, I think I'm involved.'

'In what?'

'It's . . . difficult.'

'Difficult?'

Suddenly Seb's injunction to secrecy didn't seem important any more. 'Seb's set up an operation smuggling hash into Ulster. I'm supposed to bring the stuff up off the sea bed.'

She frowned. 'And you're going to do it?'

He shrugged. 'I suppose.'

'That's it?' She appeared outraged. 'Seb tells you to, and you jump to it?'

'It's not that simple,' he replied. 'Anyway, he's fairly persuasive. I don't need to tell you that.'

There was a moment's silence, then Oonagh let out a peal of raucous laughter. 'Check out the look on your face. I slept with him six years ago, and you're still jealous?'

'I'm not jealous,' he said.

'I'm nawt jealous,' she mocked him.

'Christ!' he said.

They stared at each other.

'They take a fairly hard line on drugs across the water,' she told him. 'They're still kneecapping kids over there, ceasefire or not.'

'I'm just bringing it up and ferrying it ashore.'

'I'm sure the 'RA will take that into account.'

He shrugged. 'It's money. A lot of money.'

'What are you going to do with money? Buy some expensive rips for your jeans? You already have the entire Leonard Cohen collection.'

'I could buy the farm,' he replied, a little too defensively. 'We've been tenants here for generations. Dugald is a good farmer. He deserves a break.'

'I'm sorry,' she said. Her voice had taken on a serious tone, but the flecks of laughter in her eyes betrayed her. 'What are you doing on Christmas Eve?'

'Christmas Eve?'

'Tomorrow, remember?'

'I hadn't thought,' he replied.

'Come over for dinner?'

'I will,' he said.

'Good.'

The door was opened by Mrs Greechan, who kept house for Oonagh and looked after Sile on the nights that she was on duty.

She took a long hard look at Cal in the doorway. 'I know your brother,' she said with disapproval. 'Take off your muddy boots.'

The cottage was one of five in an isolated settlement built among the ruins of a previous settlement on the cairn on the eastern shore of Loch Ceal, a small stretch of water within sight of the sea. Behind the whitewashed cottage the moorland stretched away in the direction of Garbh. It was high and exposed. The views were breathtaking.

'Come in, come in,' Oonagh called from the kitchen. 'Don't you be bothering him, Mrs Greechan.'

Mrs Greechan tutted and shuffled across the varnished pine boards of the living room to her seat by the open fireplace, where sods of peat where burning. The smell was rich and strong.

Sile was willowy and beautiful, the image of her mother. Looking at her, it was difficult to see any trace of her violent father.

'Hello, Calum,' she said, and took one of his fingers in her hand. 'You have big hands.'

'It runs in my family,' he told her. 'Here.'

He held out the brown paper package he was holding. She took it and glanced towards the kitchen, where her mother was standing in the doorway. 'Put it under the tree,' Oonagh said.

A large Christmas tree, whose top had been sawn off, stood in the corner by one of the bay windows. It was decorated with wooden beads and stuffed cloth animals, and there was a modest pile of presents arranged beneath it.

'The wrapping is a bit plain,' Calum apologised.

'I dug the tree out myself,' Oonagh explained, going through into the kitchen, 'It was too tall. I'm still looking for a fairy to stick on it. Come in the kitchen and talk to me.'

There was a whole salmon lying on a chopping block on the wooden refectory table, and beside it a bowl of oatmeal. He stood in the doorway for a few moments. Oonagh was bending over the Aga, feeding it with wood. He could smell baking potatoes. She was barefoot, in black leggings and a cotton T-shirt. Her hair was tied back.

She looked up at him and smiled. 'Sit yourself down.'

'I brought a bottle of wine,' he said.

'Good. Help yourself.'

He drank wine and watched her fillet the fish and cut it into thick steaks which she dunked in beaten egg and rolled in oatmeal. She placed them under the grill.

'The factor up at Cual Estates slipped me this bit of salmon for plating his dog's leg,' she said. 'I've got a pile of peat outside that's larger than the house. I can't remember what I had to do for that.'

Calum raised his glass. 'Whole rivers were emptied for her. Peat bogs were stripped for her.'

'I'd be quite a catch,' she said. 'There have been other suitors.'

'Indeed?'

'Sure it's true. Lusty farmers, part-time firemen, special constables, brawny butchers. All the wives on this island think I'm a brazen hussy.'

'Madelene will be pleased,' Cal said. He immediately regretted saying it. He was trying to exclude Madelene from his thoughts, as if that would clarify his relationship with Oonagh.

Oonagh didn't seem to notice. She was feigning outrage. 'The difference is that I haven't slept with any of them.'

Madelene's occasional forays into the married men of the island were an open secret, and cause of hostility; she had been attacked on the street, spat at and kicked by hysterical wives.

He scrambled to recover his light tone. 'Keeping yourself, are you?'

'Sure,' she said, laughing. 'Enough of this shite.'

When the fish was done, she banged two saucepans together and Cal held his hands over his ears. Sile ran in shrieking, followed by an unruffled Mrs Greechan, and they gathered around the table.

They ate the grilled salmon steaks with a lemon butter sauce and baked potatoes and roast Jerusalem artichokes; and Calum couldn't remember a meal that he'd enjoyed more. Sile chattered through the meal, about her new friends and the horse that belonged to a local farmer that she was allowed to ride. She drank pop and Mrs Greechan had a glass of wine, and sucked on her false teeth through the meal, and complained when she found a bone, the only bone found that night. Oonagh looked mortified and then grinned slyly at Cal when Mrs Greechan's attention was elsewhere.

After dinner Oonagh put Sile to bed, and before she went Sile kissed him on the cheek, and said, 'It was nice to see you again, Calum.'

Mrs Greechan washed the dishes, and Cal dried them. Then she went through into the living room, sat in front of the fire in her customary seat and fell asleep and snored lightly.

While Cal was waiting he looked through the books in Oonagh's bookcase. After ten minutes she returned and stoked the fire and went through into the kitchen and came back with a bottle of Deochmore and a couple of glasses. She took his hand and led him down the corridor past Mrs Greechan's room and up the stairs to her room in the attic space.

The pine floor was strewn with rugs, and cushions, and there was a fire crackling in the grate. Red-orange light on the sloping white ceiling, candles flickering on the window-sills. Her bed was a double mattress set on a wooden palette. She put the bottle and the glasses down on the rug in front of the fire.

Cal went over to stand by the sloped window. He pressed his face against the glass and looked out across the stone ruins that ringed the cottage. 'Do you know the story of this place?'

She was pouring the whisky. He could hear the clink of the bottle. The sound of the liquid. 'Tell me.'

'There was an ancient battle here. A blood feud. Many people died. Afterwards a distraught mother built the cairn over the site of her son's death. She carried each stone herself, without help, and when she was done she laid a curse upon the stones. Later settlers came and tore down the cairn and used the stones to build houses for their families. You see the ruins outside. The curse lived on in the stones and the settlers were forced to abandon the dwellings they had built. Now you've settled here.'

'I don't believe in curses,' she said.

He swallowed hard. 'Did you mean what you said, about giving it another go?'

'You're eager aren't you?'

He didn't hesitate. 'Yes,' he said.

'Why?'

He looked helplessly out the window.

'Don't say anything stupid, now,' she said.

'I ... um ... I think ... Shit. I don't want to be a coward again. I ran away when those thugs told me to. I regret that.'

'I'm not here so that you can prove your manhood,' she said. 'Or maybe I am. Look at me.'

He turned to face her. She was naked and bold, tall as an Amazon, her clothes discarded in a pile by her feet; a resolute offering. His mouth was suddenly as dry as a lump of coal. He did not take the moment lightly.

She raised dripping fingers out of her whisky glass and traced astringent spirals round her nipples. Her breasts were high and strong and her hardening nipples were bright red; she was staring at him with an eyebrow raised, a half-smile on her face. She had always been bold. He was reminded of a song, but could not remember the words.

She massaged the smooth surface of her stomach and the taut muscles of her upper thighs so that her skin, which was offered up to him, glistened with liquor.

He went to her and she put her arms around him and drew him down on to her breasts, into the life of her, the whisky vapour rising to his nostrils like perfume, his parted lips enclosing one nipple and gently tugging. She whimpered softly. She spoke to him, and he thought she said, 'Give me.'

He squeezed his eyes shut. At that moment he really believed that there was such a thing as a second chance.

He travelled across her body, his lips brushing her ribs, his tongue chasing rivulets of whisky. He scooped his tongue across her belly, exploring the shallow cave of her navel. She bent slightly and parted her legs, encouraging him and he eased himself on to his knees.

He arched upwards, his strength focused in his tongue, darting at the folds and furls of flesh; her fingers running through his hair, gripping him tightly.

'That's right,' she whispered.

He struck as far into her as he could reach, and any further words were lost as her voice slowly but gradually rose in pitch to a strident keening. When she came her skin burned with hypersensitivity, and she couldn't bear to be touched and backed away from him with her eyes shining brightly and breathless, happy chaos written on her face.

She gathered her breath and pounced on him, her hands fumbling with his belt buckle, and pushing him towards the bed. He swept his sweater and shirt over his head, moving blindly backwards, and tripped on the edge of the bed and fell back on it. He felt wood splintering beneath the mattress. They were both laughing. She gripped the end of one trouser-leg and pulled it, and then pulled the other, his trousers coming away in her hands. She flung them behind her with an extravagant pirouette and climbed sinuously up his body with her face filled with mischievous pleasure.

'D'ya think I've woken Mrs Greechan?'

Cal said, 'The second coming wouldn't waken Mrs Greechan.'

'We'll see, shall we?' She giggled.

'If you insist,' he managed, barely able to contain himself. She rose above him, her hands on his shoulders, and lowered herself on to him, the tips of her hair sweeping across his face and her fingernails digging into his collarbones. She lifted her chin and moaned; with each thrust he pushed her higher. The bed was collapsing. She raised her arms and slapped her palms against the wall. Beads of sweat ran off her breasts on to his face. He growled through gritted teeth. She had started wailing again, the space between cries diminishing, the cries increasing in volume.

He opened his mouth and howled. He couldn't hold himself any longer – he spent himself. Oonagh shuddered, and sank down on him sobbing, her mouth searching for his. They kissed sloppily and lay back beside each other, and waited for their wildly beating hearts to settle.

Lying beside her he was as happy as he had ever been. He propped his head on his elbow and said, 'I put my arms around him yes and drew him down to me so that he could feel my breasts all perfume yes and his was going like mad and yes I will Yes.'

She cackled wildly. 'You're so literary!'

'I try.'

'Don't be trying to tell me, Calum Bean, that you read the whole of *Ulysses*. You just cribbed the last page.'

'I read the whole thing. Straight up. I was so ashamed of lying to you, I couldn't live with myself.'

She slapped his chest with her palm. 'You're a good fuck, Calum,' she told him, when she'd stopped laughing.

'You'll need a new bed,' he observed.

She giggled. 'We'll have to do this again.'

'Give me half an hour,' Cal protested.

'No,' she said, 'not tonight. It's Christmas. Sile will be up at dawn. I want you to go.'

He felt a sudden stab of desperation. She rested her head in the hollow of his neck and held him.

'I'm serious about you,' he said.

She gripped him harder.

8

He walked over the bridge to the island. There was a small wooden sign pointing to the cemetery and beside it a beaten path. MaColl was standing in the long grass by the squat pre-Christian figure. His jeans were sodden and his hair hung in dirty ringlets on his collar. He nodded for the benefit of unseen watchers as Seb approached. Seb stopped short of him, just a few feet. MaColl looked tired and rattled, as if the strain of constantly moving and the fear of the IRA catching up with him were beginning to have their effect. His eyes shifted constantly. Seb tried, by the steadiness of his gaze, to calm him; his words, though, were for the recording equipment, the questions provided for him by the voice in his ear.

'Where did you meet Dzukhokar Imayev?'

Nothing that they hadn't anticipated.

'We met at the Hotel Vitostia-New Otani in Sofia,' MaColl explained. 'That was back in the eighties. He was involved in the whole Libyan guns thing. Kind of monitoring it, you know. Now it's the same sort of thing, but privatised. Like the gas, or the electricity, you know. Christ, it was a hell of a hotel. Marble everywhere. The communists knew how to treat a decent criminal.'

'The guns,' Seb cut in. He put the briefcase down between them.

MaColl seemed to get a grip on himself. Presently, he squatted down and popped the locks. He took a deep breath and started again slowly.

'The guns are ex-Soviet army stock. AKMs with attached BG-15 grenade-launchers. AGS-17 automatic grenade-launchers and RPO rocket flame-throwers. They fell off the back of an army lorry in Lithuania, if you see what I mean. Imayev has some kind of connection to the place. They moved by rail transport to the barbed-wire factory and from there to Murmansk, and by tramp steamer bound for Limerick. They went overboard off Inishmore. I have a friend down there who owns a boat, and we brought the container up and ran it ashore in Connemara. The money to pay for the guns came from the Brink's robbery. It was carried by couriers into the Free State and from there to Cyprus and paid into an account in Limassol. Imayev may be there, for all I know.'

'Where are the guns now?'

'In a field.'

'What sort of field?'

'A green field. Get a hold of yourself, Sebastian.' He laughed, contemplating the money. He was getting into his stride now. 'Put it this way: they're safe.' He snapped the briefcase shut.

'When are they coming north?' Seb asked.

'When the big men tell me to bring them. You tell your people that they'll know as soon as I do. I've been promised twenty-four hours' warning – I expect I'll get less. The crossing is my choice, my area of expertise, remember, so I've decided the first forty guns will come through the border at Aughnacloy, buried in a lorry full of shit.'

'Shit?'

'Grade A chicken-shit. Work it out for yourself.' MaColl smiled. 'Next question?'

'The destination?'

He replied without hesitation, 'The mushroom farm at Benburb. The farmer is an old friend. He'll tie himself up in the kitchen and let us have a free run of his outbuildings.'

'Who's collecting?'

'The commanding officer and the quartermaster of the INRA will inspect a sample of the goods. It's the one chance you'll get to find the top brass anywhere near the guns. Immediately afterwards they'll be dispersed to small hides across Armagh. The killings will start soon afterwards. Right now, Gerry Adams is top of the hit list, and when they've finished with the peacemakers they'll start on the Loyalists.'

'That's it. Get out of there,' the voice in his ear instructed him.

'I'll let them know,' he said.

'You do that, Sebastian.'

He turned to leave, then turned back. 'MaColl?'

'Yes?'

'Merry Christmas.'

Seb watched the car go and turned at the bottom of the steps and looked up the face of the officers' mess at Lisburn, at the window of his own room. It was over a week since he had been there. He felt suddenly in need of a shower and a change of clothing.

As he stepped into his room he saw, half hidden by a sloping shaft of weak sunlight from the window, the figure of Claire waiting with her head propped against the chair back, pitched a little sideways in the seat, so that she could make out who was coming.

He had not expected it; he wondered what it had cost her in lost pride to be here. Her hair was wet from the shower and she was wearing his paisley-pattern dressing-gown. She rolled her head across the chair back to stare at him.

'Just what I put on my Christmas list,' he said, taking off his sodden jacket and dropping it on the carpet. Then he said, 'MaColl's given us the meat of it.'

'I heard he's told you where he's supposed to deliver the guns?'

'News travels fast,' he said warily. 'Why weren't you there?'

'MaColl isn't the only informant in Ulster,' she replied, the merest hint of indignation in her voice.

'It must have been something important?'

'The IRA leadership moved against some of the hardliners in South Armagh and Lough today. Most of the rank and file in Dundalk were picked up and questioned. The INRA leadership have gone into hiding. I've been reassuring suicidal informants all afternoon. That's why I got the job. Women make the best social workers, don't you know?' She sounded bitter.

He said, 'I hate it when you bring your work home with you.'

She almost smiled. 'You asked.'

'Who knows you're here?'

'Nobody.' She returned her attention to the window. 'Nobody at all. So tell me, golden boy, how did you beat the urine test?'

He pulled off his jumper, went over to the sink, opened the tap and cupped his hand underneath it. He drank from his palm and then ran his fingers through his unruly hair. He was tempted to tell her, to allow her a slice of his triumph, by explaining the properties of the American herb golden seal, which gives a false result to a urine test.

'I told you. I don't have anything to hide. Except now, of course. You and me, I mean. Fraternising in the festive season.'

She responded by shaking her head and smiling. She seemed to be attracted to his arrogance. 'Where are the guns going?' she asked.

She didn't know. He was surprised, and pleased. He wondered if she was already being sidelined; looking back, he believed that he had fatally damaged her during the interrogation. Now she was the outsider. He could feel the greed in her to know. It was palpable.

'I don't want to betray state secrets,' he said.

'You're a bastard.'

'The mushroom farm at Benburb.' He watched her thinking furiously. 'It's owned by a guy known as "Slab" Malloy,' he added. 'He has a fondness for dropping concrete slabs on folks' legs. Apparently he's not keen on the ceasefire. He's INLA or INRA, or something. MaColl claims he's an old friend.'

She nodded. 'They were in the H Blocks together,' she said. 'On the Dirty protest. I think they were in the same cell. How is it coming over the border?'

He hesitated.

'Tell me!'

'Buried at the bottom of a lorry-load of chicken-shit. That's how he used to bring his drugs in. He tells me soldiers are squeamish about searching in shit. MaColl isn't; I think it's some kind of scatological Irish thing.'

'You like the sound of your own voice,' she said suddenly.

'Everybody likes the sound of my voice,' Seb said. 'Fisher-King, Holdfast, all your friends with their silly codenames. They love me. Don't you?'

He walked over to stand behind her.

'They'll fly the SAS in and set a trap,' she explained. 'A loose cordon round the farm. As soon as the terrorists arrive to inspect the guns, they close the gaps and spring the trap.'

He put his hand on her shoulder and she looked up at him, searching his face. There was a barely visible penumbra surrounding her walnut-coloured irises that he recognised as the rim of her contact lenses. She looked tired but elated. He bent down and met her opening mouth with his; their darting tongues meeting and coiling.

Her bleeper went off just after midnight. He didn't react straight away; he was dressed in his uniform, sitting in the shadows on the chair that she had pulled over to the window; first, he finished his cigarette and stubbed it out on the window-sill. He had not had sex since Moscow, and now, as then, the cruelty of his love-making had surprised him; he had derived a keen pleasure from humiliating her. He looked across at her, her bright, myopic eyes sparkling in the light reflected in the window from the halogen lamps out by the perimeter fence; he knew that in her near-blind eyes he was a dark and menacing blur.

'At the age of thirty I had successively disgraced myself with three fine institutions,' he said, in rueful acknowledgment. 'School, university and the army . . . each of which had made me free of its full and rich resources, had trained me with skill and patience, and had shown me nothing but forbearance and charity when I failed in trust. Whadyathink?'

He listened to the soft rhythm of her breathing.

'Simon Raven, *The English Gentleman*,' he answered for her. 'To the point, I thought.'

He got up and went to the shredded tatters of her clothes and rooted about until he found the bleeper. He took it over to the desk and smashed it with the haft of his Purdey knife. Then he sat down and laid his cheek against the cold laminated surface of the desk, plastic shards of the bleeper pressing into his skin. He was tired, beyond exhaustion. There were no more decisions to be made, no more strategy or tactics.

'Duty calls,' he said wearily and lifted his head off the desk.

He went over to where she lay on the bed. She whimpered and curled tighter into a ball.

'There's a secure phone in brigade HQ. You can use that.'

'I can't see,' she whispered.

He had removed her contact lenses during intercourse, with the weight of his body pressing down on her spine; the rhythmic slap of their sopping loins; one fist clenched in the tangle of her hair and the other hand cupping her face, the pads of his fingers puddling in her eyes, crumpling the lenses and discarding them.

He put his hand on the bruised flesh of her buttocks. She was very still, like a wounded animal.

'I'll find you some clothes,' he said. He bent over her and brushed the flesh of her neck with his lips.

He went over to the wardrobe and fetched a T-shirt and a pair of jeans and threw them on to the bed. He picked his leather belt up from the floor. 'Here.' He flung it down on the bed. 'Get dressed.'

She dressed quickly, in the corner of the room, with her back to him, and then she turned and looked for him. He remained very still, in the shadows by the door. The jeans were baggy on her, drawn tightly round her waist.

'Where are you?' she asked plaintively.

'By the door.'

She hobbled towards the sound of his voice. 'I can't walk.'

'I'll carry you,' He picked her up; he was surprised at how light she was. She put her arms round his neck and buried her face in his shoulder. He carried her like that out of the building into the rain, across the broad tarmac apron to the red-brick building that housed 39 Brigade headquarters.

The duty watch-keeper looked up in surprise as he carried her into the Ops Room, and set her down on one of the desks next to a plastic Christmas tree.

Her voice was hoarse and broken, but it carried across the room. 'Get everybody out of here.' She pushed her hair back away from her face. One of her eyes was closed.

'Jesus,' the watch-keeper said, looking at her.

'Get out!' she screamed.

Seb looked at the watch-keeper. 'You know who she is?'

'I know,' he said. He got up out of his chair and gestured to the radio operator to join him. 'We'll be out in the corridor.'

She tried punching the buttons on the Brinton, the secure phone, but her fingers were shaking too badly and he did it for her. She identified herself to the person manning the line and listened in silence as she was briefed.

Afterwards she replaced the handset on its cradle and looked at him. 'PIRA got MaColl. He's been badly beaten.'

It welled up out of her, a single strangled sob, gathering force as it rose in her throat, shaking her whole body; she launched herself at him, raking his face with clawed hands, her broken nails gouging deep lacerations.

The Lynx helicopter circled above the wintry black-green Fermanagh countryside. Seb leant as far out of the open doorway as the harness would allow, the biting wind on the raw welts on his face, scanning the small fields and meadowlands, the thick latticework of blackthorn hedges and the scattered farmhouses with their yards full of scrap. There was still snow on the leeward slopes. Sheep huddled in the corners of fields. He identified the army checkpoints, the cordon and the incident control point, allowing the signs to lead him towards the heart of it. MaColl.

The pilot's voice crackled over the intercom in Seb's helmet. 'He's still alive. You can see him moving slightly on the infrared.'

They were losing height now. Beside him in the doorway the crewman on the machine-gun swung the barrel back and forth with renewed vigour. Seb sneered at him with an infantryman's customary disdain. On the far side of the bench-seat, Holdfast was leaning forward between the pilot and the co-pilot, watching the camera screen with interest.

The helicopter hovered above the intersection of dense blackthorn hedges at the corner of four small rock-strewn fields.

'He's in there.'

Seb pressed the transmit button. 'Is there a bomb?'

'An IED?' returned the disembodied reply. IED: improvised explosive device.

'Yes,' Seb replied wearily, 'A bomb.'

'There is no sign of a command wire, and the area has been swept with ECM for a radio-controlled device. No sign. It's clear.'

Holdfast was watching him, his expression inscrutable.

Seb said, 'Shall I go and talk to him?'

'We should like to land,' Holdfast announced.

The helicopter lifted away and set down in a field a few hundred metres away, adjacent to the lane where the command point was located. Seb jumped out of the helicopter and ran forward beneath the spinning blade across the field, and did not look back.

Richard Brannon met him by the gate, ankle-deep in mud. 'Come on,' he said, 'I'll brief you as we go.'

They trotted down the narrow mud-strewn lane, past army

Macrolon Land-Rovers and RUC Hotspurs half canted in ditches, and groups of police officers and soldiers, who regarded them with indifference.

'He was lifted from a hotel in Dundalk yesterday,' Brannon said.

'You were watching him?'

'Dundalk's in the Free State,' Brannon reproached him. Seb had noticed that Brannon affected much of the jargon of Republicanism. He found it mildly amusing.

'You can tell me,' Seb chided him, playing along.

'More than my job's wurf,' Brannon drawled, 'Dundalk's in the Souf. Different country. We don't know for sure who lifted him, or why. Can't think why they brought him across the border to dump him. He was found after a call to the confidential phone line – probably the farmer who found him. The farmer's a nationalist but anti-IRA. MaColl is threatening to set fire to himself. He wants you.'

'Joy,' Seb retorted, feigning insouciance.

'Here.' Brannon indicated a ragged hole in the hedge. 'Go easy on him.'

The blackthorn had been planted either side of a natural bund-line, a raised seam dividing fields, and the two sides had grown upwards and interlocked, forming a dense, mature hedge that concealed a hollow arch at the centre. By bending low, Seb found that he could scuttle along the top of the bund-line under the vault of overhanging foliage. The light was dappled, shadowy and green, and the earth was warmer and wetter than in the surrounding fields. After twenty or thirty metres he came up behind two of the watchers, lying outstretched on the bund-line. They were sodden and mud-caked, and shivering.

One of them, the one who called himself Bob, pointed forwards. Seb climbed over the top of them and continued on hands and knees. He could smell the petrol now, the vapour lingering in the enclosed space.

MaColl was lying in a depression, a shallow bowl, beneath the vaulted canopy of four interlocking hedgelines. He was doused in petrol; three empty cans lay beside him. His face was bruised and puffy, and one of his eyes was closed. His shirt was soaked with blood, and it stained the puddles in the rutted earth around him. He was holding Seb's Zippo lighter in his hand.

'I'll fuckin torch myself,' he yelled.

'It's me, Seb.'

MaColl studied him contemptuously as he eased himself down into the muddy bottom of the bowl. 'You took your time,' MaColl growled.

'Came as fast as I could,' Seb said, good-humouredly. 'You look a mess. What happened?'

'What the fuck you think happened?'

'Now, now,' Seb tutted. 'Don't be like that. Just let me know if you told them anything.'

'Fuck off!' MaColl spat.

Seb placed the heel of his boot on MaColl's chest and started grinding downwards. MaColl groaned.

'Yes,' Seb replied, his voice level, matter-of-fact, 'I can see that you're angry, but it really won't do. I want to know what you told them. I want to know what you're doing here.'

He lifted his boot away. MaColl wheezed and clutched at his chest. When his breathing had settled he began speaking, his voice little more than a whisper.

'I told them nothing' – he was racked with coughing – 'because they didn't ask. They beat me up and brought me here in the boot of a car and dumped me. It was just a warning. Satisfied?'

'Who did it?'

'Billy Smart's fuckin elephants.'

Seb's foot lashed out, the point of his boot impacting against MaColl's ribs. MaColl let out a whimper and curled up on himself. Seb knelt down beside him in the mud, took MaColl's petrol-soaked head in his hands, and pressed his face next to it. He whispered into his ear, the tip of his tongue flicking across the rim of MaColl's earlobe, 'Who did this to you?'

'The 'RA,' MaColl groaned. 'They've a name for themselves, Action Against Drugs or something. It was Chico and his inquisitors.'

'Why?'

'MaColl sneered. 'They know fuck-all, about anything. I was picked up because of the stunt I pulled walking down the Andersonstown road.'

'Did you tell them anything?'

'Fuck you.'

Seb bit down savagely on MaColl's ear. MaColl screamed.

'Did you tell them anything?'

'No,' MaColl sobbed.

Seb let go of his head and lay back slowly beside him in the mud and stared up at the canopy with his hands behind his head. He seemed to see lines and dappled shapes, like myriad possibilities, merge and coalesce, and he felt a surge of raw power grip him. He wanted to shout. He saw himself as the cunning manipulator of all those around him. A superman.

'Yesss,' he hissed through gritted teeth, and turned his head so that his breath was on MaColl's face. 'A terrible beauty is born.'

It was time to leave the province. To get back to Cual.

'Sorry, old chap,' Seb continued, reaching into MaColl's pocket to retrieve his Zippo, 'but as we both know there's only one way to earn my ticket out of here. Prepare yourself.'

He began punching MaColl and, after a few seconds, yelling obscenities at him. Bob was the first to reach them. He launched himself at Seb and got a grip on his jacket and they skidded around the bowl in a fan of mud, while MaColl groaned quietly.

They manhandled MaColl out of the hedgerow with a blanket over his head, and dragged him over to the helicopter and flew him away northwards.

Back out on the road, Seb explored the tender, bruised flesh across the right side of his face with tentative fingers. He winced.

Beside him, Brannon said, 'You've really fucked it now.'

Ignoring him, Seb walked over to Holdfast, who was standing next to Bertie Nugent from Special Branch, slightly apart from the huddle of policemen and soldiers. Holdfast had his hands in the pockets of his mackintosh and his shoulders hunched. As he became aware of Seb's approach he lifted his head and stared at him with his lack-lustre eyes.

'I can hear the tumbril for you, young Sebastian,' Nugent called out.

'I quit,' Seb told Holdfast.

Nugent laughed. 'They thought you were a rook. But you're not, you're a crow.'

'I don't think that MaColl will be speaking to me again in a hurry,' Seb said.

Holdfast said, 'What about the guns?'

'He says they're safe.'

Holdfast nodded slowly. 'You had better go,' he said. He

beckoned to Brannon who was hovering just out of earshot. 'Take Sebastian back to Lisburn.'

They had almost reached the car when Nugent caught up with him. 'I'll be there,' he told Seb, 'at the farm. And if I get the merest whiff of you—'

'What?' Seb snapped, rounding on him aggressively. 'What exactly will you do?'

They faced each other.

'Away ye go, Sebastian,' Nugent said, eventually.

Seb slept in the car, with his chin resting on the cross strap of the seat belt, while Brannon drove, only waking as they negotiated the vehicle checkpoint at the entrance to the barracks. Brannon dropped him outside the officers' mess.

'Don't leave the mess,' he said coldly, as Seb got out of the car. 'Someone will come for you.'

The RSM regarded him with withering contempt. Seb was unmoved; he pulled at the creases in his combat jacket and nodded. The RSM opened the door and Seb marched in. He halted in front of the desk and saluted.

The Colonel looked up from the papers on his table and stared stony-faced at him.

'In view of the serious allegations levelled at you, I have no alternative but to suspend you from duty, effective immediately. You will return to your leave address and remain there until the SIB require you for further questioning or formal charges are laid against you. You are not to leave the country. You will hand your passport to the Adjutant. Is that clear?'

'Yes, sir.'

'Have you anything to say?'

'No, sir.'

The Colonel pushed back his chair and stood up. He was a man of absolutes. He dealt only in things he had experienced. When he committed an act of violence, you knew that he had been at the receiving end of similar acts. Seb attempted to relax the muscles of his face. Although he was expecting it, the force and speed of the blow surprised him. His head snapped back. It felt as if he'd been slapped by a sock full of nuts and bolts. He struggled with every inch of his determination to show no reaction. He returned the Colonel's level gaze.

'Dismissed.'

Seb saluted, about-turned and marched out of the Colonel's office. Out of the army. There was no going back. The year was almost over and he was free.

They were standing in the kitchen. Sile had made a cake, a chocolate cake with chocolate icing and THANK YOU CALUM written on it in Smarties, and a small rotund Father Christmas and two plastic cows embedded in the icing. Since it was his cake, Cal had been given the job of cutting it. The blade was in the cake when they heard the squeal of tyres on the loose gravel chips outside the cottage.

Oonagh was closest to the window. 'It's Madelene.'

She studied his face. Cal very deliberately finished cutting a slice. He felt a sense of terrible foreboding.

Madelene pushed open the kitchen door and stood in the doorway with the wind tugging at her cashmere scarf and her loose blond hair.

'Come in,' Oonagh invited her.

Madelene took four steps into the room. The door slammed behind her. The two women faced each other. Sile looked from one to the other. Cal lifted his attention from the cake. Madelene seemed like a precious and brittle doll next to Oonagh's taller, fuller figure.

Softly he said, 'What is it?'

Madelene said, 'Al's dead.'

He seemed to stand apart from himself and listen to himself. 'Dead? How?'

'A heart attack.'

Al was twenty-six. Dead.

'Who's Al?' Sile asked.

Another dead junkie, he thought bitterly.

'I've booked us on the ferry,' Madelene said, defying him to refuse her. 'It leaves in an hour.'

He shrugged. He didn't want to think. He wanted to curl up.

'You better hurry,' Oonagh told him, and put her hand protectively on Sile's shoulder.

'I'm telling you, Jibby, it's got Dadaist rubbish, surrealist sex, Cubist objects ... pubes, menses, dead skin,' Ed shouted, as he spilled out of the taxi with a cellphone clamped to his ear. He skidded on the muddy grass between headstones. 'It's got emotions and ideas, and best of all it's not fucking abstract, Jibby. It's the future babe, no one knows it better than you. Look, I better ring you back, I've got a funeral. Ciao.'

Cal had his hands on the length of cord and was easing it through his fingers, helping Al's father and brother and one of his uncles lower the pine box into the ground. Al's father was red in the face and dripping with perspiration from the strain of the weight. The broken veins in his nose stood out bright purple. Billy, Al's squaddy brother, sneered at Cal across the grave. His eyes were small and black and sunk in folds of skin. The uncle looked embarrassed and angry. The tension looked like turning to violence. Most of the family had stayed away. The mourners were divided into two hostile camps: immediate family and Al's friends.

Al's mother had begged him to be a pall-bearer. 'I don't want there to be any trouble,' she'd said. She looked much older than the last time he'd seen her; shrunken. Reluctantly he'd agreed, knowing that it would make him a focus for the wrath of her estranged husband, Stan, and her thuggish weedjie son.

It was raining, and there were few umbrellas among Al's friends. The dark woollen suit that Calum was wearing was sodden and heavy. It was Dugald's and it was too large for him. The trousers were spattered with clay from the graveside.

He had mentally divided Al's friends into those who were using heroin and those who weren't. There was Brun from Muirhouse, a tall, wasted zombie; and Shug, who was recently out of Saughton and using already; and Dode, who was HIV-positive. All of them Edinburgh junkies. There were three others from the Brew Crew, two men and a woman. He recognised one of the men from the party in Stoke Newington; the others were strangers. They had all come up in a van with Kelly.

Kelly was dazed and stoned, her face flushed and bloated with crying. Her fingers kept fluttering at her side. Andy was standing at her shoulder looking uncomfortable, sure that if, as a black man, he made an effort to comfort her it would be misunderstood. There were already angry mutterings from the family side.

Then Ed and Madelene arrived. They had been snorting coke

all morning, and arrived late as the body was being lowered into the ground, the taxi dropping them at the entrance to the graveyard. She was wearing a black wraparound dress and her black leather boots, and with each measured stride across the graveyard she revealed a glimpse of stockinged thigh through the division of her dress, and the pine box hung unnoticed above the hole while the mourners watched her approach and listened to Ed yelling into his cellphone.

Kelly stared at Madelene, and her face reddened and became twisted with hatred. So Al had been sleeping with Madelene again. Cal felt like howling in frustration.

Afterwards Al's mother begged him, 'Calum, cum up the hoose, fir Kelly's sake.' The house was on an estate on the outskirts of Dundee. The junkies had departed quickly after the box was in the ground. Cal and Andy took Kelly in a taxi up to the house, Andy didn't want to come in, but Kelly had to be helped out of the taxi and into the house. Madelene and Ed followed in another taxi. There were bottles of whisky and cans of Export on a side table and a green plastic Christmas tree with multicoloured fairy lights in the corner. The trouble started as soon as they were in the house. In the front room the brother, Billy, muttered sullenly from a corner.

Al had never got on with his brother.

'Nigguh cunt,' Billy swore.

Al's mother bustled up to them with whisky. 'It's jest his wey. The boy's upset.'

'Ahm fae here,' Andy protested. 'Ah was born in Dundee.'

'Ah know, son,' she said.

Cal threw back his drink. It burned his chest and throat going down. His stomach was empty, and the strength of it went straight to his head.

'I cannae stand these weedjie cunts,' Andy muttered, and gulped at his whisky. He grimaced. 'Christ, Bells.'

Al's father staggered up to them; his eyes were red and glazed. He brought his fist up in front of Cal's face. It had SCOT Indian-inked on the fingers; LAND was on the other hand. His breath stank of whisky.

'Lissen, son, ahv clocked you, ya university smart-ass cunt. Ah don't like your sort. Yer no differen fae thae junkies fae

Muirhouse. Worse even. Listways they're honest aboot it. They're scum, yer scum dressed up as lamb.'

Calum stared evenly at him.

At that moment Madelene swept in, her second delayed entrance. She brushed past him, trailing heady scent, and went straight up to the table and poured herself a huge measure of whisky. She downed it in one. The mourners watched, their mouths agape.

'I hate fucking Dundee,' she groaned, in her imitation Jerry Sadowitz voice.

'It's vile,' Ed agreed, looking around. He was slight in a midnight-blue satin suit by Prada, with his hair gelled in some sort of Britpop pudding-bowl style. 'Takes me back. Shankill kitsch.'

Al's father backed away across the room from Madelene as if she was some kind of witch. Then Kelly started giggling hysterically. Everyone turned to stare at her.

Andy hissed at Cal, 'Fir fuck's sake do something.'

Cal went over and helped Kelly up out of her chair.

'Ahv pished missel,' she said loudly.

There was a damp patch down the inside of her black tights. Her shoes were slick with urine. Al's mother grabbed her by the arm, and steered her out of the room.

Andy said, 'Ahm gaun.'

'Ye can't,' Cal pleaded. 'We can't leave Kelly here.'

'Is awright fir you, white boy. Much mair bevvie n these cunts wul string me up. Look at it, it's a fuckin Klan gathering.'

The flush on Billy's face went up into his scalp; under his short-cropped hair his head shone bright red. He'd taken off his jacket and rolled up his sleeves, he had the red hand of Ulster tattooed on his left forearm, and UVF scrappily inked on the back of his left hand. Behind him, his hatchet-faced and heavily pregnant wife was scowling at Madelene.

Kelly forced her way back into the room with Al's mother hanging on to her. She put her arms around Cal's neck.

'Ah want you Calum,' she said. 'Ahv eywis had the hots fir you. Yer my man. Kiss me like ye did at the bus station.'

Cal tried to disentangle himself but she was clinging on tightly; her breath reeked of whisky and there was a strong ammonia smell rising off her.

'It's the bevy,' Cal explained, looking desperately around him. Andy was backing towards the front door, appalled.

'Ahm glad he's dead,' Kelly said, her voice rising. 'He was crap. Ah havenae been shagged fir six months. Cum oan, Cal, take us to the lavvy n shag us.'

Al's mother was sobbing now, tugging at Kelly's arm.

Billy advanced across the room. 'What's the fuckin score here?' he growled.

Kelly fondled Cal's balls through the material of his trousers. 'Ye can stick it intae ma arse,' she told him.

'Yer fuckin fucked,' Billy snarled.

Ed put himself between Cal and Billy with his thin arms out in front of him, barring Billy's way. 'Ease up, pal,' he said, loosening into his Belfast accent. 'I mean, the girl's upset.'

'Fuckin stay ootay this,' Billy spat. 'It's fuck-all tae dae wi you.' He jabbed a finger at Calum. 'Git ootay hir, ur ahm gaunnae gie ya a kickin you'll remember, n take the fuckin jungle bunny wi yer!'

'You're degrading yourself,' Ed informed him. 'You're in denial. I know where you're coming from, but your brother's dead. It's a fact. No one can change it.'

Cal had backed up against a wall, missing the doorway.

Kelly let go of him and yelled at Billy, 'Away n batter yir wife, is all yer good fir.'

Billy surged forward. Ed put his hands on Billy's chest, palms outwards, and pushed him back. 'Don't fuck about, pal,' Ed told him.

Billy stopped, and rolled his head to one side.

Andy stared at Ed, aghast. 'I thought you said he was from Belfast.'

'I think he's lost touch with his roots,' Cal replied.

Billy's eyes were narrowed to slits and the muscles of his jaw were taut with tension. Cal could see what was coming.

'Ed . . .'

Billy swung his head round and launched it, slapping his forehead into Ed's face. Blood sprayed from Ed's nose. He crumpled. Cal heard the sound of glass breaking somewhere.

Billy was triumphant. 'Ya cunt ya!' he yelled.

Al's mother was on the floor screaming, with her arms around Kelly's ankles. Kelly was standing very still. Calum took a deep breath. Events seemed to have radically slowed. He took two deliberate steps forward so that he was standing directly in front of Billy.

'Come oan then,' he said evenly, balling his hands into fists.

Madelene took a step up to Billy and glassed him. After a split second's hiatus of shock, he screamed and dropped on his knees. Blood gushed out of his face between his fingers.

Cal said, 'Fuck.'

Madelene turned to face the rest of the family, showing them the glass, its rim of bloody palaeolithic blades. 'Any more?' she asked.

Calum put his arm round Kelly and together they stepped over Al's mother's prostrate body and backed out of the room and through the front door to where Andy was waiting by the gate; after them came Ed, holding a handkerchief to his bloody nose, and, finally, Madelene.

Beyond the gate they broke into a run, and didn't stop until they were off the estate and on a main road. Andy used Ed's cellphone to call a cab.

Calum found that his hands were shaking with the loosening tension, and he fought the urge to gabble. Only Madelene seemed untouched. She affected glacial disdain.

'That wis fuckin rage,' Andy said, once they were all in the cab.

'Orange bastards,' Kelly screamed.

'He bwoke my dose,' Ed mumbled, with his head tipped back against the headrest and his crusted handkerchief held against the ballooning mass of his nose. It had turned a spectacular lilac. No one paid him much attention.

'We need somewhere to crash,' Cal said.

'We're going to the gallery,' Madelene told them.

'No way,' Ed protested.

It was an expression of infallible faith and considerable psychological power. It was Madelene and all her seductive fantasies, fixed for a moment, inside and out.

The gallery was a loft space in an eighteenth-century cotton trader's warehouse in the grid of streets east of Glasgow City Chambers.

'Very eighties,' Andy pronounced, standing beneath the sandblasted portico.

There was a small and unassuming sign beside the entryphone

that belied the grand conceit of its title, The Madelene des Esseintes Museum, and beside it a roughly handwritten note: 'Closed for Christmas'.

The loft was a hundred-foot open space with maple floorboards, whitewashed walls on three sides and a floor-to-ceiling pane of glass on the fourth, with the city beyond it.

As they emerged from the freight lift, their nostrils were filled with the smell of tannin, and their eyes were drawn upwards to the vast animal hide curving above them. Entitled *Everyone I Ever Slept With*, it was somewhere between a flag and a tent, suspended from the ceiling by steel hawsers and lit by carefully placed spots that made the raw-sienna coloured hide seem almost translucent. The columns of names branded on it stood out crisply black.

Names and dates, for anyone to see. More than Cal could ever have imagined. His own name and beside it the day of the month of the year. He felt unreal.

'Boo,' she whispered in his ear. Involuntarily, his hands went up to his face, his palms rubbing at the taut skin. Madelene drifted away, chuckling. He dream-walked across the polished floor, across the word 'Striptease' that she had burnt into the floorboards, passing a row of shoes – many of them familiar – reminiscent of the television images from the Filipino presidential palace in the aftermath of the Marcoses' hurried departure. Row upon row of Imelda's shoes, only these were Madelene's. Beyond them were racks of clothes that smelt of her, an earthenware vessel containing soiled underwear and countless stacks of pickling-jars labelled by contents: fingernails, navel fluff, teeth, snot, eye-grit . . .

Somewhere off to his right Andy was pointing and whispering, 'Wat's zat?'

On a narrow plinth there was a small bronze casting, vaguely mushroom-shaped and with the thick stem of a boletus. Cal picked it up and turned it over in his hands.

Andy said, 'Mebbe it's an alien, eh?'

'It's my vagina,' Madelene told them.

A silence followed, broken only when Cal expressed what they'd all been thinking. 'How exactly?'

'A Femidom,' Madelene explained. 'And malleable wax.'

She opened a cabinet and produced from her pocket the broken glass that she had used on Al's brother. Inside, the cabinet was divided into small compartments, with each compartment displaying an item of significance, a knife, a hat-pin, a corkscrew, a cigarette. It was entitled, *Acts of Violence*, each item was the clue to a confrontation. She set the glass, still crusted with blood, in one of the few empty compartments.

She turned round and found that she was the centre of attention. 'Usually, there's a charge for the eyeing of my scars,' she informed them.

'What are you doing?' Cal asked.

'It's a fashion thing,' Madelene answered. She seemed in a better mood. 'It's my wave. Let me surf it.'

'It's a sicko's theme park,' Kelly sneered.

'Anger, frustration, longing, envy, jealousy, even boredom. I get almost every reaction in the book,' Madelene told her, at her most condescending. 'You know, I think it's almost as serious a method of communication as sex.'

'Fuck off,' Kelly snapped. She turned her back and went over to stand by the window. She hugged her upper arms.

Madelene chuckled.

Ed emerged from a small kitchen at the back of the gallery, clutching a block of ice, a pick and a dishcloth. He went over to a desk by the elevator, swept its surface clear of a sheaf of catalogues and a basket filled with violet and scabious, and tipped the ice on to it. He started jabbing bad-temperedly at the ice with the pick. When he had broken off enough pieces he threw down the pick, scooped the shards into the dishcloth and pressed it to his nose. He groaned extravagantly.

Andy grinned, stuck his tongue in his cheek and started pumping a closed fist up and down. Wanker.

Cal continued his circuit of the gallery. On the back wall, by the kitchen, was a row of framed prints, which proved on closer examination to be photographs of gutted buildings. He recognised the charred ruin of the Mermaid fish bar on Cual and beneath it the legend 'My first job – Mermaid'. After it, 'A new home – Murbhach'. He looked across at Madelene, but she was watching Ed.

From somewhere, he had produced a fist-sized hessian sack that he set on the desk. He untied the drawstring one-handed, and shovelled his hand down into its contents. It came back up with a palmful of caked white powder. He flung away the icepack and started grubbing at the hollow of his palm, sniffing and snorting with increasing desperation.

'Buck!' he screamed. 'Buck! Buck! Buck!'

He was covered in it. There was white powder in his eyebrows and on his lips, and encrusted in the bloody mass of his nose. He stopped abruptly as he realised that everyone was staring him.

'Smile,' Andy told him. 'Yir oan *Candid Camera.*'

'I need something,' Ed yelled. 'Cumb on, Maddy, it buckin hurts. What about a needle? I'll inject it. Give me one of your needles.'

Needle. The word left a swathe of silence in its wake.

Calum watched Madelene. She looked furious, never-seen-before colour rising in her cheeks. Abruptly, she turned her back on them all and strode to the spiral staircase in the far corner of the room, the heeltaps of her black boots punctuating her fury. She disappeared in the direction of the bedrooms.

Andy mouthed the words to the Velvet Underground song. 'She's a femme fatale . . .'

Ed scurried after her, trailing flurries of white powder.

'Check that oot,' Andy said. 'Council wul hav to git a grit lorry in after him.' He sauntered over to the desk, put his finger into the powder and worked some into his gums. Presently, he smiled. 'Cocaine, amigo, Colombia's finest export,' he said. 'Usually it's against my religious principles, but under the circumstances . . .'

Cal shook his head grimly. 'I need a drink,' he said. He went through into the small kitchen and started randomly opening cupboards. Soon he located the liquor cabinet; it was stocked with scores of unopened bottles. He found a bottle of special vintage Black Deochmore.

'It's Christmas all over again,' he said, deadpan. He leant through the doorway and showed the bottle to Andy. 'Two hundred quid a bottle.'

It took him another few minutes to find the glasses, huge bowl-sized tumblers in clear handblown glass. He poured the liquorice-coloured fluid into them. He stopped by Andy who was emptying handfuls of cocaine on to the table.

'It's black,' Andy said, when he paused to look in the glass.

'Well observed. I'm telling you, this is a rare opportunity. Black Deochmore.'

'I thought I was the only black in Deochmore.'

'Not back in 1964, when this was laid down in sherry casks. The sherry must have been rich as tar.'

Cal walked over to the window where Kelly was standing. The district was still and silent. He rested his forehead against the glass, and watched her from the corner of his eyes. She was crying, the tears running down her cold reddened cheeks, and sniffing occasionally.

'Whisky?'

She accepted the glass and cupped it in her pale hands. She affected a laugh. 'Calum's cure-all?'

He smiled. 'Never fails.'

'I won't cry any more,' she said.

'Don't mind me.'

'It's her I mind.' She took a large mouthful of whisky and gulped it down. She had stopped sniffing now.

'You want to talk about it?'

She nodded. 'It was the crash that killed him. When he came oaf that bike. It broke his spirit. They filled his legs so full of pins he'll be setting off metal-detectors in a hundred years. Fer a whole year he wasnae hisself. The pain was bad.'

She looked at Calum. 'I needed a break so I went home to my ma n pa in Thurso. I thought he'd be awright.' She took another gulp of whisky. 'But Madelene pitched up at the squat in her fancy racing car while I was away. She was wanting to buy a gun, fir fuck's sake. A gun. You know Al, he'd fix up anybody. She's playing up to his hardman Mr Fixit image. They take a Sunday drive up to Manchester, because Al kens a man in Moss Side. They buy a gun on the Alexandra estate, but that's just the start of it, because she's shagging him by now. That's how she controls weak-willed men like Al. She's goat loads of friends squatting in Hulme, and takes a room. And now Maddy and Al are awae oan a chemical holiday. They're outlaws now in their little minds. Mickey n Mallory.' Her face was hard, and her voice bitter with vitriol. 'She put him on to it, and he never came oaf.'

Cal stared at her, appalled.

'She's goat another sucker up there now.'

'I'm sorry,' Cal said, shaking his head.

'You're sorry?'

'She's not using, Kelly.'

Her face twisted in outrage. 'What?'

'She's not on smack. She may have a lot of faults but she's not a junkie.'

'You know that do you?'

'Come on, she looks so healthy.'

'She's careful,' Kelly sneered.

'Kelly, there's not a mark on her.' He could have kicked himself. 'I'm sorry,' he said.

'So yir shagging her as well, are ye? Christ!' She stepped violently away from him. 'Men! Yir so fuckin pathetic!' Grabbing her coat from one of the chairs, she stormed across to the elevator.

'I was wrong about you, Calum Bean,' she said.

'Good one,' Andy told him, after she'd left. 'You outdid yirself.'

'Where will she go?'

Andy shrugged. 'She has friends round about. She'll be fine. Cum oan, have some coke and a smile. Ed cannae very well git it up his nose now, can he?'

'Fuck it,' Cal muttered, suddenly reckless, 'have you got a note?'

'Fuck that,' Andy said. 'Just git yer hooter in it, n start hooverin.'

Cal got down on his knees, put his nose in it and started sniffing. 'Fuck, it's strong,' he yelled.

Then Andy went down on the pile. 'Wheeee!' he squealed.

They started dancing rhythmically in place, flailing their arms in strange gyrations, wildly intoxicated.

Andy had collapsed on the floor surrounded by opened bottles, half-empty glasses and swathes of coke like stardust. All the lights were off, just a few guttering almost-spent candles dotted across the floor and on the desk. Cal stood barefoot half-hidden in the shadow cast by the tent, reading the name over to himself. That one name. Sebastian. He felt paranoia and exhaustion coiling inside him like two opposing snakes. Had she really slept with Seb?

He heard her footsteps on the stairway. She was wearing a silk robe and it gleamed in the candle-light. She crossed to the sink in the kitchen and opened the faucet, and cupped her hand beneath the jet of water. She lapped at the water in her hand with her tongue. It was unsettling to watch, not quite human.

He came away from the shadows, took a few hesitating steps towards her. She looked up abruptly, letting the water run between her fingers.

'Who's there?' she called softly.

'Me. Calum.'

She straightened up. He saw that the tie at her waist had half unravelled, and the robe had opened loosely, revealing a deep V that reached to the sparse, short-cropped hair of her pubis. He felt a strong desire for her, but experienced it as if at a distance. He felt disembodied.

She gathered the robe round herself, clutching the fabric together above her tiny breasts.

He stopped in the doorway, just a few feet from her. 'How is he?' Meaning Ed.

'Unconscious,' she said.

He bit his lip. 'Did you knock him out with something?'

'Don't be stupid' she said.

'I want you.' He blurted it out, without thinking about it.

She smiled, the candlelight picking out her bright white teeth. She taunted him, 'It turned you on, didn't it? The violence. It scares you and excites you.'

He shook his head, as if to shake off the confusion that dogged him.

She snarled, 'What about Oonagh?'

'I don't know,' he replied slowly, taken aback by the anger in her voice. It had never occurred to him before that she might be possessive. 'What about Seb?'

She laughed derisively. 'What about him?'

'His name, it's up there. Is he the one you love?'

'Everyone I slept with, Cal, not everyone I had sex with. Did you never share a bed as a child?'

'I'm sorry,' he said.

'Anyway, he's not the only person with that name.'

She turned her back on him and walked towards the stairs. He watched her, her swaying hips, the shimmering silk on her buttocks. He swore at himself and went after her, following her up the stairwell and down a thickly carpeted corridor. She paused with her hand on a door-handle. He had no words to say, no other way of expressing his desire; he put his hands on her waist and slid them up her ribs, reaching for her breasts.

'Stop it!' she hissed, and she spun around to face him. Surprised by her vehemence he dropped his hands and backed away.

'Take your clothes off,' she said.

He stood still.

'Take them off. I want you naked.'

He undressed, loosening his tie and pulling it over his head with the shirt; he kicked off his muddy suit trousers and pulled down his boxer shorts, discarding them in a pile at his feet. He stood naked and erect in front of her. She looked at him with approval. 'Turn round,' she commanded. 'Now face the wall.'

He laid his palms and his forehead against the cold surface of the wall, the plaster was creamy white, lit by subtle floor-level lighting.

'Don't move,' she said.

He heard a rustling sound as she shrugged off the robe and it floated down to the carpet. She was behind him now; he could feel her breath on his spine. She hooked a leg through one of his, and he felt her pubic hair brushing the back of his thigh; forcefully she tugged his legs apart.

'That's better,' she said, her voice low and seductive.

Her lips travelled across his shoulders. She bit into the flesh between his shoulder-blades. He squirmed against the wall. He heard the sound of her spitting on her fingers, and then she reached round and slid her moist fingers through his pubic hair. The plaster was damp where his mouth had moved in an arc across it. His hair was charged with static electricity.

'That's how you want it.' He heard her spit on her other fingers. 'Isn't it?'

He felt her fingers sliding down the cleft between his buttocks, the fleshy pad of her finger tracing a circle at the mouth of his anus. She slid two fingers in; he tensed for a second, and then they were in and sliding back and forth.

She told him, 'You just wanted to be fucked.'

He was moaning. He shuddered as she withdrew her fingers. His hands scratched at the wall, and he stood back from it trembling. The door closed behind her; she was gone. He didn't know what to do. His whole body was shaking. He knew she was in there with Ed. He banged his fist against the wall in frustration.

He ran the back of his hand across his face, and opened the door. She was lying naked on the unmade bed, surrounded by candles. Ed lay on the floor in his crumpled blood-stained suit, with his mouth slightly open.

Cal went over to Ed and knelt beside him. He rested two fingers against his neck to check his pulse.

She gasped, in outrage. 'Did you think he was dead?'

He shook his head slowly.

'Fuck me.'

'What?' he said, shocked, not moving.

'Fuck me right now.'

He wasn't strong enough not to look at her. Once he had looked at her, he could not refuse.

'You're mine,' she said. 'You'll always be mine.'

9

The morning was awkward. Ed was in pain and became bad-tempered when he discovered that they had raided his coke stash. 'You got no respect,' he mumbled. It was true, but he was too frightened of Madelene to do much more than sulk. She packed him off to the hospital in a cab, threw a blanket over Andy and took hold of Cal's hand.

'Come with me to Edinburgh?'

Cal had left the bedroom at dawn, easing himself out of the tangle of her limbs and stepping over Ed's prostrate body. Now he felt used and abused. He asked her, 'Why?'

She laughed. 'Don't be so suspicious. Brun's promised me some hash for Hogmanay. Anyway, it'll be fun.'

There was no way of telling what Madelene's idea of fun might be.

The MG would be too conspicuous in Muirhouse so they parked it short and walked the last mile through Leith, crossing the dual carriageway to the housing estate, coming in at an angle through a blind spot in the newly installed video-camera array on the perimeter. They crossed the open and empty tarmac spaces between the ugly housing blocks.

Brun's apartment was at the end of a dark passageway of abandoned apartments bolted shut with sheets of steel. The floor was covered in broken glass and stale pools of urine. 'Shooting Gallery' was spray-painted in bright pink lettering on the door.

'You advertising?' Cal asked when Brun opened the door.

Brun was thin as a stick, with weeping grey skin; he was nearly bald and of indeterminate age. He shrugged half-heartedly. 'Wee schemies,' he said. 'Whit til I git a hoal ov they cunts. C'moan in.' He shuffled two steps away, stopped and lifted his bowed neck and peered uncertainly at Madelene, at her beautiful, unforgettable face.

'Brun, I feel wretched.' Her voice was slow as syrup, hoarse and breathless – she was fully aware of the effect – pressing her hand against the wasted flesh of Brun's upper arm. Cal, rendered invisible, irrelevant, followed on. 'Damage's Lepers' he has called them in the past, the scabrous, depleted ranks of her suppliers. They fell over themselves to pander to her whims; heroin-dealers forgot all about a mark-up to find her hashish, Coke-dealers promised her speed, Ecstasy dealers scoured their filo-faxes to procure her Valium.

'Look at me. I'm shaking.' She wasn't. 'Al's death was just the last straw. Let's smoke a joint.'

Madelene sat on the couch next to Brun and Cal sat in a worn-out armchair opposite them. In the other chair next to him, the recently released Shug studied Madelene with predatory curiosity. The room was stifling – the streaked windows were painted shut – and stank of cigarette ash, stale milk and vinegar. There was no agonising preamble; a block of pressed hash was produced from a plastic bag under the coffee table; ashtrays and half-empty greenish milk bottles were shunted aside.

Cal watched her roll a joint, crumbling a sizable lump of hash in the well of her palm; her sharp-pointed tongue travelling up the seam of a cigarette, splitting it open, and sprinkling the strings of tobacco into her palm. She massaged the hash and tobacco together for a minute or so and then fed the mixture into the opened-out cone of king-size papers – she was extravagant in her use of papers. She was extravagant in everything.

When she was finished, she held upright, in the pinch of her slender fingers, the joint's long slightly warped spear-shaft; and flicked her wrist, as if she was ringing a hand-bell.

Satisfied, she inserted it between her lips and lit the taper. She dabbed at the hot coal with the moist pad of a finger, toked on it and rolled her eyes in mock ecstasy at her three rapt observers. The room quickly filled with the cloying aroma of the drug.

'It's awright,' Brun said.

She nodded slowly, and passed the joint to Cal.

The hash was strong, its effect almost immediate. Cal's breathing seemed to become leaden and his stomach writhed.

At some indeterminate point Madelene stood up and as if by arrangement so did Brun and they went through to Brun's bedroom, Madelene taking her bag with her, pulling the plastic partition door closed behind them.

Shug lifted his eyebrows in a grotesque parody of surprise, and then broke into a smile, displaying a single yellowed front tooth. 'Wish ay had a fairy godmother.'

Cal offered him the joint, but he shook his head and continued to smile.

Roiling paranoia. He contemplated the detritus littering the table; his mind was full of all sorts of nasty possibilities. He wanted to get up and open the partition, but his head was rushing savagely. He smoked more of the joint. It occurred to him that he hadn't eaten since the bacon sandwich back on Cual.

Shug was smiling and nodding. He looked like something unpleasant in one of Madelene's formaldehyde boxes; some floating scrap of surrealist genitalia. It came as a sudden revelation. The flat and its inhabitants were an experiment, a piece of performance art with decay as the theme.

'I ken yir face, fae Sativa?'

'No,' Cal said. He knew the club though he had not been there for some years. 'I was a friend of Al's.'

'S'at right?'

'Aye.'

He continued smiling and nodding. 'Good gear?'

'Aye,' Cal said.

'Strong?'

'Aye.'

'It's good.'

'Aye.' Cal nodded. He was terrified.

'Yu shur ye wernae at Sativa?'

'Aye.'

'Ay'm shur I eyeballed you.'

'No.'

'You calling me a liar?'

'No,' Cal said, slowly.

Shug smiled. 'Yir oaf yir wee trolley,' he said.

Madelene pulled back the partition. Brun loomed behind her, red-eyed and wasted.

'Let's go,' she said.

Cal got up and swayed over the table.

'The hash,' she reminded him. He packed it in his bag,

which he slung over his shoulder, and followed her out of the apartment. They walked across the empty parking spaces and out of Muirhouse.

In the car he asked her, 'What were you doing in there?'

She glanced across at him. 'Winding him up.'

When she didn't elaborate he asked, 'What d'you mean?'

She laughed. 'He's clockwork, don't you know?'

He didn't understand. He said, 'What now?'

'When we get back we're going to see Dougie. Seb's expecting you to sort out the boat. Where's the money?'

Cal stared at the dash. It was time to commit. 'I can get it.'

The ferry rose and fell with the waves, water sluicing across the smeary surface of the portholes in the bar on the lower deck, and Cal gripped his glass to stop it from sliding across the table. Madelene watched him from across the table. She was sitting with her legs crossed and her arms outstretched on the back of the bench seat.

'You're so transparent,' she said, and laughed. 'I feel like I'm seventeen.'

When they were seventeen they had tumbled in and out of bed as the mood caught them. He had always derived a certain pleasure from screwing her while she was supposed to be involved in a relationship with someone else. That was then; it was different now, it seemed more like a compulsion. He wasn't looking forward to going back to the island. He didn't know what he was going to say to Oonagh. It felt as if there was a tight band of metal pressing against his forehead. He was stoned and exhausted.

'Don't . . .' he pleaded.

'Do you remember the first time we fucked? In the windmill. I was your first. Seb was furious.'

'Please . . .'

Andy came back from the toilets, groaning, and slumped on the seat beside them. His face was as grey as ash. 'I don't remember anything,' he moaned.

The ferry continued to rise and fall with relentless monotony. Cal felt sicker and sicker. Eventually he stood up and said, 'I'm going outside for some air.'

Andy had his head resting on the seat back and his eyes firmly shut. Madelene looked at Cal with amusement. 'Don't be long, lover,' she said.

He went out on deck and over to the railings and stood into the wind so that the spray struck his face. He rolled his aching shoulders. Madelene had thoroughly unsettled him. He stood that way for five minutes, and watched as the wind stripped away the murk and rain, and the fractured black cliffs of the Og were revealed as if for the first time.

Even at this distance he could hear the crashing waves in the whirlpool at its base. For a second, a shaft of sunlight caught the top of the outcrop and flashed on the gravestones in the cemetery. Even now, thinking of his mother, it filled his heart with desolation.

Once again, he'd screwed everything up. He'd taken his chance with Oonagh and pissed it in the wind. Now there was nothing left but the smuggling.

As he turned to leave, something caught his attention. Another passenger, the only other passenger out on the deck, a motorcyclist sitting on the wooden-slatted seat, still wearing his black-visored helmet. Cal remembered having seen a black 900cc Ninja bike when they loaded. There had been something familiar about the man's gait as he climbed off the bike on the car-deck and climbed the steps. Now it seemed odd that he hadn't removed his helmet. Too tired and depressed to think on it further, Cal stumbled back inside.

At Port Claganach the bike was off before them; he only heard the roar as it accelerated away through the almost deserted town.

They dropped Andy off outside his mother's house. 'See you at New Year,' he said and ambled inside.

'Well?' Madelene demanded, looking across at him, the rain pattering on the MG's soft-top.

'Your place,' Cal told her, 'if you want the money.'

He instructed her to park halfway down the gravel drive, just short of the ruin of the castle. 'I won't be long,' he said, evasively.

Madelene shrugged.

He went quickly through the castle and the walled garden and beyond into the rhododendrons, dropping down into the dripping defile, making his way down to the hidden cove and from there across the rocks to the trench that held Seb's cache. He located the scratch marks in the moss, and lifted the stone under which the old ammunition box was buried. He removed the plastic bag of money and stuck it in an inside pocket. He set off back to the car.

He found Madelene in the ruins of the castle. He got the feeling that she had been following him. She was staring upwards, through the collapsed floors, at the blackened roof timbers.

'Why did you set fire to it?' he asked.

The tiny lines under her eyes crinkled as she read the expression on his face. 'Is that what you think?'

'Well?'

'You're very bold today,' she said. She turned her back on him and walked out of the ruin.

Graeme Hogg's farm was located on a barren and stony cliff edge, among broken rocks and marsh grass, on the north side of the Og. The tarmac road climbed up out of the shelter of Port Claganach on to the bunched fist of rock.

The farm was at the end of an exposed three-mile hardcore track that turned off the road before it reached the cemetery. It was hard going in the MG, and Madelene drove slowly, with her teeth biting down on her lower lip.

First they saw the wheeling crows, battling with the wind sweeping across the cliffs, and then about a mile up the track they passed two vehicles in a field, one of them owned by a local farmer and the other Oonagh's Subaru. They were parked next to a broken crush and a pen that contained a few skeletal blackface sheep; as they passed Oonagh looked up from the sheep she was holding down and stared at the car. Some dark shade of animosity filled her expression. Cal willed the seat leather to swallow him up.

The farm was in a ruinous state. Shattered roof slates littered the yard; there were gaping holes in the roof, with exposed and rotting beams. They got out of the car and went across the mud to the kitchen door, starved-looking cats scattering before them.

The house was like a cave, an animal lair. Its walls and roof were blackened with smoke and a thick layer of grime and everything reeked. Dougie Hogg looked up slowly from the table, and studied them with red-rimmed eyes; around him on the flagstones were sheets of newspaper and coils of dried-out dog turd. The only light came through a single smeared pane of glass in the window, surrounded by Sellotaped cardboard. Thick PVC sheeting was strung across the hole in the partition-wall, the remnants of a doorway, that led through into the rest of the house.

'Give him the money,' Madelene said, putting her bag on the table.

Cal opened out the plastic wallet and removed the notes. He counted them out on the table and then pushed the bundle across the table-top towards Dougie.

'Where is he?' Madelene asked.

Dougie tilted his head towards the doorway. Madelene slung her bag over her shoulder and went through into the adjoining room. She pulled back the opaque sheeting for only a few seconds but Cal managed to catch a glimpse of a body lying on top of a wooden board balanced on oil drums. The body was surrounded by motes of dust in a shaft of sunlight falling from the open roof.

'Wir d'ye wan it?' Dougie asked.

Cal turned towards him. Dougie was pushing the ownership documents across the table towards him.

Distracted, Cal asked, 'What?'

'The boat, man.'

Cal considered this. Seb had been quite specific: 'Bring it round to the cove at Murbhach.' In the cove it would not be visible to any casual observer from either land or sea. 'Say you're going away to the mainland.'

Dougie nodded slowly.

There was a long pause. Cal stared at the PVC sheeting that divided the rooms.

'I ken yir Dugald's wee bruther?'

Cal looked down at him. 'Aye.'

'Ir ye a farmer as well?'

'No.'

Eventually Dougie said, 'Hir bruther was here.'

'Madelene's brother? You mean Sebastian?'

'Aye, the suldjer.'

'When?'

'A while back. He sed ye'd come fir the boat.'

Madelene came back through the partition, pulling it across the opening behind her, and went straight over to the table. She peeled six fifty-pound notes off the top of the bundle and dropped them in her bag.

'Is there some left fir me?' Dougie asked.

'It's by the bed,' she replied. 'There's a dead dog in there. It stinks.'

'Aye,' Dougie said.

She looked at Cal. 'Let's go.' And to Dougie: 'You stay out of sight until this is done.'

Cal stood up and gathered up the documents.

In the car, on the way back down the track, Cal said, 'That was Graeme Hogg through the back, wasn't it?'

'The islanders think he's on the mainland,' she said.

Cal looked across the car at her. Her eyes were fixed on the road.

'What are you doing?'

'I'm making sure they keep their mouths shut,' she told him.

'Christ.'

As they came back down the track they saw that the cars had gone. The sheep were dead: the pile of carcasses covered in a mass of crows. The crows scattered as they drove past, circled briefly, and plunged back down on to the pile behind them.

That evening he went to the ringing telephone, abandoning a half-empty bottle of whisky, pulled the hallway door closed on Aulay's panel-beating, and lifted the receiver to his ear.

'It's me,' she said brusquely.

He rested his forehead against the door-jamb. Oonagh was the last person he wanted to speak to.

'You know I could point to a hundred farms on this island and say that farmer loves and cares for his beasts. Tell me, why is it that I get called out to the one really bad farm and I see you there? Why is that?' He could hear barely controlled fury in her voice. 'What were you doing up at Graeme Hogg's farm?' she demanded.

He hesitated. 'Looking for his brother, Dougie.'

'Do you know where Graeme Hogg is?'

'I think he's on the mainland,' he said lamely.

'You didn't see him?'

'No.' He paused and squeezed closed his eyes. 'We didn't see anyone. We went up there. Nobody was there.'

'Wait till I get a hold of him. The bastard hasn't fed his sheep for days and the crows have been at them and pecked out their eyes. They were blind and near dead. All I could do was kill them.'

'I'm sorry,' he said quietly.

There was a long silence.

She sighed. 'No. I'm sorry. It's not your fault.' Another silence, and then a softening in her voice: 'How was the funeral?'

'Bad,' he told her, not wanting her to go on, not wanting to explain. He wanted her to stay angry with him, so that he could feel he was getting what he deserved.

'He was no older than you. How come he died?'

'He was a junkie.' He shook his head; it seemed like such a simplistic statement. 'He overdosed.'

'I see. You know many people using heroin?'

'I didn't used to know any,' he said.

'Does it not make you angry?'

'Yes,' he said tersely.

'You don't want to talk about it?'

'Not really.'

'You could come over here,' she said tentatively. 'I've a stale slice of cake waiting on you.'

'Not tonight,' he said.

There was another uncomfortable silence.

'Will I see you?' she asked.

'Yes. I'm sorry. Its just . . .' He struggled for words. 'Nothing.'

She tried to remain bright. 'Madelene invited me to the New Year's party.'

He was confused. 'When did she do that?'

'About a week ago.' She sounded curious. 'Why?'

'I just thought you two didn't get on,' he said stiffly.

'Is there some reason why we shouldn't?'

'No,' he said. 'Look, I'm tired. I can't think straight. I'll see you at the party.'

'All right,' she said softly and put the phone down.

He stood for some seconds listening to the sound of the broken connection, and then he swore at himself and went back to his whisky.

He walked up out of the field past flaming thuribles on bright lengths of chain; the brazier-cups spinning past the bare, tattooed flesh of Shuard's arms as he whirled them in elaborate patterns; the dog Kali howling and sprinting around him, and Organ staggering backwards beneath a smoking chillum. It was New Year at Murbhach and the lorry-mounted soundstacks were playing the Orb. Bonfires crackled all around him. Down in the corner of the field near the windmill a tent was burning, and a group of people were trying to stamp it out. Cal took another pull on his whisky bottle. Sile ran past him in a flurry of travellers' kids, stopped and ran back to him.

'Yer for it,' she said.

'I know,' he replied miserably.

She ran off.

He went across the courtyard to the stable block, lifted the latch on the door to the kitchen and went in. Madelene's room was filled with seated people and the sound of Burning Spear.

Cal caught sight of Andy. He stepped carefully between supine forms, knelt beside him and shouted in his ear, 'Have you seen Oonagh?'

'Aye.' Andy pointed down the length of the attic space towards Seb's room. 'I saw her go that way.'

'Cheers.'

She looked across as he ducked through the hanging. She'd been studying the photos of Seb on the wall; Madelene's shrine to her brother. He joined her by the wall, so that she was within reach. He wanted to put his hand on her waist, but he knew that he had lost that right.

She said, 'He's beautiful, isn't he? A feudal lord?'

'Yes,' Cal replied frankly. 'Yes, he is.'

'Achilles?'

'He thinks so.'

She turned her head towards him, her fierce eyes displaying no humour. 'And who are you?'

He shrugged, tried to introduce a hint of levity. 'I thought I was Odysseus, the crafty one, or even Homer himself.'

'What about the prat who gets himself killed pretending to be his friend?'

'Patroclus,' he said.

'Yes.'

She looked hard into his face. She said, 'I'm not staying.'

Suddenly he wanted to go back to before the funeral. He wanted to start again. 'I could come with you,' he said hopefully.

'I got a phone call, about two hours ago, from Madelene. She asked me to bring some needles.'

'I'm sorry,' he said.

'Have you been having sex with her?'

He breathed out hard.

'Don't lie to me.'

'Yes,' Cal admitted.

'How could you?' she asked, maintaining her unclouded gaze. Calm.

'I don't know. I don't understand myself.'

'They'll destroy you, Seb and Madelene. They'll eat you up and throw you away, like a bone.'

'I'm sorry.'

'Goodbye, Calum.'

'Don't go. Give me another chance.'

'A third chance? Fat chance. Fuck you,' she whispered. 'You know, you nearly had me fooled. I nearly got my wires crossed. Thought you were different.'

And the first of the explosions went off, a flash of piercing blood-red and orange light flooding the window and the room, followed almost instantly by a concussive boom.

Sudden silence, broken only by the background beat of the soundstacks.

'Christ!'

'Seb,' Cal said.

He took her hand and they went through the doorway, and through the mass of dazed and struggling people under the white striplight – Andy who also saw the significance of the explosion had hit the light switch – leading a crowd of the bold and the curious, spilling out of the stable block.

Crump. The fireball folding upwards and outwards; a red-orange stamen lunging into the clear night sky, and a mush-rooming cloud of acrid red-lit black smoke. A nuke among the apple trees.

An oil-drum with the top cut off, filled with diesel and petrol in equal parts and buried in the ground to the rim, surrounded by a loop of det cord and with a waterproof bag immersed in the fuel mixture. In the bag a fist of plastic explosive and more det cord, plus some gunpowder and fireworks; the sealed wire-cable coming up out of the bag and leading away to the detonator. All of it camouflaged by leaves and branches.

There was no doubt about the identity of the bomber; it

occurred to Cal that Seb must have been on the island for at least one night to have organised such a dramatic entrance.

If the two nukes were to get attention, then the finale would be the windmill. Looking across the courtyard Cal saw that the seventy-five-year-old Hugh MacCoinneach had emerged from his house clutching a bottle of brandy. He was wearing a faded, once bright-red, mess jacket with gold braid on the cuffs and lapels, a crumpled white shirt and bow tie and a pair of too-tight tartan trews; and with his widow's peak of silver hair, and flanked by travellers, tribespeople and islanders, he looked like a bizarre lion rampant surrounded by infidels. He took a few diffident steps in the direction of the mushroom cloud.

Behind him, in the doorway, Cal saw Breeze; the firelight on her oil-black hair and glinting in her dark oval eyes.

The windmill exploded. First the chocks; two small puffs of smoke and the whole conical structure teetered unfettered for a second, and then the sails flamed from stem to peak and fell away, and for another second it seemed an anti-climax. Then the bulk of it exploded; caulked timbers spun like matchsticks through the air, chased by blossoming fire.

All around, Cal people had begun clapping, just a few at first recovering from the spectacle, and then it was taken up and everybody was clapping and cheering and hugging each other. It was New Year.

Seb walked out of the shadows, almost unnoticed; he seemed shy at first, eyes down. Cal took a couple of hesitant steps towards him but Seb lifted his head and gave him a brief lopsided grin and stopped Cal in his tracks. Seb went past him to his father and stopped in front of him. They stood face to face, all straight-backed martial bearing. Words were exchanged, although Cal could not hear them. The father nodded. Seb reached out with opened arms, and father and son embraced.

Glancing around, Cal saw that Oonagh had gone. He swore softly to himself. Beyond her father and half-brother, Madelene was standing watching him, her expression one of naked triumph.

Cal loafed around the farmhouse for two days, waiting for a visitor or a summons, feeling dispirited and restless. He begrudged the sheep and the cattle the trips out to the barn to feed them. He watched television, old Bond movies that he had seen a thousand times before and other festive-season repeats; he tried writing about the battle for Claremont Road but found that he couldn't remember people's names or the things they had said. He was too confused about his own feelings to set them down straight. He thirsted for some kind of action.

In the event it wasn't Seb or Madelene, it was Oonagh. She called him in the middle of the night. He stumbled down the stairs and picked up the phone and listened to the torrent of mangled gasps and undecipherable words.

'Stop it,' he said firmly after half a minute. 'Start again, slowly this time.'

'He's escaped from Whitemoor,' she sobbed. 'It was on the radio. He'll come, I know he will . . . he'll come for Sile. I know it.'

The father of her child, the convicted IRA terrorist, was loose and probably heading her way. A knot twisted in his guts. The upper arch of his jaw started to throb painfully.

'I'm so fucking scared,' Oonagh said.

He struggled for words of reassurance. 'He . . . he wouldn't be so stupid.'

'He thinks I touted on him. He wants to hurt me . . . he means it. He's on his way here right now. I know it.'

The fear of death had come back for him with a vengeance; he wanted to cling to the ground. But he could not live with himself that way.

'I'm coming,' he said and slammed the phone down and grabbed some clothes, spitting words of violent bravado.

The pick-up wouldn't start. He banged his fists against the steering wheel in desperate frustration. He climbed out of the cab and ran round to the front and lifted the bonnet and saw that the starter motor was gone, or rather he'd been looking at it in pieces on the kitchen table for the last two days.

'Aulay!' he screamed.

He ran two miles through the rain to Droch and borrowed a car from Dylan who worked at the abattoir, getting him up out of his bed and demanding the keys and having to give some kind of a breathless explanation.

He drove at break-neck speed across the island, sluicing through the water-filled curves and accelerating wildly on the straights, his fist on the horn to scatter grazing cattle and sheep. He lost control of the car beyond the turn off at Kentraw, on a sharp bend, the car climbing the low bank and tumbling over into the marshland beyond, where it was hidden from sight. The rain continued unabated.

He had no way of telling how much time had passed when he regained consciousness, it was still dark though, and it had stopped raining. The wind had cleared the cloud cover and the sky was bright and clear. The car had tumbled right over and was upright in the marsh, sunk to the level of the wheel-rims. Cal lifted his head off the dashboard. He ran his tongue across his lips and tasted iron. Blood. He groaned, and tenderly dabbed at his forehead; a skein of flesh hung off it like a strip of kebab meat.

Muddy brown water pooled around his ankles. He wound down the window and climbed out. He immediately sank to his thighs in the marsh. He lurched across to a tussock of grass and pulled himself free, and climbed the bank to the road.

He started walking. Blood ran off his forehead into his eyes, so he rubbed them with his hands, and got grit and mud in his eyes and could hardly see.

It took him an hour to reach Carndonald. He arrived too late; the black Ninja bike from the ferry was parked diagonally across the loose gravel driveway. The house was dark.

He stopped in front of the door, and because he couldn't think of anything else he banged on it with his fist. He took a few steps backwards and looked up at the roof of the cottage, the Velux window in the slate roof. His fear was almost unendurable.

A light came on. He heard footsteps on the wooden stairs.

The door opened; Seb stood naked on the doormat.

Cal stared at him in open astonishment.

'What do you want?' Seb asked.

Cal's voice was so quiet as to be almost inaudible. 'Where is she?'

'She's fine,' Seb replied coldly.

'I want to see her.'

'No. She's asleep. She doesn't want to be woken.'

'I don't understand.' Cal shook his head.

'I've sedated her. She's asleep.'

He struggled for comprehension. 'Sedated her?'

'Yes.'

'Let me see her.' Cal moved to go past him, but Seb put out his hand so that it rested against Cal's chest.

'You're too late, Cal. She was in shock. I dealt with it.'

'She phoned me.' Cal pushed Seb's hand aside, and wedged a foot in the door. 'I want to see her.'

Seb struck him on the chest. Cal was knocked back a few steps.

'Don't fuck with me,' said Seb, his voice low and threatening. 'Go away and sort yourself out. You look like shit.' He closed the door.

Cal sank slowly to his knees in a rut in the gravel and began shaking, the vibration coming up through his legs and travelling across his shoulder-blades and down his arms to his fingertips.

The light upstairs went out.

He remained that way for some time and then, bowed and defeated, he climbed to his feet and stumbled down the road in the direction of the coast road and the dawn.

The following night, with the starter-motor fixed and back in the pick-up, he went out to the bothy at Murbhach to confront Seb. He packed an axe-handle on the passenger seat. He spoke harshly to himself all the way there, and when he parked the pick-up at a passing place short of the bothy and turned off the engine, he was forced to wipe a blob of froth from his lips. He got out of the vehicle, taking the axe-handle with him, and walked the last mile up the rutted track to the isolated cluster of buildings.

The black motorbike was parked outside. Lights glowed through the curtains in the cottage windows. Keeping to the grass he walked past the coal-shed towards the nearest window, intending to look inside.

'Ssssth!' Somebody hissed.

He stopped and spun round.

Madelene was standing, barely visible, in the shadows at the mouth of the coal shed. She sniggered. Suddenly self-conscious, Cal let the axe-handle drop. He realised how ridiculous he must look. Pathetic.

'Fuck's sake,' he whispered angrily, and then, 'How long have you been here?'

She shrugged.

Cal considered this information. 'What is he doing?'

'Fucking.' She sounded amused. 'He's on a roll.'

'Who?'

She gave him a withering glance. 'Breeze, of course.'

'Breeze?' he whispered, in shock.

'Everything is going right for him, so he's doing all the fucking he can. Yesterday Oonagh, today Breeze. It would appear that my mighty father has returned to Seb what was his by right of rape and conquest. Or maybe he doesn't know? What do you think? Do you think my father knows about this?'

Cal didn't reply. He felt an almost overwhelming desire for a cigarette.

'You look like shit,' Madelene observed. 'You need some stitches.'

'I crashed a car.'

'I told you you should learn to drive.'

'So you did,' Cal said. 'Are you going to tell your father?'

She dismissed the suggestion with a flick of her hair, a disdainful curl of her upper lip.

'What now?' he asked slowly.

'I'm not fucking you, if that's what you mean,' she said.

'No,' Cal said, 'I don't think that's what I meant.'

He went back past her and between the car and the motorbike.

'Don't sulk,' she hissed after him.

He guided the blowpipe freehand, holding it at an angle against the plate and tubing, slashing through the steel with the thumb of his leather gauntlet down on the oxygen lever, the high-pressure oxygen from the central bore-hole of the cutting nozzle spraying molten oxide out the downside of the cut – the kerf – the separating pieces clattering away on the concrete floor of the shed.

He shut off the red valve on the shank and the flame was extinguished with a pop, and then the oxygen valve on the cutting attachment, and finally the oxygen valve on the shank.

He pushed his goggles up on to his forehead, taking care not to catch them on the line of stitches in his hairline. He stared at the twisted heap of steel that was to have been a bedstead for Oonagh.

'That looks like a cure for anger,' said a voice behind him that set his teeth on edge. Ignoring it, he turned off the cylinder valves and then opened the valves on the shank to release any gas in the hoses. Seb was the last person he wanted to speak to.

'I didn't know you were sleeping with Oonagh,' Seb explained. 'I wouldn't have stood in your way. I apologise.'

Cal squatted down and turned over a piece of metal with his pliers, observed the wash of colours, yellow to blue, on the underside.

Seb continued, 'She was hurt and angry at you, and then she was terrified, but you didn't come. So she phoned me. You can see the logic in her thinking. Her ex-boyfriend is an IRA man, I'm a soldier; she wanted some protection. You weren't there. You'd already let her down once.'

'By sleeping with Madelene?'

Silence. A nasty covetous whiff, some frisson of unacknowledged jealousy; the truth was Seb didn't seem to like people having sex with his sister.

Seb said, 'You know they've caught him. He's back in prison. It was on the radio.'

'Was he coming this way?'

'I don't know.'

Cal hung the torch on a hook on the cylinder trolley and looped the hoses round the regulator gauges. He removed his gauntlets and went over to the tap.

'I paid Dylan to fix his car,' Seb told him.

Cal considered this as he splashed water on his face. 'I guess I owe you for that.'

Seb said, 'You know you don't owe me anything.'

'Do I know it?'

'You remember the vows we made.'

'I remember a vow not to touch heroin. I don't remember anything about fixing cars.'

'It was implicit,' Seb protested. 'Always to help each other out in a crisis. Trust, that's what it boils down to.'

Cal looked at him for the first time, the first time he'd got really close to him since his return to the island; he observed the nail marks gouged on Seb's cheek, his pale face and tired, zealot eyes. The implicit violence.

Seb said, 'I spoke to Madelene. You know what she told me? She said you said I was a psychopath.'

Cal reddened. 'I was stoned,' he said.

'It implies that I act in an unpremeditated way. That I'm somehow unprofessional.'

'I guess I didn't think it through.' It sounded lame, defensive. He should be standing up for himself. He watched Seb's emotional register swing from hurt pride to weary familiarity. Seb watched him with calm, sleepy eyes.

'When was the last time we really spoke? I mean without any hangers-on? Just the two of us?'

Seb held out a cigarette, the filter towards him. Cal accepted the cigarette and Seb lit it for him using his recently recovered bronze Zippo.

Cal was curious, wondering what Seb was up to now. He took a few drags on the cigarette and settled his behind against the anvil. Seb started walking up and down the length of the barn, staring up at the cross-beams.

'After the Gulf War,' Cal said reluctantly, 'you were angry that you hadn't been able to go the whole way.'

'It was bad karma,' Seb explained. He crushed the butt of his cigarette under the heel of his boot, and immediately lit another. 'To stop when we did.' He stared at the lighted end of the cigarette, holding the tip of the filter in three fingers. 'I went to Hong Kong a few days later.'

He stopped. His walking back-and-forth had been gradually slowing; the energy seemed to be leeching out of him. 'Cal?'

'Yes.'

'You want to know who I slept with last night?'

'Maybe,' Cal suggested, 'you don't want to talk about it.'

'You don't want to hear?'

Cal hesitated. 'No.'

Seb shook his head slowly. 'I've been out of control these last few days. I've been bottling things up. It all came out, that's all. Sometimes,' he said, 'I don't think I feel much of anything, except rage. I feel rage, and lust and humiliation.'

'You're tired,' Cal said.

'I am,' he conceded with a thin smile. 'It's the price of keeping a grip on things.'

'You're still into it?'

'Sure,' Seb said. 'That's why I'm here.' He paused. 'I mean on the island. I'm here now because I'm hoping you'll help me out.'

Cal laughed. He felt flushed; there was pain in his eyes from all the booze he'd been drinking the past few days. 'I should hit you, not help you.'

'I understand,' Seb said. 'But you've always helped me in the past. You know you're wrong about when we last talked. You know we've talked since then. You gave the plan its name, the Freedom To Live.'

'I got beaten up. You wanted to blow up a house.'

'We went ahead and did it,' Seb observed. 'You helped to make it happen.'

'You don't need me to make it happen. I'm not one of your international contacts.'

'You're my conscience. You see things I don't.'

'That's why you want me along?'

'Yes.'

Cal frowned. 'Let me ask you a question?'

'Anything,' Seb said.

'I know you want to do it but why are you doing it? Don't tell me it's because of money.'

'It's not.'

'So what is it?' Cal asked.

'I had the idea, in southern Iraq, in the Zone. Thinking it made me really want to do it. Because it was possible. I didn't want there to be any gap between the thought and the action.'

'Are you sure you're not just doing it because you're bored?'

'No,' Seb said, emphatically, and then, with a winning smile, 'Never admit to being bored.'

There wasn't any way that Cal could resist. There never had been. He had tried before to get away from them but it hadn't worked. Madelene was right: they owned him.

'I want to get off the island,' he said, after a pause.

'As soon as the boat's ready.'

'What am I supposed to do?' Cal asked.

Seb produced a computer disk from his pocket and handed it to Cal. 'For the Trackplotter on the boat. There's no buoy to mark the spot, so you'll have to drag back and forth until you find it.'

'The boat?'

'Is down at the cove.'

Cal considered this information. Then he said, 'I'm not having Dougie Hogg on the boat. He's a liability.'

'You're right. But you'll need two of you.'

'I'll take Andy. If he'll go.'

'That's fine, but you pay him out of your share and you don't tell him any more than you need to.'

'How much is there?'

'Eight barrels. One ton.'

'That's a lot of hash,' Cal said, and after a pause. 'It is hash?'

'Don't start on me. Of course it's hash.'

'All right,' Cal said.

'I'll be there on the beach waiting. After that it goes over the border.'

'Who's taking delivery?'

'Ed Crowe's people,' Seb replied.

'They're cool?'

'They're tight. Secure, I mean. And mostly in the dark. The whole thing is broken up into hermetically sealed parcels. Everyone has a piece but no one has a clue. The hash is Afghan but it came in on a Russian barbed-wire boat. The source is Chechen and the money that bought it was stolen in America. The cross-border smuggler is Catholic but the end-purchaser is Protestant. The ceasefire has come and swept away all the old certainties. People are wondering about the future. Times of anxiety nourish the belief in conspiracies of evil. A Republican splinter group think they're going to kill Gerry Adams and MI5 think they're going to save the ceasefire. It's a Gordian knot; beautiful chaos.'

BOOK TWO

UNDERWOLVES

1987–1995

They [the Scots] live in huts, go naked and unshod. They
mostly have a democratic government, and are much addicted
to robbery. They can bear hunger and cold and all manner of
hardship; they will retire into their marshes and hold out for
days with only their heads above water, and in the forest they
will subsist on bark and roots.

Romaika, Dio Cassius, AD 197

1

Cal coughed, hacked and unzipped his sleeping bag, releasing an accumulation of noxious fumes that made his head reel. He groped about on the bare and splintered boards with the heel of his palm and finally located the alarm clock and silenced it. Bodies shifted in sleeping bags or under piles of blankets around him. Someone groaned; someone called out in their sleep. He lifted his legs in a drift of leaking duck-down and rolled out of the bag, his toes slipping across newspaper greasy with chip fat. He cursed and rolled back on to the bag and got up on all fours, shivering in the early-morning cold, and reached down into the bottom of the bag for his clothes, dragging them out in a bundle. He dressed quickly, standing to tug up his army-surplus trousers and easing his loosely-laced trainers on one after the other. He pulled a T-shirt over his head. He scratched at the fine patina of week-old stubble on his chin and mussed at his clots of hair and looked around. There was dew on the scabrous surface of the lath-and-plaster walls, glistening on the livid flesh of the Tank Girl mural and on the few remaining window-panes. He crossed the room, stepping gingerly over huddled sleeping bodies, and went out on to the landing and down the great stairway, with one hand on the balustrade, skipping the missing or dangerous steps. He went across the hall, smoothing his hair back from his forehead with his fingers, collected a knapsack from a hook by the studded double doors, pushed one wrist-thick oak door open and went out into the cold, steaming dawn.

He jogged across the gravel drive, and up the steep bank between ancient stands of beech trees, and eased himself over a drystone wall and went across the fields past the deep ochre gash, filled with silent yellow JCBs, that would someday be the Dalkeith bypass. He scaled a barbed-wire fence, scrambled down a steep bank on to the forecourt of the Esso station and ran, almost doubled over, to the shadows at the front of the shop. It wasn't a twenty-four-hour station and the attendant wasn't due till seven. The daily delivery truck had already been, and the two bread crates of fresh sandwiches were stacked by the pile of newspapers outside the door. Quickly Cal emptied the contents of one crate – BLTs and chicken tikkas – into his knapsack and after it stuffed the *Independent*, the *Guardian* and the *Sun*, though he knew the *Sun* was the only one sure to be read; back at the castle they displayed the slacker's fascination with watching events drift by in trashy newsprint.

He slung the rucksack over his shoulders, slipping his arms through the loops, and sprinted back across the forecourt, up the steep bank and over the fence, and within minutes was jogging back through the fields towards the castle with the day's food.

It was his first day back in Edinburgh after six weeks' inter-railing across Europe with Andy – five weeks of peeling sunburn, camping out in railway stations and drinking litre bottles of wine, followed by a week sheltering in an old German bunker on Cap Frehel in Normandy with nothing but half an ounce of hash and seven tins of beans for company. They had received their exam results over the telephone in Istanbul and had both made the grade for Edinburgh – Cal to study English Lit and Andy to study Electrical and Mechanical Engineering. Back in Britain they had made a bee-line for Edinburgh and the 'Jah Palace', an abandoned castle in the woods by the River Esk where Organ and Seb, and a floating population of others – public-school drop-outs, musicians, Rastas, teenage runaways – had been squatting for the last year. Seb had already completed his first year at university – though there was some doubt whether any of his tutors would recognise him up close, and he had spectacularly failed all his end-of-year exams.

Cal had first come to the Palace in June when his exams were over and school had been consigned to an unpleasant memory. He stayed a month and watched the students come and go and shift from bed to bed, and thought that this must be heaven. Now it seemed tense and frail . . . there was an introspective urgency to the partying that he did not remember from before. He was particularly worried about Seb.

Seb's brother Rory – madcap fresh-faced Rory with the gridlock teeth – had died in July. Two down, if you believed the prophecy. Rory had, on the night of his death, according to the rumour circulating at the Palace, consumed a cocktail of heroin, Temazepam, cocaine and whisky and then thrown up while riding pillion on the M1, and drowned in his motorcycle helmet. The driver had apparently reached Leeds before realising that his passenger was dead.

Cal received the news in Istanbul with the results of his school-leaving exams. It was hardly surprising. Rory had been on a self-destructive binge ever since losing his job with the McLaren team. A few weeks before his death he had destroyed his lovingly restored Aston Martin on the Deochmore road, and prophetic mutterings had been heard to issue out of the bar of the Loch Intake Hotel along the lines of: 'That boy's not long for this world.'

Seb had been steeling himself with a vicarious enthusiasm for alcohol, drugs and cigarettes. After the death of his mother, and in the absence of any consolation from his father, Seb had come to rely heavily on Rory for his emotional stability. Grief was almost unbearable for Seb; now it seemed, once again, that he might not survive the struggle of coming to terms with it.

With the exception of his morning run, Seb hadn't – to anyone's knowledge – been off the estate since the funeral. He lived out a daily ritual of a morning run, followed by a day of getting paralytically stoned, and a night-time's orgiastic drinking. It was true that he wasn't the only one; Organ, and another old Etonian named Dom, and a black Rasta from Aberdeen called Norton all shared the same state of stoned immobility, but Cal believed they took their lead from Seb and Seb's destination was anyone's guess – Cal was inclined to think he had death in mind.

He climbed the drystone wall marking the boundary of the Melville estate and headed down through the beech trees towards the castle. Once back, he dumped the pack at the top of the stairs, and went back across the room through the sleeping bodies and climbed back into his sleeping bag.

Waking, Seb saw aqueous light dancing on the crumbling yellowed plaster ceiling and for a few seconds he could not locate himself; there was a painful brightness that informed him it was morning. Recollection came soon enough; it was the September sun on the algae-clogged stretch of the River Esk outside.

Autumn; the wind-down after the summer. 1987. The smell of stale alcohol and cigarette ash. He raised himself on to his elbows and studied the girl beside him, naked on her belly, a patina of fine dark hair visible at the base of her spine. She was Irish – a student at the university – but he struggled for her name. He recalled the night before. She'd cornered him by the bonfire, her eyes like black opals in red-rimmed cups. She had screwed him aggressively; kneeling astride him on the mattress on the floor – one hand stroking herself and the other planted on his sternum. Her hair down over her face, she panted – working herself into some kind of personal and private fulfilment; his hands crossed behind his head, staring upwards, preoccupied with the death of his brother.

It occurred to him that she might not remember his name. It seemed better that way. Carefully, he climbed out from under the pile of blankets, picked up his lens case and padded naked across the bare boards out on to the landing and down the stairs, judging the steps by memory – he was almost blind. He went out to the tap in the sunlight, and rested his lips against the spout, gulping greedily at the cold water. When he looked up he saw his blurred reflection in a shard of mirror propped on a ledge. His swollen, dissipated eyes. He rinsed his fingers, and then put in his lenses, a daily ritual; left eye then right eye. The cleaning solution stung his eyes, squeezing tears from beneath his tightly closed eyelids. He shook his head. When he opened them again, his face emerged from the blur and he contemplated his reflection in quiet desperation.

He went back into the castle, and ran up the stairs two at a time, pausing briefly on the landing to confirm that the day's food was in, and glanced into the big room. There were sleeping bodies everywhere. He was one of the few with their own rooms. He went back to it and dressed in jogging pants, hooded top and trainers. The girl did not wake.

He spent ten minutes out on the lawn stretching, loosening his muscles in gathering anticipation, and then ran five miles, following the paths through the dew-drenched ruins of the castle gardens, dodging between overgrown rhododendrons and avenues of beech trees, leaping down the embankment and across the old railway line, crossing two farms – hurdling electric fences and scattering heifers – making a loop round the council landfill and coming back with the sun in his streaming eyes. Sprinting, his churning knees rising almost to his chin. The urgency in him was not something that he could control. Remembrance twisting painfully in his guts. The last time he saw Rory alive.

He gritted his teeth while a fat knuckle ground at his eyeball. The pack heaved through the brackish mud, dragging the side of his head across the face of the bricked-up arches. He could hear cars on the far side of the wall on the road to Slough. He could feel the contact lens twisting and crumpling in his eye. Then it was gone; half his vision gone.

Somewhere above, on the top of the wall, pale and cadaverous and shrouded in a black greatcoat stood his brother Rory. St Andrew's Day at Eton. Wet November. Rory had appeared after months of absence, to watch his brother, Seb the scholar, play the Wall Game. Rory MacCoinneach, who was the only person to have scored at the Wall Game in the past twenty-five years. Rory the legend. Rory who was forced to leave Eton when the money ran out – not an indignity suffered by Seb, who was a scholar and had his fees paid just as seventy other scholars from College had each year since Henry VI opened the school. Rory the racing driver with potential. No more. Rory, the junkie on the brink of death.

The pack fractured. College had the ball. The Oppidans falling back towards the wooden door that is their goal. The lurking presence of Rory above him. He moved his head from left to right, the focus of his one good eye sweeping across the moving bodies. His bad eye blurring and focussing just inches in front of his face. The focus switching from left to right; good eye to bad eye and all the details slipping. The ball flew. He caught it with his good eye. He was just twenty yards short of the door. A clear shot, the sort of opportunity that comes once in a blue moon. Not since his brother. Not since Rory. Everyone is screaming, 'Score!'

He threw. Bad eye focused. Missed.

He screamed in desperate frustration.

Cal scratched his head – his hair was peppered with plaster from the ceiling – shuffled across the landing to the window and rested his forehead against the rotten window-frame. He contemplated the opaque green surface of the River Esk twenty feet below, and after a minute or so he unbuttoned his fly and peed into it. Exquisite relief.

The door opposite opened and a girl with thick red and chestnut hair emerged from Seb's room. She was painfully attractive.

'I swam in that river yesterday,' she protested. Her accent was Irish. Northern Irish; harsh and at the same time stirring.

'I pissed in it yesterday,' Cal admitted, buttoning himself up.

'Charming,' she said. 'I've always fancied cholera.' She shook her head, clearly angry at herself. 'To go with the gonorrhoea I've probably caught.'

Cal said, 'It's a breeding ground.'

'Not that as well. I've one child already, thank you very much. What was in that punch?'

'Some acid, I think.'

'Jesus,' she said.

He watched her lace her black boots, bent at the midriff, with the cloth of her blouse billowing out. He stared down at her hanging breasts, the red points of her nipples. She looked up at him through her fringe.

'Big boots,' he said, uncomfortably.

'Big eyes,' she said. She straightened up.

He asked, 'Are you really a mother?'

She laughed. Her nostrils flared. 'Are you for real?'

'I'm hung over,' Cal protested.

She started down the stairs.

'Will we see you again?'

She stopped and looked at him. 'We?'

'Me,' Cal said. 'Will I see you again?'

'I don't know who you are.' She nodded in the direction of Seb's room. 'I don't know who he was.'

'Sebastian.'

'Don't tell me.' She put her hands over her ears and went further down the steps.

'I'm Calum.'

'I'm appalled,' she said.

'Mind that step,' he warned her, following her down.

She went through the rotten wood and sank to her ankle. 'Shit!'

'Here let me.' He put out his hand and she gripped him and levered herself out.

'Thank you.'

'Don't mention it.'

'I won't again.' She turned her back on him and limped down the rest of the stairs. He followed her to the door and stood and watched her climb in her car, a lime-green Hyundai, start the engine and skid away down the deeply rutted gravel drive. He remembered Organ had tried to rouse a work-party to rake the gravel back in June, but the suggestion had been vetoed scornfully. She didn't even look in her rear-view mirror.

He sat on the steps and stared at the trees.

Seb appeared a few minutes later, running through the trees. He came down the bank, ran across the forecourt past the dried-out fountain and stopped at the bottom of the granite steps. He walked back and forth, grimacing, with the flats of his hands resting on his kidneys, refusing to double over, drawing long draughts of air through his nose.

Cal watched him closely. Seb came over and squatted beside him on the steps.

'She's gone,' Cal informed him.

He was looking out over the trees as if there was something he could not quite put his finger on. He stuck out his lower lip. 'There's not much to say.'

Cal asked, 'When are your re-sits?'

Seb shrugged and grimaced comically. Seb's end-of-first-year exams were a standing Palace joke; he'd spent the night before each exam on a different beach – Gyle, Crammond, South Queensferry – tripping on mushrooms and building sandcastles. This was in the days before he had given up all drugs but cannabis. He had arrived at each exam in a state of exhaustion and promptly fallen asleep. Having done it a couple of times, it had become a matter of principle and the challenge had been to find a new beach each time and build ever more baroque sandcastles.

'Next week,' he replied.

'You going to take them?'

He stared heavenward. He stood up briskly. His eyes narrowed. A small police car had appeared and was slipping and sliding down the track towards them. It parked by the fountain and two uniformed policemen got out.

Seb leant over and spat.

One of the policemen called out softly, 'Awright, Mr MacCoinneach.'

Seb greeted him, 'Plod.' Seb had a prejudiced view of policemen; he considered them stupid. Cal was inclined to agree.

'Very original,' the policeman said, without visible expression. 'Go and fetch Mr Morgan-Ruthven, there's a good chap. Tell him his daddy's been scoffing cream buns wi' the Chief Constable again.'

Seb shrugged and went off into the castle in search of Organ. He found him asleep on a sofa in front of the TV with two four-foot speakers either side of him pushing out sizzling white noise. The end of a 3 a.m. stereo showing of *Apocalypse Now*, another nightly ritual. Organ could recite the film from beginning to end.

Seb nudged him with the toe of his trainer. Organ groaned and turned over. Seb kicked him harder, in the ribs this time.

Organ cursed and started waving his arms. He eyed Seb suspiciously.

'The rozzers are here,' Seb warned him. 'Your dad's been hassling the Chief Constable again.'

'Interfering cunt,' Organ muttered indignantly. He gripped his head in his hands. He hadn't spoken to his father, other than through lawyers, for years. A family trust, controlled by Organ's father, owned the Palace – and his father was the prime force behind the attempt to evict them.

By the time they got back out on the steps, there were people hanging out of all the windows and taunting the policemen, who had retreated to their car.

'Leave this to me,' Organ mumbled.

Seb laughed. 'Don't worry, mate. It's all yours.'

Organ staggered across the gravel.

Seb turned and looked at Cal. 'I'm joining the Paras.'

Cal was genuinely surprised. It was out of the blue. 'Really?'

'Never been more serious. I went into Edinburgh last week for the medical. Ran all the way. Didn't tell anyone. I'm not hanging around here. Here's one for you: "This loose behaviour I throw off".'

His outstretched arm took in the ruinous castle – the Jah Palace, its motley inhabitants and the police car – but it seemed to Cal that the gesture encompassed a wider frame; his whole life up to that point, Cual and his family.

Madelene arrived that evening in her MG. She nearly ran him over. He was wandering out of the trees carrying a stack of firewood when off to his left he heard the MG's growl on the crackling gravel. He kept walking, blithely assuming that he had the right of way. Next thing he knew he was bowled arse-over-tit in a shower of branches.

Madelene regarded him with what he guessed – it was always guesswork trying to read the unmarked oval of her face – was genuine bafflement. Which he took to mean: I can't believe that I keep screwing you.

'Get up, Calum,' she said, those tiny lines under her eyes crinkling. 'Look where you're going.'

'Madelene' was all he could think of to say. She didn't have the nickname 'Damage' back then. Which isn't to say she hadn't earned it; it was just that he hadn't thought of it. He climbed clumsily to his feet. She made him feel clumsy; she had that power. 'That,' she said, pointing, 'is my cousin Calum.'

Her tanned and freckled passenger regarded him boldly from behind dark sunglasses.

'This is Ed Crowe. I found him in Brighton. He's Irish, and African too. He's a producer.'

Cal realised that he had no idea what being a producer meant. Ed lifted his hand, complete with Rolex Submariner on his wrist, a couple of inches off the doorframe. A too-cool greeting. Cal barely nodded in return as vehement dislike rushed unbidden to his aid. She had that power, too; the kind of visceral beauty that started wars.

Madelene roared off towards the castle. He started collecting the wood into a pile. He told himself that he wasn't jealous; that after six weeks sleeping on cold floors in railway stations and Second World War bunkers, it was hardly surprising he was feeling out of sorts. It was a time of great change for him. University. Leaving home. He was just impatient for it to happen; the start of the academic year, a new place to live, away from the claustrophobic social structures of Cual, perhaps a girlfriend. An opportunity to find an alternative to Madelene.

There wasn't enough wood, and despite a late-night foray into the trees for more, slackness prevailed and more of the floorboards were ripped up for the fire – the doors were long gone – and the number of available bedrooms was further reduced.

Ed Crowe was greeted with the suspicion shown to any unknown male who showed his face at the Palace. It was only when he produced a bag full to the brim with multitudinous drugs that he was offered a measure of acceptance. Seb, who wasn't one to show that he was impressed by the size of anybody's stash, subjected Ed to a thorough interrogation, while the other occupants of the Palace looked on, yelled encouragement and helped themselves to Ed's drugs. Ed seemed unfazed, and made no mention of payment. It turned out that he was an Irish Protestant from the Shankill area of Belfast, whose family had pulled up their roots when he was a teenager, and emigrated to South Africa. Seb pounced on this with some enthusiasm. Ed explained that the reason for their leaving was his father's growing disenchantment with the Loyalist paramilitaries.

'These days it's hard to find a UDA man who can string a sentence together,' Ed explained. 'I know. I went to school with half of them. Saying that, the Afrikaners weren't much better.'

His comments were greeted by a roomful of stoned, blank faces. The world beyond the Jah Palace was truly an incomprehensible place. Only Seb seemed to have any idea what Ed was on about.

Seb came tall and pale through the trees, wearing a thin and ragged T-shirt and charcoal-stained jeans. Cal watched him coming; from where he was seated Seb was silhouetted by the dappled flames reflected in the castle windows. Cal watched the shifting shadows of dancing bodies on the ceilings, the winking fairy-lights strung around the fountain. Beside him, on the far side of the small bonfire, Andy lay on his back with his eyes closed.

Seb squatted by the fire. His glossy, careless red-black hair shone. He offered the bottle he was holding and Cal passed him the joint he'd been smoking. Seb dragged on it hungrily and then pressed the heel of one palm against his face. He seemed to be in pain. When he lifted away his hand there were tears running down the narrow planes of his face. It was difficult to tell if it was merely his eyes that were bothering him.

'Don't ever let me down,' he said without warning. Staring at Cal over the fire, his eyes sparkling like mercury, tiny as pins. There was a dangerous, drunken intensity in his face.

'I won't,' Cal said, after a careful pause. The impulse to placate was something that Seb seemed to bring out in people.

'I'm serious.' Seb blinked. And again. 'You're like a brother to me,' he said. 'A real brother.'

Cal said, 'I'm sorry about what happened to Rory.'

It was a few months now since Rory had died, but it seemed to be hitting Seb harder with each passing day. He drew back, swaying slightly, his forehead furrowed scornfully. 'He was a wanker.'

He produced a knife. It had recently been sharpened and the edge was bright steel-blue. 'I want to clear the air,' he said.

Cal made as if to speak but then stopped, without anything to say. He watched the knife-blade hovering above the fire.

'I want you and me to seal a pact. With blood. Never to touch heroin. So I don't ever have to think about it again.' He stared at Cal. He looked violent and fragile at the same time. The whole Palace lived by Seb's moods. It was a question of trying to elicit a good one.

'All right.'

Seb didn't seem to hear for a second. He continued to stare at Cal as if he wished to shape him to his will, and then he understood and his face was instantly split with the rictus of a wild and barbarous grin. 'Good man,' he said.

'Do it quickly,' Cal told him, deadpan stoned.

Seb set the knife-point against the meat of his thumb, pushing his pointy tongue out between his teeth, and with one stroke sliced it from knuckle to wrist. Blood, black in the firelight, welled out. He held out the knife by its handle.

Cal took it and turned it over and inspected the blood-slicked blade. He set it against his skin. The knife was truly sharp, and the cut was almost painless, a brief stinging sensation. They gripped hands and Seb twisted him one way and then another, and then let go and staggered back into the fire, and was sheathed in bright sparks. He stumbled away through the woods.

Cal inclined his head, stuck his palm in his mouth and sucked at the wound.

On the far side of the fire Andy said, 'Was I dreaming?'

Cal shook his head.

'Far out,' Andy said. 'He's fucked up.'

'He just doesn't know if he has what it takes to endure.'

There was a pause.

Andy said, 'Well profound.'

Cal shook his head, surprised at himself. They both laughed.

They had sex in a potting shed, with Ed's Ecstasy grinding at his face and Ed himself blundering around in the darkness calling out her name. There was an ugly inevitability to the act. Madelene stripped naked, discarding her clothes among the piles of broken terracotta pots and hiked herself up on a bench.

'Fuck me, boy,' she urged, with her eyes squeezed closed.

There just wasn't any way to refuse.

Cal loomed above her in fury and self-loathing as he thrust into her; her face thrown back on the rough table surface, her lips pulled tightly across her teeth, and the veins in her throat standing out like cords. He put his thumbs on her eyelids and tried to force her eyes open but she bit his forearm. He pulled back but she gripped him harder and came back with him, and he lost any semblance of self-control and dragged her back and forth in a flurry of wood shavings and terracotta chips while she hissed and snarled like a fighting cat.

Afterwards she hopped down off the table and he ran his palm down the bare flesh of her buttocks and removed the splinters lodged there.

When it was done, and she was dressed, she reached up and kissed him. 'Thank you,' she whispered, her eyes bright.

He was taken aback, confused by this unaccustomed expression of tenderness. He said, 'What do you mean?' But she was gone.

He stood alone in the darkness.

Sometime after dawn Seb shook him awake and waved a set of keys in front of his face. Cal scooped at his gummy eyes and sat up in his sleeping bag. He stared at the canopy of trees above him and the embers of the fire beside him.

'What time is it?'

'Time to drive me to Aldershit.'

Cal scrunched up his face. 'What?'

'You heard.'

'You must be joking.'

'Never been more serious. I'm due to report to Depot Para this afternoon. Madelene's lent us her car. She wants it back here by tomorrow.' Seb nudged him with his foot. 'Come on, get moving.'

Seb handed him his boots and watched him tug them over his tatty socks. Reluctantly, Cal bundled up his sleeping bag and staggered with it through the drifts of leaves and down the bank to the MG.

'Where's Aldershit?' he mumbled.

'Aldershot, really. Enemy country. England, South of.'

'Fuck's sake,' Cal hissed.

'There's sperm on your jeans. You've been fucking my sister again, haven't you?'

'Give it a rest,' Cal groaned.

'She's got a boyfriend. She doesn't need you.'

'I think that's her decision.'

'He's a good bloke.'

'He's a drug-dealer,' Cal pointed out. 'You met him yesterday.'

Seb snorted. 'Aldershot,' he said. 'And don't spare the horses. I've just swallowed a quarter of an ounce.'

Seven hours later, Cal halted the car on the broad concrete esplanade at the entrance to the depot. Seb got out and slung his bag over his shoulder. Behind him, beyond the chain-link fence, a Second World War-era Dakota plane was parked on the grass. He imagined Seb falling through the darkness. Howling.

Seb stuck his head in through the window.

'This is it.' He grinned impishly. His eyes were almost closed, he was so wasted.

Cal wanted to shout at him, 'This is the last thing Rory would have wanted,' but he knew there wasn't any point. Seb had decided.

'Thanks for driving me down, mate.'

Cal shrugged. 'That's OK.'

'It's just something I have to do.'

'I know. You're a MacCoinneach.'

He straightened up and strode towards the concrete chicane at the entrance, without looking back.

Cal wound up the window and sat still for a few seconds, gripping the steering wheel. Now that Seb had gone, the smell in the cab was overwhelmingly of Madelene. Her dusky odour, redolent of eroticism. He started the car and drove north.

He slept that night at a motorway service station, curled up in his sleeping bag in the cramped cab, enfolded in the traces of Madelene.

He woke early, in the last dark hour before dawn, and walked around the tarmac esplanade to rid himself of stiffness and then sat in the restaurant and ate a rasher of bacon, which had been curling under the heat lamps for too many hours, in a spongy white bap that tasted like cotton wool. The coffee was foul. He watched a coach disgorge its cargo of sleepy students and other travellers on to the forecourt; they hurried towards the building through the early-morning cold.

He felt a strong sense of loss, as if Seb's decision to join the army had broken that close tie – something more than friendship – that had bound them since their mothers' deaths. Now he would have to make his own way in the world. He finished his coffee and went back to the car and drove north again, into what he imagined was a new life.

He arrived back at the Palace in the early afternoon. Most of its inhabitants were still asleep. He went to find Madelene and discovered her curled up asleep in Seb's bed with Ed Crowe. He put her keys in one of her boots and didn't wake her and then he went and found Andy and together they caught a bus into Edinburgh and registered at the university.

They found a flat that day on the Easter Road in Leith, and moved in within a week and were joined by a third, named Al, who was an old schoolfriend of Andy's from his days in Dundee.

Cal heard later that the 'Jah Palace' had been gutted by fire, which seemed like a fitting, MacCoinneach way for events to come to an end. He came across Organ now and again with his coterie of stoned Etonians, outside a lecture hall or maybe in the café under the David Hume building – he had a puppy with him, a husky named Kali – but without Seb there Cal found he had little to say to them. He heard occasional news of Seb, mostly through Madelene: he heard that he had left the Paras and gone to Sandhurst, and subsequently joined a Highland regiment; that he was a platoon commander in Northern Ireland.

2

A knot of skinny and sweating white guys in baggy denim glided past them in the bar at Pure, their jaws rolling with ecstasy and the beat from the dance floor. One of them lifted his fist displaying his rings. 'Nuff respect.'

Andy rolled his eyes. 'Awright.'

Cal snorted into a pint of snakebite, his sixth.

Andy was outraged. 'Yo no tink I'm a Yardman?'

'The closest you've ever been to a Ranks is a taxi-rank on the Lothian Road.'

'Very funny. I'll have you know my da's fae West Kingston.'

'And yer from Dundee. Your accent is stronger than mine.'

'That's right, posh boy.'

'Me posh?'

'Aye, hanging aboat wi' yer aristocratic cousin Sebastian fae McBrideshead. We all know yer accent was ditched the day you turned up at university.'

'Away n shite.'

'Posh boy,' Andy muttered under his breath, and he took a sip at his pint. He grinned.

'I'd hate to share a flat wi' you two bickering all day,' Glen said. Glen was an editor at *Student*, Edinburgh University's magazine.

'Takes a brave man, like,' Al grunted, his hand snaking out across the beer-sodden table for his vodka.

Then he saw Her on the dance-floor; the flick of her mane of chestnut hair; a glimpse of white teeth; her long lycra-clad legs pumping with the bass beat, anchored in big shit-kickin boots. He wasn't sure for a second, and then he knew it was her; without a doubt.

She came off the dance-floor at the end of the song blanketed in sweat. There were two other girls with her. They walked across to a table and sat down.

Cal pointed. 'Who is she?'

Glen shook his head. 'Don't even think about it.'

Cal was indignant. 'What?'

'I'm serious.'

'Aye right, Mr "I've got my ear to the ground" Gonzo-journalist. Come on, then, know-it-all, tell us.'

Andy said, 'Aye. Wat's the score wi' her?'

'She's an Irish Catholic,' Glen explained.

'That,' Al said, slumped half comatose on the bench-seat, 'is nawt a virgin.'

'I don't think she's saving herself,' Cal agreed.

'I mean she's connected.'

'What, you mean like the Pope's her brother?'

Glen said, 'She's got a boyfriend.'

'That's a challenge,' Cal told them.

'He's in prison.'

Cal shrugged. 'So he's not around. All the better.'

'He's a convicted IRA man.'

There was a pause.

Cal was scornful. 'You do talk a lot of shite.'

'Straight up. Last year she complained to her tutor aboot police harassment. It went all the way up to the Vice-Chancellor. Apparently guys from Special Branch had been following her around the university. I'm just saying what I heard. She's a vet student. That's how I know. The tutor's shagging one of his students; it comes out as pillow-talk. You know the score.'

Cal stood up. There was an attendant rush of blood to his head. 'What's her name?' he shouted when the room stopped reeling; the music seemed to be getting louder.

'Oonagh. Her name is Oonagh O'Hara.'

They were all looking at him.

'Right,' he muttered.

Al grinned. 'This may call fer a bit of whizz.'

'And tequila,' Andy called after him.

She clocked him as he approached, a brief glimpse, no more, and continued talking to the dark-haired girl beside her; the other girl, the redhead, was heading for the bar. He noticed Andy moving to intercept her. He felt an unfamiliar surge of predatory elation. She looked up at him.

'Hello again,' he said, his face loosening into an easy grin.

She did a double-take, initially hostile and then an element of cautious enquiry. She couldn't place him.

He slid on to a stool beside her.

'The Jah Palace, you remember that?' He was angling for a response, letting his grin widen. 'That falling-down castle out at Loanhead. Two years ago.'

'Oh, my God,' she laughed, horrified.

He laughed with her.

'I don't do that kind of thing,' she protested.

'It was a bit of a surprise,' he said, 'to look up and see you dancing.'

'Christ!' She shook her head.

Andy returned from the bar with the redhead and a round of tequila. Al eased himself into the group. The table was close to the dance-floor and it was necessary to talk loudly, to lean into each other's faces. He huddled next to her. She seemed reluctant to drink, but was egged on by her friends. They all downed the tequila; it was harsh and seemed to carry him to a crest of drunkenness, of single-minded intent.

'My name's Cal.' He held out his hand to her.

'Oonagh.'

He took her hand in his, it was hot. Suddenly, he hadn't a clue what to say. 'You have . . . um . . . legs. They're—'

'Useful,' she said. 'Mostly for walking.'

'No,' he said. 'I mean they're . . . fantastic. Sexy.'

'Look, I don't do this,' she said abruptly.

'You don't do what?'

'You know what I mean. I'm not even sure who you are.'

'You don't remember?'

'I mean . . .' She tailed off. It occurred to him that she had him confused with Sebastian. It filled him with a heady rush of confidence. 'You look different to how I remember,' she said.

He smiled easily. 'It was two years ago.'

'I was terrified that you'd given me some kind of disease.'

He laughed out loud. Too loud. 'My mother taught me always to wash behind my ears.' He fell suddenly silent. It felt like a cheap shot. His mother had said no such thing to him, in fact he couldn't remember a single piece of advice she'd left him with.

'What's the matter?'

'Nothing,' he said.

She put her hand briefly to his face and looked at him with sympathy; an understanding of some shared grief. 'You look sad.'

Glen arrived with another round of tequila. Cal saw that Al and the dark-haired girl on the far side of Oonagh were snorting speed off their fingernails. She saw it as well.

'One more drink,' he urged. He closed his eyes and opened them again. It was gone. They drank the tequila. He was back on the wave, riding in Seb's slipstream. How would Seb do it? He'd connect, with his eyes and his hands, with his daring and cunning. Give it blag, Seb would say, courage and effrontery.

'We'll talk about sex between strangers, about strange and powerful compulsions,' Cal told her.

'I really have to leave. They'll be closing soon.'

'I want to do it again.'

Her eyes studying his face. She didn't seem outraged. 'Why?'

'Don't you believe in compulsion? Have you seen yourself dancing? You're so . . . sexy.'

'I'm not trying to be sexy. I was just dancing.'

'I love your voice.'

She laughed. 'I don't believe you.'

'There's no time for that. Seize the day. Come on, talk to me.'

'Talk about what? You're living in cuckoo land. This isn't real.'

'I saw you dancing. That looked real, Oonagh.'

'I can't do this.'

'Can't or won't, Oonagh?'

'Jesus, you're exasperating.'

He let his mouth run with it. 'I saw you, your legs, your hair; it was like two years was nothing. Where have you been? Why did you just leave? Now I'm telling you I want to make love to you again. You're sitting there, totally uninterested. Even that's a turn-on.'

'I'm not uninterested. I'm just . . .'

'I want you to want me the same way I want you.'

More tequila arrived. They were surrounded by dense plumes of smoke that encouraged intimacy. He put his hand on the upward curve of her thigh, his thumb pressing against the hard sinew. She continued to watch his face. He saw that her grey-green eyes were flecked with streaks of gold.

The music stopped. The overhead lights came on, the glare was horrendous. He took his hand off her thigh. He saw Al and the dark-haired girl in animated discussion. Andy and the redhead were coming off the dance-floor. Glen was nowhere to be seen.

They gathered their coats and spilled out on to the street in the drizzle with the crowd and were carried over to the pavement on the other side near the darkened steps up to the railway station. He edged her against the wall and kissed her. She looked away, saying she wanted to go the other way, back up under the bridge on to Princes Street for a taxi. He pulled her down towards the underpass, where Al and the dark-haired girl huddled against each other under the orange sodium light. A freight train rumbled overhead.

He pressed her against the wall and tried to open her coat. She said she had to get home. He put his hand between her legs, against the sheer lycra, and she seemed to fall against him, pushing at his fingers with her head turned against the wall. He put her hand against the bulge in his jeans. She broke away, running past a skip and a pile of scaffolding and went uphill, along an empty street past a row of industrial units. He caught up with her and put his arms round her from behind and she stood motionless. He moved his hands over her belly and the arch of her ribs, describing spirals around her nipples.

'Stop it,' she whispered.

They could hear voices behind him, amplified by the underpass.

He moved his hands down her belly and ran his fingers into the crease in the lycra that divided her labia. He pressed against her buttocks, spooning her.

'Stop it.'

She stamped downwards on his shin with her heel and he groaned and hopped backwards. She reached out for him and he put one hand against her shoulder while gripping his shin with the other. She ran her hand up across his back to support him and drove her knee up into his groin. The air rushed out of him. She stepped back and he slumped against the pavement, gagging. It felt like his balls had leapt upwards and were lodged like pebbles in his throat. By the time Andy found him, curled up in a pool of vomit, she was long gone.

*   *   *

Kelly rang the doorbell at 6 a.m. and Cal, who was curled up in the hall under a kebab-stained greatcoat, went to open the door. She stood in the darkened stairwell and stared at him. She looked as if she'd been walking for hours; all the lacquer had run out of her black-dyed hair.

'You look awful,' she said. She was short of breath from the climb up five flights of stairs.

'So do you.'

'I couldn't sleep,' she said. She wanted to see Al.

'He's not here,' he said.

'I'll sleep in his bed, then.'

'No,' he said. 'It's occupied. Friends.'

She studied him sceptically. 'Well, can I come in?'

'Sure.' He stepped back and she came into the hallway and dropped her donkey-jacket. He followed her into his room.

She lit a candle. 'I'll have this half of the bed,' she said.

Cal scratched his head. 'All right.'

She took off her jumper and unbuttoned her skirt and left them in a pile on the mildewed carpet. She got under the duvet in her Dead Kennedys T-shirt and black woollen tights and curled up. Cal stripped to his boxer shorts and climbed in after her. He blew out the candle.

She snuggled up against him. 'It's cold,' she said. 'And your breath smells.'

'Sorry.'

Before she went to sleep she asked, 'Who has he got in his bed? Do I know her?'

'No,' he replied, but she was already asleep.

Cold November. His knees were red and sore where they poked out of the holes in his jeans; he'd been meaning to sew patches on for weeks. He had his black leather jacket zipped up to the throat and his locks tied in a bun under a ski-hat. It was bitterly cold. At the end of a tutorial, he fought his way against the wind across Buccleuch Place and down Newington Street into Thins the booksellers where, as he did at the end of each month, he stole books for the rent, stuffing them into a Thins bag he had saved for the occasion. Then he went down Drummond Street and stopped at the Drummond café for a bacon-and-egg roll. He struggled against the wind to the Pleasance and stood outside the crèche. He stamped his feet; his toes were wet from the splitting seams in his Doc Martens. He blew on his fingers.

She came out soon enough. Her daughter was wrapped tight against the cold: a fake-fur jacket in dark blue dotted with bright yellow butterflies and a thick grey scarf and blue mittens, the kind that are attached by a length of wool that runs across the shoulders. Her burnished-bronze hair poked out from under a hat the shape of a tea-cosy.

He squatted down in the slush and said, 'Hello. What's your name?' Her nose was pointy and red and moist. He looked up at her mother. 'Hi.'

The little girl clung to her mother's legs and peeped out from behind a knee, and said quietly, 'Sile.'

'That's a pretty name.' He stood up.

Oonagh said coldly, 'I didn't expect ever to see you again.'

'I came to apologise.'

She pursed her lips. Her thick hair was wet and it glistened in the light of the emergency exit.

'I behaved badly,' he said.

She shrugged. 'You were drunk.'

'Can I walk you to your car?'

She pointed. 'It's over there.'

She was forced to shuffle forward with Sile's head poking from between her knees and her arms looped round Oonagh's thighs.

'What are you reading?'

He stared at the bag for a moment, nonplussed. He put his hand in and drew out a book. '*Ulysses*,' he said.

'Have you finished it?'

'I haven't started it yet. Its coursework.' He wasn't due to read Joyce until the summer. He resolved to read it immediately.

'I'd like to talk,' he said. 'Try again, maybe.'

She opened the rear passenger door of her car and set Sile in the child-seat and fixed the harness. Sile stared at him with bright eyes.

She straightened up and closed the door. She faced him, some cold and bitter memory pinching her face. 'Don't come here again,' she said.

'I'm sorry,' he said. He stared at her. 'I just wanted to make amends.'

She gripped her hair with her fist and turned away from him. She groaned loudly.

'I'll go,' he said, backing away.

'Fuck you for coming here,' she said. 'No. Stand still and listen. Every night I used to walk out of here and there would be two men in a car sitting there watching me like a couple of reptiles. Gloating. I still feel fear when I walk out that door. They used to follow me back to my aunt's. I thought they were police, but who knows for sure?' She shook her head and spoke bitterly. 'He was on the run. A regular fucking outlaw. He'd shot an off-duty UDR man on his tractor and created another widow, and wrecked more children's lives. Did they think I was a part of that?'

He could not meet her eyes. He felt inadequate in the face of her anger.

'I'd run away from all that. Penniless and pregnant. You know, I got it together. Yes, I had some help from my aunt, but most of it was me. It wasn't easy, but I thought I'd got it behind me. Then those lizards sitting there in the car park, like they were threatening to take my daughter away. You have no fucking idea.'

'No, I haven't,' he said simply.

'That's right you haven't.'

She turned and opened the driver's door.

'What happened?'

She looked at him. 'What?'

He gestured across the car-park. 'They're not here now.'

'No, they're not,' she said grimly.

'Why?'

There was a long silence.

'They caught him,' she said. 'At Holyhead. He had a train ticket to Edinburgh. He was coming here. To wreck my life over again. Excuse me, I've studying to do.'

She climbed into the car and slammed the door. He had to jump out the way as she reversed backwards in a flurry of slush. He stood shivering in his sodden trousers as she drove across the car-park and went under the arch and out on to the road. He walked back to the flat on the Easter Road, filled the bath with pots of steaming water from the hob and lay in it with his eyes closed.

Cal made his first, less than satisfactory, foray into the world of drug smuggling later that week.

Rab grinned and blew on his fingers. 'Welcome to Dunfermline,' he said. 'Or, as it's known to a select few operators, Drugs R Us.'

He slid across the back seat and eased himself out of the car, and slunk with his head off at an angle down a skeletal privet hedge and into a darkened alleyway, and was briefly illuminated by the orange aureole of a street-light on the edge of a patch of grass.

Cal shivered and sank further down in his seat with his head resting on the dash. His teeth chattered. 'Christ,' he groaned.

Kelly drummed her fingers on the steering wheel and stared furtively around. 'Sit up straight,' she hissed.

'I've got flu,' Cal complained. 'Turn the engine on.'

'No.'

'It's freezing in here. I'm dying.'

'We'll draw attention to ourselves.'

Two teenagers rambled past, one of them dragging a skateboard on its rear wheels. They glared suspiciously at the car's occupants. Seconds later a cigarette butt landed on the bonnet. They stared at its red burning eye.

'Do you think that was the last skateboard in Scotland?'

Cal said, 'This isn't Dunfermline, it's a fuckin time-warp. Whose car is this?'

'A friend's.'

Cal glared at her through his locks. 'Are you insured?'

'No.'

'Great!'

'Will you stop moaning! I'm regretting ever bringing you.'

'I'm regretting coming,' he grouched. 'Dunfermline!' He closed his eyes and sank further down into the seat, feeling miserable. Five minutes of leaden silence followed.

'Where the fuck is he?' Kelly hissed.

Cal said, 'Let's go home.'

'I'll put you out and you can walk.'

'Crawl, more like.'

'Stop your moaning.'

There was another long pause.

'There he is.'

A skinny shape scuttled out of the shadows, clutching a heavy plastic bag. The rear door was tugged open and Rab dropped on to the back seat. He pushed the plastic bag under the driver's seat.

Kelly started the car and turned it in the cul-de-sac.

Rab kept staring over his shoulder out the rear window. 'Step oan it,' he said.

Kelly screeched through the gears. 'I'm trying.'

The car lurched out of the close, and on to the ring-road circling the estate. Rab spat out high-octane directions and jittered back and forth across the back seat.

On the high street in the rush-hour traffic, he said, 'Pull over.'

As soon as the car was beside the kerb he jumped out. Cal lifted his head off the dash. Kelly wound down her window. 'What are you doing?'

Rab leant in the window. His eyes were bright cherry-red. 'Ay'm gaunnae take the tren. I'll see yas back at the flat.'

'You can't do that,' Kelly protested, her voice edged with panic, but he was gone, bobbing through the crowd next.

'Shit!' She slammed the heels of her hands down on the steering wheel. 'What are we going to do?'

'Drive,' Cal said.

She wedged the car back into the traffic. Cal was up and staring about. A police car passed them, cruising in the opposite direction.

Cal asked, 'How much dope is there?'

'I don't know.'

'Christ!'

'Think of something.'

'We'll just have to do it.'

They followed a back road, chosen at random, out of Dunfermline. For a while a Ford transit seemed to follow them and they panicked. Kelly accelerated through a red light and pulled up a farm track and they waited for it to pass with their hearts pounding. They doubled back into town and followed the signs for the M90 and the Forth Road Bridge.

Kelly stalled the car fifty metres short of the toll booths. A car-horn blared behind them and cars began to swing around them and feed into the booths. Red and green lights winked on and off in front of them. There was a police car parked on the broad tarmac esplanade on the far side. Cal contemplated grabbing the plastic bag, running back to the bridge and flinging it into the sea. Would they send divers down for it?

Kelly seemed to be having problems breathing. 'Have you got forty pence?'

'What?'

'The toll. I haven't got any money. Forty pence.'

'Christ.' He started frantically digging in his pockets. 'Christ!'

Kelly ran her fingers along underneath the seat, searching for change. 'What are we going to do?'

Cal rummaged in the glove compartment and in the ashtray. They found thirteen pence.

'Shit!'

'What are we going to do?'

'Will you stop fuckin saying that!' Cal yelled. 'Think! Think!'

'Think what?'

'Think anything! Think! I've got it! Yes! You'll have to write a cheque.'

She stared blankly at him. 'Can you do that?'

'I don't know,' he said, through gritted teeth.

She started the car and it rabbit-hopped forward.

'Calm down,' Cal yelled.

'You fuckin calm down,' she retorted.

They stalled again, at an awkward angle against the booth.

'Awright, hen,' said the woman inside, 'It's a cold night.'

Cal watched the police car. There was one man inside and he was talking into his radio.

Kelly said, 'Ay'm sorry. I'll have to write a cheque. Is that all right?'

'Aye,' replied the woman wearily.

A momentary tide of relief swept across Cal's throbbing brain. Kelly rummaged in the murky interior of her bag for her cheque book. What came out was the skeleton of a cheque book, its cover ripped up for roach material, and the few remaining cheques stained and half legible. It flapped in her hands like a broken wing. She lifted up her head; there were frantic tears gathering in the corners of her eyes.

'Do you have a pen by any chance?'

The policeman had stopped talking into his handset and appeared to be watching them. Suddenly Cal understood the point of memorising songs, or rhymes, or even dates. There were moments like these when they could keep your head from exploding. He knew very few songs. He might remember one verse and a scattered mass of words with spaces between. He wasn't even much good at whistling. He felt that his head really was going to explode.

On the far side of the car the woman sighed, and handed over her pen. 'Aye, hen, there you go. Forty pence.'

Kelly's hands shook as she wrote out the amount in tall, spidery letters. She had to open the door and undo her seatbelt, and half climb out of her seat to get close enough to hand over the cheque with her card.

The woman wrote down the number on the back and passed back the card. 'On you go now, hen.'

Kelly closed the door and looked across at him. He was staring intently at the windscreen wipers, muttering 'Fuck' over and over again.

Cal's father, Angus was on his own in the kitchen. Aulay had, in the last year, taken to working on cars in the kitchen; it was considerably warmer than one of the sheds. Angus Bean seemed to have no objection to this arrangement, especially as Aulay brought him cigarettes and fried him lunch.

More and more often, Cal would return from university to find the kitchen filled with stripped engine parts, and rainbow pools of oil on the quarry tiles, with his father on regular duty in his large armchair by the stove, at ease, perhaps with his slippered foot resting on an engine block.

His father greeted him, 'Like a bad penny.'

Cal shifted the pile of tools in the sink to reach the taps, and filled the kettle. 'Tea?'

'You know what I find difficult to stomach?'

'Illuminate me,' Cal said wearily. He had already had to endure the jibes of the crew all the way over on the ferry.

'The fact that a Bean got caught. I feel a profound sense of shame. I gave you your independence, I allowed you to make your own way. This is how you repay me.'

Angus Bean was uncommonly proud of the fact that in his days of whisky-smuggling and poaching he had never once seen the inside of a police cell.

Cal said, 'I didn't intend to get caught.'

'Are you sure?'

'What do you mean?'

'You're influenced by your mother's moral qualms. Do you have a cigarette?'

'No.'

'Yir a thoughtless child.'

'Give it a rest,' Cal said. He was feeling excessively perse-cuted.

'Your cousin Madelene came to see me,' Angus continued. 'She smokes.' He tended to value people by the amount of nicotine they consumed. 'I told her you were involved in some half-arsed drug deal.'

'Thanks.'

'Sebastian's gone off somewhere to war.'

'The Gulf.'

'No, she said the Middle East. Are you sure you don't have any cigarettes?'

Cal slammed the kettle down on the draining board. He gritted his teeth. 'I'll go and buy you a pack.'

'Don't go on my account.'

'Don't worry.' He stamped out into the rain.

He paused at the entrance to the barn, unslung his bag from his shoulder and set it on the flagstones beside him. He watched her as she stood with her eyes closed and her head cocked to one side, in front of the painting.

'Earth to Madelene.'

She opened her eyes very suddenly. The rims of her eyeballs were as yellow as old ivory and flecked with veins of toffee. She was wearing a pair of paint-spattered overalls.

'Behold the criminal,' she greeted him, flourishing her paint-brush like a rapier. 'What did you get?'

He sighed. 'Community service. I wasn't the one the Polis were after.'

This seemed to satisfy her; he wasn't much in the mood to recount the whole painful debacle.

'Back for Christmas?'

He sighed. 'Well, yes. And no. Can I stay here?'

The canvas loomed huge and raw behind her, ten foot by ten foot, as if skewered on the barn wall. Corporeal, glistening.

'My bed's full right now,' she told him.

'I've got to finish my play,' he said, after a pause.

The play had been chosen for the Scottish Student Drama Festival on the basis of his proposal, and it was due to start in rehearsal at the beginning of term. He had an entire act to write.

Madelene didn't express a flicker of interest when he mentioned his play. He was getting used to it. Nobody seemed to take his writing seriously.

He asked, 'Is that real skin?'

She nodded. 'Peelings on encaustic. Last year's sunburn in fact. What do you think?'

He thought her painting was as extravagant, and gluttonous, as her love-making.

'It's . . .' He struggled, troubled by the image. 'Violent.'

She made a sound, an abrupt click of tongue and teeth, that he recognised as an expression of annoyance.

'Art has always been about violence. Defilement.' There must have been some shade of doubt in his face that angered her further. 'Look at it. Titian's *Marsyas*. Goya's *Disasters of War*. Museums are littered with corpses and crucifixions, decapitations, tortures, firing-squads, rapes, butchery – all in beautiful oils.'

She was more beautiful and more terrifying than her canvases would ever be. She turned back to the canvas and laughed self-consciously – or seemed to. 'I think it's sexy. Tactile.'

He stood beside her. 'What's it called?'

She gave him a look. '*Skinned.*'

'Yes,' he said, feeling slightly foolish.

'Seb's agreed to leave me his body,' she said.

After a while he said, 'I don't think I got that straight.'

'If he dies in the war I get his body. He's written a will. He favours something heroic and Stalinist, social realism in a formaldehyde tank. A bumper erection. I thought something stripped bare; a lampshade or two from his skin, his right foot a paperweight, his face a fine linen, maybe a bar of soap—'

'And I eat men like air,' he finished for her. 'Sylvia Plath.'

'Whadyathink?' she said.

Cal said, 'I don't think they'll let you.'

She laughed. Her fingertips stroked his forearm, and a spark of static seemed to jump between them. 'I approve of your hair,' she said, brazenly flirtatious. 'You know, you look pretty cool, maybe even a little dangerous.'

'You're making fun of me,' he said slowly, thoughts of sex rushing unbidden to the forefront of his mind.

She studied him for a few seconds; she sighed, 'You're too

transparent.' She looked back at the painting. 'Have you heard from Seb?'

'No. Have you?'

'He wrote to Dad. His longest letter ever. He's anticipating a battle. We think Torq's out there as well.' She shook her head. 'Dad's furious. Apparently he's an old buddy of Saddam's from before the Iran–Iraq War. He keeps shouting down the phone at people in Whitehall, and threatening to go over to Baghdad. They may yet end up on different sides of the battle-line.'

'He thinks he's going to lose his sons,' Cal said.

She mocked him. 'The curse?'

Cal shrugged. 'They believe it. Maybe that makes it true.'

She said, 'What should I believe?'

He reached out and gripped her upper arm and gathered her towards him. He buried his face in the dry honey-coloured hair behind her ear, the whiff of turpentine rising off her skin. He kissed her neck and put his hands under her breasts, on the bulky paint-stiff material of her overalls.

She shifted and gave him a pitying smile. 'You're a funny wee fucker.'

He was nine inches taller than her. He'd never been called a funny wee fucker before. It rattled him. He stepped back from her, feeling resentful.

Her eyes were shining brightly. She pressed an index finger to his lips. 'I have to work,' she said. It was true that she was single-minded about her work. Then she said, 'I don't love you. I don't think I ever will.'

He sighed.

She studied his face. 'Self-pity doesn't suit you,' she said.

'I think I'll go back home and make up with my dad. Write my play.'

'You do that.'

The bus dropped him en route to the ferry, and he walked up the track and gave the Collie With No Name a wide berth.

'You took your time,' his father greeted him.

'I bought you two packets to be on the safe side.'

His father grinned broadly. 'You're covered in paint.'

Cal looked down the front of his leather jacket at the ochre and umber palm prints, flecked with red, displayed like Stop signs on his chest.

'Sure, it looks to me that the island's temptress has given you the push.'

'Fuck off, Dad.'

He went up to his room, opened one of the drawers of his desk and removed an unframed black-and-white photograph. It was one of the few photographs of his mother in existence. She was sitting with her twin sister, Mary, on a boulder on the summit of one of the Paps of Garbh. He carried the photograph over to the bed, lay down and contemplated it. The two young women were wearing shorts and hiking boots, and canvas backpacks. They beamed in ruddy health at the camera. It was nine years now since she'd died and she seemed alien to him. When she died he had tried to fix certain memories of her in his mind, but they were becoming indistinct – certainly they bore little resemblance to this photograph of her in her youth; she had been thirty-nine when she gave birth to her youngest son, Calum, and fifty-two when she died.

Madelene held a dinner party that New Year to mark what she called her father's 'Great Misfortune'. The invitations, in silvered lettering on black card, described the dinner as a Huysmans Black Funeral Feast in memory of The MacCoinneach's virility. Her father was, she claimed, impotent; though whether this was literal or metaphorical impotence was not made apparent. Certainly The MacCoinneach was smarting from being refused a place on Edward Heath's diplomatic mission to Baghdad in which the former prime minister had negotiated the release of British hostages but failed to find a peaceful solution to the crisis.

Mocking her father's superstition, Madelene draped the dining room at the farmhouse in black cloth, spread crushed charcoal across the flagstones, and served a variety of black foods to her guests by flickering candlelight. They ate caviar and Greek olives on Russian rye bread as a starter, and as a main course pheasant in a bitter-chocolate and hashish sauce the colour of boot polish.

Madelene's other guests included an American mime artist from Paris called Troy, a voluptuous Goth from Brighton named Tania, and a young proctologist from the Royal Infirmary in

Edinburgh who was collaborating with Madelene on her latest artwork.

They drank Guinness, porter and kvass from a mismatched selection of glasses, jugs, vases and mugs that were clustered around each place setting.

Though Cal's recall of the sequence of events that followed was disordered, he was fairly sure that The MacCoinneach saved his appearance for the plum pudding; there was no commotion to announce his arrival, no slamming of doors or clatter of segged boots on flagstones. There was nothing of Seb in the deliberate and menacing silence of his movement. Hugh MacCoinneach merely paused for a moment or two longer than might be expected, silhouetted in the doorway, while their voices trailed away into silence and then, assured of their undivided attention, he prowled across the room in his magenta smoking-jacket with a cigarette trailing ash in one hand and a large whisky clamped in the other. He sat in the empty chair at the head of the table, downed his whisky in one gulp, and glared out from beneath his livid black eyebrows at the assembled company.

Cal reflected that, with his startling blue eyes and stark widow's peak of hair, his martial bearing and preternatural good looks, it was not difficult to sympathise with the view, most often expressed in the bar at the Loch Intake Hotel, that Hugh MacCoinneach was the devil incarnate.

Madelene broke the silence. 'DD,' she said, which in her father's parlance meant dead drunk.

The MacCoinneach sneered.

Madelene asked, 'The Foreign Office kept you on hold again?'

'Greensleeves,' he replied, in a drawn-out sibilant hiss. 'Seventy-six minutes.'

Madelene was delighted. 'Yesterday some young thing at the FO had the audacity to tell our father it was about time we proved we are serious about not arming future enemies. Can you imagine? No guns to the rag-heads and no knighthood for Daddy.'

But The MacCoinneach wasn't listening; he had fixed his attention on Andy. 'Have you blacked up on my account?' he enquired.

The proctologist gasped. Andy looked across at Cal, who was equally at a loss.

Eventually, Andy said, 'No, I'm black.'

'Really?' The MacCoinneach drawled. He stubbed out his cigarette on the table and immediately lit another. 'I didn't know we had any piccaninnies on the island.'

'Ignore him,' Madelene cut in. 'He just needs a good screw. The widows of the island have long since grown tired of the lecherous old fraud. He wants something young and nubile to flatter his ego, and give him a new set of sons to replace the ones he has so carelessly mislaid.'

'They're not all dead yet,' her father observed.

'Seb's written a will,' Madelene informed him.

A subtle hardening of the mass of crow's feet round his eyes was the only indication of the old man's anger.

'What crime exactly was it that you committed in Ethiopia all those years ago? How did you earn the curse?' Madelene demanded.

'Can't remember,' her father muttered.

'The story I heard,' she continued, 'is that you received advance intelligence that the Italian Air Force were going to drop mustard-gas canisters on a village in the highlands but you chose not to warn the inhabitants, what with mass murder being a powerful incentive to the locals to join your little rebel force. What do you say, Daddy? Is that about it?'

The MacCoinneach rewarded her with a lean and murderous smile. 'Spot on,' he said.

'I'm out fer a walk,' Andy said, and stood up.

Which was about when Tania squeezed Cal's thigh under the table. He wasn't sure at first, because he was losing touch with parts of his body; but then she started walking her fingers along the inward curve of his thigh. He didn't know whether to stand up or stay put.

Andy left the room.

'Why don't you find me a woman?' The MacCoinneach challenged his daughter.

'Please!' Her face was stricken with disgust. 'Don't make me puke.'

The MacCoinneach sighed. 'My darling daughter,' he said, 'you have the grace of an angel but you speak the discourse of the devil. Your parts do not fit well together.'

'My parents did not fit well together,' she retorted.

'How old is your father?' Tania whispered loudly.

'Nobody knows,' Madelene sniggered. 'Not old enough.'

The MacCoinneach switched his attention to Tania, and rewarded her with his most predatory smile. 'What about you?'

'I'm spoken for,' she replied, and leant over and pushed her tongue between Cal's lips and into his mouth. Madelene howled with laughter and started clapping.

It was only later, flat on his back beside the swimming pool with a mild concussion, seconds after being blown out of the pool by an irritable electric eel, that he reflected on the exact nature of his bad luck.

'Wow,' said the girl on the tiles beside him.

Someone had filled the pool with black ink.

'That'll teach you,' Madelene told him afterwards, stroking his forehead indulgently.

Edinburgh. Two months later. Madelene leant forward over the row of dusty bucket-seats and whispered huskily in his ear, 'This is merry shit. It's very good.'

He concentrated on the activity on the stage, the actors fine-tuning their movements; he refused to be distracted by Madelene's warm breath on his neck. The theatre was freezing. There was no money to heat it for rehearsals. Madelene was stroking the hair on the nape of his neck with her fingernails.

Eventually, he muttered under his breath, 'Are you patronising me?'

'Don't be so sensitive.'

The director glanced over his shoulder at them from two rows ahead. Madelene smiled at him. He blushed and hurriedly turned back to his stage directions.

'How do you do that?'

She closed her eyes. 'I'm sorry, Cal. Do what?'

'Intimidate people.'

'Ssshh, I want to watch the play.'

Cal hunched his shoulders and sank further down into his seat, burying his nose in his scarf. It was painful giving up to another's interpretation of something he had written, and yet it was also a relief. Finishing the play had been a nightmare of frantic caffeine-assisted scribbling; nocturnal pacing and pen-chewing in his bedroom back on Cual. Now he didn't have to worry about it.

Madelene slept with him that night, which he took to mean that she really had enjoyed his play; that, or she was reeling him back in, reminding him of her control over him. He preferred to believe the former. The following afternoon, when he stumbled out of bed with a mammoth stone-over and waded through the mouldy coffee cups and plates crusted with ketchup, she opened an eye and contemplated him with a wasted smile.

'Good luck, lover,' she said, and went back to sleep.

He sat at the front of the bus, staring out across the spires of the city, feeling profoundly optimistic. It was his time.

The bubble burst that night. The director had been unhappy with a scene and insisted that the actors repeat it again and again. Cal had suggested a few changes. As a result he didn't get back from the rehearsal until well after midnight. He turned down the offer of a drink at the Traverse with the cast and hurried back down the Easter Road in the biting cold.

He stood for a few seconds in the darkened hallway with his key in the lock and listened to one of Madelene's more vocal expressions of pleasure issuing out of Al's room. There was no mistaking it. He went dejectedly to his room, and, reflecting on the piles of used plates, cups, Rizlas, empty bottles, roaches and cigarette butts, he noted that the only memento she had left him, by which to remember another night of violent passion, was a used tampon in a coffee cup beside his pillow.

He woke with a start to find the flat filled with heavy black smoke and the sounds of hysterical laughter. He stumbled out of bed and pulled on some boxer shorts and hopped out into the hall. Al's bed was on fire, the bright orange flames leaping five feet in the air. Al and Madelene were backed up in the corner of the room, stark naked, and cackling and coughing dementedly.

'Do something,' Madelene squealed, her eyes streaming.

He passed Andy standing in the hall with his head in the smoke. 'Something up?' he asked.

'You could say that,' Cal muttered, hurrying for the kitchen.

He tipped up the washing bowl, emptying its rancid soup of potato peelings into the sink, filled it with water, took it to the bedroom and tipped it over the bed. Andy followed up with the bathroom rug, smothering the remaining flames. Al jumped up and down on it a couple of times and the bed-frame collapsed. Cal opened a window.

Madelene produced a cigarette from somewhere and lit it.

'Damage,' Cal said. 'Everywhere you go you cause damage.'

She gave him a withering look.

Al scratched his head and sent an apologetic look in Cal's direction. 'I don't s'pose we could stay in your bed the nite, mate?'

'No.'

'Fair enuf.'

'Now the fun's over,' Andy said, 'I'm oaf to bed.'

Madelene flicked her cigarette out of the window and followed him out of the room. Al watched her go open-mouthed. Cal felt a grim satisfaction.

Al leant forward and pointed a finger across the breakfast things, raising his voice above the sound of the radio. 'Ur you saying you didnae have sex with her?'

Andy sipped his coffee. 'Jus wat I said, Al. I didnae have sex with her.'

Al was appalled. He looked at Cal. Cal shook his head; it was beyond his reckoning.

Al demanded, 'Why not?'

Andy pulled a long face and scratched his stubble.

Al shouted, 'Cum oan!'

'Don't fancy her, I s'pose. Not my type.'

'Nobody, I mean *nobody*, says no to Madelene.'

'I wis knackered.'

'No wonder she left in such a bad mood,' Cal commented. 'I don't suppose this has ever happened to her before.'

'Iz this sum kindae black thing?'

'No,' Andy said. 'It's not any kindae thing.'

'It disnae make any kindae sense, that's fer sure. I mean, a chance like that disnae come round very often. Am I exaggerating?'

Andy groaned in exasperation. 'You should take a look at yourselves. She's a flame, man. Youse flutter round her like moths.'

'Very profound,' Al sneered.

Cal was distracted, shifting his chair towards the radio on the counter.

'It's not personal,' said Andy.

'Of course it's personal. It's a fuckin insult!'

'Ssshh!' Cal said. They looked at him. He explained, 'The ground war's started.'

3

Tremendous noise. Seb lifted his cowled head off the vision blocks and observed surface-to-surface missiles cruise overhead like angry bees. The sky was lit with the lambent glow of hundreds of burning well-heads and, out on the fracturing horizon, the relentless strobing of arc-lights.

He was in a state of spasm deferred. Nothing heard, seen or felt pierced the carapace of his enforced calm. He observed, recorded and behaved. In front of him a US Humvee flashing FOLLOW ME in garish neon peeled on to the column and led them into the minefield. He rolled his wrist again to see the time. The fluorescent dots stood out starkly against his black neoprene glove. 14.05 hours, G plus 1. 25 February.

The Breach. They passed armoured bulldozers and groups of Americans in chemical suits standing on the dunes and the shattered hulk of a Humvee that had strayed on to the mines. The Warrior's headlights picked out a row of vast creosote letters that seemed to float above the sand-berm; WELCOME TO IRAQ, COURTESY OF THE BIG RED ONE. This was the place for gas, while the vehicles were in the bottleneck. He'd seen the film taken by an Iranian film-crew who went into the Kurdish village of Halabja just hours after the Iraqis had dropped chemical weapons: four thousand corpses littering the streets.

He mouthed, 'Or close the wall up with our Scottish dead.'

He saw his first POWs, lines of shabby, stick-like Iraqis with their hands crossed behind their heads, being shepherded down a safe lane by US Military Police. Hollow-eyed and starved-looking, the Iraqis had no gas masks. He could not summon any feelings for them, neither hate nor pity. He shifted his charcoal facelet and his nose was filled with the stench of diesel fumes.

Out on the crest of a dune a scrawny dog fox, apparently

unaffected by the noise, loped along, shadowing the column for some minutes.

He felt numb, as if the months of anticipation had built a bulwark against any pre-emptive rush of excitement. The Knife – that expression of malignant vigour – waited, barely noticed, at the edge of his senses. He had come to understand that his utmost could be delivered only for a few seconds. Consequently, it was to be hoarded and only at the right moment unsheathed.

The rest of the crew were electric with excitement, had been since they left the staging area. He consulted his map, which resembled a sheet of fine-grained sandpaper. He mouthed a list of objectives; Copper, Brass, Steel, Zinc, Platinum, Tungsten . . .

A sudden plume of sand on the crest of the dune marked the spot where the fox hit a mine.

The Humvee peeled away to the left, its crew waving them on, and they headed out towards the open desert. Half an hour later, fifteen kilometres beyond the breach-head, they crossed phaseline New Jersey and the US Cavalry screen, and for the first time everything out in front of them was enemy. It began to rain; hard metallic sheets drumming on the compacted surface of the sand.

He ran round the front of the Warrior, ducking under the steady chatter of the 7.62mm machine-gun, and charged into the hail of hot brass cases cascading off the turret. They struck his smock and skin, stinging the exposed flesh. He had the butt of the rifle up into his shoulder against the flak jacket and fired twice, but the Iraqi was already out of view around the back of the Warrior. It turned sideways abruptly, and the heat of the diesel engine swept across his face, the roadwheels spinning towards him.

He surged forward and outward, rounding the corner as the vehicle slewed. Wildly inaccurate automatic fire kicked up sand at an oblique angle to him. He grinned savagely. The Knife unsheathed.

ThunkThunkThunk. The Warrior's main armament pumped cannon shells into the Iraqi trench-system. He wiped the sweat from his eyes and breathed out hard. He took a skimming glance round the corner while a glissade of sand poured off the storage bins. He saw Warriors and Challengers churning up bunkers and the ragged flags of sandbags that marked a trench-line not twenty metres away, and nearer to hand his own Iraqi backing away and changing magazines, with his Kalashnikov pointing at the sand. He had stiff, unwashed hair and a full black moustache that drooped at the corners. Catching sight of Seb, he flailed away round the front of the Warrior.

It was like a chase from *Tom and Jerry*, round and round in a cloud of comical dust. Absurd, hysterical. Time to end it. Quick.

He changed direction and sprinted back round the bulk of the Warrior and was on him in a second. The Iraqi picked him up in his peripheral vision and turned his head, his mouth open and his sour breath in the air between them, but by then it was too late. Seb swung his body into him and with one stroke hammered him in the temple with the butt plate of his rifle. He could hear the crunch.

The Iraqi dropped on to the sand. There was blood all over his pitted, acne-scarred face; blood from the scalp wound at his temple and a froth of blood from his nostrils leaking into his moustache. Blood welled up out of the crust of grime in his right ear.

Seb tipped his rifle downwards and slid the bayonet between two ribs, twisted it and pulled the trigger. The body heaved beneath him.

There, he thought, I've killed a man.

He leapt up off the sand, sprinted forward to the trench and dropped into the bottom of it as the Warrior swept over him, the spinning roadwheels just inches above his head; sand cascading down on top of him from the collapsing trench-walls. He rolled on his back and tugged out the pin on a L2 grenade and popped it around the first zigzag. He flipped the lever on the rifle to automatic. Counting, he squeezed his eyes closed.

Crump.

Shards of wriggly tin, and strips of sandbag peppered the far wall. He rolled round the corner and emptied a magazine into the black smoke.

He was completely deaf. Moose, bowling over the top of him, stamped on Seb's helmet, banging his upper and lower teeth together, so that he knew to stop firing. He lifted his finger off the trigger. Events telescoped. He ran forward to Moose, fluidly changing magazines.

Crump.

The lever mechanism of an L2 spun away over his head. Smoke engulfed him. Moose was firing. It felt as if boulders were grinding in his eyes. His head was pounding. He went over the top of Moose, kicking him as he did so, and squeezed into darkness between shattered timbers. Nails and splinters ripped his clothing. His helmet scraped a concrete ceiling. He was in a bunker. He punted himself spider-like along a fractured wall. A western woman's face, cut from a glossy magazine, smiled at him just inches away. He stumbled as the wall dropped away and pulled himself back; he'd reached a doorway. He could hear gunfire; he wasn't sure which side. He told himself to stay calm. Wait a beat.

He pulled the ring from a phosphorus grenade and posted it carefully through the open doorway. He curled himself tight against the wall.

Pffsssssss . . .

Blinding white gobbets of phosphorus fell like sleet around him. Somebody was screaming. He went fast and low into the room and emptied another magazine. Sand blasted his face. The barrel of his rifle glowing dull red. He skidded blindly in something liquid, and fell against a table-edge, opening a flap of skin on his cheek. He scuttled crab-like under the table and used a charger to fill a magazine. He shouted to Moose, but couldn't hear anything above the roaring in his ears, and crawled across the floor and over the charred hummock of a body, feeling for a doorway with outstretched fingers.

He dug in his pouches for the egg-shape of another grenade, pulled the pin and threw it overarm into the next room. He folded his arms under his chest and pressed his face flat against the rough sandy floor.

Crump.

An iron hand gripped his collar and yanked him backwards through a typhoon of dust, his rifle still kicking at his shoulder, and suddenly a mouthful of fillings and slathering pink gums was screaming in his face.

'Stoap fuckin firin!'

He lifted his finger off the trigger.

The Sergeant-Major appeared out of the dust, his face black

with cordite burns, and contorted with fury. 'They fuckin Iraqis've fuckin surrendered!'

He let go of Seb, who staggered backwards and slid down a bunker-wall, grinning.

'Yer a fuckin loonatic!' the Sergeant-Major screamed.

For a fraction of a second Seb considered shooting him – they had never seen eye to eye – but instead he applied his safety-catch and lowered his rifle. He reached inside one of his pouches for his vial of eye-drops. His hands shook as he squeezed out the liquid and it ran down his face like tears.

He noticed that his hands were covered in blood. He didn't know if it was his own or had once belonged to someone else.

'I don't want this ever to end,' he said.

Four days later he climbed the crest of the Mutla ridge where the highway out of Kuwait City narrowed from six lanes to four – the bottleneck that US F-15s had sealed with five-hundred-pound bombs – and surveyed the smouldering devastation beneath him.

The traffic was backed up a mile and spread out over half a mile of soft sand. The burnt-out wreckage of fifteen hundred vehicles which had borne the brunt of all the weaponry that the aeroplanes the US Navy, Marines and Air Force could muster; Landcruisers, sports cars, school buses, delivery vans and fire engines. Anything with wheels that would carry the fleeing Iraqi army out of Kuwait.

Ever since they had stopped the advance he had been turning over in his head a fragment of a nursery rhyme that his father had sung to him as a child:

How many miles to Babylon?
Three-score miles and ten.
Can I get there by candlelight?

At night the well-heads seemed to burn like vast candles on a wooden table-top. The first vehicle he passed was a Chinese mortar vehicle which had been hit by a cluster bomb and perforated like a colander. The ammunition in the two vehicles had brewed up and there were body parts spread over two hundred square metres. He trod carefully.

When they had arrived, on the morning of the 28th, they found American soldiers moving amongst the bodies, dispatching the most severely wounded. Now the burial details were at work. He was looking for Moose. He knew he was on the right track when he passed a lorry packed with looted TVs and VCRs, boxes of Levi's and Pampers; the charred carcass of the driver had a fresh cigarette poking from between its lips. He'd once seen a cigarette in the mouth of a dead cat on the Kennedy Way in Belfast; a week later he noticed that the cigarette had been smoked halfway to the filter and then returned to the cat's mouth. It was a Jock thing.

The ground was littered with cartons of cigarettes. He split one open and pocketed a couple of packs.

Moose was supervising a detail who were throwing body parts into body bags. He saw Seb approach and walked up to him. He pushed his facelet up on his forehead and immediately lit a cigarette. 'It gits ye at the back ov ye throat,' he complained.

It was true the smell was getting bad.

'Give ye yer fuckin military cross, did they, suh?'

Seb shook his head. 'The Sar'nt-Major blocked the citation. Told the RSM I got out of hand. It went all the way up.'

'Fuck that,' Moose said, sucking fiercely on his cigarette. 'You mean ay put all that fuckin hard work in and yer nae gunnae steal the fuckin glory?'

'That's right.'

'Fuck that!' He was outraged. 'Some mash cunt fae England wul git it. Thas wurse than you fuckin gittin it!'

'Tell me about it.'

'Ah, fuck it. Youse wan a smoke?'

'Picked up a pack en route.' He tore the cellophane with his thumb-nail, and extracted a cigarette. Moose lit it for him.

'Can youse bilev they Iraqis? Sure enuf if the swag wasnae nailed down they fuckin swiped it. You gotta hand it to they rag-heads. Fuckin helping themselves, too rite.'

'There's a vehicle coming,' Seb observed.

Moose followed the direction of his gaze. A stripped-down Land-Rover was driving erratically between the wrecks towards them, kicking up a storm of dust.

'There's a MILAN mounted on that.' The humpbacked outline of the anti-tank missile was clearly visible.

'Ay,' Moose jeered. 'Fuckin SAS. Scudbusters. They Rambo

fuckers ave bin comin back ova the border all day. Stoppin off fer a few holiday snaps, and back to Kuwait City fer a bath n a brew n a stack ov medals.'

The Land-Rover braked in front of them. It was coated in a thick layer of ochre dust, and the heavily armed passengers were swathed in muddy ponchos and *shemaghs*. The driver pushed his goggles up on to his high forehead, and loosened the length of *shemagh* that obscured his disfigured mouth.

'Hello, Torq,' Seb said, after a pause.

Torquil looked him up and down. 'Got you cleawing up, have they?'

'Something like that.'

Torquil curled the pink combs of his upper lip in a sneer. 'Thee you later.' He drove off.

Moose said, 'Whose zat flash cunt?'

'My brother.'

Cal caught sight of her across the crowded foyer of the theatre, smiling at him. He excused himself from a conversation and eased himself through the crowd spilling out of the café. She spoke briefly to delay her friends, who were standing out on the steps, waiting to leave. She came towards him. In an act of unaccustomed decisiveness he took her elbow and steered her over to a space at the foot of the staircase that led up to the balcony and the director's box. He reasoned that he had nothing to lose. She allowed herself to be led.

'I liked your play,' she said.

'Good,' he said, finding himself smiling broadly. He didn't have a clue in the world what he was going to say, so he said, 'Oonagh,' savouring the sound of her name.

She laughed at him.

'What?'

She shook her head.

'Will you . . . um . . . have a drink? There's a cast party. Bring your friends.'

She shook her head again. 'I've got my finals coming up.'

He grimaced. 'Me too.'

He hadn't even opened a book. He had three overdue essays to write. It wasn't worth thinking about. She made him want to be enthusiastic about it.

'I have to go,' she said.

'I'm sorry about what happened before,' he blurted out.

'That's all right. I think I've changed my opinion of you.'

There was a pause.

'That sounds good,' he said.

'I liked your play. It wasn't what I expected.'

'Stay,' he said, emboldened.

'I'm behind with work,' she said steadfastly. She laid her mittened hands against his chest. 'Goodbye.' She turned her back on him and went down the steps and joined her friends.

He gripped his forehead and groaned.

It took him a week to summon the courage to go looking for her. This time he avoided the crèche, and instead tracked her down to the Dick Vet library. He walked the length of the library a few times. Finally, he retraced his steps to where Oonagh was reading behind an imposing rampart of manuals and files, and sat in the seat opposite her. She looked up, and their eyes met.

'Fancy seeing you here,' he whispered.

She scrutinised him for what seemed like a long time.

'Doing a little research,' he explained. 'For a play.'

'Really?'

'No,' he conceded.

She smiled. He took it as a cue. 'Coffee?'

'A quick one,' she said, and spent a few moments packing away her things with a thoroughness that caused him much envy. If she was that serious about taking a break, she must be that serious about settling down to work. Cal rarely managed to unpack his rucksack before he was heading for the coffee shop. However hard he strove to immerse himself in study, he invariably found himself distracted. He told himself that when it came to studying he was a lost cause.

'Are you thinking?'

He looked at her, confused. 'What do you mean?'

'Were you having a thought, just then?'

'I was thinking how badly I'm going to do in my finals.'

'Good.'

'Why good?'

'You have a way of staring, with your mouth slightly open. It makes you look dreamy. Or retarded. I was trying to work out which.'

'I wonder myself,' he said.

In the café they split up, Oonagh finding a table while Cal went off to queue for the coffees. When he returned with them, a tall dark-haired man with the build of a rugby player was standing over the second chair. He stared at Cal suspiciously.

'Its all right, Mike,' Oonagh told him. 'I know him.'

The rugby player backed off. Cal sat down. 'What was that about?'

'The vet students are protective of me,' she explained. 'I've had problems with strangers.'

'I don't look much like the Polis,' he said.

'Nor an IRA man,' she replied seriously.

It was a stark reminder of her circumstances. She watched his face, gauging his reaction.

In response, trying to lighten the tone and demonstrate that he was not intimidated, he asked, 'What do I look like?'

She laughed freely. 'Youse look like a frigging scarecrow.'

'Well,' he said, 'stick with me and you won't have a problem with crows.'

'I'd be more worried about mice,' she retorted.

'There are no mice in my bed.'

She lifted an eyebrow. 'You're jumping the gun, aren't you?'

'I'm sorry,' he said quickly, berating himself for getting carried away.

She seemed pleased. 'You're very keen.'

'Yes,' he said.

'I come as part of a package,' she said. 'Child, dog, convict, et cetera.'

'I know.'

'It doesn't bother you?'

'Not so far.'

'Maybe you are retarded,' she said, and then, 'Come over for dinner tomorrow night. I'll meet you here at five. Now I have to work.' She drained her coffee and stood up. 'See you tomorrow.'

For one strange, unreal moment he thought that they were driving out to the Jah Palace. Back in time. He sat in the passenger seat of her rust-bucket Hyundai and watched the old slag heap on the outskirts of Gilmerton go by, and then they were over the top of the Edinburgh bypass and on the A7 to Dalkeith.

She took the turning for Melville Farm, and skidded through the ruts up a mile-long grass track with 'Boops' by Sly and Robbie thumping out of the sound-system.

She threw back her head and exposed her teeth: 'Fire . . .'

They skidded across the farmyard, past a snarling Alsatian on a chain and a shed full of cattle, and came to a halt next to a small cottage. There were lights on and twists of smoke coming out of the chimney, and when he got out his nose lifted to the familiar, welcoming smell of peat. There was a motorcycle next to the door and another dog barking.

He followed her into the damp porch, and was greeted by a grey lurcher that jumped up and laid its paws on his chest and sniffed him as if searching for some sign of bad character. A further line of defence.

She said, 'That's Fly.'

'I see.'

The dog dropped down and seemed to shepherd him through into a dark hallway, toward a closed door framed by orange light. She pushed the door open against a resistant vermilion carpet, and they were in a small, comfortable room with a large fireplace. In front of the fire, and surrounded by pieces of a farmyard jigsaw, Sile sat cross-legged on a *dhouri* beside a young woman with a dark plait and a brightly coloured mohair jumper.

Discarding her jacket, Oonagh scooped Sile up in her arms and hugged her. 'Have you been good?'

'The best,' replied her daughter.

The young woman stood up and smoothed her jeans down over her Doc Martens. 'Your father called.' Her accent was Irish.

'What did he want?'

'He didn't say. A reconciliation, I figure.'

Oonagh snorted. 'He'd be as well to howl at the moon.'

The young woman picked up a motorcycle helmet off a chair. 'I'll be off.'

'Thanks,' Oonagh said, and then, 'This is Calum. You know.'

She looked him up and down as she brushed past, the ghost of a smile on her face. Oonagh stoked the fire and then squatted on her heels beside the jigsaw and picked up a piece.

'This is a realm of women,' Oonagh informed him. 'We don't have many men here.' Sile was scrutinising him with her arm looped through her mother's; she had her mother's way of staring brazenly at you. He listened to the sound of the motorcycle starting up outside and the dog barking madly.

'I'm honoured,' he said.

She laughed freely, distinctively, chaotically; it was a heartening sound.

Carefully, he unslung his backpack and opened it. 'I brought a bottle of wine and a book.' He'd stolen it that morning from Thins, and then had second thoughts on Nicholson Street and gone back and returned it to the shelf and browsed a while, and then taken it to the counter by the door and purchased it legally. For no reason that he could put his finger on, he had decided that a genuine present should leave a hole in your pocket. It was a Ladybird book: *Butterflies and Moths.*

'The last time I saw you you had butterflies on your coat,' he explained. He went down on one knee and offered it.

Sile took a few hesitant steps away from her mother, took the book from his hand and retreated with a shy, gap-toothed smile. 'Thank you,' she whispered.

'The pig's ear,' Oonagh said.

He said, 'I'm sorry . . . ?'

'Your foot.'

He looked down and saw that his boot was resting on a piece of jigsaw; a geometrical slice of a pig, an eye and ear, and a cock's beak and wattle.

'Right. Shit. Yeah,' he said, and shifted his foot and picked it up. 'Shall I?'

Sile nodded. Carefully, he leant forward and slotted it into place.

Oonagh said, 'You know if you put polish on your boots they last longer.'

After a moment, he endeavoured to nod gravely. 'Really?'

She laughed again. 'I'm sorry. I'm terribly bossy.'

'Not you.'

She took the pin out of her hair and shook it down. 'Sile and I will have a bath,' she said. 'You watch the fire, and open that wine. We won't be long.'

He got up again, and went over to the fire and piled a few more sods of peat in the grate. He stood with his back to the fire and warmed his legs; and, staring about him, he read the signs of her presence. Like many of the cottages on the outskirts of the city, it looked as if it had last been decorated in the seventies, but Oonagh had clearly done her best to disguise the bright purple and orange wallpaper with fabrics and rugs. Simple things that seemed to indicate an independence of mind; two cotton bobbins used for candlesticks, an old galvanised watering-can with a fern growing out of it, an unusual-looking length of wood, shells from the beach, found and salvaged things.

Browsing the shelves of the bookcase he caught sight of a couple of black-and-white photographs tucked beneath a copy of the poems of W. B. Yeats. The first was of Oonagh, in school uniform, looking lanky and toothy and self-conscious; in the second she was wearing jeans and an anorak and standing beside a tow-headed youth with a sparse moustache, acne and an almost concave chest. Was this her terrorist ex-boyfriend? Sile's father? It was difficult to see any sign of a family resemblance, or of any implicit threat in his guarded, nervous expression.

He chopped onions at the table and drank wine while she slipped back and forth between the oven and the sink, where she was de-bearding a bucketful of mussels, and Sile ran up and down the hall in her pyjamas and dressing-gown, chasing the dog. Oonagh's hair was damp and shiny. Her shirt was rolled up to her elbows, and revealed her tightly veined forearms.

'How was your play?' she asked.

'We won,' he replied. 'The show goes down to London in a couple of weeks. Two nights at the Almeida.'

'You must be pleased.'

'Aye.'

'You don't sound over the moon?'

'It's not really my baby any more, you know. It's not private anymore. I have mixed feelings. Do you understand that?'

'I think so. Here, chop some garlic.'

He watched her. She moved with athletic, and unselfconsciously erotic, grace. It occurred to him that she would maintain this elegance throughout her life. She'd look this good at fifty.

'Tell me about your family,' he said.

'Jesus.' She rolled her eyes.

'Go on,' he prompted.

'Where do you want me to start?'

'Wherever.'

She narrowed her eyes, and a slight crease furrowed her forehead. 'Its not ... some kind of picaresque – poteen and cattle-rustling.'

'As long as I'm entertained,' he joked.

'All right, then,' she replied, flecks of anger in her eyes. 'My grandmother was an Irish-speaker, from Donegal. She was bought at the hiring fair in Strabane at the age of thirteen. The farmer who bought her was Protestant, of course. They were all Protestants, the farmers. She milked, washed, cooked, and churned and she didn't get a day off for six months and at the end of that six months she was paid five pounds. That's all. Five pounds. She couldn't read or write. She slept in a pen like an animal.'

'Sounds like slavery.'

'It was poverty. Don't romanticise it,' she snapped. 'Every six months she was hired again, until she reached nineteen and married. Her husband was hired as well. After the ceremony he went back to the farm. He didn't see her for six months. That was their life. He died at thirty-five, and she had to go back to work as a labourer to support her children. Five children. They got out, emigrated to America, except my father.' She sighed. 'My father's a self-made millionaire. A Thatcherite wet dream in bandit country. He owns a cement factory in Lamclough. That's South Armagh. They call it bandit country,' she explained. 'He started off delivering gravel, and diversified into concrete blocks and tiles; now he controls twenty per cent of the market, North and South. That's the official biopic.'

'It sounds as if you don't like him.'

'I don't. He's a bully, and a thug. And a bigot and a snob.'

'What about your mother?'

'Spineless. Wifely.'

It was a cruel dismissal. He waited, but she did not elaborate, so he asked, 'What about you? What brought you to Edinburgh?'

'I just wanted to get away.' She said it with a firmness that invited no further questions. She tipped his onions and garlic into a frying pan. They sizzled. 'What about you?'

He shrugged. 'Not much to say.'

UNDERWOLVES

241

'Say it anyway. Here, open this wine.'

'I come from an island. Cual. Population four thousand. Then there are forty thousand geese, and the seals, and the mermaids . . .'

'Little People?'

'Only the Cradden. A few boarded-outs left over from the war.'

The cork popped out. He handed her back the bottle and watched as she poured most of it into the pan.

'There's a huge lump of rock, almost a separate island, called the Og. It has the cemetery on top of it and a whirlpool at the bottom of it. My mother's buried there.'

'I'm sorry,' she said.

'It's not a bad place to be buried,' he said. 'It smells quite strong sometimes, because of the goats.'

'That's not what I meant.'

He smiled. 'I know.'

'Tell me about your family.'

'All right,' he agreed. 'I'm the youngest of three. My eldest brother, Dugald, runs the farm, and the middle one Aulay, is a mechanic of sorts. The Beans have always lived there. We were a slave clan originally. Now we're tenant farmers.' He chewed at his lip. 'My mother died when I was eleven, in a car crash. She had run the farm. My father was a fisherman. After she died he just gave up. He stopped working, stopped getting up in the morning.'

'That must have been difficult for you.'

'Not really. When I look back I'm surprised at how easy it was. My father never really knocked much of a dent in my life. There wasn't much to miss. To be honest, I don't know what my mother saw in him. Anyway, it's old news. Dugald took over the farm after Mum died. That's the way it's been ever since.'

'And you?'

'Me? The first to go to university, and probably the last. I went to school on Cual, helped out on the boats in the holidays. Worked on the ferry. Did a bit of welding. Read too many books, you know. Dreamt of the wider world. The usual.'

'Wrote plays?'

'A few.'

She emptied the bucket of mussels into the liquid, and they

clacked and rattled as she scooped them around with a wooden spoon. She put the lid on the pan.

'Just a few minutes.'

'I'm starving,' he said.

They had supper by candlelight on the carpet in front of the fire, eating the mussels from bowls, sopping the liquid with homemade garlic bread and discarding the shells in the pot, and drinking wine. Sile had a small bowl of mussels and a glass of orange juice, and described her day. Afterwards she said goodnight and her mother put her to bed, and standing at the end of the hall he could hear the sound of Oonagh reading aloud to her.

After listening for a few minutes he went and settled on the sofa. He heard the sound of the light being switched off and Oonagh's soft footfall in the hall. He felt a sense of gathering anticipation.

She entered without speaking and went straight to the fire, then turned and contemplated him. A silent message travelled between them.

'Come here,' he said, quietly confident.

She straddled him. She sank her fingers into the fibrous mass of his hair. They kissed.

Later, after coming up for air, he said, 'I've been looking forward to that.'

She smiled. 'You're funny.'

He frowned. She tugged at his jumper. 'What's the matter?'

'I was remembering the last time someone called me funny. A funny wee fucker.'

She had a quizzical look on her face.

'I'm sorry,' he said.

She sank back down on top of him. Half an hour later, naked on the sofa, he suffered an uncomfortable premonition as she gripped the tip of his penis between her forefinger and thumb and scowled at him. He tried to look open and innocent.

Her expression hardened, 'You're not the one I slept with that night.'

He blanched. 'I can explain . . .'

She tightened her grip. He squealed.

'You shit,' she said. 'Who was he?'

It came out in a rush. 'My cousin Seb you wouldn't like him he's a soldier.'

'I don't think I like you.'

'I was the one peeing in the river the following morning. You fell through a hole in the stairs. I helped you out.'

'That's an excuse?'

'An explanation . . . ?'

'Not a very good one.'

'I'm sorry,' he said. 'Really sorry.'

For a minute or so he thought he'd lost her, but then she shrugged and said, 'Come on, then.'

They made love by moonlight on her lumpy single bed, which was ringed with clumps of dried flowers and scented candle stubs, while the Cowboy Junkies played 'Misguided Angel' on her sound system; and she came after the longest time with tears in her eyes and sighed and said, 'Crimson.' Which she later explained was the colour of her coming. He marvelled at the firmness of her body, her belly and buttocks, and the corded muscles of her arms. They clung to each other like the last two people alive. He traced the spray of freckles on her back.

'You'll have to be patient with me,' she said softly. 'Don't misinterpret me, I don't want sympathy; but if you want this to go somewhere you'll have to be patient.'

'Sometimes I feel like the most patient person in the world.'

She held him tighter and then gradually her grip loosened and her breathing steadied. His hand remained on her head, gently stroking. The tips of her hair shone like molten brown sugar in the guttering candlelight.

He felt as if he had had a glimpse of everything that he wanted in life; and he had a sudden premonition that he might never be this happy again.

'He was a fighter for freedom, my own teenage Che Guevara,' she said with bitter irony. 'It was guaranteed to make my father mad. I mean, the old man was a Sinn Féin supporter; he paid his dues. More than that, he was well connected in the IRA. That was the price of living in Lamclough, of being a successful businessman. He played some kind of intermediary role during the hunger strikes. I guess I mean he's up to his neck in it.

'But he didn't have it in mind for me, I was going to get out.

Education would be my passport out of Ulster. And it was. He went ballistic when he found out. His own convent-school daughter pregnant by some snotty little thug from Crossmaglen. My man was a killer by then. Eighteen and a killer. His first off-duty UDR man; shot him off his tractor in the middle of a field.'

She let out a scarcely audible sigh. 'The further away you are the more insane it seems. The stupid, pointless deaths. It's so medieval.'

Although he was aware of sectarian hatred in Scotland, it had had little impact on his life on Cual or here in Edinburgh. Northern Ireland seemed like another world to him, beyond his comprehension.

'I ran away, went to Belfast. The city. I stayed in a house on Arizona Street. Arizona – it sounds exotic, doesn't it? It wasn't. It was a cul-de-sac, in more ways than one. I lasted a couple of months; I was sick of it and filled with morning sickness and bile. So I said bugger the lot of you and fled the country. I haven't seen sight of them since. My aunt, who lives here in Edinburgh, took me in and I lived here and finished school and made the grades for the Dick Vet.'

'Will you go back?'

'I swore I'd never set foot in Ulster again.'

A week later he left for London. Oonagh drove him to the bus station and stood on the platform holding Sile's hand while he waved from the top deck. He slept all the way, and in the morning took the Tube to Islington and walked to the Almeida Theatre to watch the rehearsal.

The play went well, and received a favourable review in the *Guardian*, and at the party after the second night he was pressed for what he was going to write next. The truth was he had no idea. It made him feel vulnerable about the future. He retreated to the kitchen and shotgunned a couple of beers.

While he was standing with the ring-pull in his fingers and his lips curved around the puncture in the base of the second can, the window, on the fourth floor of a flat in Oxford Gardens, was flung open and his cousin Seb climbed in.

'All right, lover,' Seb greeted him. 'Give me a squeeze.'

They bear-hugged, all bulky jackets and segged boots skidding on the linoleum.

Cal handed him a beer. 'Gone off the stairs, have you?'

'Scaffolding, mate,' Seb grinned. 'Easier than trying to persuade someone to buzz me in.'

'How did you find me?'

'Made a few phone calls, followed the spoor, you know. Playwright. Ha!'

'When did you get back?'

'This morning. Flew out of Riyadh a couple of days ago. A quick stop-off in Germany to do my dhobi. Come on, let's go sit out on the ledge.' He produced a bottle of twelve-year-old Deochmore from inside his jacket. 'Scotch holiday?'

Cal fetched some glasses. They climbed out on to the scaffolding and sat with their backs to the outside wall, and looked out across Notting Hill.

Seb opened the whisky and poured them each a measure. 'Slainte.' He tipped back the glass and smacked his lips. 'All that time out in the desert and nothing to drink. Making up for it now. I spoke to that chick, what's she called? Al's girlfriend?'

'Kelly.'

'That's it. She said you've got a girlfriend.'

Cal nodded.

'Cunning,' Seb said. 'That's what I need. A rampant fucking.'

Seb was still in 'the company of men' mode. Wide of the mark. Or so Cal thought. Instead, Seb was searching his face; he was always conscious of the effect his words had. 'You're really serious?'

Wrong-footed, Cal nodded.

'That's a turn-up for the books.' Seb said. 'I'm pleased.'

'Thanks. How was the war?'

'Shite.' He sighed. 'We should have gone the whole way.'

'You mean Baghdad?'

'Sure. Why not? Stop Saddam gassing and burning his own people. I mean, who gives a fuck what Syria or Saudi Arabia thinks? Their precious coalition.' He glanced across at Cal. 'I'm sorry I missed your play. Congratulations.' They clinked glasses.

Cal asked, 'What was it like?'

'The war? Crude. Neat. Both, in fact. Beautiful, really. A fast and furious extravaganza.' He became thoughtful. 'The truth is I didn't want it to end.' He frowned. 'Is that sick?'

'I don't know,' Cal said. 'I guess I'd have to have been there. I saw the pictures of the Basra road.'

Seb nodded thoughtfully. 'We got there just after the planes had finished their work.' He paused. 'It was unreal. I don't mean it was surreal or weird; it just wasn't war. It was as if someone had opened a scrapyard but failed to put a fence round it. A vast, rambling, stinking mess. It wasn't my war.'

'What was your war?'

Seb took a long pull on the bottle. 'There's a funny thing about killing. It's not that it's addictive – that would be going too far – but it certainly gets easier, more attractive. After you've done it once you begin to understand that the only way to feel normal about it is do some more, to blur the distinction between one killing and another. It didn't take me long to get used to it. The length of a tunnel. Five minutes. You get better at it. And then you can look back and laugh at the person you were before it started, the person who was afraid. Once you're good, really good, you don't want it to end. That's what I meant, when I said that I didn't want it to end. You'd have understood, if you had been there.'

They sat in silence passing the bottle back and forth.

Eventually, Cal said, 'What now?'

Seb smiled. 'You mean my illustrious army career? I'm going for 14 Company.'

'What's that?'

'Undercover work in Northern Ireland. Special Forces, you know. I start selection in a month's time. I've got my fingers crossed. What about you?'

Cal sighed. 'Finals.'

Seb shook his head. 'Fuck that fer a game ay sodjirs.' Then he said, 'I'm flying to Hong Kong in the morning.'

'Leave?'

'Yeah. I've got myself booked on an RAF flight. I'm off on a quest in search of an Asian babe. Come on, let's go clubbing and get mortal. I'm paying.'

'Sounds good,' Cal said.

'Huge potatoes growing from your ears?' Cal frowned at this and focused on Oonagh, the steam rising off her skin and the beads of sweat on her upper lip.

She threw a sponge at him in friendly remonstration. 'I've been talking to you for five minutes and you haven't heard a word.'

Sile loomed over him holding out a tea cup from a child's play set. 'It's your coffee,' she said, with sparkling eyes.

'Thank you,' he mumbled. He set the lip of the cup against the upward curve of his chin and let the bathwater dribble out. He made contented slurping noises.

Sile grinned.

Oonagh said, 'What's the matter?'

'Nothing,' Sile said.

'I'm sorry,' Cal said. 'I was thinking.'

'I'm not blind. What about?'

'Seb.'

'Who's Seb?' Sile asked, clambering back over her mother's legs.

'The soldier,' Oonagh said. 'The one I . . . ?'

He nodded. The room was thick with steam.

'What is it?'

He sighed and shifted his legs to make them more comfortable. It was a tight squeeze, fitting them all in the bath. Sile asked, 'What's the matter?'

'I got a phone call from Madelene yesterday.'

'Who's Madelene?' Sile asked.

'A girl I know,' Cal replied. 'In fact, my cousin. It's complicated.'

Oonagh lifted an eyebrow at that. 'And?'

'Seb came back from leave in Hong Kong with a girlfriend. A Chinese girl. Taiwanese, in fact.'

'Which girl?' Sile asked.

'A girl from far away, who had to come in an aeroplane,' Cal explained. 'He took her to Cual to the estate and apparently things got weird. Well, actually pretty straightforward. She ditched Seb and moved in with his dad.'

'Charming,' Oonagh said.

'Seb's father is kind of a strange character. I think he's an arms-dealer. He's into free love and stuff.'

'I didn't know the two were connected.'

'What?'

'Free love and arms-dealing.'

'Oh. Well, they are in him. Seb's stormed off the island. Nobody's heard from him since. Madelene's worried.'

'Why?'

'Well, he's kind of unpredictable. I mean, I think he might blow something up.'

Her eyes narrowed speculatively. 'With a bomb?'

'That's what he does. I think he might blow up a building.'

'Christ!' Oonagh said, 'What is it with me?'

'What's the matter?' Sile asked. 'What did you say?'

'I don't think he'll hurt anyone,' Cal said quickly, not really convinced. 'I hope not, anyway.'

He woke to moonlight, and traces of phosphorescence behind his eyes. He was sure that he had heard a dog barking. At first he could make no sense of it.

Oonagh was asleep beside him, the covers fallen away from her chest. Cal peered into the moonlight, pressing his face against the glass of the window. It was difficult to see anything, but there seemed to be the silhouette of an unfamiliar car parked on the grass.

'What's her name?' a voice said, with weary familiarity. Seb was sitting in a chair, his feet up on the end of the bed. Moonlight lit half his face. 'I never did find out her name,' he said.

She was awake. She raised herself on to her elbows and stared at him with a boldness that caused Cal an almost physical hurt. She made no effort to cover herself. 'You must be Seb?'

A tongue of flame seemed to leap from his fingertips, and after it came a whiff of petrol. The light from his Zippo made devilish horns of his eyebrows. He lit a joint, the sweet smell of hash drifting up the bedcovers towards them.

'I never did thank you for that night,' he said. He passed her the joint and she took it. Their fingers brushed in the moonlight.

'I enjoyed fucking you immensely,' Seb told her pleasantly. 'I'd never tasted Irish.'

Her startled gasp was followed by an abrupt exhalation and a fit of coughing. Seb sniggered.

'Madelene phoned me,' Cal said, with a hint of peevishness.

'So you know that my father has acquired a new girlfriend. Soon to be his wife. Took her without asking,' he said wryly. 'Seems to me that it's open season on Seb's girls.'

'I'm nobody's girl,' Oonagh said defiantly. She passed Cal the joint, and he inhaled hungrily.

'I was kidding,' Seb said. 'It's called irony.'

'I was being hard and unfeeling,' Oonagh replied, with a smile. 'It's called steely.'

'I was a reddish-brown tinge,' Cal added, passing Seb the joint. 'It's coppery.'

'I'm insolent and brazen,' Oonagh retorted. 'Brassy.'

'Brass is an alloy,' Seb informed her.

Cal said, 'So is steel.'

'Therefore the girl loses,' Seb announced. 'She pays a forfeit.'

'So what do I have to do?' she asked archly.

'Come get in my car, drive away with me. Leave this sad, ugly bastard.'

'I have responsibilities,' she said. 'A kid.'

Seb said, 'I'm sure Cal will look after it.'

'I don't think so,' she said. 'I don't go off with guys on the rebound.'

'I'm not on the rebound,' he snapped. He kicked his feet off the bed and jumped up out of the chair.

'I'm not bitter,' she mocked him lightly.

There was a pause. It was difficult to gauge his reaction by moonlight.

'You've got a big mouth,' he said, finally. He added: 'I'm leaving.'

'Where are you going?'

'An undisclosed location in Herefordshire. They want to take a look at me and see if I'm suitably sneaky.'

'Is that the SAS?' Oonagh said. 'Or the SS?'

'14 Company, they call it,' he replied.

'How very understated of them,' she said. 'How very British.'

'So what do you think?' Seb asked. 'Is Seb secret squirrel material? Sufficiently stealthy?'

'I heard the dog barking,' Cal observed.

'I didn't think it would be polite to strangle her dog,' Seb replied.

'I have a name,' she said.

'Perhaps you'd like to share it with me,' he countered.

'Oonagh.'

'Oonagh.' He said it over to himself. 'I like it.'

He was smiling, the moonlight sparkling on his teeth. 'Have fun,' he said, gently. Then he was gone.

They heard a car door slam, and, a few seconds later, an engine start and wheels churn up the gravel.

Cal's final exam passed without fanfare, and as he drained a pint afterwards in the beer garden at the Pear Tree, surrounded by his fellow students, he reflected on the fact that in four years of studying English Literature he had made no close friends with which to celebrate its end. Oonagh still had a week to go and she was refusing to see him. Cal made an effort and shared some speed he'd been saving with one of the students from his tutorial, but it made him feel jittery and paranoid. He stayed for a few pints and then excused himself. No one seemed sad to see him go.

He thought that he would sit in the park but it had begun to cloud over and it no longer seemed like an agreeable idea. Instead he went into Deacon Brodie's on the Royal Mile. The courts had emptied and the bar was filled with witnesses and defendants, mostly overweight girls pushing buggies and pale, tattooed men in ill-fitting shiny suits.

Cal drank his first pint quickly and immediately ordered another.

Beside him, on a bar-stool a woman began mouthing words in venomous silence; she clenched her fists in rage. The barman paid no attention to her.

Cal was halfway through his second pint when she looked up at him.

'Is it you?' she asked.

'No,' he said. She smelled vaguely urinous.

'It isnae you,' she acknowledged, clearly disappointed.

Two long-haired youngish men came in and sat at the bar. One of them had a beard.

'Thair evil! Ay telt these cunts the score,' the woman told him. 'Naebody better try again, cause like ah sais, ah'll be right doon here n makin a loat ay allegations.'

Cal glanced at the bearded man, who was sniggering unpleasantly. The second man was younger and fair-haired. When Cal looked at him he raised the point of his chin and bared his teeth threateningly.

The woman yelled, 'Ah'm nae invisible!'

The barman was standing opposite the two men. He told them they couldn't sit there if they didn't order a drink.

They paid no attention to him. They were staring intently at Cal. Eventually he turned on his stool to face them. He and the two men looked at each other for a considerable period; when the exchange was over they slid down off their stools and left. He felt that they had come in for no other reason than to intimidate him. He felt truly paranoid.

'Ah mind what happened. I saw it aw.'

He didn't finish his pint. He backed fearfully out of the bar.

'I know,' she called out after him. 'I know.'

Tourists gave him a wide berth as he stared around him. The sun was out again and he had to squint against the glare. He was starving and he resolved to buy a baked potato on Cockburn Street but in the event he went into the City Café, thinking that Al might be there. He wasn't. He drank another pint alone. He phoned the flat from a payphone but it was engaged. He tried again from the railway station, after a whisky at the Hebridean, but it was still engaged; it was his guess that Al had left the phone off the hook. He cashed a cheque at the bureau de change after the cashpoint refused him. He bought a half-bottle of whisky in a brown paper bag and opened it as he crossed the roundabout by the Playhouse and staggered down Leith Walk.

He was just beyond Bostons, passing an open doorway, when a man put his hand on his shoulder. Turning, he felt a cold thrill of recognition dance on his spine.

The bearded man said, 'We've things to talk about.'

He did accents. No. He was really Irish. He nodded in a sinister and purposeful fashion. Cal felt the sharp point of a knife pressing into his kidneys.

The one with the knife, behind him, hissing with rancid breath, 'Move!'

Cal dropped the bottle and it shattered on the pavement. People stood and stared.

'Shit!'

They shoved him through a doorway into a darkened stairwell half filled with garbage sacks, and he skidded through a pool of recent vomit and fell over. The first kick caught him on the side of his jaw and broke several teeth. After the second or third kick he went into a sort of glide; the damp flagstones seemed to fall away beneath him. He knew what was happening – they were going to kill him.

They turned him over and the fair-haired one straddled him. His face was a sack of venom. The point of his knife hovered above Cal's right eye. 'Which eye, fucker, left or right?'

Cal shook his head. He felt cold; his tongue went up into the bloody pulp of his jaw, exploring the broken shards of teeth. The pain was like chalk on a blackboard.

The bearded one said, 'Cut the bastard up.'

The knife flicked through the gristle of his nose, spraying blood like red mist. The fair-haired one wiped a blob of froth from his lips with the back of his hand. He looked up at the bearded one. 'Shall I?'

'Enough,' said the bearded man. He squatted down beside Cal. 'Give me some nice simple answers.'

Cal nodded.

'Your name is Calum Bean, am I right?'

'Right,' Cal said, through a mouthful of blood.

'You're a student?'

'Right,' Cal said.

'Are you Catholic or Protestant?'

'Catholic.'

'Fucker. You go to church?'

'No.'

'Are you scared?' The fair-haired one stroked Cal's cheek with the tip of the blade.

'Yes,' Cal said. 'Yes.'

'Stay the fuck away from Oonagh O'Hara.'

Cal looked up at the bearded one in terror.

'Swear!'

'I swear . . . I swear . . . I'll stay away.' There were tears pooling in his eyes.

The fair-haired one seemed embarrassed. 'Let's cut him up some more.'

The bearded one said, 'You wouldn't lie to us, would you, Calum? You wouldn't go and phone her or arrange to meet her, would you?'

'No,' he whispered.

The bearded one nodded. He held out his hand. 'The knife.'

Reluctantly, the fair-haired one handed over the knife. He

glared at Cal for a full minute and then he went berserk. He punched him repeatedly and then shoved him under the stairs and began kicking him, the rubbish bins and the walls. Cal scrambled through a pile of loose garbage sacks and collapsed. After they had gone he began to crawl towards the door on to the street.

He could hear the buses on Leith Walk.

4

He heard the sound of approaching footsteps in the ward distantly, distorted as if he was submerged in water; they seemed to go on for a long time. His eyes travelled slowly across the high white ceiling and he explored the broken roots of his teeth with the tip of his tongue. Now the shadow of someone was leaning over the bed. Cal squinted through blackened, puffy eyes.

'What the fuck happened to you?'

'Seb,' he croaked.

'Never mind that.' There was a razor edge to Seb's voice: *The knife.* 'What happened?'

'I got beaten up.' He felt desperately humiliated. He whispered miserably, 'I'm not without courage.' His tongue was as uncomfortable as a lump of coal.

Seb was oblivious, furious. He snarled, 'Who by? We'll get them.'

'They're long gone,' Cal managed.

Seb was insistent. 'Gone where?'

'Back to Ireland.'

'Ireland?' Seb frowned, and just as suddenly the anger was gone, or rather redirected; stored with all the other fury roiling behind his ice-cold azure eyes. You had to know him to see it. 'That's too much of a detour. We don't have time. Come on, let's get you out of here. Sister!' He started rummaging in the cupboard by the bed for Cal's clothes.

Cal was sick of lying in bed. He'd been there for two days now and it was enough. Now he wanted to be out of Edinburgh. He sat up and swung his legs off the bed. 'Where are we going?'

'I've got a better idea for revenge. Something long overdue. Come on, get dressed.'

Seb gulped at the jug of water by the bed, and then thrust his hands in up to the wrists and ran them through his hair.

'Jock wash,' he explained. 'I've been sleeping in the car.'

Cal eased himself into a T-shirt.

'We're going on a road trip,' Seb told him.

Fifteen minutes later, despite the protestations of the nursing staff, they walked out of the Royal Infirmary on to the Edinburgh streets.

Seb strode round to the front of the hire car, into the oncoming traffic. He ripped the parking ticket off the windscreen, crumpled it in his fist and pitched it down into the well of the passenger seat, where it joined all the others.

'Get in,' he snarled, over the roof of the car and then, with that savage glint in his eye, he fixed the full force of his gaze on Cal. 'Let's burn tarmac.'

Cal dumped his bag on the back seat amongst the debris of newspaper meals, bolt-cutters and mud-caked boots, and climbed in the front seat and put his boots up on the dash.

'You mean Tarmac?'

'That's exactly what I mean.'

'Good,' Cal said, grimly.

Seb was intent. 'Give it a bit of wheel-spin, then go.'

They accelerated out of the parking space into the traffic amid a flurry of horns and squealing brakes. In town Seb drove as he spoke, in short, violent pulses; with the toe of his cowboy boot floored, on either the accelerator or the brake.

'Tosser,' he screamed out the window and gave someone the finger.

Cal asked, 'What's happened?'

Seb glanced across at him. 'What d'ya mean?'

'What's the matter?'

'Is it that obvious?'

'To me.'

Seb gripped the steering wheel harder. 'You know how difficult it was to find a red Calibra to match this one at short notice?'

'No,' Cal said, watching him.

The words rushed out of Seb as if he was using them as a bulwark against his gathering emotion. 'I found one two days ago off the Edgware Road, outside a detached house. I checked the electoral register: a Mr Abdul Arif. A British rag-head. An unexpected bonus. We're wearing his number plates; gathering parking tickets and speed-camera fines for him.' His voice was louder and more strident. 'I've opened a cell-phone account for Mr Arif. No proof of identity required. I reckon we've got seven days of free calls. The phone's on the floor somewhere. Give Madelene a call. She's in London selling paintings. The number is in the glove compartment. Tell her we'll meet her at Glastonbury in a couple of days. In the green field. Meanwhile, let's find you a butcher and get you a slab of meat for that eye. There's a brick of hash under your seat.'

Cal said, 'Tell me,'

Seb howled.

Cal shouted, 'What?'

Seb braked violently. Cal snatched at the dashboard. Seb slammed the horn with the heel of his palm. 'Fucker!'

He swung right in a U turn, pulled over to the side of the road and stuck the gear into neutral. He took his feet off the pedals.

'I failed 14 Company. I got thrown off the course yesterday. They said I wasn't fucking stable enough!'

Cal had never seen him so desperate. 'I'm sorry,' he said.

Seb was crying. 'I'm fucked. Truly fucked.' He paused and wiped his eyes. 'It was my one hope. What chance do I have now? I'm not a graduate. No one's going to make me a general.' His voice rose again, the fury welling up out of him. 'Special Forces, that's the only chance I had. The fucking SAS wouldn't take me because of my eyes. My fucking cripple eyes! I hate my eyes!'

'I had the crap knocked out of me. I feel like a fucking mental case. I'm not putting up with it. I'm leaving.' They were slumped on a walkway high in the scaffolding on the clock face of the North British Hotel, with Princes Street Gardens beneath them and Edinburgh all around them. 'Fuck them all,' Seb agreed, popping open another bottle of Beck's with his Swiss army knife. The beer and the long, dangerous climb seemed to have calmed him down.

'I'm never coming back,' Cal said. 'You can call me a coward if you want.'

'They've gone,' Seb said. 'There's nothing you can do now. There's nothing either of us can do. We're in desperate straits.'

Cal shifted among the empty bottles littering the walkway. 'What are you going to do?'

Seb shrugged. 'What does any fucker do? Hang on. Fight off the day I have to take a McJob. What about you?'

'I just want to be left alone,' Cal said miserably.

'I want to do something immense,' Seb countered. 'Huge. The biggest fucking thing.'

'I want to disappear off the face of the earth.'

'I want to be special.'

The only thing about Cal that felt special was the degree to which he experienced the shallowness of his personality and the emptiness of his own words.

'I want money so that I don't have to think about it,' he said. 'I don't want to be frightened or scared. I just want to live. Survive. I want the freedom to live.'

Seb lifted his bottle. 'The freedom to live. You've got be committed if that's what you want. You've got to be prepared to grab the wolf by the ears.'

He howled at the sky.

Cal woke up, lifted the raw steak off his eye and looked around. The windows were obscured with mud. Seb switched on the windscreen wipers, and they squealed and slowly scooped an arc of glutinous brown mud off the screen. It was dark outside.

Seb was howling with laughter. 'We're a sorry pair of fuckers.'

Cal acknowledged the comment with a wry smile. He asked, 'Where are we?'

'A field.'

Cal scratched his head and peered through the smeary windscreen. He nodded with his lower lip out. 'A field.'

Seb agreed. 'A fuck-off big field.'

'Why?'

'Mud,' said Seb with customary certainty.

'How much mud?'

'Too much. More than I really wanted. I got a bit carried away with the mud motif.'

'Not a dusting, then?'

'More like a bath. We couldn't just pitch up at Glastonbury in a pristine red hire car. Think of the embarrassment. We needed character. Fucker doesn't even have four-wheel drive.'

'Really? I don't think it comes as standard in hire cars.'

'I had to know,' Seb said, emphatically.

'Don't you get enough of this stuff at work?'

'You can never have enough lying about in the mud.' He flexed his shoulders, his lips twisting in a smile, or an apology, or some combination of the two. 'Well, when I say that, I don't include this situation.'

Cal considered this, then wound down the window and dropped the steak out of it. He turned back to Seb. 'Push?'

Seb snorted. 'Down to the axles, mate. Halfway to China. Don't worry, I phoned the AA. Fancy a swim?'

They waded through the mud that surrounded the car and Seb opened the boot and took out a chamois-wrapped package. He unfolded it and revealed the original number plates.

'We better put these back on,' he said.

Before he closed the boot, Cal caught a glimpse of a propane gas cylinder nestled among twenty-five-kilo fertiliser bags.

'You take the front,' Seb instructed him.

After switching the plates they struggled through the field to the track that ringed it and followed it under a railway line and up on to the road. They sat on a crash barrier and smoked cigarettes.

Cal said, 'You're serious about Tarmac.'

'I've got all the ingredients,' Seb agreed.

Cal considered this for some time. Beside him, Seb smoked patiently.

'Nobody gets killed, right?'

'Right.'

'I mean it.'

'So do I.'

Cal nodded. 'Count me in.'

He was rewarded with a familiar Seb grin; that impish combination of mischief and disingenuous humility. He was limbering up.

'I'll do the expressions,' Seb warned him.

When the AA man arrived he turned out to be from Dundee, ex-Black Watch, square and blocky like an industrial fridge-freezer and covered in what looked like millscale but turned out to be tattoos.

'High jinks, eh?'

Whether he was referring to the state of the car or Cal's face was not revealed. Seb grimaced winningly.

The AA man ratcheted the car out of the field by hand, pumping the lever with the blue-veined fencework of his forearms and biceps. They watched in open admiration.

'He's a big fucker,' whispered Cal.

'If he takes a shine to you,' Seb said, 'remember to fake an orgasm.'

'Awright,' pronounced the AA man, slightly short of breath, as the car mounted the track. 'I'll be on my way, then. Don't forget to give us a call the next time you get stuck in a field.'

'You'll be the first to know,' Seb assured him, and slipped him a tenner. 'You'll keep this under your hat, eh? A simple breakdown, something electrical. Nothing much to remember.'

'My mind is blank,' the AA man agreed.

Back in the car, Cal asked, 'Where to?'

'Southbound. London first. Then revenge.'

They parked in Kensal Rise, beneath a broad-leaf lime tree in a street of suburban semi-detached houses that had been broken up into flats.

Seb produced a house key. 'Media types. I know him from school. Sometimes I crash here. Sleep on the floor, you know. Thought I might as well get a key cut. They're in Dublin making a film about the IRA. Stephen Rea's in it. It's fucking ironic when you think about it. Piquant.'

The flat took up the ground floor; a bedroom, a bathroom, a small kitchen and a sitting room with French windows taking up one wall. Staring through the glass Cal saw that there was a small garden overgrown with rose bushes. The room was bright and comfortable, filled with hand-printed fabrics in primary colours. He walked through the flat. On the bedroom walls there was a set of framed photographs of a naked man and woman. They were blonde and good-looking, and clearly unselfconscious.

Seb opened a bottle of wine.

They carried the fertiliser in under cover of darkness and used a coffee grinder to reduce it and the caster sugar to a fine powder. Seb built the timer in an ice cream carton, using nails, batteries, twinflex, a wooden dowel pin and a parkway timer. When he had finished and taped it to the main body of the explosives, he said, 'Well I'm not hanging around here. I've arranged to meet Ed Crowe at the Market Bar on the Portobello Road.'

Nothing unpleasant ever seemed to pierce the bubble of Ed's karma. A smile was rarely far away. He acknowledged the state of Cal's face with an expression of bland incuriousness and proceeded to take Seb by the upper arm and steer him between tables towards the back of the bar.

'There's something I want to talk to you about,' he said. 'A proposal.'

Seb asked, 'Here?'

Ed laughed. 'No, not here. These are just marketing people and trustafarians. The anthropologically interested. You want a bottled beer?'

'I'll have a pint,' Seb said, jutting out his chin, and raising his nose as if to catch a scent. 'Introduce me to some of the chicks at that table.'

'That's my boy. One of these girls is doing a marketing job for the Lebanese Tourist Board. Explore Beirut, that kind of thing. No mean feat.'

Cal followed them, reluctantly.

'Shakti, Alice, Tara, this is Seb,' Ed said, to the men and women gathered round the table, 'and this is his friend Frankenstein.' He slapped Cal on the back. 'Only joking. These guys are from the Hebrides.'

'Really?' enquired the girl called Alice, between puffs on a Silk Cut. She was wearing a black silk puffa jacket and had a swathe of strong blond hair. Her voice was hoarse and expensive. 'I've just been to Iona. It's so spiritual.'

'Aye, right enough. There's a lot of spirits on Cual,' observed Cal.

'Seven distilleries, in fact,' Seb added dryly.

The man who called himself Shakti said, 'We were at school together.' Everyone at the table watched him. He pushed his lank shoulder-length hair away from his face and sniffed. 'You scored at the Wall Game.'

'No,' Seb said coldly.

'Yeah, it was you.'

'It was my brother.' His searching gaze was already drifting away across the bar.

Cal regained consciousness late that morning curled round the bomb in the kitchen of the flat in Kensal Rise. Someone had thrown a jacket over him. He got up and opened the door. Alice gave him a cursory glance as she passed him in the corridor. She was wearing a bathrobe and chewing on a cigarette. Ed followed her out of the bedroom and grinned smugly at Cal. Alice went into the bathroom and turned on the shower.

Ed asked, 'You want some coke?'

Cal shook his head. Ed shrugged and wandered through into the sitting room. Cal went after him. Seb and Tara were playing backgammon at the table, surrounded by crumpled notes, cigarette packets and beer bottles. Seb looked up as he entered.

Tara let out a stifled scream. 'What is this shit? Who is he?'

It seemed like an excessive reaction to the state of his face. Obviously she didn't remember him. It was like he'd been invisible all night.

'He's a friend,' Seb explained, lighting a cigarette. Ed flopped down on the sofa and closed his eyes. Tara glared at Cal for a while, but then seemed to lose interest. She returned to staring at the backgammon board.

Seb rubbed his eyes. 'I'm knackered,' he said. 'And broke.'

Tara managed a wasted grin.

'This bitch,' Seb said cheerfully. He drank his whisky. 'You guys better take this party elsewhere. Cal and I have some revenge to do.'

Ed nodded slowly. He stood up lazily and shook himself like a dog shedding water. 'That's cool.'

'You better drop those two off,' Seb told him.

'I'll take care of them.'

Alice emerged from the shower and got dressed without comment.

When they had all filed outside, Seb stood in the doorway looking at Ed. 'I'll see you again, in a few days.'

'Sure enough,' Ed replied. 'We'll talk. I'll run some more ideas by you.'

They heard an engine start up outside. Seb closed the door and went back through into the sitting room and lay on the sofa.

Cal asked, 'What was that?'

'Stuff. Ideas and plans,' Seb explained. 'Money-making schemes.'

'What kind of schemes?'

'Ed wants me to go into partnership with him. Moving weight, you know.'

'Drug-smuggling?'

'He thinks I'd be good at it.' He pressed a cushion against his forehead. 'I'm going to get a couple of hours' kip. Then we'll head down to the coast.'

Cal asked, 'Are you going to do it?'

Seb lifted the cushion off his face. 'What's with all these questions?'

Cal shrugged.

Seb said, 'I told him I'd think about it. Maybe, you know. Hell, why not? I've got nothing to lose.' He replaced the cushion and was almost instantly asleep.

The wind off the Channel snapped at the yew trees and crows shifted and squawked, despite the darkness and the rain. It was a seventeenth-century manor house, set back from the road and surrounded by trees. The road was quiet and they drove past it several times without headlights.

'This isn't quite what I expected,' Cal said hesitantly. 'I mean, I thought we were going to blow up some offices. Maybe a lorry park, a factory.'

'No,' Seb told him. 'We're going to the top. Executive director. Where the buck stops. These characters rake in share options and bumper dividends but they don't take personal responsibility. It's time they did. They call themselves the captains of industry. It's a fucking insult.'

'What about the driver?'

Seb replied with chilling zeal. 'The driver died of a heart attack last year. He'd had three strokes and five years of anonymous hate mail. He was a lackey. Who worked him into the ground? Who made him work longer hours? Who killed my mother? Who killed your mother?' He pointed at the house. 'That's the man.'

Cal said, 'I'm not participating in murder.'

Seb regarded him in self-righteous silence. Then he said, 'He's on holiday in Provence with his family. Two weeks in June. Every year.'

'All right, I believe you,' Cal stated. He sighed and added, 'You know, things aren't great right now. Not for either of us. I don't know what I'm capable of, let alone you.'

Seb dismissed this remark with a curt nod. He had turned his attention to the stark black outline of the hexagonal brick chimneys. 'Fire for fire. We're going to burn down his house.

Destroy all those irreplaceable mementos. Cinder his kids' toys and his wife's tapestries.' He glanced across. 'That's what I'm capable of – what about you?'

Cal was still sweating from all the alcohol working its way out of his pores. 'Are we going to get away with this?'

Seb nodded. 'Oh yes. Thanks to the Justice Department.'

Cal had heard of the Justice Department. They were a cell of animal-rights activists already responsible for a number of bombings across the country.

'It's tidy,' Seb explained. 'Our man's master of the hunt. It seems the local hunt's awash with the nouveau riche.'

'OK, Seb.'

They went back through the empty village, past the church, and followed the road leading out to the dual carriageway. A mile short of the junction Seb turned off the road on to a narrow, overgrown track that went up a steep incline on to the Downs. He parked next to a stile.

'We walk in,' Seb said, pulling two pairs of gloves out of the glove compartment.

'Let's get it over with,' Cal said.

Cal hefted the propane cylinder onto his shoulder while Seb loaded the bomb and the detonator into a backpack. He navigated with the aid of an Ordnance Survey map and a pencil-thin red-filtered torch. There was no moon. As they reached the crest of the Downs, the wind off the Channel whipped at their legs and the exposed flesh of their faces. The rain had reduced to a light drizzle.

'Two more miles,' Seb said.

Cal groaned beneath the weight of the cylinder.

The valley was spread out beneath them, dense, dark clusters of trees and houses like islands surrounded by a sea of broad, featureless arable fields. Somewhere in the distance were the Channel and the Seven Sisters. The outline of the manor house, with its huge chimneys, was clearly distinguishable.

They followed the path down through a sprawl of gorse and across a field of rape, scaled the flint wall and found themselves in a flowerbed in the grounds of the house.

Seb pointed at a shadowy alcove on the floodlit terrace. His teeth gleamed white in the darkness. 'There's the door. Ready?'

Cal said, 'Sure.'

Seb produced a crowbar from his pack. Cal felt a sudden rush of excitement.

They went low and fast across the lawn and up the stone steps on to the terrace. Seb used the crowbar to force the lock of the glass-panelled door.

They went down the narrow wood-panelled corridor until they reached the main hall. Seb unslung his backpack and reached in for the bomb; he slapped it against the side of the gas cylinder, and the magnet held it.

He consulted his watch. 'Seven minutes.'

Cal frowned. 'What?'

'We tripped the alarm. The police take nine minutes to get here.'

'Shit!'

Seb removed the lid from the ice-cream box, connected the battery and ran his fingertips in a slow and orderly action across the circuit, the pins and wires, as if he was reading Braille.

Cal struggled with what seemed like a reflex. Run.

Seb grasped the end of the dowel pin between the forefinger and thumb of his right hand. He grinned at Cal. 'Happy?'

'Ecstatic.'

Seb looked at his watch. 'Now,' he whispered. He removed the pin.

The parkway timer started to click as it turned.

Click.

Seb replaced the lid on the box.

Click.

'Run.'

Click.

Cal paused for a breathless second on top of the wall at the end of the garden and looked back down the valley at the flashing blue light of an approaching police car. It was still a couple of miles away.

Beside him, Seb grinned. 'Dead on time.'

They were halfway across the rape field when the bomb exploded. A few minutes later, standing on the top of the Downs, at the highest point for miles, they paused and looked back at the firestorm.

'For Mum. For both of them.'

Cal nodded, too out of breath to speak.

*　　*　　*

UNDERWOLVES

'That,' Seb said, pointing at the car, 'sounds like a skeleton wanking in a dustbin.' The rattling had started as they tore up the M23 towards London. By the following morning it was pronounced, a death rattle. 'I say we torch it.'

They were leaning against the bonnet, in the forecourt of a Safeway in Wandsworth, contemplating the car; it was dented and filthy. The cleanest thing about it was the number plates – the pristine originals restored to their rightful place.

'Best thing for it.' Cal was jittery and exhausted and running on left-over adrenalin. 'Torch the bastard.'

They rested for a few minutes – they still hadn't slept – and then Seb walked around the back of the car and removed his backpack from the trunk. Whatever he thought they might need or might identify them as the bombers he stuffed into his backpack. Cal recovered his bag.

Seb filled a syringe from his pack with petrol from the can and squirted it into the radio-cassette. He waved his Zippo back and forth in front of it until it started to waft smoke, and then he climbed out of the car and called out halfheartedly, 'Fire!'

He walked in a wide circle around the car. When an over-enthusiastic shelf-stacker rushed out with a fire-extinguisher; Seb was forced to trip him up and send him sprawling into a row of trolleys.

'Sorry old chap,' he said. 'Didn't see you coming.'

People started rushing out of the supermarket. Cal sat on a bench at a safe distance and watched the burning car. Seb joined him. 'Here goes.' The petrol tank exploded. 'Exquisite,' he drawled. He looked at Cal, and arched an eyebrow.

Cal said, 'Thanks, Seb.'

Seb grinned loopily. 'Don't mention it.'

'I mean it. Thanks. It was good to do something – about Mum, I mean.'

'I know what you mean.'

Eventually the fire brigade arrived. After they had doused the wreckage Seb called the rental company and they delivered a new car within an hour. They were back on the road.

It was a great night, except that they couldn't find any hitch-hikers to pick up. They slept that day at a service station on the M4, Seb in the front and Cal spread out across the back seat, and when they awoke it was night-time and Glastonbury had started. They broke open a bottle of whisky, drove west and pulled off at every junction and petrol station searching for hitch-hikers but, to Seb's increasing frustration, they found none.

'It's outrageous.'

'It's a shame.' Cal struggled, and then folded over, coughing, surrounded by smoke. They'd been making serious inroads into the hashish since waking.

'I mean I've got drugs, I've got drink. Where the fuck are they?'

'It's the wall,' Cal whispered, his eyes watering. 'It's keeping them away.'

'I'll throw them over the wall!' Seb shouted.

They skirted police roadblocks, abandoned the car in the car-park of a pub in East Pennard and hiked down a re-entrant on a compass bearing. The rain had lifted and the night was starry. They crossed one of the tributaries of the River Whitelake, climbed the bank and spent five silent, motionless minutes in a hedge listening to someone coughing, until they both dissolved into giggles.

'Cows.'

They ran across the field, and over the old railway track and were at the ten-foot wall. Seb was first to the wall, turning as he struck it, the shock of techno beat coming through the surface of the wall and across his shoulder-blades, hands forming a stirrup on his knee, lifting Cal up and on to the wall.

Seb took a few steps back while Cal steadied himself on the crest of the wall, skylined by strobe-lights, then took a running jump and the momentum carried him into Cal's grip. Cal pulled him up and together they dropped down into the site and within seconds were surrounded by milling ravers and strobe-lights. Ecstasy.

They whooped like Red Indians.

Cal followed the dirt path toward the top of the field, past haphazard clusters of tepees and tents and the low murmuring of those still awake as they huddled round bonfires – it was just after dawn – while the thumping beat drifted up from the larger fields beneath them.

Madelene was holding court around an enormous bonfire,

flanked by a posse of New Age admirers. Cal went right through the centre of the bonfire and slumped in front of her. She gathered his head in her hands, and the tips of her fingers moved across the surface of his bruised and blackened face, exploring his nostrils and mouth, tracing the broken roots of his teeth with gathering wonderment. Her head darted in and within seconds the tip of her tongue was probing the wound. They slumped back on the grass and she rolled over on top of him. Cal was dimly aware that someone was cheering.

'Have you got them?' She clung sinuously to his chest.

He knew exactly what she meant. 'My teeth? No. I wasn't really thinking of art at the time,' he explained.

She pouted.

'I'm fine,' Cal said. 'Nice of you to ask.'

She grinned. 'Of course you are. Ed told me. He's here somewhere.'

'Really?' Cal said dryly.

'You don't like him, do you? He can be tiresome. Where's Seb?'

'Asleep by a fire, down there somewhere.' He pointed down the path in the general direction.

'My wounded hero,' she said huskily. 'My very own.'

He essayed a smile. 'I came to say goodbye.'

They parted on Sunday night, at a junction on the M4. Seb pulled over to the side of the roundabout and let him out. He clutched his backpack and a small cardboard sign with 'Cornwall' written on it in black marker pen.

Escape.

Madelene was furious – he could read it in the mask-like stillness of her skin – angrier than he had ever seen her. He didn't understand.

'You'll let us know where you are?' Seb said.

He nodded, but more out of reflex than agreement. 'I'll find a job on the boats. When I'm settled . . .'

Seb looked away, and tapped the steering wheel in irritation.

Cal stepped back from the verge.

Seb called, 'You want to leave it like this?'

'Like this.'

He began to tremble, for no reason that he could fathom. His eyes followed the cars heading for the M5 and the South-West. 'I better get going,' he said. 'I'll miss the light.'

'You're mad,' Seb told him.

Cal saluted him. 'Crazy motherfucker,' he said. Suddenly, he felt strangely elated.

Seb was smiling. 'You can't just disappear.'

'Try me.'

Madelene hissed, 'Drive.' She would not look at him.

Seb waved. 'Be careful,' he said.

They went out of his life.

5

It was a game they played. They lounged on the bonnet of the sand-caked Landcruiser, affecting unconcern.

'Mountains,' Mukhambetov said. 'Ravines.' He had his gaze fixed on the shimmering, gelid haze in the indistinguishable distance. It was probably Iraq, but it was difficult to tell; there was no clearly delineated border. Major Shamil Mukhambetov, United Nations Monitor, was thinking of his home in the north Caucasus.

Chechnya. Not Russia. At the farthest edge of Europe, a war just waiting to happen.

'Forests,' Seb returned, savouring his own memories. He shook the sand out of his goggles. 'This time of year Kintyre is silver and red and bright orange like an autumn bonfire.'

'Wild pear and hazelnut,' Mukhambetov mused. 'There was a time when your country, also, was upon the outermost edge of the civilised world.'

Seb adopted a scholarly tone and added, 'Scotland is the furthest place from paradise on the *Mappa Mundi*.'

A camel spat. The bedou, mostly young boys cradling Kalashnikovs, watched the jewel-studded Rolex on Mukhambetov's cable-thick wrist with predatory interest.

'This place is pretty medieval,' Seb added.

The other six members of the team, the Bangladeshi, the Pakistani, the Argentinian, the two Americans, the Chinese, were retreating; putting as much space as possible between them and the bedou with the anti-tank missile, a Russian-made RPG-7.

'But with the entire range of modern weaponry,' observed Mukhambetov, and then, 'So . . . ?'

Seb shook his head, smiling. 'Your hardware. You sold it to them.'

'The Russians sold it to them.' Mukhambetov corrected him.

'I'm sorry. I keep forgetting. Is that not a Russian army uniform you're wearing?'

Mukhambetov gave him a withering glance. 'So I understand that if it was a piece of British hardware you would go?'

'Of course.'

'If I die you must visit my aunt who lives in Grozny,' said Mukhambetov, his English slow and deliberate. 'She will make you a cup of tea.'

'I'm gasping for a cuppa,' Seb agreed.

Mukhambetov eased himself down off the bonnet, and started walking in his distinctive loping stride towards the bedou, who was striking the diamond-shaped nose of the RPG-7 missile against the hard-packed sand.

'Maybe he's drilling for oil?' Seb called out.

The big Chechen dismissed him with a wave.

Seb watched as he stood over the small wiry bedou with his hands cupped. The bedou studied him suspiciously and then with some reluctance handed him the missile. Mukhambetov squatted down beside him, and for five minutes turned the stalk of the weapon over in his hands, pointing out features; the sight mechanism and trigger housing. He stood up and set the missile against his shoulder in demonstration. He handed it back to the bedou. A minute later they were enfolded in a blanket of dark smoke and kicked-up dust. The missile streaked away across the demilitarised zone into Iraq. The bedou emerged from the smoke, grinning through the blackened stumps of his teeth.

Mukhambetov sauntered back to the Landcruiser.

The Pakistani slammed the door of the Portakabin that served as a communal eating area and hurried to catch up with the Bangladeshi. He had a large white bandage covering his ear. Seb and Mukhambetov, seated on a rock, watched them hurry across the sand to their Portakabin. Mukhambetov removed the cap from a bottle of Absolut and flicked it at the chain-link fence that ringed the UN compound. He never put the cap back on a bottle.

'They're furious,' Mukhambetov explained, with great weariness. 'The Americans are cooking pork sausages again. And beans. In the microwave. They are so typically, effortlessly American.'

Tonight it was the Americans' turn to cook. It was an occasion that came round every seven days and few of the members of the UN mission looked forward to it.

'You're not eating?'

'I'm an unruly savage from the mountains,' Mukhambetov replied. He tipped the neck of the vodka bottle at Seb and swigged a mouthful. 'A secularist, but religious too. I don't eat pork. Here.'

Seb took the bottle from him. 'I hate beans,' he said. 'They remind me of school.'

'Ah yes, the harsh regime of the English public school. The playing fields of Eton, buggery, communism.'

'Give it a break,' Seb said with the bottle held to his lips. The astringent liquor burned his throat, and turned his empty stomach. He passed the bottle back. 'What happened to his ear?'

Mukhambetov looked at him. 'You don't know?'

'I've been sleeping. Then I went for a run. You're the first person I've spoken to.'

'A camel spider made a midnight snack of him.'

'Jesus,' Seb said, disgusted. He had a thing about camel spiders and had already incinerated a couple of them with a makeshift flame-thrower he had constructed from an aerosol can. Their venom was supposed to be a powerful local anaesthetic; they paralysed their prey and then ate it at leisure.

'He didn't secure his door properly. He woke up with the spider on his face.'

Seb shook his head. 'This place.'

'I am leaving tomorrow,' Mukhambetov announced.

Seb was surprised. 'Really?'

'I have a new job in Kuwait City as a translator. I'm sick of the desert.'

'You don't speak Arabic.'

Mukhambetov shrugged and took another swig. 'I'm a Muslim so they think I speak Arabic. I lied. I'll hire some Bangladeshis to do the job for me. Kuwait's awash with them. It will leave me more time for outside interests.' He grinned wolfishly. He meant more time to make money. 'Don't worry. I still have to come out to the desert for business.'

Seb was aware that the Chechen bought alcohol, among other things, from the travelling bedou market that operated in the demilitarised zone, and sold it on, with an astronomical mark-up, to certain well-established clients in Kuwait City. He had a feeling that this was not the full extent of Mukhambetov's activities.

Seb said, 'I'll miss your garlic beef and pitta.'

'You watch out for spiders,' Mukhambetov told him.

'All routes to money are devious, Sebastian, and none guaranteed.' Mukhambetov pushed the brick of black Afghan hashish across the glass-topped table. Afghanistan was the dark destroyer in Mukhambetov's imagination. The deepest, darkest place. As a reconnaissance company commander, working in the Kandahar region and dressed as a Mujahedeen, he had been responsible for ambushing guerrilla bands and torching native villages. Villages full of fellow Muslims. Women and children. When he had drunk enough vodka, at least a bottle, he was prone to start describing the atrocities that he had participated in. It had caused a great deal of tension out in the desert.

He was sober now.

'I still have colleagues in Kandahar,' he said.

Beside him a Bangladeshi fed thousand-dinar notes into the hopper of an electronic money-counter and noted his findings in a child's exercise book. Between batches he paused, sipped at a tiny cup of espresso, and deftly snapped a rubber band round the bundle before tossing it into a cardboard box. The blue-and-white tiled floor of the hotel room was littered with cardboard boxes stacked with bundles of money.

Mukhambetov's fingers had grown chunky with a line of gold rings since the last time Seb had seen him. He explained, 'They're all forged; dropped by the CIA on southern Iraq during the air war to destabilise the economy. I recovered a whole palette of dinars.' He wrinkled his nose and grinned. 'The bedou give me a rate and offload them in the north on the Kurds. Thank God for America. How much hash you want? One tonne, a hundred tonnes?'

It was some time since Ed Crowe had made his proposition in London. At the time Seb's reaction had been deliberately open-ended and vague. He had no desire to work for Ed; his sense of self-preservation required a greater degree of control than that. But the proposition had intrigued him, and he remembered deciding he might be able to utilise some of Ed's contacts in the drug world if the right opportunity presented itself.

Since his failure to pass selection for 14 Company, and his subsequent posting to the demilitarised zone, the hunger in him to risk everything on some heroic scheme had been growing stronger with each day. He had come to understand that anything was possible.

'You want to smoke some hashish?'

Seb declined.

'Come on,' urged the Chechen. 'You're on leave.'

'I have to see the Colonel first, sign the leave book,' Seb told him. He still maintained a rigid separation between his two lives; it was, as he often stated, the secret to his survival in the army. 'Maybe afterwards.'

'How long have you got?'

'Nine days.'

Mukhambetov sank back on the sofa, with his arms outstretched. 'Come to Chechnya.' He seemed to be studying him shrewdly. 'There's someone who wants to meet you.'

Seb considered this. 'Who?'

Mukhambetov grinned. 'A friend.'

'KGB? Whatever you call yourselves now? Federal Security Bureau?'

Mukhambetov laughed in his face. Politely, he joined in the laughter.

'You shouldn't listen to folklore,' Mukhambetov said.

Seb tried to stare him down.

'However,' Mukhambetov conceded, 'it's not inconsistent that these people were once KGB. Now they are for the free market. Most of all, for independence in Chechnya. You see, they know about you because I told them. In something like this, moving weight I mean, they have to know.'

'Sure,' Seb said, gnawing his lip. 'They'd have to know.'

'So come.'

He looked back at Mukhambetov and found him grinning. 'What are you doing to me?'

'Don't worry,' Mukhambetov said. 'They'll take a look at you, talk to you, show you the product, and then if you are happy they will disappear. You are not supposed to know about them, and they don't want to know about you. It's just you and me. They will not bother you.'

'Unless I fuck you over?'

Mukhambetov smiled. His eyes seemed as flat as a snake's. 'It's the way we do business. Are you coming?'

He was aware that he had reached a defining moment in his life;

if he accepted what was offered, forces would be unleashed that might prove impossible to rein back in. Seb in the whirlwind.

He had been kicked back at every turn, overshadowed, badly used and undervalued; now was his chance to define himself in unique terms. To take the offer was to begin again from nothing, to live anew. I'll take it, he thought.

'All right.'

'I have to go out to the desert first. You take a flight to Cyprus, book into a hotel in Limassol. Put that down in your leave book.'

It was dawn and Seb was preparing to leave Cyprus. The plane's turboprops were turning, its landing-lights switched on. He recognised it as a Soviet-era Cub An-12, a four-engine transport aircraft. He recited its features like a reassuring mantra: speed 777kph, combat radius 3600 km, capacity ninety troops or two armoured personnel carriers. The belly of this aircraft had disgorged just three men in black leather coats and fur hats. They had scurried down the steps and across the tarmac to the waiting Mercedes, each carrying a bulky suitcase.

'Cash deposits,' Mukhambetov muttered, his eyes following the car as it sped away. He was wearing an immaculately pressed uniform and peaked cap.

His cellphone beeped, and he answered it. 'That's us,' he said.

They ran towards the fuselage door. In the cockpit a white face was staring at them without discernible expression. The inside of the plane was bare except for bundles of webbing, and steel crates lashed to the side bars for seats. They taxied for take-off, the air howling in the cavernous space, and then they climbed, banking steeply.

'It is a surprise to me that there is any money left in Russia to steal,' Mukhambetov yelled as he dropped down beside Seb and handed him a flask of vodka.

'Those were your people?'

'No! Cossack scum.' He smiled. 'We're just a couple of stowaways. Let's hope there's enough fuel.'

'To hell with getting old.' Seb drank deeply, and returned the flask. He leant back against the webbing and closed his eyes.

Hours later, responding to a change in the plane's engines, Seb shook himself awake. They were losing height rapidly.

'It's a rare talent,' Mukhambetov said, 'to be able to sleep in such conditions.'

Seb scratched his head. Mukhambetov was grinning, his eyes shining brightly. Seb guessed that he'd made serious inroads into the flask of vodka. He wondered if it was any indication of the amount of danger they were in.

The plane was hurtling through immaculate blackness. 'They have runway lights here?'

Mukhambetov shrugged. 'Maybe they didn't pay their electricity bill.'

The lights came on at the last possible moment. The plane didn't so much land as slamdunk; it was as if a fist had taken hold of it and slapped it down on the tarmac. The passengers were flung forwards by the impact.

'Welcome to Russia,' Seb muttered, extricating himself from the webbing. It felt as if his arms had been dislocated.

'Dagestan,' Mukhambetov corrected him. He opened the fuselage door, and together they peered out. The plane taxied, engines roaring, past a row of Hind ground-attack helicopters.

'A place called Kizlyar. The Russians refuel their fighters at the airbase here, and they use helicopters from here to insert so-called mercenaries to stir up trouble in my country.' He looked thoughtful and sober. 'Someday I'll come back here.'

'How about concentrating on getting out of here first,' Seb suggested. Mukhambetov only grinned.

He dropped to the tarmac and Seb followed. As they trotted warily across the tarmac, an army jeep raced towards them out of the darkness. It screeched to a halt in front of them and the driver, in a long grey overcoat, jumped out and embraced Mukhambetov. A swift conversation followed. The man in the overcoat climbed back in the jeep, and Mukhambetov and Seb climbed over the tailboard into the back. The jeep took off across the air base. Mukhambetov remained silent. They passed rows of single-storey barrack huts and playing fields and a squad of Russian soldiers in tracksuits jogging on the road. Seb wondered how he was going to explain being arrested on a Russian airbase in the Caucasus.

The jeep slowed as they neared a checkpoint barrier. The driver stopped the jeep and waited for the sentry to approach.

He wore a thick grey overcoat like the driver's and he was carrying a Kalashnikov. He stared impassively through the window at them. Mukhambetov removed an envelope from inside his uniform jacket and passed it over the driver's shoulder. The envelope changed hands quickly, and the sentry stood away from the jeep and the barrier rose.

Within minutes they were careering down the main road towards Chechnya. Mukhambetov started to remove his uniform.

Chechens in camouflage fatigues, guns resting on their shoulders, came up through the wooded ravine towards them. They moved silently, like wraiths in the early-morning mist. Mukhambetov and his companions stood up from the campfire and waited to greet them. Seb climbed self-consciously to his feet. The arriving Chechens propped their Kalashnikovs and hunting rifles against a beech tree, and the two groups threw arms around each other in the traditional Chechen greeting. It was, he imagined, like watching scorpions mating.

The tallest of the newcomers stopped in front of Seb. He wore a Sufist's grey beard that obscured his mouth and long, straight grey-white hair that reached below his shoulders. Secured to the crown of his head was a small beaded skull-cap with a tassel. His eyes were startling, so clear that they were almost colourless. Seb looked into them, and what he saw there, the cruelty and coldness, did not seem human at all. It put Mukhambetov in the shade.

'Welcome, Sebastian MacCoinneach,' the newcomer said in clear and precise English. They embraced. A stale, dry smell came off his skin like camphor.

'I am Dzukhokar Imayev.'

The Chechens sat together around the campfire. Only Imayev, Mukhambetov and Seb remained standing.

'You know what I have been reading?' Imayev said. 'I have been reading your father's file.'

Mukhambetov appeared embarrassed and would not look at Seb. Imayev shook his head thoughtfully. He looked, not unkindly, into Seb's eyes. 'What shall we do with you?'

It occurred to Seb that he was about to be shot as the son of a spy and probably dumped at the bottom of a ravine for the wolves to fight over. He'd seen wolf prints while brushing his teeth down at the river that morning. It seemed a fitting punishment for being so naive. By rights he should have something snappy to say, a final exclamation mark, but he couldn't think of anything.

'I think I have made a mistake,' he said eventually.

The silence thickened. Eyes sliding, then sliding away. He could feel the colour rising in his cheeks, a snake of sweat at the back of his neck.

Imayev said, 'You think every Chechen is a gangster?'

'No,' Seb said, swallowing.

'I think maybe so.'

Seb shrugged resignedly.

Imayev chuckled. 'Sit down.'

They sat side by side in front of the fire. The others watched in silence. Imayev spoke briefly in a language that Seb did not understand and Mukhambetov replied in the same language.

Mukhambetov said, 'He wonders if it is a mistake to trust you.'

'What can I say?'

'I told him that you are a Highlander, a man of the mountains, like our people. You have a proud spirit.'

Seb decided to light a cigarette. Imayev was amused and laid his hand on Seb's knee. After a couple of drags Seb said, 'I'm a wild and wicked Highlander. It's written on my heart.'

They laughed. Imayev clapped his hands together. One of his party opened his knapsack, took out a large square package wrapped in newspaper and held it out to him. The newspaper in which it was wrapped was *Izvestiya.*

Imayev said, 'This is the price of freedom.'

He set it down on the dark earth beside the fire and folded back the newspaper. There were two brick-shaped plastic packets wrapped in black masking tape. Imayev peeled away the tape to show that the packets were filled with heroin.

'Look at it,' Imayev said, 'the destroyer of worlds.'

Seb looked at the heroin. He had been a naive fool. He looked at Imayev, who was watching him with predatory caution; his eyes held a measure of contempt, a measure of menace.

'Try it,' he said.

There wasn't any alternative. Seb put a finger into the powder and worked some on to the nail. He sniffed it.

Imayev watched him. 'It's pure,' he said.

Seb rubbed his nose.

'American dollars, Russian weapons and Chechen spirit will

keep us our independence,' Imayev told him. 'You bring us American dollars, we give you heroin. Dollars, Sebastian, it's all about dollars. Dollars are freedom when the Russians come.'

'Will they come?' Seb wondered. He could feel a faint cold easing down from his sinuses, spreading across his cheeks, and numbing his fear. He wiped the sweat from his eyes.

'It is inevitable. The Russians will find no peace while a single Chechen remains alive. Stalin tried to solve the problem by deporting the whole Chechen nation, exterminating half of them. He failed. Yeltsin will fail.'

Seb was suddenly aware that he had stopped sweating. He swallowed, fighting a wave of nausea. 'Fuck,' he said.

'It doesn't matter how many Cossacks or Ossetians he has,' Imayev continued, seemingly oblivious of Seb's condition, 'how many tanks or helicopters. He can level the cities. He will still fail.'

Imayev retaped the bags and wrapped them up again in the newspaper. One of the Chechens took the package from him and returned it to the knapsack.

'We will be ready,' Imayev said.

Seb rolled over on his hands and knees, letting his head loll down between his elbows. 'Fuck,' he said.

He heard the distinctive click-clack of a gun being made ready, and then felt the cold O-ring of the muzzle against the flesh behind his ear. Time seemed to uncoil and become limitless.

'Look what I have done to you,' Imayev said. 'Look at you. You think you can really play my game?'

He was dead. It took everything he had, every last shred of his being to speak. 'Fuck you.' Mucus spooled out of his mouth.

Imayev laughed. 'Perhaps you can,' he said. 'Perhaps you can.' He removed the muzzle and stepped away, chuckling.

'Go back to your people. Raise the money. When you are ready come to me – in Moscow.'

Seb turned over and eased back, resting his elbows on the soft earth. He watched the Chechens collect their weapons and move off up the densely wooded slope towards the mountains. The whole encounter had lasted less than ten minutes. Beside him Mukhambetov dug at the earth with the toe of his boot and wouldn't meet his eye.

'Fuck you,' Seb whispered.

6

E d said, 'What's the definition of a fanatic?' Madelene sat absolutely still on the edge of the couch, as though what was on offer was so fragile that she had to be careful not to disturb even the air.

'Someone who doubles his efforts when he's forgotten the point.' Ed laughed at his own joke and continued recklessly chopping cocaine on the glass-topped table with his Amex card. Recently, when he found himself in company, Ed had taken to denying that he took cocaine – after all it was passé. Here, he maintained no such pretence. 'Come on,' he urged, without subtlety. 'You have mixed emotions. It's understandable. A giant leap, and all that.'

'Spare me,' Seb scowled.

They were in Ed's quarter-of-a-million-pound flat in Notting Hill and Seb had come, at Madelene's prompting, to listen to what Ed had to say. Ed was enjoying the attention.

'You went to Russia, or wherever, with a noble plan,' Ed said, with a roll of his wrist that sent his Rolex down from under his Nicole Fahri suit. A long way from the too-tight jeans and trainers of his Shankill childhood, or the khaki shorts and scrappy moustache of his teenage years in South Africa. Ed was a master at re-inventing himself.

'We all crave remarkable and heroic schemes,' Ed said. 'I know I do. But that's not how it panned out. Shit happens.'

Seb watched him hoover lines of coke through a rolled-up hundred-dollar bill. It was theatre. Seb despised cocaine.

Ed rubbed the knuckle of his right forefinger against his right nostril, then his left. 'Shiit,' he spluttered, the carefully suppressed harshness of his accent coming through, as it always did when he was high. He shook his head. 'The ethics of it even make me sick.'

Seb slapped him very hard across the side of the face. He did it dispassionately, without any hint of the malice he was capable of. 'I'm not in the mood for your cod morality,' he told him.

Ed fell back with a soft plop into his leather chair. He held his hand to his smarting cheek. 'Animal,' he said.

Ed was right. Seb had an animal's wildness in him, but he had a tight rein on it. Only Madelene had seen the real black mood, the mood that he had brought back with him from Chechnya. His black dog.

'It's the way of the world,' Ed retorted peevishly. 'It's no good getting high and mighty. Everyone's at it.'

Seb lit a cigarette. 'I'm not,' he said. He could feel the reproach in Madelene's stillness. 'Not yet, at least,' he conceded.

Ed laughed, and after a few seconds Seb grimaced sheepishly.

Madelene broke her silence. 'Tell him about your man, Ed,' she said.

'Not my man,' Ed insisted, as if he was issuing a disclaimer. 'A man.'

'Tell him, anyway.'

'Put it this way, he fits the profile. I mean, he *is* the profile.' Ed leant forward, dropping his voice as he did when negotiating contracts. 'He's got experience smuggling weight into Ulster. He knows the border, and he's got the capital we need to set the deal rolling. And, best of all from our point of view, he needs us.'

There was a pause, during which Seb felt Madelene staring at him, willing him to engage.

'Why?' he asked, reluctantly.

'He's got no friends,' Ed explained, pitching the deal. His method was to move his hands in short, prancing gestures; now pointing, now forming a circle with thumb and forefinger like an over-enthusiastic chef. He had slender wrists, easily broken. 'He's on the run. He got himself involved in a robbery over in the States. A bank job. He was the inside man. He let the bandits into the building. They were Noraid; the US arm of the IRA, only more militant these days.'

'I know who Noraid are,' Seb snapped.

'Of course you do.' Ed conceded indulgently. He was a marvel to watch. 'They promised to look after him, but of course when the job was done and the money shared out they didn't want to know. Threw him to the lions. He's damaged goods, you see. Now there's an international warrant out for him. His share of the robbery was sort of medium. Enough but not enough, if you see what I mean. Not enough to set him up for life. He wants more, and he's prepared to put the money up from his share of the Brink's job as capital, but obviously he can't afford to stick his head above the parapet, not with the warrant. Which is where we come in.'

Seb's eyes narrowed. His mind was racing now. 'What's your connection to this guy?'

Ed shrugged. 'Business. We had a go back in the early nineties, bringing E and whizz to the drug-starved masses of Ulster. He was one of the foot-soldiers, the Catholic side of the operation. Only it wasn't the right time. Too many old prejudices. The IRA kneecapped him.'

'So he's no friend to the IRA?'

'Definitely not,' Ed replied. 'Used to be one of their brightest. Did time in the cages with Bobby Sands and Gerry Adams. Later the H blocks. He knows the people and he's in on a lot of the secrets. You know, border crossings, secret tunnels, that shit. Didn't stop them kneecapping him. He hates them with a vengeance now. You could use him, if you choose to.' He adopted a mollifying tone. 'There's no harm in meeting him. You can change your mind later. After all, nothing is written in stone.'

But it was written in stone; the decision had been made.

It was three o'clock in the morning. The bar was in the basement of an unexceptional house with flaking stucco in a row of shabby neo-Georgian façades. Taking their cue from Ed, they had walked past it several times. Then Ed's ever-present cellphone chose to beep. Ed swore. Seb sniggered. Ed whispered heatedly into the phone. The conversation over, he took a last look up and down the road.

'It's cool,' he said. He shoved the rusting gate and went down the flagged steps that led under the main porch to the basement flat. A buzzer was set into the doorframe. He pressed it and they waited. Seb pointed to a video camera set in a recess in the stone.

A disembodied voice issued from the grille, and Ed replied with his name. The door clicked open.

They went down a narrow hallway and through a door into a small dimly lit room. A haze of blue smoke floated at head height, obscuring the ceiling. The corners were filled with shadows. There was no one else in the room. Ed went over to a sideboard and opened a bottle of Johnny Walker Red Label.

Seb lounged on a sofa, looking about him. 'What now?'

Ed held out a glass to him. 'We wait.'

'I need a piss,' Seb announced.

'It's through there,' Ed said, pointing towards a door.

The back room was the substance of the place; five or six small square tables topped with green felt, with shaded lights dangling on flex above them. The blue smoke was denser and seemed to fill the spaces between the tables. The only sound was the clatter of poker chips moving back and forth and Seb's segged boots on the polished wooden boards.

As he was passing a table a player looked up. Their eyes met for the briefest time. Seb felt the cold shiver of recognition. He was a big man, with lank brown hair and heavy brows. Distinctive eyes. Oisin MaColl. I know you. I pulled you out of a ditch. MaColl shifted in his chair, a suspicious, hunted look on his face. Christ, thought Seb, he's recognised me. Keep walking. He told himself that there was no way that MaColl would recognise him, as an individual or as a soldier, that all he would remember was the uniform, the helmet, the gun; and, just maybe the voice, the English accent that identifies an officer amongst the brogue of the Jocks. Nothing that could, at this moment, be connected with Seb; unless there is some sign, some significance of posture, that says to a man brought up in the ghettos of West Belfast: army.

Seconds later, standing over the bowl, watching his slightly too yellow stream of piss splashing in the bowl, he felt a surge of excitement. This wasn't some sterile rehearsal in Herefordshire. This was it.

MaColl was still in his seat, Seb noted, as he walked back through the tables, but watching him.

Seb closed the door behind him. 'I don't think this is a good idea,' he said, crossing the room and picking up his jacket. 'I know that man.'

Ed stared at him, dumbfounded.

The door opened behind them. MaColl stood framed in the doorway, surveying the room.

'I know you, Ed Crowe,' he said, and then, looking at Madelene, 'I don't know you, but God I'd like to.' And finally to Seb, 'you seem familiar. I don't know where or when, but we've met before.'

'I doubt it,' Seb said.

'Nevertheless.' He grinned roguishly and looked about him again. 'Since it doesn't seem I'm about to be arrested, perhaps you'd like to have a drink with me?'

'I don't think so,' Seb said.

MaColl was puzzled. 'What have you got to lose?'

Everything? Nothing that wasn't lost already? He had no way of knowing. He was launched into the darkness, the unknown.

Afterwards, in the days that followed, it started to make more sense. He knew MaColl: they were bound together. After all, MaColl owed him his life. There were even moments when it seemed there must be some outside force guiding events. It amused him to think he had destiny on his side.

Madelene went with him back to Scotland. They spent a week of his army leave in the Glasgow gallery surrounded by her collections, her artwork. Gradually he came to understand that she wanted to take possession of him; to add him to her bell-jar specimens, to brand his name along with all the others on her animal hide. He let her.

'Ed's found us a buyer,' she told him towards the end of the week, when she had put him sufficiently at ease. 'I spoke to him this morning. It's some schoolfriend of his from Belfast.'

He did not respond. She slipped out of a pair of heels, with her hand resting lightly on his shoulder. His skin was still tanned from the Kuwait sun.

'The buyer wants to meet you.'

He rubbed his jaw with his thumb as he chose another pair of shoes from the selection on the rack.

'Whomsoever this shoe fits shall be my bride,' she said mockingly.

She rested the arch of her foot in the palm of his hand. He stared at the beauty of her, hardly daring to breathe, trying to feel his own wish for mercy kindle an answering mercy in her.

There was none. She was insistent that they smuggle the heroin. She would not go anywhere with him without money, and he wanted her to go with him more than he wanted anything else in the world. He pressed his thumb against the scarrified blue-black marks between her lacquered toes.

'You can live a long life on heroin,' she told him. 'It's like embalming fluid. It has a preservative effect. It's not heroin that kills, it's contaminated additives, liver infections, AIDS.'

He eased the shoe on to her foot.

His cellphone beeped. He snatched at it. It was Ed, of course.

'Has she spoken to you?' Ed asked.

'Yes,' he said dully. He listened to himself as if he was suspended outside himself, a witness, disassociated.

'Our friend represents strong interests. He'll take a full ton. Set us up for life, like you said.'

Strong interests? Connections behind connections. He wondered if he was approaching the time when he would no longer want to know the identity of those who were to benefit from his plan. He wondered if it might become necessary not to know.

'He wants to meet you,' Ed continued. 'He's over here on other business. Near to where you are now. In Scotland, I mean.'

'Yes.'

'I'm at Heathrow. On my way there.'

'Yes.'

'Get yourself a tracksuit and some trainers. Our man likes jogging.' Ed laughed. 'Like the President.'

He felt the helpless serenity of one who has accepted everything and anything.

Someone had spray-painted 'UFF' on the roadsign at the centre of the roundabout leading into Carluke. He was no longer troubled, or even serene. Instead he was angry, as if the problem had ceased to be a moral one. The plan had somehow shifted realms, from the fantastical to the actual. The congruence of events and personalities had given it clothes. And he was angry.

Ed was almost apologetic. 'Of course, Truth's questionable. He's a dedicated psychopath, after all, a Protestant workaholic assassin. It devastates the mind. But he's also extremely security-conscious. There are no informers amongst his lot. I'm telling you, he's paranoid beyond belief.' Ed grinned. 'He thinks the army is out to kill him.'

'They probably are. What the fuck is he going to think of me?'

'Don't worry. We grew up together. I used to live two doors down on Hazelfield Street in the Shankill. We used to hang around the same chip shop at night. We were in the same gang.' 'Did a bit of burglary, you know,' he added, mocking his old accent. He became reflective for a moment. 'Teenage kicks. Most of the gang are dead now, or in the Maze or Maghaberry, or they've found Christ. It's weird. You wouldn't believe the number of convicted killers and born-again Christians that I know. It's mind-boggling.' He seemed genuinely mystified.

'I wanted to be a hardman, once,' he said. 'But I didn't have the necessary attributes. I could talk, though. I could negotiate. That was my salvation.'

'Fuck's sake,' Seb hissed, finally losing his temper.

Ed was taken aback. 'Look, don't lose your cool. Everything's fine. Truth's people sometimes come over and provide security on big deals that go down in London. He knows the money and the power that's there for the grasping. It's a case of, if others get it, why can't I? And he trusts me implicitly. It's a Shankill thing.'

Ed parked the convertible by a rubbish skip at the entrance to a park.

'And another thing, he's due to go down. They're getting him under the new statutes, for directing terrorism and membership of an illegal organisation. He'll do years and years. You see, he wants some money coming in, so he's set up when he gets out. It's that simple.'

'He's going to think I'm a plant,' Seb said.

'What, like a marigold?' Ed kidded him.

'You are *so* fucking stupid,' Seb said.

'Listen, calm down. I told him all about you.'

'Christ!'

'He had to know. In something like this it's necessary. You may have to do something to satisfy him that you're kosher.'

'Like what, for instance?'

Ed shrugged. 'I don't know.' He laughed suddenly. 'I remember a dealer once in Brixton. The first time a customer went to him, he'd make them swallow a goldfish. He had a whole tank of them in his front room. Little wriggly things. Did he think an undercover cop would refuse to swallow a fish?'

'Shut the fuck up,' Seb snapped. He was trying to get it straight in his head, the nature of the man that he was about to meet. 'What's he doing over here?'

'Networking. He has friends in Combat 18. Listen, if he gives you any leaflets – you know the kind of thing, eugenics, the holocaust-hoax, niggers stealing our bodily juices – just humour him.'

'I suppose you told him I'm a Catholic.'

'I didn't know you were a taig,' Ed said, in mock horror. He punched Seb lightly on the shoulder. It was an impertinence. There was something about Ed that made you want to burst his balloon. Seb got out of the car. He laced his trainers, slowly and deliberately.

'I'll wait for you,' Ed told him. He started punching numbers into his cellphone. 'Give Truth my best regards.'

Seb straightened up. He was ready for combat. He jogged into the park.

The minders came at him from five different directions. Almost immediately. Three of them stopped short of him, and formed an attentive perimeter, while two, youngish, with shoulder-length hair, came in close. The bearded one took him by the arm to lead him further into the park. Just for a moment, Seb lost control of *the knife*, its cool power uncoiling, racing across his shoulders, down his arms and into his hands. The bearded man felt it also and flinched as if he'd been struck.

Then he smiled, insinuating a violent kinship. 'You're the maan,' he drawled, with a distinctively rolling Belfast accent.

Seb was unimpressed.

The fair-haired one took his other arm. He was smiling. There was a moistness to his lips that Seb found repellent.

They led him to a secluded part of the park, where they stripped him naked and methodically searched his clothing and trainers. It was getting repetitive; this constant intimacy with strangers. He had come to regard it as an unavoidable necessity. Smuggling required it.

'I don't think I've ever seen such a big dick,' the fair-haired one said. 'Have you ever seen such a big dick?'

The bearded man smiled indulgently.

'Turn round,' the fair-haired one said.

As he did so, Seb felt the hairs on the back of his neck rise, then, seconds later, fingers mussing his hair and sliding under his armpits.

'Do you have to stand so close?' Seb asked.

'Sure, I do. Bend over. I'm going to look up your hole.'

When he was done, the man rested his palm against the back of Seb's thigh for a few seconds. 'He's clean. I'd say verging on the virginal.'

Another, more authoritative voice, instructed him to turn round. If having him naked was intended to make him feel ill at ease, they had miscalculated. It merely accentuated the difference in height between them. Stevie Truth's build said it all – he was a wee Shankill Road man, with Neanderthal shoulders and a cannonball of a head with cropped ginger hair and the faint hairs of a moustache beginning to show under his nose. He was wearing a blue Adidas football shirt and his bare arms were covered in Loyalist tattoos.

'What are you smiling at?' he asked.

'Nothing,' Seb replied. 'I have amiable features.'

'Have we met before?'

'I stopped you once,' Seb said. 'You were jogging down the Donegal Road.' It was common knowledge that Truth picked out his victims by jogging into Catholic areas to recce houses and escape routes.

Truth eyed him suspiciously. 'Ed has been away from Belfast for a very long time,' he said. 'You can get out of touch when you go across the water. It's easy to lose your roots.'

Seb said nothing.

'I don't trust you,' Truth said.

'You could stand some watching yourself,' Seb said evenly.

Truth blinked once. He was obviously so unused to anyone standing up to him that he had forgotten what it was like. Eventually, he laughed, a loud and harrowing sound. 'Sounds like a sound basis for a partnership,' he said. 'Put your clothes back on. We'll go for a jog, you and I.'

They matched each other, stride for stride, through the park for twenty minutes, then stopped by a stand of trees.

'Sometimes, you have to use the forces of the devil to undo the work of the devil.' Truth was walking back and forth, with his hands on his hips. Rivulets of sweat ran out of his hairline and down his livid temples. 'Winston Churchill said that.'

'Or something similar.' Seb forced his head up, making his breathing settle.

'What?'

Seb shook his head. 'Nothing.'

'There are thousands of smackheads in Dublin,' Truth informed him. 'They sell the stuff at bus stops, you know.'

'Listen, in twenty years time there'll be more Fenian voters in Ulster than Protestants. It's a question of demographics. You think things can go on as they are. Baaallicks, they can.'

He paused for a long time, and Seb wondered if he was being invited to comment. But he said nothing. He had little sympathy with the Loyalist cause: he had more respect for the IRA than he did for any Loyalist organisation. He felt that whereas the IRA were intelligent opponents worthy of his attention, the Loyalists were merely opportunist murderers and gangsters. It did not surprise him that Truth was interested in heroin. It merely confirmed his opinion.

Truth said, 'We're the ones struggling for survival, struggling for the heart of our nation. It calls for desperate measures.'

Seb couldn't see the connection.

'This whole business may not look good from one side,' Truth continued, 'but from the other, it's governed by careful rules. The important rule is don't shit on your own doorstep.'

'So where are you going to shit?' Seb asked him.

Truth blinked again. 'It's simple,' he bragged, 'so fuckin simple. Smackheads don't breed. Smackheads don't vote. I'm going to swamp Andersonstown, Ballymurphy, Poleglass, Twinbrook. I'm going to stick a needle full of cut-price scag in every taig forearm in this city. I'm going to turn every Fenian fucker into an addict. They'll drop like flies. Heroin will be the Third Force.'

It was laughable, the idea that you could use heroin as some kind of sectarian weapon and confine it to one side of the community. Heroin was indiscriminate – it would break out all over. It was obvious that Truth knew nothing about drugs. He was an innocent. An innocent psychopath. He deserved whatever was going to happen to him.

'I have vision,' Truth said.

You're blind, Seb thought.

'And strong interests supporting me. I don't want to spill the seed of my idea on barren ground,' he said. 'I don't want to find I've been fucked by the SAS. You see what I mean?'

'I think so,' Seb said.

'Like I said, I don't trust you.'

'I won't take it personally.'

Truth stared at him. The moment of truth. 'I want you to do something for me. A bond of trust.'

'What?' Seb heard himself ask.

Truth grinned savagely. 'A head job.'

As simple as that. Straightforward. Murder.

'It is necessary that you kill someone.'

Seb swallowed. He was face to face with the final thing. It wasn't such a big thing – after all, he had been to war, he had killed before. It was merely a sequence of movements and gestures: the Knife unleashed.

'One of my boys will give you a piece of paper, with a name and an address in Glasgow. Do the job and we have a deal. You bring the devil's food to me in the Shankill and I'll fill your pockets with other men's cash.'

'He's so fucked up, it's stunning.' Seb crumpled the cigarette packet and threw it out of the car. 'He wants to fire off needles like cruise missiles.' He dragged hungrily on the cigarette. His hands were unsteady. He shook his head, and the motion continued and became frenzied like a sudden wind passing through him. After a few seconds he got control of himself again. 'We can use that to our own advantage.'

They drove on the motorway into Glasgow.

'It's perfect,' Seb announced.

Ed grinned.

'Where's MaColl holed up?' Seb asked.

'Amsterdam,' Ed replied. 'I thought it would be safer.'

'Get on to him. Warn him I'm coming. I want access to the money.'

Ed said, 'Then what?'

'Moscow. Madelene and I will go, to meet the Chechens.'

'So it's happening?'

'It's happening,' Seb agreed. Suddenly his heart filled with optimism. He had a supplier, a smuggler and a buyer. He had the logistical set-up and the money was in motion. There was no stopping him. 'It's really happening.'

'It'll go down in history,' Ed said.

'We're going to have to do a shitload of preparation, here and in Ulster, if we're going to pull this off.'

'It's no problem,' Ed assured him. 'So what did he want you to do? To prove yourself?'

For a split second, Seb thought that Ed knew, that he was mocking him. Cold rage churned in his guts. Then he realised that Ed genuinely didn't know.

'Mind your own fucking business,' he said softly.

He made every stroke count, he put his shoulders into it and did not hurry. After every few strokes he put down the file and ran his thumb across the edge of the entrenching tool. It was sharpening up nicely. He had bought it that morning from Bostons on Leith Walk in Edinburgh. He had delved through piles of junk to find it. No one would remember his face. That was the way of it at Bostons.

It all seemed to Seb a lushly textured dream. He thought about it often; even the smallest details were remembered with clarity. The coldness of the muzzle of a gun pressed against the flesh behind his ear. The cruel knowing in the Chechen's voice: 'Look what I have done to you.' That fraction of a second in which he felt the terrifying certainty of extinction. The strobe-like whooshing of his pumping heart. Then laughter.

There was a bead of blood on the palp of his thumb. He raised it to his lips and sucked on it, thoughtfully.

The time for introspection had passed; now it was time for action. He felt a savage elation. He had died and been reborn unburdened, free, invulnerable.

Opposite him, Madelene shifted in the tangle of sheets on the bed. She had never been troubled by moral qualms. She was truly invulnerable. Since the moment when he had first set eyes on her, beneath the smooth black surface of the sea, and had mistaken her for a mermaid; since that moment he had been captivated by her entirely. He laid the file down on the varnished pine flooring. The tool was ready. Everything he did, he did for her. Soon she would wake, and hit herself with the first needle of the day. By that time he would be standing in the hallway of a tenement block; the filed blade flickering in the smoky light. The moment suspended. Waiting for the door to open a crack.

Ease back a little to allow room to swing. Three steps. Swift and balletic. Float like a butterfly . . . bring the tool down in a whistling slash.

And afterwards? A coffee? Maybe some whisky? Definitely a cigarette. And soon after that a flight to Moscow.

7

The call came around midnight: a few softly spoken words on the telephone. 'Get dressed,' Seb told Madelene. 'This is it.'

Ten minutes later they strode through the hotel foyer, past the plainclothes security men in bulky black suits and with close-cropped hair, and went outside, down the steps past the uniformed guard and the boys covering the arriving and departing cars, through the cluster of dollar-prostitutes and beggars.

Moscow was exhilarating, liberating, and with every step he was recreating himself. He no longer had any objection to heroin. Heroin was a commodity like anything else. Fierce demand required a fierce supplier. It was the most free and evolutionary trade – no tax, no excise, no insurance. No constricting morality.

His oath to Cal seemed paltry now, irrelevant. Madelene had made it clear to him. She clarified everything. Even the Glasgow murder seemed unreal. He had emptied himself of all compassion.

She slipped her arm through his and they strutted together down the dark and cobbled street past rows of muffled elderly women squatting in front of a few miserable items for sale.

For two days they had prowled the streets, waiting for a message from Mukhambetov, while scabrous shapes lurked in the shadows. They had purchased a gun from an army conscript, a deserter who'd climbed fearfully out of a drain cover to offer it. Seb had his hair cut close to his head in imitation of the Moscow mafia style. He wore a mink hat and cowboy boots. As a libertarian, an avowed capitalist, and as a soldier he was proud to have been, in some small way, responsible for the collapse of the Soviet Union. He liked this new town. It was in your face.

Seb chain-smoked as he walked, lighting each cigarette with

the stub of the previous one, flicking the douts under passing cars.

As they were passing a darkened alleyway between two warehouses, a Mercedes cut in front of them and two men in rollnecks, cradling machine-pistols, jumped out and frisked them – their fingers and palms moulding their upper bodies, crotch, thighs and ankles. On finding the gun they flung it away down the alleyway. Apparently satisfied, they gestured to them to climb in.

The back of the car was large, but crowded. Shamil Mukhambetov, newly demobbed in an expensively tailored suit and even more gold jewellery, was established in the leather upholstered seat opposite. The two bodyguards wedged Seb and Madelene in against the partition dividing the limousine. They set off, weaving between the potholes in the road.

Mukhambetov wagged a ringed finger. 'I think you bring your woman to make her walk in front of you? Am I right?'

Seb lit another cigarette. Mukhambetov wanted to play. Seb was wary of him; he had not forgiven him for what had happened in the mountains. Oblivious, Mukhambetov reached forward and put his hand on Madelene's knee.

'You know, I was in Afghanistan, just recently, I mean. In connection with our business today. Anyway, I met an anthropologist. He was very excited because he thought that the civil war had led to the emancipation of women. Whereas before the war the women were forced to walk behind the mules, now they were accorded the right to walk in front of the mules. So what do you think?' The big Chechen grinned, his prominent yellow teeth almost in her face. 'It is not so bad to lose a wife to a land-mine, but a mule, well that is not so easy to replace.' He let out a slow rumble of laughter and slouched back in his seat.

Seb shook his head. Madelene licked her lips, and gave him her cool arrogant stare.

Mukhambetov switched his attention to Seb, who returned his gaze.

'You know, I think a leader, a true leader of men could do anything he wanted with you,' Mukhambetov told him. 'Make anything happen.'

They emerged from the Mercedes outside Night Flight on Tverskaya Street, and swept past the pavement kiosks and prostitutes and the sour-faced policemen patrolling the pavements in their shabby body armour, fiddling with their AKMs. The bulky security guards at the entrance to the bar wore smarter black flak jackets and Spetsnaz T-shirts, and ran their portable metal detectors over them as they entered. Madelene received particular attention. The bodyguards checked in their weapons and coats.

Inside, floorshow strippers walked amongst the tables while diners bid for the right to undress them. The big prizes were going to a table of five bankers gathered around a chilled bottle of imported Smirnoff. A stripper gyrated in front of them with an expression of bland, fathomless contempt.

The bodyguards indicated two empty booths with a commanding view of the bar, and waited patiently while they seated themselves. A waiter brought them imported vodka – nobody was drinking Russian vodka.

Mukhambetov was amused by the bankers. 'They speculate against the rouble. Moscow is a rotten city, feeding off foreign money.'

Seb was beginning to relax. He said, 'How is civvy street?'

Mukhambetov laughed and waved a bundle of money in a girl's direction. 'In Moscow I'm a pariah. Nobody trusts me.'

'So what are you going to do when this is over? Fight for your country? Find a place in the sun?'

Mukhambetov said, 'Don't laugh at me.'

'I wouldn't dream of it.'

'I'm learning Arabic. I have started to read the Quran. I want to atone.'

'Christ,' Seb said.

'He was a prophet,' Mukhambetov agreed.

Seb said, 'I see you're still drinking.'

'One step at a time, Sebastian. Remember, I have to live with myself. What about you? What are you going to do with your millions?'

Seb downed his vodka and lit a cigarette. He hooked his arm round Madelene's shoulders. 'I'm going to retire gracefully with my girl. Somewhere they don't ask too many questions.'

He saw that Madelene's violet lips were parted, perhaps smiling.

There was barbed wire everywhere. It sprouted in ugly tufts from the ground. It snaked along the high walls that surrounded the squat red-brick workshops. It sagged in thick strands from rusty posts, and huge coiled bales of it were stacked on the waste ground beneath the wooden watch-towers.

'Establishment III-391/36,' Mukhambetov said, and then in explanation, 'A gulag. You know, a prison camp. They make barbed wire.'

Seb yawned and stared out the window. They had driven five hundred miles through the night, on some of the worst roads he had ever encountered, to this grey, polluted outpost of the old Soviet empire, on the Volga river. The Mercedes swept through the gates and halted in front of a low brick building.

'The party's over. In eighty-nine they were producing two tons a year. When the Berlin Wall came down the bottom dropped out of the market, and then, to make it worse, Yeltsin used foreign razor wire on the White House siege last September. These fellows can't compete. The machinery is ancient – it was plundered from the Germans after the last war.'

They got out of the car and stood in the icy slush. The bodyguards fanned out.

'It has passed into history. Now it is a shrine. We used to surround everything in barbed wire. It was like an article of faith. The pillar of communism.'

'You getting sentimental on me?' Seb said.

Mukhambetov laughed heartily. 'I like the irony of it.'

'So how much am I buying?'

'One hundred tons, at sixty-five thousand roubles a spool. Practically nothing. There is still need for barbed wire in Ireland.'

'The troubles may be over,' Seb observed.

'You don't change things quickly over there. You don't shake the world in a few days like we do. You have slow revolutions. Meantime, you need barbed wire.'

'I'll take your word for it.'

'The merchandise will travel with the spools of wire. By rail to Murmansk and then by tramp steamer to the port of destination. The merchandise will go over the side in the general location that you indicate. I'll be there with you – don't worry about how I get into the country, that's my problem. I'll give you the exact grid reference then. You recover the load and bring it ashore. When you're happy, your Irishman can pay me. Then I leave.'

They found Imayev standing beside a drained swimming pool. He was holding a Leica camera. Beside him, looking nervous, was a thin, ferret-faced man with the lardy complexion of a minor Russian bureaucrat.

'That's Ivanov,' Mukhambetov said, 'the director.'

They joined them at the lip of the pool to watch the frozen tableau beneath them. There was a man kneeling on the bottom surrounded by streaks of vermilion scum. He had lank black hair and was wearing a cheap imitation-leather coat. A second man, a Chechen, stood behind him, holding a Kalashnikov levelled at the back of his head. All was still and silent.

'Tell me, do you recognise him?' Imayev asked.

'His name is Busygin,' Mukhambetov replied, without hesitation. 'He is a journalist with *Moskovskiy Komsomolets*.'

Imayev received the news without visible reaction. He was turning the camera over in his hands. 'He was taking pictures as we came out of the building. His curiosity has got the better of him.'

'He could damage us,' Mukhambetov said. 'People believe what he writes.'

Imayev nodded. 'Shoot him.'

There were three shots, one after the other, methodical and unnecessary. The first killed him. He seemed to drift sideways, spraying red mist, for a fraction of a second before pitching forwards into the muck. His heels kicked up behind him. The Chechen stepped forward, pressed the muzzle against the base of Busygin's shattered skull and fired twice more. The crack of each shot snapped back and forth in the pool's hollow chamber.

When it was done, Imayev took a photograph of the corpse.

'Take him back to Moscow,' he instructed Mukhambetov. 'Throw him in a river.'

He turned to Seb and regarded him with a savage intensity, holding him with his will. There were charcoal flecks in the grey skin under his eyes, like gunpowder. He seemed to be laughing. He threw the camera to Madelene, who caught it awkwardly in her left hand.

'You like death?' he asked her, still watching Seb.

'Yes,' she replied, clutching the camera to her chest. 'I like death.'

The heroin was piled in neatly wrapped sacks in one of the

warehouses, like bags of cement. One ton didn't look so much stacked like that. Millions of pounds' worth. Freedom.

They were stacked above Schiphol, waiting for a runway to clear, before he told her he had found Cal. He had been staring out at beads of water snaking across the dull silvery surface of the aircraft's wing. The sky was grey and leaden. Uncomfortable grit rolled on his lenses. Flying always made his eyes bad.

They passed over the huge crescent apartment blocks that ringed the airport. The flight captain was speaking over the intercom; apparently the flooding was bad in Holland. Somewhere down there, on the flooded Dutch coastline, Cal was struggling with a sinking rig.

'I hired a private investigator,' Seb explained.

He didn't know how she was going to react. He didn't know how he wanted her to react. She had been furious in the aftermath of Cal's disappearance. He was only now beginning to get the measure of her possessiveness, and her vindictiveness.

'I've got a full report,' Seb said.

He could feel her watching him. He didn't want to look at her: he was frightened of what he might see in her face.

'His brother's getting married,' he protested. 'Somebody had to track him down.'

Unnerving silence.

'He can bring the stuff up off the sea bed,' Seb persisted. 'He knows his way around a boat.'

How much easier it would be if he excluded Cal from his plan. He pressed his forehead against the perspex window, looking for words with which to convey his meaning precisely. The truth was that Cal was inextricably linked with the whole affair. There wasn't any way of leaving him out.

'I really need someone I can trust for this,' Seb said. There, he'd said it. He sat there in the cold, carefully controlled environment of the cabin, waiting for her to speak. The plane banked and began its descent. He had a week left before he was due in Belfast. A week in which to cram all the final details, before the plan was finally, irrevocably, set in motion.

'You want someone to watch over me,' Madelene replied softly.

It was a painful admission; that he didn't trust her, and he didn't trust himself with her. He required Cal's calm rational eye.

'We just don't tell him it's heroin, that's all.'

'All?' She echoed his thoughts.

They parted in the transit lounge. She was going on to Glasgow, and from there to Cual. He was going to Left Luggage to collect MaColl's money, and after that he would hire a car and go looking for Cal.

'I'll send him to you,' Seb said stiffly. He wanted to tell her not to sleep with Cal – but it would cost him too much in lost dignity. He wanted to understand her, to beg her to tell him what she thought.

A few hours later, and Cal stood sodden and dripping in the splintered doorway. Beside him, the plywood door flapped loosely on one hinge.

'Flew into Schiphol,' Seb explained. He was lying on the bed with a glass of duty free and a cigarette. 'A few hours to kill. I'd heard you were here so I thought I'd come and see you. You look like shit.' He whipped off his sunglasses. 'Well?'

'The rig sank,' Cal said. 'I'm dead.'

'You're exaggerating,' Seb assured him. He jumped up, pulled Cal into the room and propelled him down on to the bed. 'Here, sit down.'

He watched Cal sigh and rub his face in a vigorous circular motion that was familiar to him. It was great to see him. For a few moments things seemed simple, like they had been before Madelene.

'Where have you been?' Cal asked, halfheartedly. Clearly he wasn't going to ask how Seb had found him. That would be uncool.

'Moscow,' Seb replied, and let his mouth run with it for a while. But Cal wasn't really listening. He was frowning. 'Not work then?'

'Definitely not,' Seb told him. 'This is something else entirely. More your line. Moving weight, I mean.'

That grabbed Cal's attention. Something was badly wrong. Seb said, 'What have you got yourself into?'

The telephone rang. Cal picked up the receiver and Seb watched his face grow significantly paler.

Afterwards, Seb said, 'Tell me about it?'

When Cal had explained about the lost hash, Seb replaced his sunglasses to hide his streaming eyes. 'Let him come, mate. I'll show him.'

Byron flailed sideways like a crab. Cal stood breathless on the far side of the hotel room. Three lightning strides and heightened awareness in Seb had given way to something closer to absence. Narcolepsy. A new form of *the knife.* Presence or absence, it mattered very little to Seb. He had accepted that it was beyond his control.

His Purdey blade had left matching vertical slashes on the man's cheeks. He didn't remember doing it, but the evidence lay before him. A soft throbbing like the distant sound of drums filled his ears.

'I can hear your heart,' Seb told Byron, in wonderment.

It was over. He smiled. He reached out and laid a hand on Cal's shoulder. They were together again; bound tighter by this expression of violence. He felt a savage elation. 'Excellent, lover.'

He stepped away and lit himself a cigarette. This called for a grand gesture. He opened up his rucksack and tipped a shower of stolen twenty-dollar bills over the bloody body on the carpet. Pay the man off: best not to leave loose ends. He quoted something that seemed appropriate. Cal, as usual, did not recognise the source. Seb kicked the body and heard ribs crack.

Then, without warning, he was spent, faint. A mist of blood descended like a curtain behind his eyes. The adrenalin was gone. All he wanted to do was stick his head under a tap until he was back with the living.

'I think I'll wash my hands,' he said.

He had to grip the taps with all the strength of his resolve to stop himself slipping down on to the floor. The extravagance of his aggression was beginning to frighten him. He searched his reflection in the mirror for some visible sign of weakness, a crack in his armour. He wouldn't last five minutes in the tightly monitored environment of Belfast if he didn't get himself under control. Only total self-mastery would see him through to the end of the plan.

'Get a hold of yourself,' he said.

When his breathing had settled, he removed his bloodied shirt and scrubbed his flesh until he felt clean and ready to face Cal.

Seb strutted round the pool table, a coffee-shop skunk joint hanging on his lower lip, flourishing his cue like a rapier. He had come full circle, and he was back on a high. He bobbed down to dispatch balls into pockets. He took his shots without hesitation, always with one eye closed. He rarely missed.

'I'm on a mission from God,' he announced. He was in his stride. He swallowed a mouthful of lager from a tall glass. 'I had a dream back there in the desert. In the Zone. I want to get the good burghers of Belfast out of their minds. I want everyone to get high.'

'You just keep thinking, Seb,' Cal said, smiling. 'It's what you're good at.'

'I'm serious,' Seb protested.

'I'm sure you are.'

'Don't use that tone, man. I'm telling you. A whole ton.'

'Of what, exactly?' Cal asked.

Seb squeezed an eye closed. White ball to striped ball to pocket.

Lie.

Now. He took the shot. Pocketed the ball.

'Hash.'

It was done.

Cal eyed the table and asked, 'From where?'

'Afghanistan,' Seb replied. He caught the look on Cal's face. 'Fuck's sake! You want the shit to come from the Lebanon? Kurdistan? Iran? Face it, stable regimes don't encourage dope-growers. I thought you were an anarchist? This stuff is grown in an area controlled by students. They call themselves the Taliban. Guys in rope sandals, with those Mujahedeen hats.'

He decided not to tell Cal that the Taliban were Muslim fundamentalists. There was no point sowing doubt in his mind. 'Shit. For all I know, they grow the stuff organically.'

'You're taking the piss out of me,' Cal replied.

'All right,' Seb said, holding up a placatory hand. 'Listen. When I was in the desert I met some of the right people. Chechens in the Russian army. They were Afghan veterans. They had worked undercover there. While they were there they forged links with the growers. They have a logistic network, international connections.'

'Mafia?'

'Freedom fighters,' Seb corrected him. Then he added: 'They can dump a ton of the stuff off the coast of Ireland and we can bring it in. You can bring it in. We'll get a much better price in Ulster than we would in London or Glasgow. A whole ton. A one-off. A lightning strike.'

He jabbed two fingers at Cal, trailing smoke and ash. 'A thrust, mate, with a sharp blade into the corridors of wealth.'

BOOK THREE

BLIND

February 1996

Half drew she him
Half sank he down
And nevermore was seen
Traditional nursery rhyme

1

The Cessna crossed Malin Head at three thousand feet, flying parallel with the Donegal coastline, before turning into Sheep Haven. Seb lifted the door in the fuselage and shied for a second from the blast of cold air, an instinctive and fearful reaction, then looked out at the seething mass of water in the estuary, the whitecaps racing for the shore. Somewhere, out there on the ocean, Cal was struggling towards a rendezvous with the drugs.

Seb reached out with gloved hands for the strut under the wing, and put a cramped and tingling foot on the wheel. He shimmied with his fingers out to the end of the strut. Breathing deeply, he kicked out into free space and hung for a few seconds by his fingers, cruciform in the slipstream, and, enjoying himself now, he grinned across the chasm of air at the dog Kali. She was panting in the doorway, her eyes bright as mica in the darkness, her snout raised to the wind. The plane swept over the black mass of land below. Organ was shouting and giving him the thumbs up. He let go, arched his back, splayed his arms and legs, and plummeted towards the earth.

Freefall. The wind's claws in his eyes. Howling. Aaaaaaaoooouuu . . . !

Counting . . .

By the numbers, he reached for the drogue shoot with his right hand.

Counting . . .

He flung it away, and the main body of the parachute was tugged out after it, billowing silk unfolding above him. Everything slowed. He drifted slowly, with his hands on the risers, towards the surface of the earth, his eyes scanning for the bonfire. Numb and protesting muscles loosened and stretched. It was about to rain, or maybe snow; black clouds were drawing in off the sea.

He'd spent the previous twenty-four hours bent almost double in a sleeping bag, under a pile of cardboard boxes in the cramped confines of Organ's Cessna, after sneaking on to the airfield on Cual at midnight the night before to ensure that no one saw him leave. Now Ireland, snow-clad and hostile, was rising towards him.

The updraught from the bonfire gave him a last moment of lift and swept him, like a monstrous black shadow, close over Madelene's head. He landed with his ankles together, skidded in a dark slush of snow and recently spread muck, rolled over on his shoulder and went sliding like a curling-stone across the field.

When he stopped, he climbed unsteadily to his feet and started hauling in his chute. The first fat drops of hard rain struck the back of his neck. The chute shifted in and out of focus in front of him.

'Attention all shipping, especially in sea areas Malin and Hebrides. The Meteorological Office issued the following gale warning to shipping at 0100 GMT today. Malin and Hebrides, south-easterly severe gale force nine increasing storm force ten soon.'

He had felt at home in the darkness. Lying, dressed in oilskin brace and bib bottom, on top of his folded-out sleeping bag, it occurred to him that, in the blink of an eye, he might return himself to a Dutch hotel room, and discover that everything in between – the rig sinking, Byron, Seb's master plan, Al's death, Oonagh's appearance on Cual – had been a dream or a flash of acid. He could wait silently in the darkness and all these things would evaporate like mist. He had made such a mess of things. He felt that, with Oonagh, he had been offered a chance to escape from Madelene's influence, but he hadn't taken the chance. He had no clear explanation for it. Surely it was more than just sex. Part of him wondered if it was that he needed to see this whole thing through to the end, as if a puzzle had been set in their childhood and an answer was only now coming within reach.

The radio broke his reverie. The kettle was whistling behind the fiddle rail. Andy would want a mug of tea. He was back in the here and now.

The mobile phone beeped. Cal reached for it and held it against his ear. It was Ed, across from Limerick harbour, watching the Irish Navy's solitary coastguard vessel, silent at her moorings.

'All's well,' Ed said and broke the connection.

The time for second thoughts had passed long ago. Cal swung his legs off the bunk and slid them into his wellington boots. He shrugged himself into his oilskin jacket and in the narrow space between beds he poured two sugary cups of tea and carried them up the short ladder to the wheelhouse.

Andy was listening to Linton Kwezi Johnson on the ghetto-blaster and staring intently out the window. The boat was riding huge swells and there was green water over the bow.

'I'm no happy.'

'Have a cup of tea,' Cal replied. He glanced at the Trackplotter. They were in thirty fathoms of water. The contours of the sea bottom were clearly visible on the flickering green computer screen. 'We're as close as we're going to get without the exact grid.'

'It's a shambles oot there,' Andy informed him.

'*Dread beat 'n' blood,*' said Linton Kwezi Johnson.

'I'm glad it's dark,' Cal said.

A brutal wind lashed the coastline; spruce trees on the hillsides above the walled estate were torn down. The rain was getting harder; it filled Seb's eyes and blurred his vision as he strode across the cobbles from the main house to the converted eighteenth-century barn that contained the recording studios. He gripped Madelene's shoulder. The band had gone into Derry for the night with the film crew. Seb's band of smugglers had the estate to themselves.

They ducked through the narrow portal in the iron-studded oak door, and entered a large white room. At the centre of it six-foot yucca plants clustered beneath a high skylight. It was warm and humid.

Mukhambetov got up out of a cream leather couch and sauntered across the reception area towards them, coming up on Seb's right side, his arm raised in salute. Platinum discs burned brightly on the walls. Seb started as Mukhambetov got close, as if he had not noticed him, and Mukhambetov's step faltered for a second, as if he was unsure of Seb's response.

Seb mastered the set of his face. He smiled. They bear-hugged. Mukhambetov took a step back, took in Madelene, and held out his arms.

She sidestepped him easily and disappeared into the building.

Mukhambetov shrugged good-humouredly. Seb flicked a glance at his Rolex, squinting slightly. The muscles in his arms kept seizing and relaxing.

'We're on schedule. The boat should come ashore in the next hour.'

Mukhambetov fell into step beside him. 'So you've fooled the establishment?'

'It looks that way.' Seb laughed, edgy and tense. 'And I didn't go to Cambridge. Or join the Communist Party.'

Mukhambetov mocked him: 'Sebastian MacCoinneach, the enemy within.'

They pushed through a set of double doors.

'The ceasefire is holding,' Mukhambetov observed.

'Of course it is,' Seb replied. 'It's axiomatic. People want the good life. They don't want to buy their booze from behind bullet-proof glass. They don't want their children hobbling around on dud knees. They want to shop at a decent supermarket. You want something to eat?'

'I had a Big Mac in Dublin,' Mukhambetov told him. 'You know, it really does taste the same in Moscow. Of course, you don't have to queue so much in Dublin.'

They were playing the game again. Seb said, 'I see the Russians flattened Grozny.'

Mukhambetov shrugged.

'How is your aunt?' Seb asked.

Mukhambetov shrugged again, casually.

'You still reading the Quran?'

'No.'

Seb glanced at him. They laughed reflexively, without mirth.

Mukhambetov said, 'I don't have time for that any more. Too many other things to be afraid of. War, for instance. The Russians.'

'You know, since the Gulf, I don't get scared any more.'

'That is your big problem,' Mukhambetov advised. 'You're too excited, and not frightened enough. You think you have a monopoly on hatred; you underestimate the power of other people's hatred.'

'Nobody hates like me,' Seb said.

He opened the door to the sound-stage. It was large, big enough for an orchestra, with sound-proofed walls. There was a chemistry set lying on a black ash table at the centre of the room, and beside it a bottle of Absolut and a glass.

Seb said, 'You shouldn't have to wait long.'

Mukhambetov walked over to the table and picked up the bottle. 'You think of everything,' he said, dryly.

Above them, from behind the mirrored glass of the control room, Seb knew that Madelene was watching them. 'It's business,' he told Mukhambetov.

Mukhambetov's eyes seemed to glaze. He stared into space and scratched his chin. 'I think I'll grow a beard, Sebastian, an imam's beard. What do you think of that?'

'Great. That'd be great.'

'Fuck you, Sebastian.'

Seb waited, half expecting some expression of violence. They stood facing one another.

'You got a good deal,' Mukhambetov informed him. 'Very favourable.'

'I know.'

'There are no absolutes, Sebastian. No thing is better or worse than any other thing. Heroin, hashish, barbed wire, groceries, plastics – it's all the same.'

'Is this an apology?'

Mukhambetov smiled thinly. 'An explanation.'

Seb's uneasiness about Mukhambetov began to dissipate.

'You want the grid?' Mukhambetov asked.

'Sure,' Seb said.

Mukhambetov rattled off the eight numbers. Seb produced his mobile phone; he held his breath and dialled. Cal answered on the second ring. Seb repeated the numbers and broke the connection. There, it was done. He lit a cigarette. It occurred to him that Mukhambetov was nervous in his presence. This cheered him immeasurably.

The storm continued unabated.

Cal looked back across the swirling deck at the wheelhouse, at Andy's face glowing unearthly green above the instrument panel, but he found no consolation. It was terrifying. A fifty-foot swell. There was no horizon, just surging green water and the roll of the boat to tell him which way was up.

He struggled forward at a crouch, swaddled in oilskins, with one hand on the gunnel to stop him being swept overboard. In his other hand he carried the weight of the barbed steel hook – the creep – that he would use to drag for the hash.

Andy was dodging the weather; riding with the stern to the waves and the engine idling. With each wave the stern was lifted up and Cal cowered against the deck until it passed.

Bracing himself against the A-frame, he attached the creep to the spool of yellow polypropylene rope on the hydraulic sheave-hauler, and swung the pulley out over the sea and let the rope run and run till it hit the bottom.

He waved frantically at Andy. He could feel the creep bouncing on the sand at the bottom. He fought to maintain tension on the rope. This was the worst part of it. Twice before he'd brought hash up off the sea-bottom, but that was off the coast of Cornwall and there had always been a buoy to mark the location of the haul. He'd never tried dragging blind, or in this kind of weather.

He imagined the watertight barrels floating about a metre off the sea-bottom, each of them attached to a strop or 'leg', which was in turn attached to a 'lane', a steel hawser running along the sea-bottom, and anchored at either end. It was a question of finding them.

They criss-crossed back and forth dragging the creep, while Andy kept one eye on the monitor as it tracked their course across the grid and the other eye on the radar, watching for any sign of other shipping. The scanner had already picked up the warning to all small craft to head to port.

After half an hour of having his face lashed with salt spray that stung like nettles, and clinging desperately to the A-frame with numb fingers, and cursing Seb over and over, Cal felt the rope come fast and then the sheave-hauler begin to labour as it reeled in.

'Yes!' He shouted, the rope rushing up through his fingers.

Suddenly the boat pitched forward with a massive wave and the stern rose to almost vertical. The tension on the rope increased dangerously, the sheave-hauler squealed. He punched the STOP button and listened, half expecting the rope to snap.

The moment passed, the wave was gone; but, when he switched the hauler back on, the rope was running easy. He had lost the catch. He brought the creep up to the surface to check, but there was nothing attached. They were forced to turn back into the swell.

They wallowed briefly, side-on to the waves, and then they turned again, dodging. He let the rope run.

Then he had it. The hauler groaned.

'Up you come. Up you come. Yes! Yes!'

He grabbed the hawser. As the fluorescent-orange barrels bobbed up out of the water and were hauled on to the pulley he cut the strops holding them with his bait knife and dropped them through a deck-hatch into the cold-water tanks.

When it was done, he fought his way back to the wheelhouse and dragged the door closed behind him. He shook his hands to get the circulation back into his fingers and swept back his hood and rubbed the exposed surfaces of his face.

'I don't think I'd cut it as a seal,' he said, smiling weakly, the relief uncoiling in him. He found that he was shaking uncontrollably.

Andy lit him a cigarette. 'That wiz fuckin intense!' he said. 'Twice there ay thought ye'd bin swept away.'

'So did I,' Cal said, watching the cigarette bobbing and weaving with his hands.

'Ay'll tell you, ay could do with gettin stoned,' Andy said.

Horizontal sheets of water were striking the wheelhouse.

Cal shook his head.

Andy protested, 'You said yersel, every other time the first thing ye do is cut yersel a share o the haul. Too right.'

Seb had been firm on that point. The last thing he'd said, standing at the end of the jetty, was 'Don't touch it. There's no time to repackage it. The whole thing works on a tight timescale. You heard what I said, back at the beginning: we do this right or we don't do it at all.'

The nicotine was making Cal's head spin, or maybe it was the boat that was spinning. 'Seb said no. That's the end of it,' he said.

Andy shook his head. 'You'se shud stand up tae him.'

Cal ground out his cigarette. 'This is not the time.'

Andy said, 'Come oan, there's never gaunnae be a right time.'

'I'm not going back out there.'

They ran with the sea.

*   *   *

BLIND

Hard rain lashed the jetty, and boiled off the surface of the arc-lights that had been 'borrowed' for the night from the video production company, and off the deck lights on the boat. Cables snaked back and forth across the wooden planks.

As they pumped out the tanks the nose of the boat rose towards the jetty. Andy untied the boom from where it had been fixed against the wheelhouse roof wheelhouse, and when he was done, Cal hooked the first barrel on to it and they swung the boom out over the jetty and lowered the barrel on to the bed of the pick-up truck parked there.

'Victory!,' Seb yelled, milk-churning the barrel down the bed of the vehicle.

Cal was beyond exhaustion; punch-drunk from the waves.

When the last of the barrels had been transferred to the pick-up, they refilled the tanks and secured the boom. Andy switched off the electrics.

On the jetty Seb grabbed Cal in a bone-crushing hug. 'You did it!' He grinned manically, his head tilted at an unfamiliar angle.

'Are you all right?' Cal asked, struck by a sudden misgiving.

'Never been better,' Seb replied, without hesitation. 'I'm on top of the world. How are you?'

'Fine.'

It was absurd, Cal reflected, how easily Seb managed to lift his morale. It showed how easily people adapted to circumstances out of their control; they looked for something familiar and latched on to it.

'I'm knackered,' he said.

Andy leapt the gap between the boat and the jetty, and hurried to the pick-up with their backpacks. When they were finished, they squeezed into the cab of the vehicle and took the steep track up to the house. Gulls wheeled sideways over the windswept heights. Seb drove with his fists clenched on the top of the wheel, moving his head from left to right as he struggled to see through the rain.

'I've fixed you up with a bed for a few hours,' Seb said. He glanced across at Andy. 'You're booked on a flight out of Dublin in the morning. The studio's laid on a complimentary car to the airport. All you've got to do is behave like a musician. I'm sorry, but you'd stick out like a sore thumb in Belfast. They don't go in for blacks there.'

Andy shrugged. 'Nae bother,' he said.

Seb made no mention of his plans for Cal.

The unloading bay was in a cul-de-sac between the main house and the studios. There were three vehicles parked on the slick cobbles beside the emergency exit – a black, bullet-shaped Audi convertible, a brand-new white Bedford van and a muddy eight-ton six-wheeler Mercedes truck. Seb parked the pick-up and they hurried against the roiling wind to the large double doors. The pungent stench of ammonia buffeted them.

'Jesus,' Andy protested, 'what's the smell?'

'Chicken-shit,' Seb yelled.

'Chicken-shit?'

Seb paused before ringing the bell, a conspiratorial smile on his face. 'The merchandise is going over the border buried in a lorry-load of chickenshit.' He grinned. 'What's kept in the dark and fed on shit?'

Cal shrugged. 'You mean, apart from me?'

'Very droll,' Seb replied. 'I think you'll find mushrooms is the answer to the riddle. The merchandise is being delivered to a mushroom farm—'

He stopped mid-sentence; there was some kind of disturbance inside the building. Madelene was shouting. Seb unzipped his leather bomber jacket and shifted the Desert Eagle tucked in his jeans, turning the grip towards his right hand. He pressed the bell.

Madelene opened one of the doors. Despite the darkness, she was wearing sunglasses. There was a streak of blood leading from her mouth across her face. Seb pulled out the gun and pushed past her into the corridor with one of his eyes closed. Cal followed.

MaColl was kneeling on the carpet squares, pressing a bloody handkerchief against his cheek. The rest of his face was still livid with the bruises inflicted by Seb and, before him, the IRA. For a second it seemed that Seb could not locate MaColl, even though he was kneeling just a few feet away; frustration warped his face as he searched for him, and then, abruptly, his head swung round and he had MacColl in his sights.

Cal sucked at the air, gasping with sudden insight; Seb was blind on his right side. He must have lost a lens.

'What the fuck happened?' Seb demanded, reholstering the pistol.

'The bitch bit me,' MaColl protested.

'What?'

'I was just being friendly, like. Passing the time with the girl.'

'Piece of filth,' spat Madelene.

Seb spun round on her. 'You keep a grip on yourself.' Then to MaColl, and equally aggressively, 'You concentrate on the job.'

Madelene stood in front of Cal. She reached up and ran her hand across his scalp, scissoring her bloody fingers through his newly cropped hair. 'Did you keep your locks?'

He nodded, suspicious of her attention.

She teased him gently. 'Stripping yourself down to essentials? Preparing for battle?'

'Who's with Mukhambetov?' Seb demanded, his voice rising.

'He's drunk most of a bottle of vodka.' She shrugged. 'He's not going anywhere.'

Seb groaned and punched the wall. 'Why don't they do what they're fucking told!'

'We're not soldiers, Seb,' Cal replied, too tired to be sympathetic, not taking his eyes off Madelene for a second. She was giving off a heady and atavistic aura. It was no wonder that others were picking up on it. Now she was directing it at Cal. She was so unpredictable. Just days before she had spurned him, now she was being seductive again. She took him for granted. He felt imprisoned by her.

Behind her, Seb sighed wistfully. 'You think soldiers do what they're told?'

'Smoke a cigarette,' Cal advised.

'Come on,' Seb said. 'Let's get you to bed.'

Madelene smiled. Cal could feel his head, his whole being, sinking towards her.

At the table Seb watched the streak of mercury climb the thermometer with a sense of rising excitement. 'The children are in bed,' Ed announced, closing the door behind him. He was carrying a large suitcase. Cal and Andy had been provided with sleeping bags in one of the other rooms in the complex and encouraged to go to sleep. Deliberately excluded. 'Only the corrupt and the crazy remain. How does it look?'

'Ninety per cent pure,' Madelene replied. 'The world's finest.'

'Copacetic.' Ed smiled. He wiped the back of his hand across his nose. It was swollen and rotten-apple-coloured. They were all marked by violence – except Madelene. She was untouched.

Seb jumped up from the chair that he had been straddling, and ran his fingers through his swept-back hair. Nostrils flaring, he paced back and forth in front of the map-board, between plastic-wrapped sacks of heroin.

Across the room, Mukhambetov grinned, and rolled his thick neck. His face was flushed with alcohol. 'What did I tell you?'

Seb nodded curtly.

Ed set the suitcase down on the floor. 'Your money,' he said. 'Fresh from the Limassol launderette.'

Mukhambetov got up from the far side of the table, swaying slightly, grinning from ear to ear.

Seb consulted his watch again. 'We're on target.' He pointed a hand, spade-like, at MaColl. 'I want you on the road inside a couple of hours.'

MaColl nodded. Seb stopped in front of Mukhambetov. 'You're out of here.'

'Good luck,' Mukhambetov said, his hand held out.

Seb dismissed the remark with a swift shake of the head. 'I don't need luck.'

He took Mukhambetov's hand, and in one violent action, spun him round and snapped his arm up behind his back, forcing him down on to his knees. With his free hand he pulled the Desert Eagle out of the waist of his jeans and rammed the muzzle into the back of Mukhambetov's head.

'You motherfucker,' Seb hissed, child-like with spite. He pressed his thumb over the oiled spur of the hammer, and cocked it back. The workings locked into place with a sound like a dry stick snapping.

A single commingled breath drawn in a long aspiration. An eddy in the smoky room.

'How might a prince of my great hopes forget,' Seb said, 'so great indignities you land upon me? How does that grab you?'

Mukhambetov was breathing heavily and rivulets of sweat were running out of his hair and into his eyes, which he kept opening and closing. Madelene leant forward in her chair, with her chin resting on her knuckles, an expression of amused curiosity on her face.

'Hey, man,' Ed protested, 'what the fuck are you doing?'

'Playing the game,' replied Seb, apparently calmly. 'The rules require tit for tat.'

Madelene's light laugh tinkled like a wind-chime. 'Eliminate the fucker,' she said softly.

Abruptly Seb stepped back and let the pistol hang by his side. After a few seconds, Mukhambetov climbed slowly to his feet. He stood, biting his lower lip fearfully.

'It was nothing personal,' Seb said. 'But you put me in a bad position before, on your ground, and here, on my ground, I couldn't let it slide.'

Mukhambetov rubbed his face, shivering the thick gold chains on his wrists, lifting a film of sweat on the palms of his hands.

'You can go now,' Seb told him. He believed they were all frightened of him now. He had bent them to his will. He felt magnificent. His eye was no bother to him. He was in the ascendant.

Mukhambetov nodded slowly. He seemed more relieved than angry. He waved one hand in a feathery gesture and went out of the room through the thickly padded door, taking the suitcase with him.

'You're crackers,' MaColl said.

'Shut it!' Seb hissed. 'Now, let's get this stuff repackaged and loaded.'

Cal twisted and turned in his sleeping bag, stalked by amorphous and not unfamiliar fears, by the feeling that there was something out there in the dark, something threatening. As a child, in the aftermath of his mother's death, he had spent many nights shivering under the covers, filled with fear, listening to the windows rattling in the wind. Something of the same feeling crowded him now.

When Seb came for Andy and flipped on the striplight he got up on his elbows and stared blearily across the room, but Seb told him to go back to sleep, and his last memory of Andy was of him putting his hand on his shoulder and whispering, 'Good luck.'

A sinister eroticism plagued his dreams. The bodies of those familiar to him writhed in sexual congress; they parted, switched partners, and came together in a slow and self-conscious ballet, and it seemed to his unsettled mind that the exaggerated positions of their limbs conveyed a meaning beyond his understanding.

After waking one too many times he gave up trying to sleep. He slipped out of the bag, put on his boots and went out and patrolled the anonymous carpeted corridors.

There had been no resolution to his encounter with Madelene. Events – Seb's manic behaviour and his own tiredness – had conspired to keep them apart. He didn't know whether to be grateful. She seemed more strange with each encounter.

He found the door to the control room and went in. A stream of low-volume invective was issuing out of the intercom, announcing to the world that Oisin MaColl was the real mastermind controlling the operation. Curious to hear more, Cal sat down in front of the mixing desks and looked through the glass at the sound-stage below.

MaColl was speaking straight into Madelene's face. 'Don't make me laugh, sweetheart. Your plan? *Your* plan? You think I'm just here to smuggle your shit over the border? Wake up and smell the fuckin' coffee. My money, my shit. My plan. Your precious brother's only here to keep the spooks and the shock-troopers off my back long enough for me to get to Belfast. That's it. Period.'

'Our supplier, our buyer,' Madelene snarled back at him. 'Our plan.'

MaColl laughed at her, and she flinched as a gob of spit from his mouth landed on her cheek. He started backing her up towards the table. 'Girl, your supplier is history. Packed up and pissed off back to Russia. Crowe said you were gullible. You think Stevie Truth wouldn't deal with me direct? You think he trusts you more than me? Because I'm a taig and he's a prod? Baaallicks. This is business. You Brits have no fuckin' idea. Your brother will be lucky if I let him keep his kneecaps. And as for you, you're a convenience and nothing more. A perk of the job.'

He pinned her arms with one red-mottled hand and with the other, the bandaged one, he reached into the opened leaves of her cashmere skirt. 'You're everybody's meat.' Remorselessly, he bent her down over the table, using his bulk against her slight frame.

Cal adjusted the volume and the box-like room was filled with the sinister whistle of MaColl's breathing; his churning lips close to her ear. And as she sank beneath the onslaught, it seemed as if her features were replaced by an absence of features, a seamless mask from which all trace of humanity was erased.

He could not bear to look at it. He reached across and pressed down on the transmit button.

Very slowly and deliberately, he said, 'Get her off.'

MaColl took a quick step backwards and whirled round fearfully. Madelene dived for the floor, reaching for something unseen. MaColl lurched across the stage, his chest heaving. Madelene came up holding a pistol straight out in front of her with both hands. Cal remembered his conversation with Kelly after Al's funeral, when she told him that Madelene had bought a gun.

'OK, OK,' MaColl said, backing away. 'OK, for Christ's sake.'

Madelene said, 'You're dead.'

'I don't blame you for being angry,' MaColl said, switching his attention between her and the mirrored bank of windows above him. 'But think about it for a second.'

'Fuck you,' she said, advancing.

'You won't get your money without me. You're fucked without me. Think of all that juicy money.'

'You're filth.'

MaColl was gaining in confidence, playing to the unseen watcher. 'I'm the man from the 'RA, the man who'll carry your shit across the border. You remember that.'

Cal fully expected Madelene to shoot him. In his experience she cared little for the consequences of her actions; but, somehow, inexplicably, the moment passed. Sneering, MaColl turned away. She remained with her hands out stiffly in front of her.

'You'll pay for this,' she called after MaColl as he left the room. When he was gone she turned the pistol around in her hands, staring at the barrel.

Cal watched her until she put the pistol down and then he went down to her, to comfort her, but she would not let him touch her.

'Are you OK?' he asked.

She stared at him wide-eyed. Her stare was devastating; utterly without warmth, without recognition – as if he was an insect, a cockroach.

2

Beyond Clady the road narrowed to a single lane as it climbed Fearn Hill. The fields were slushy and wet, full of heather, furze and rushes still clad in melting snow. A few scrawny sheep grazed among the rushes. As they passed, the sheep pricked up their ears and stared warily after them.

The turn leading to the border was blocked with wire, but there were footsteps in the snow beyond it, leading across the hills; the makings of a path. They climbed over the wire. Cal caught himself and left a line of snags like tooth-marks in his jeans. The faintest suggestion of a smile crossed Seb's face; but his very clear, azure eyes remained cold. Unmoved.

They walked side by side, divided by the weight of matters unspoken. Cal balked at the idea of giving voice to the fear that had grown in him during the night, because he feared the outburst it might precipitate; he was certain that, just as Seb permitted no unhappy memories spoken aloud, so any question-ing of his actions or judgment would be regarded as the most profound treachery. For no reason that he could think of, other than cowardice, he maintained his silence.

As they followed the path over the hill, it widened into a track. They could see a couple of isolated farms sited on natural vantage points with long lanes running to the farmhouses. Away in the distance there was a farmer in a tractor in a field. He stopped the tractor as they crossed the crest of the hill. Watchfulness seemed to be the spirit of the place.

He didn't even know why he was crossing the border with Seb. The original agreement had been that he would bring the stuff ashore and then leave. Instead, Seb had woken him the next morning, said, 'Coming?' and that was that. The company had split up, each of them heading for a separate border crossing. He had come because, in truth, there was no question of him not coming. It was just one more example of the control they exerted over him.

'Are we in the North or the South?' Cal asked, stiffly.

Seb frowned. He pointed at a dip in the track. 'I think maybe that's the North. And maybe the South beyond it.'

'I guess I expected a wall,' Cal said.

Seb glanced at him coldly. 'This isn't Berlin. There's fuck-all on the map.'

Seb's cellphone beeped three times, and then went silent. 'MaColl's met up with the truck,' he said.

There was a pile of broken-up cars and electrical appliances lodged in the heather at the steep bottom of a field. They climbed a hedge and followed a tarmac road for two miles, hurrying against the wind. They passed a cottage, and an elderly man came to the door and stared at them as they went by.

'I hate this fucking place,' Seb said.

They passed a Garda checkpoint. The Garda watched them without apparent interest.

'I guess we're in the South,' Seb admitted.

There were no road signs. Seb looked back down the road at the checkpoint, and then forward again, as if he was searching for some visible mark that might indicate the border. Growing frustration twisted his face.

'Now we're in the North, I think.' Seb stopped. 'I kept thinking that the land smelt queer,' he said, vehemently. 'It was the smell of blood, as though the soil was soaked with blood.' He looked across at Cal, who shrugged, not recognising the source.

'Jung,' Seb told him. He pointed down the road. 'The piece of Ireland which passeth all understanding?'

Cal had no wish to play the game. He was tired of Seb's bullying tone of voice, the hectoring quotations, the 'command presence' he had honed so successfully as a child, and stuck with through everything. Cal was convinced that this semblance of arrogance was the reason why Seb had achieved so little satisfaction from his life.

After an uneasy silence, Seb said, 'Murbhach is being repossessed.'

Cal closed his eyes, and sighed.

'No coming back from the brink this time,' Seb explained, sudden bitterness in his voice. 'The old man's lost it all at Lloyd's.

While he was standing up for Uncle Saddam, his syndicate was going under. He didn't listen, didn't get out when they gave him the wink. They're throwing the old man out on the moors.'

It seemed unthinkable that someone else might live on the estate.

'You can pay off the debt, with the money you make,' Cal said.

'Is that what you're going to do with your money? Bail out the Bean family? Buy Skurryvaig farm?'

Cal bridled at the hint of condescension. 'So what are you going to do? Abandon the estate?'

Seb glanced at him. 'I'm taking off, lover,' he said, without a trace of humour in his voice, 'disappearing off the face of the earth. I remember you once wanted to do the same. Look, everything has changed. I don't think you realise how much. I have no obligations to anyone any more. Not to the army, not to my father, and not to Murbhach.'

He stopped abruptly. The shadow of some involuntary ferocity crossed his face. '*The knife*'. Cal felt a sudden and distinct sense of physical danger. He turned round. There was a British soldier staring at them from a ditch just a few feet away. He was aware of others in the nettles and thistles around him, and more in the field beyond.

'Hello,' said the soldier, a Geordie. His wide smile was utterly unnerving.

'All right,' said Cal. It had occurred to him that Seb might be carrying a gun, that he might be preparing to use it.

'Where are you going, man?' The soldier asked.

'Castlederg,' Cal replied, after a moment's hesitation. Beside him Seb remained silent, tense. Cal elaborated quickly, 'We've been hiking the Ulster Way. Took a bit of a detour.'

'What happened to your faces?'

Seb shifted almost imperceptibly.

'We had a bit of a scrap,' Cal explained. 'A disagreement over a lassie.'

The soldier nodded cheerfully. Just as suddenly everything was going to be fine.

'You're a Jock?'

'Aye.'

They went on down the road. There were cows in the fields now, bunched around piles of winter feed.

'Ulster Way,' Seb said. 'Cunning.'

'Jesus! I thought you were going to shoot someone.'

Seb stared at him, refusing to be drawn.

Cal strode down the road, rubbing his face. 'Fuck! Fuck! Fuck!'

'Calm down,' Seb said softly.

'What the fuck do you think you're doing?'

Seb shook his head. 'What are you talking about?'

'The whole fucking shebang. The big con trick. Smuggled weapons, terror groups, MI5. Christ, MI5!'

Seb laughed dryly. 'You know they say in Ulster that if you play the part, you can get away with anything once.'

Cal was silent for a while. Seb's confidence was breathtaking, literally.

'I'm serious,' Cal insisted.

'So am I,' Seb retorted. 'Around here, everything is seen; and just as incomers aren't welcome, so no one will talk against their own – at least not openly. That's what we need MaColl for; he's one of them, he reassures the watchers on both sides. They expect certain things, like guns and bombs. Give them what they want; let them see what they want to see. It's a feint, a classic military manoeuvre. Hannibal at Cannae.'

Cal shook his head. 'You want to beat them at their own game, Seb, prove you're better than they are.'

Seb regarded him coldly. 'I am better than them. I'm beyond the range of their understanding.' He didn't seem to have any sense of proportion at all.

'You're blind,' Cal said.

'I've lost one lens, if that's what you mean.'

'That's not what I mean.'

'When this is over, I think you should go back to Oonagh.'

Cal was taken aback.

'That business with Oonagh,' Seb continued. 'I want you to understand that she slept with me to get back at you. Yes, she was frightened, but that wasn't all of it. It was revenge, I guess.'

'This isn't about that,' Cal said. 'That's the one thing it's not about. It's everything else.'

Seb didn't seem to be listening. 'We never had secrets, did we? That was the point of it. You and me. It wouldn't matter how bad it got, because you'd understand.'

They passed a small brick bungalow just beside the road. There was a woman standing at a window with her back to them.

'If you're about to tell me that you're running off with Breeze, don't bother,' Cal said. 'I know all about it. Madelene told me.'

Seb let out a sudden bark of laughter. An explosive release of tension. The woman in the window spun round in fright and screamed at the top of her voice.

'Christ!' said Cal. It was difficult to know what to do. The woman had been joined by other women, all looking at them suspiciously.

'Let's get out of here,' Seb said.

They hurried along the road, Seb striding out ahead, almost running.

Cal struggled to keep up with him. 'What is it?'

Seb glanced at him. 'You think I'm taking off with Breeze? You're more naive than I thought.'

'I'm naive enough to be following you.'

Seb turned on him. They were shoulder to shoulder, thigh to thigh. 'Go, then,' Seb said. 'Turn your back on me.'

Cal met his gaze.

'All right.'

Seb reached across and put the palm of his hand against Cal's chest. Cal tensed, expecting Seb to push him away; but the palm remained where it was, resting above Cal's heart. An unbreakable connection.

'I'm sorry,' Seb told him.

'Forget it,' Cal snapped.

'No.'

'Fuck you,' Cal said bitterly.

Seb winced and hung his head. 'Don't . . .'

'Don't what? Don't leave you and your crazy plan.'

That brought his head up. 'Don't you have faith?'

'Sure,' Cal sneered. 'I believe in virgin birth. In water into wine. That Sebastian MacCoinneach can con everyone, everywhere. Including me.'

'I'm not conning you,' Seb replied. 'It *is* possible. The money is there for the taking. The plan *will* work. Christ, we've got this far – all the way from Afghanistan. The only barrier to success now is disbelief. Have I ever let you down? Have I?'

A pause.

'This isn't about that,' Cal protested.

'Have I ever lied to you?'

Another pause.

'No,' he conceded reluctantly.

'We burned Tarmac. Nothing can stop us. Nothing.'

'I don't trust them,' Cal said. 'Ed, MacColl. Those are only the ones I've met.'

'You think I do?'

'I don't know.' It felt as if his resolve was slipping, as if he was losing an argument. He didn't have what it took to stand up to Seb. 'I don't know why this has to be so complicated.'

'It's big money,' Seb countered. 'The biggest. That's what they care about. All they care about. Think about it. They won't jeopardise the money. So they won't jeopardise me, because I'm the only one who can pull this off.'

He caught the look on Cal's face. 'I've got surprises up my sleeve,' he explained. 'I've got watchers watching the watchers. I've got bangs!'

'So why do you need me?'

As soon as he said it, Cal knew that he'd given in and that he'd be seeing the plan through to the end.

Seb was astonished. 'You're my friend. It was your idea. We made an oath.'

Cal groaned. The incredible, expanding, all-consuming oath.

Seb was smiling. 'Lover.'

Now Cal just wanted to get walking. To get it all over and done with. 'Come on, let's go,' he said.

They walked. As they went down the hill into Castlederg, they caught sight of a white Bedford van parked beside the road, and ringed by traffic cones. Cal recognised it from the parking area outside the recording studios. He noticed that Department of the Environment decals had been added to the sides.

'It's Madelene,' Seb said.

They approached the van warily. There was no other traffic on the road.

When they were within a couple of metres of the van, Madelene, who had been watching them in the wing mirror, got out of the cab wearing DoE overalls and a baseball cap disguising her hair. She went around the back of the vehicle and opened the double doors.

Their eyes met as Cal came abreast of her, and whatever she saw there made her glance quickly at Seb, standing beside him. Seb merely shrugged and climbed into the van.

Here take this.' Seb flung Cal a flak jacket, and after it some DoE overalls. 'Put the overalls on over the flak jacket.'

Looking around him, Cal saw that the van was filled with equipment; flak jackets, torches, overalls, balaclavas, piles of strops and karabiners, a heavy-duty pallet-truck, a generator and a power winch.

'We're going down into the bowels of the earth,' Seb explained. 'We're going at them from underneath.'

He consulted his watch. He forced his hands together as though he was trying to hold himself in on the centre of something. 'Come on,' he whispered.

Something was happening, beyond Cal's understanding. All he knew was that he was in the back of a moving van that he could not see out of, and that his destination was a mushroom farm.

Seb's cellphone beeped twice. His eyes seemed to get smaller and more finely focused.

'MaColl's arrived at the crossing point,' Seb explained, his voice level, almost monotone. 'Ed's watching from the housing estate opposite. He rings Organ in Dublin. Organ is never still, he moves from place to place. Organ rings me. Three rings. Two rings. One ring. No connection is made.'

Cal asked, 'What if it goes wrong?'

'Five rings. Everyone scatters. Separate escape routes, like in the plan.'

He had a cigarette in his mouth, but hadn't lit it. He was staring at his watch. 'If they stop the truck we're fucked.'

'Will they stop the truck?'

'Not if I'm right. Not if they're holding out for the big fish.'

'The big fish?'

'The hardliners who want to kickstart the war. The hardliners who are due to take delivery of the guns at the farm. The spooks and secret soldiers stop that truck for more than a few seconds at that checkpoint and they give the game away. The whole thing folds like a house of cards. You see, Ed is not the only person watching. All sorts of lowlife are watching that crossing point, just watching for the merest nuance, the merest sign that it's a trap.'

Seb's cellphone beeped once.

'Yes!' He leant back against the side of the van and lit his cigarette.

They descended into the storm drain, bulky in their flak jackets, wheeling the pallet-truck slowly forward by torch-light, the white ellipse of light skimming the algaed surface of the maintenance walkway and the river of snow-melt coursing beneath them.

They were due to turn off two kilometres into the tunnel. Seb went out in front of them, pacing the distance with his pistol drawn, the knot of karabiners on his belt clinking like loose change, his shadow like that of a hunchbacked silent-movie villain. Madelene giggled, and the sound was picked up and echoed by the water as it tumbled across the haphazard lumps of concrete and tree branches that obstructed its flow. It was not a pleasant sound. There was an oppressive aura in the tunnel; flecks of paranoia and claustrophobia. Nobody spoke.

After forty-five minutes, Seb stopped abruptly and consulted his map. He pointed his torch down the bore of an unused side-tunnel. It was older, Victorian-era, brick-lined and dripping with moisture.

'This is it,' he said.

They unloaded the winch and the generator and carried them into the tunnel. It was smaller and without a walkway, so they sloshed forward at a crouch, through umber-coloured sludge, their heads brushing the roughly textured ceiling of the tunnel.

A hundred metres down the tunnel Seb stopped and played his torch-beam across the glistening walls around him. There were clusters of snails on the bricks. At shoulder height on the north side there was a spray-painted yellow arrow pointing downwards.

Seb passed Cal his torch, knelt down beneath the arrow and started exploring the dark crevices between the bricks. Cal saw that the grouting had been dug out and the bricks loosened. The bricks came away easily in Seb's hands; he started removing them and throwing them away up the tunnel.

When the hole was large enough, Seb crawled through and shone the torch down a line of old and sagging wooden props, just a few feet off the tunnel floor, revealing the horizontal shaft of an old lead mine.

'Look at that,' Madelene said.

'Bingo,' said Seb.

The walls of the shaft were covered with graffiti. Slogans and expressions of revolutionary solidarity, spray-painted by those who had been forced to lie there in hiding, and those who had paused while passing through.

'Fire up the generator,' Seb told Cal.

Cal yanked the whipcord on the ignition and the engine caught immediately and roared, making an unconscionable noise. Hurriedly, he connected the generator to the power winch, pressed the feed button on the pistol-grip and passed the hook through the hole to Seb, who attached it to his belt and started crawling away up the shaft, the hawser unspooling after him.

'Remember,' he called behind him, 'two tugs.'

Madelene paused for a second in front of the hole and looked at Cal. Her eyes shone brightly in the darkness. She reached out to touch his face and he recoiled. They stared at each other.

'No,' he said.

She didn't seem to hear him. She reached out and traced the outline of his cheekbones as if he was unfamiliar to her. She turned away from him and crawled through the hole into the shaft.

As soon as they were out of sight, the urge rose in his throat like bile.

Go.

A two-kilometre jog down the storm drain. The keys were in the van.

Go.

Seb's words, 'Go then. Turn your back on me'.

Cal flicked his torch on and off. It was fine; it didn't make any difference; he could do it in the dark. Although he had been plagued by nocturnal terrors as a child, he had never let his fear of the dark paralyse him. He could find his way back to the mouth of the tunnel, just as he had found his way across his own house, time after time, in total blackness.

He imagined the forces of law and order gathered above him. A steel necklace strung round the farm. It was folly for Seb to imagine that he could triumph over such forces. An untenable arrogance. Suicide.

Go! There was nothing stopping him.

He could taste it, like sulphur in his mouth. But.

In the end there wasn't much to believe in except friendship and loyalty. He had run before, but it had led him back to a dark place. Now he had to stand firm in this dark place. It was not one of his own choosing, but it was all there was. Calum's last stand.

Thinking it made him smile with dry humour. Fuck it.

He was here and he would ride the whirlwind to the end. After all, he had given it its name; he had unleashed it. Seb's grand gesture. Screw the lot of them: the army, the police, the IRA. Screw Edinburgh and Eton. Screw his family.

Perhaps Seb *could* make it, somewhere. Perhaps he was wrong, after all.

He had a cigarette, breaking the cellophane on a fresh pack. The flicker of the lighter seemed to suggest movement close to him. Spooked, he turned the torch on and swung it up and down the tunnel. A rat eyed him suspiciously. After a while it scampered away. He switched the torch off again. The tips of his fingers on the hawser were numb. He was getting cold very quickly. As he grew colder he felt the fear gathering around him.

There wasn't a chance. At the same time, there wasn't anything else.

He felt the hawser jerk twice in his hands. He punched the button on the pistol-grip and listened as the motor started winding in the hawser.

The moment of truth.

He heard a flutter, and then suddenly there were black shapes whistling close over his head, striking his face and shoulders. He fell back and cowered against the muck on the floor of the tunnel – quivering in shit.

Bats. It was only bats. He was ashamed.

There was a rough dragging sound from the mine shaft.

He'd lost his torch. He suffered a moment of panic, searching around in the sludge at the bottom of the tunnel. His fingers connected with it. He composed himself, switched the torch on and pointed it into the shaft.

A grey beast in a vortex of dust slouched towards him.

The first hundred-pound backpack burst out of the shaft in a shower of loose bricks and dust, and others started to tumble after it, crashing into the winch and generator and tearing the pistol-grip out of Cal's hands. Seb was dragged out on his back; hard extraction, he called it. As he emerged, he unhooked the karabiner attaching him to the hawser, and rolled free. MaColl was next, in a flail of arms and legs, landing in a heap on the pile of backpacks. The winch seized, and the hawser went slack. Cal hit the STOP button. Seconds later, Madelene crawled out of the shaft.

The absence of sound was startling. Torch-beams flicked back and forth in the swirling dust, like searchlights at the scene of a natural disaster.

'Victory!' Seb hissed. A stray beam of light revealed that his overalls were in tatters, and there were crusts of blood on his arms. 'Up, up, up!'

He cut the strop on a backpack, grasped the harness, and started dragging it down the tunnel toward the storm drain. 'Come on!' he barked. 'Get working!'

MaColl was shaking his head back and forth as if stunned. Cal shouldered him aside and grabbed hold of a backpack. The weight of it tore at the sinews of his arms. He knew what he had to do.

He was halfway down the tunnel, his chest screaming with the effort and his torch bobbing like a firefly, when Seb scuttled past him on his way back up. 'Any minute now, it's going to blow,' he yelled.

For a moment, Cal didn't understand what he meant. He reached the end of the tunnel and hefted the pack on to the pallet-truck beside the one already there. He paused, waiting for his breath to come back. When it came, he saw it clearly – a bomb. One of Seb's bangs. There had to be a bomb: it was inevitable. He headed back into the tunnel, hurrying after Seb.

Too late.

The shockwave came barrelling down the mine-shaft and knocked him flat, and after it came a scaring wind that clutched at his lungs and left him speechless.

Sound roared in Cal's ears. He sat up and pointed his torch up the tunnel. Incredibly, Seb was on his feet, stumbling towards him with a backpack, a bright white grin on his blackened face.

'That'll freak them,' he croaked. He stepped over Cal, dragging the pack behind him. 'Sorry if I didn't mention it in my plan. Bit of a surprise, don't you know. The decisive moment!'

There was nothing to do but carry on. Cal staggered after another pack, passing Madelene and MaColl on their way down.

MaColl was shaking his head. 'What the fuck?'

'A bomb!' Seb yelled.

When the tenth and final pack was piled on the pallet truck, Seb swaggered back and forth in front of the tunnel entrance in naked triumph.

He stretched, turned on his heel and punched the darkness. 'Yessss!'

He pissed up against the brickwork.

'Fuck you!' he yelled hoarsely, flipping a finger in the direction of the mine shaft. 'I've won!'

MaColl slid down the concrete wall, grinning like a clown. 'A ton. A whole fucking ton of heroin. Hur fucking rah.'

Heroin.

There was no mistaking it. MaColl's words.

'Heroin?'

Seb stopped pacing back and forth.

A terrible truth emerged. It seemed too painful to consider, a deeper and darker place than any other; nevertheless, Cal repeated, 'Heroin?'

Silence.

A vacuum in which the tension grew towards the intolerable and the cold realisation that Seb had been lying to him from the very beginning, from that moment when the masterplan had first been raised over a pool game in Amsterdam.

Everything is permitted – no, not everything!

Suddenly Seb's torch was in his eyes. 'We don't have time for this,' he growled.

All Cal could see was after-images, a field of red static and dancing prisms of green and purple.

'Heroin?' He took two hesitant steps towards the truck and reached blindly for a pack. He unclipped the flap and reached inside.

'There's a whole fucking army on top of us.' The frustration was clear in Seb's voice.

'Tell the kid to wise up,' MaColl said, indignantly climbing to his feet.

'Leave it,' Seb pleaded, but they both knew he had no power beyond the persuasion of his own words to compel Cal. He never had. Cal had always acted of his own volition. He'd never seen it so clearly before.

He peeled back the oilcloth wrapping, dug his fingers into the hessian sack, and came up with fistfuls of fine white powder.

It was betrayal. Treachery. Beyond belief.

'We'll talk about it later,' said Seb softly, imploring.

'We'll talk about it now.' His voice sounded unreal in his ears, incredulous. 'What did you think you were doing?'

But Seb was speechless, rolling his head back and forth, in the light from Madelene's torch.

'You lied to me,' Cal said. He jabbed a finger into the centre of Seb's chest. His voice rising, the anger swelling, spilling over. 'You. You lied. You said it was hash.'

That snapped Seb back into the present. He matched Cal, anger for anger, snarling, 'Of course it's heroin. It had to be heroin. There wasn't any choice. You understand that.'

'No, I don't fucking understand,' Cal spat.

'Don't be so naive!' Seb punched the backpack sending a swathe of heroin fanning across the walkway. 'You think we were going to make any money on a ton of hash?'

'This is heroin, Seb. *Heroin.*'

'It doesn't matter what it is!' Seb yelled. 'It's just a product. You don't have to think about it.'

'What about the oath?'

'No!'

'People will die,' Cal said. 'Like Rory died. You'll be responsible.'

Seb howled. The sound seemed to explode from his throat, his head was thrown forward, then back, then forward again in uncontrollable spasms. It was as if he had broken free of the constraints of his own body. His howling was as atavistic as that of a predator deprived of its kill. Motes of dust, scraps of lichen and moss knocked off the ceiling floated downward, blurring the beam fixed on him. In that light, he seemed hardly human. Abruptly he head-butted the wall, and slumped into the muck.

MaColl growled, 'There's no time for this shit.' He pointed at Cal. 'Forget him. He's served his purpose.'

Seb stared up at MaColl, a gout of blood leaking out of his hairline, an expression of childlike incomprehension on his face.

The crack of the bullet was ear-splitting. MaColl crumpled.

Blood from the artery in his groin squirted in a twenty-foot arc across the storm drain.

'Christ!' Seb screamed.

Madelene's eyes refracted the light, insect-like. Implacable.

'You stupid cow!' Seb yelled.

MaColl looked up at her, silently imploring her, his face deathly white in the torch-light.

Seb was gripping his head like a vice, yelling, 'Where the fuck did you get that gun?'

'Moss Side,' Madelene replied, calmly. 'The numbers are burnt off.'

'Christ,' Seb moaned.

'He's bleeding to death,' observed Cal softly.

She shot MaColl again, in the back of the head this time. His dead jaw gaped.

'You've just killed a man,' Cal said.

Madelene pointed the gun and the torch at his head. Cal's heart beat fearfully. A flak jacket had not saved MaColl. He imagined her smiling. Beside him, Seb chewed at the knuckle of his forefinger, in rage and despair.

'Lover,' she said, in that special tone of voice.

Seb flinched as if he had been struck. For one blind moment Cal imagined she was talking to him, not Seb, and then it was clear as day. They were lovers.

Madelene knelt beside the body and, after a moment's silent contemplation, inserted a curious finger in the wound in the back of MaColl's head.

'What are you doing?' Seb asked, appalled.

She shrugged and then rolled the corpse off the walkway. MaColl slipped into the flood water and floated for a few seconds, his overalls puffed up with air, before disappearing under a cascade of dirty foam.

When they emerged from the drain Ed was on the slipway, wearing the overalls of a DoE employee. It was dark, and cold. Ed stopped mid-stride when he saw them, a questioning look on his face. Cal was pushing the truck, with Madelene behind him, her gun pressed into the back of his neck. Seb was lagging behind; the confrontation with Cal seemed to have robbed him of all volition.

Ed asked, 'Where's MaColl?'

'He's not coming,' Madelene replied, with an air of wonderment. 'In fact, he's dead. I shot him. In the head.'

Ed laughed, as if he was conscious of missing some secret hilarity. To Cal it seemed unlikely that Ed was going to survive either; which left Seb and Madelene. It was as if a caul had been lifted from his mind, and for the first time he saw things clearly, free of the self-imposed restrictions of loyalty and family; he had become acquainted with a heedless greed.

'Seb?' Madelene demanded.

Seb looked up. 'Stevie Truth?'

'He's waiting for you,' Ed replied, fixing on the subject with some enthusiasm. 'With the money.'

Seb nodded, as if it was what he expected.

'There's something else,' Ed said tentatively, as if unwilling to put it into words. 'Something weird. Maybe nothing.'

'Spit it out,' Madelene demanded.

'It's like there's too many people on the streets in the Shankill. It's sort of clammy.'

'Clammy?' In Moy it was raining.

'Something's happened,' Ed said. 'There's no radio in the van. Do you want me to make some phone calls?' Seb's restriction on the use of phones was clearly putting an almost intolerable strain on Ed.

'Just do what you're told,' Madelene said.

They loaded the van under Madelene's direction, while the rain washed the blood out of their hair and torn clothing. When they had finished they climbed in the back, on top of the stack of backpacks that reached almost to the ceiling. Ed closed the door on them, and they were in darkness.

The ceasefire was over. The RUC were throwing up roadblocks across the province. They were stopped at a checkpoint before they had travelled five miles. Soldiers watched the vehicles through the sights of their rifles from the ditches by the side of the road. An RUC man, bulky in body armour fresh out of storage, walked up the line of cars towards them.

'What shall I say?' Ed whispered through the grille, his head shivering back and forth from all the coke he'd taken. Seb didn't seem to notice. He didn't seem aware of anything.

'Tell him you're going to a burst water main. Find out what's going on,' Madelene commanded.

The van was wearing the plates of a genuine DoE vehicle and the RUC man seemed satisfied with Ed's over-eager explanation.

Ed asked, 'What's happened?'

'There's been a bombing in London,' the RUC man said, with weary resignation. 'Two civilians killed.'

In the back, Seb groaned softly.

They drove on into the darkness, towards the motorway and the route into the city; cocooned among bundles of heroin.

'You're a liar,' Cal said accusingly.

He wished he had his torch with him, but he'd dropped it at the mouth of the drain. He wanted to point it in Seb's face, to fix him with the beam, and demand a reply.

'Why?'

'I didn't have any choice,' Seb whimpered. 'Don't you see that? Once I was in I couldn't get out. Everybody was saying do it, do it. I didn't have any choice at all.'

'You lied to me.'

'Leave him alone,' Madelene said.

'No.' Cal told her. 'You should have left him alone.'

She snorted contemptuously. 'What difference does it make?'

Cal shook his head slowly. 'Anything is permitted. That's right, isn't it?'

'Don't be so moralistic,' she said.

'It's only heroin?'

He heard her click her teeth in irritation.

'It wasn't meant to be like this. You needn't ever have known.' Seb paused. 'I love her.'

Cal was aghast. 'You think she loves you?'

'I don't know,' Seb replied. 'It doesn't matter any more. It's all over.'

'It's not over yet,' said Madelene.

'It's over for him,' Cal pointed out. 'He's pulled off his magic trick. He's shown he's smarter than everyone else. So, Seb, what do you think Rory would say? Well done? Pity about the smack, but at least you fucked over the establishment?'

Madelene laughed. 'Rory would have loved us.'

Cal kept his attention fixed on Seb. 'Sure, you could have been his supplier. You could have had him in the palm of your hand. Think of the power.'

He shoved the long, silvery scar on the meat of his thumb into Seb's face. 'Easier than this?'

Seb's face contorted beneath his hand, as if riven by some silent tumult.

Madelene wedged her pistol between Cal's teeth. 'Shut the fuck up,' she hissed.

Stevie Truth was waiting for them on the second floor of a car bodyshop in the Shankill in Protestant West Belfast. They came into the city on the motorway, passing the Catholic ghettos and the broad slope of the Milltown cemetery on their left side. They turned off on the Crumlin Road and dropped down on to the Shankill. They saw army Land-Rovers with muffled, nervous soldiers leaning out the top.

Truth didn't seem especially pleased to see them. Methodically, he locked and bolted the garage doors as they spilled out of the van and stripped off their flak jackets and overalls.

'I didn't think you'd make it,' he said. He clapped his large white hands together to get the dust off. He was wearing a football shirt over a pair of jeans, and Nike trainers. His florid skin shone under the striplights. To Cal, who was seeing him for the first time, he looked short and barrel-shaped like a snub-nosed revolver.

'Hello Ed,' Truth said, acknowledging his schoolfriend without humour, while at the same time eyeing Seb and Madelene's handguns warily.

When they started unloading the van, he cleared his throat and raised a hand. 'There's no need for that,' he said. 'It's not going anywhere.'

He gestured to them to follow him. They stared at him.

'It can't do any harm,' Ed said.

They looked to Seb, who shrugged in acquiescence. Madelene looked furious. She prodded Cal with the muzzle of her pistol. There was a bell beside the door at the top of the stairs that led to the offices. Truth sprinted up the steps two at a time and then stopped and waited for them. He rang the bell and a voice called out from inside.

'Yeah?'

'Who'd ya think,' Truth snapped, with the first hint of irritation.

They heard the sliding of a lock and a bearded man stood before them in the office's fluorescent light, squinting. As soon as Cal saw him he realised that he was one of the men who had beaten him up in the hallway in Leith over two years before. The realisation alarmed him so thoroughly that he tried to force his way back down the stairs. Seb lunged at him, clamped a hand around Cal's throat and pinned him against the wall.

'What are you doing?' Seb wondered, an other-wordly quality to his voice. He seemed surprised at the speed and vehemence of his own reaction. He relieved some of the pressure on Cal's neck. 'I'm sorry,' he said.

Cal was too shocked to speak. For the briefest moment he had witnessed the unleashing of *the knife*, and for the first time he had been on the receiving end. It was terrifying.

Madelene screwed the muzzle of her gun into his face. 'Don't try anything,' she snarled, unnecessarily.

He got the distinct feeling that she wanted him to try something. Her expression carried the same intensity of purpose as when she was painting. It was as if she had found, in killing, an art form at which she excelled, and she was eager to do it again.

They were both abhorrent to him.

They led him down the hallway to an office. The office was grey and sparsely furnished with a linoleum-covered desk and two chairs, and, in one corner, a grey metal filing cabinet. Stevie Truth and the bearded man seemed to find the situation embarrassing and distasteful. Truth went over to the window. He rolled his short, blunt head on his shoulders.

'Things change,' he said with apparent regret.

Seb went over to stand beside him. Ed followed, wringing his hands. His accustomed confidence had been replaced by a wheedling paranoia.

'Everything is cool?' Ed enquired hopefully. 'I mean, before, you said it was cool.'

Seb looked out at the drab street below; a row of tightly packed second-hand cars sweeping into focus as he moved his head from left to right, a woman struggling with a buggy on the cracked pavement and behind her a tramp slumped in a cardboard box in a doorway.

'I remember an IRA bomb on the Shankill,' Stevie Truth said. 'Two kids were killed. The first two kids. Your father decided to get his kids out. My father decided to stick it out. Why did you come back Ed?'

Ed looked mystified. 'What are you talking about, Stevie?'

'The circumstances have changed,' Truth explained. 'The ceasefire is over.'

'That's politics,' Seb replied, calmly, 'not business.'

'I've just lost my distribution network.' Truth was looking out over the city, in the direction of the Republican stronghold of the Falls Road. He shook his head. 'A stone's throw away.'

Seb frowned. 'So?'

Truth shrugged. 'We must re-negotiate the price.'

'The price stands,' Madelene insisted.

Truth laughed. 'Did you think I'd say, "Hello, my name's Stevie Truth, and I don't know you, but here's a few million quid in a suitcase"? You thought it could work like that in Belfast? You think this is some kind of banana republic?'

'That's how it works,' Seb said, 'anywhere else but here. It's a great equaliser.'

The bell sounded in the hallway. The bearded man went out and returned a minute later with a young fair-haired man. The other half of the duo who had beaten Cal. His mouth had started throbbing, the scars on his face burned. His sense of danger continued climbing sharply, in near-vertical swerves.

Truth spoke in a soft and reasonable tone. 'There aren't enough junkies in Northern Ireland. We're way behind. You see, it's not the drug of choice. I was going to have to go out and create a market. A long-term strategy, something that would have required a stable political situation. Now I can't see how I can do it.'

'We're not interested in your problems,' Madelene said.

'Our problems,' he countered. 'Unless you want to take this stuff away with you.'

'This isn't business,' Seb said softly.

'Yes it is. That's exactly what it is. In Ulster politics is business.'

'Perhaps,' Ed suggested, 'we should listen to Stevie's proposal. Re-negotiate.'

Cal said, 'I'm leaving.'

Nobody reacted, so he said it again. Seb stared at him.

'You had me beaten up,' Cal said.

Seb blinked. 'No.'

'These are the two men who put me in hospital.'

Seb seemed genuinely surprised. The fair-haired one recognised Cal. 'I'll be damned,' he said, with good humour. He sauntered over to him and pointed at the scars on his nose and on his cheek. 'That's my work,' he said. It took all Cal's willpower not to flinch.

Seb looked at Truth, who shrugged his thick, simian shoulders. The fair-haired man was giggling. He nodded to Ed. 'See, we earned every penny.' The bearded one was more cautious, watching Seb to gauge his reaction. Seb could tell he was armed. Probably not the only one. Truth would be armed.

Ed was backing up against the wall, frightened of the expression on Seb's face. Ed had always been the weak link, weaker even than MaColl. Spineless. 'Madelene asked me to fix it,' he explained. 'I made a phone call. That's all.'

Seb shook his head sadly. 'Madelene?'

Cal was watching her face, just inches from his own. Her toffee-coloured eyes, masking an inscrutable intent. 'Why?' he asked.

She shrugged, showing no sign of remorse, 'Because . . .'

Cal shuddered. 'Because of Oonagh?'

'Maybe I was in a bad mood.'

'You're sick,' he told her.

'Madelene?' growled Seb, demanding an explanation.

She flicked her hair in annoyance and bared her throat. 'I don't need to explain myself.'

'You're insane,' Cal said.

'Spare me,' she sneered.

'I'm not staying here.'

'You take one step, it will be your last,' she told him.

Cal stared into her eyes. 'I don't think so.'

She seemed to falter, as if she had seen some unexpected reserve of defiance in his eyes. Then Seb was pointing his gun at her. The bearded man had drawn a large square pistol. It was a businesslike gesture, and he didn't seem to want to point it at anyone. Stevie Truth watched the proceedings incredulously.

'Let him go,' Seb told her, deadly serious.

Madelene pouted. 'You wouldn't.'

'Believe me,' he said, 'I would.'

Cal looked at Seb. 'Come with me,' he said. 'This isn't you.'

Madelene mocked him: 'Just say No?'

'It's too late,' Seb said, with infinite sadness. 'Now, the only way out is through.'

'Don't,' Cal pleaded.

Then, suddenly, he did it. Seb smiled. That brilliant infectious smile, transforming everything into some shared gruesome joke. A conspiracy against the dunces.

'Preserve thou the righteous. Let vengeance take the wicked.' He laughed. 'Go, for Christ's sake.'

When Cal stepped out into the hallway, Madelene did not shoot him and Seb did not follow. He experienced an odd feeling – almost relief. Before, when they had beaten him, he had run, but now he was walking of his own volition. He understood now that he was not a coward, he was just a normal, weak person who had allowed himself to be possessed. He had stood at the chasm's edge.

Now he was free.

All the lights were on in the workshop. As he went cautiously past the van he saw that its tyres had been slashed. As his own face had been slashed. It saddened him. He did not expect to see Seb or Madelene alive again. They had made their choice. There was nothing else that he could do. They had cast themselves out. Kicked loose of the earth.

He unbolted the door and went out into the rain.

He was halfway across the road, pausing on the white lines, when he saw Torquil. He stopped. Torquil was slumped in a doorway directly opposite, wrapped in damp cardboard and tatters of newspaper, with filth in his matted beard. In the semblance of a tramp. He was staring directly upwards, ignoring Cal, and muttering into his sleeve, to unseen listeners.

Cal turned and looked up at the window in the building behind him. He saw Seb's pale, distorted face swimming behind the glass. As he watched, Seb raised a hand and pressed his palm flat against the glass in a gesture of farewell or surrender, Cal couldn't decide.

A car horn beeped at him. He walked away.

'You should have taken his advice and gone with him,' Stevie Truth said grimly. 'You're way out of your depth.'

Carefully, not trusting his one good eye, Seb squeezed it closed and then opened it again. The instant remained. Down in the street Torquil continued to stare straight up at him. He held his breath.

He wondered if he would live. He did not think so. It had been a rapacious and pitiless folly. His own folly – it was pointless blaming Madelene. They were staring at him.

He pointed and asked wearily, for the record, 'Who is he?'

Truth followed the direction of his pointing finger.

'Look at him. He's just a tramp,' Ed said, hurriedly.

'Care in the Community like,' the bearded one explained. 'A social worker comes out to see him from time to time. Been there for months. He can't talk like. Just funny noises.' He began to mimic the sound.

Truth let out a soft and plaintive sigh. He put his hand on the gun in his jeans.

'It's an ambush,' Seb told them.

'SAS,' Truth growled softly. 'You traitorous fucker.'

Whatever else, now that the plan had failed, it seemed important to punish those who had breached security. 'All I ever asked, was to keep it tight,' Seb said.

He saw that he had been foolish. He had been so intent on making a fool of the security forces that he had not paid sufficient attention to Ed's side of the operation.

Ed was trembling. He knew he'd failed. 'My Da always said that bloodshed was lazy,' he said. 'Bloodshed was failure.'

Whatever Ed saw in response, it appeared to give him little comfort. He bowed his head in resignation and closed his eyes.

Crack.

Seb shot Ed on principle: the buck had to stop somewhere. After that, the air shimmered and swirled with bullets. Crack. Crack. Crack. He blinked, and each time he blinked, he did not know if he would be sighted or blind afterwards. There was no pattern. He kept blinking and firing. He imagined an officer, in an operations room far from this location, receiving a nod from the RUC and speaking into a microphone. 'I have control. Stand by . . . stand by . . . *Go!*'

Soon men in black would fill the room. He would die.

He felt a great weight strike his shoulder. The man with the beard had shot him. Seb swung the barrel around, took a few steps, and fired a round at him. Then he fell flat on his face. As he stared at the tight grain of the floorboards, it seemed that a part of him had detached itself and was falling away between the boards into infinity. He blinked. He realised that he had lost his other lens. Now he was all but blind. Somewhere deep inside him something soft and feathery was turning, and waking; he could feel its malice.

Madelene reached down and touched his arm. There was blood on it. 'How are you?' she asked.

He was glad she was still alive. He saw that she was still wearing her flak jacket; he realised she had always intended to survive. His body stiffened in a sudden spasm. He raised himself on his knees and brought up the pistol.

'You're beautiful,' Madelene told him.

Seb swung the pistol around, nudged Madelene aside with the barrel, and fired at the fuzzy shape of a man crawling towards them. Stevie Truth.

'Reload,' he told her. She reached into his pocket for a magazine. There was a hot metal smell in the air. He listened to Truth take a deep exhausted breath, and die.

'These paltry fuckers,' he said.

'You got them,' said Madelene. She smiled. 'The mass of dolts.'

'There are more of them outside,' Seb told her. 'A whole army of like-minded people. My family.'

Madelene shook her head. 'I'm your family.'

He was grateful that she was there. They deserved each other. He didn't think he could bear the pain by himself. Which was not the way it was supposed to be. He reached out with his strong arm, grasped her shoulder and eased himself on to his feet. Standing up hurt very much. He was surprised and relieved that the SAS had not broken down the doors. Perhaps they were letting evolution do its work. Waiting for the fittest to emerge from the bear-pit.

I'm coming.

'We are going to drive out of here,' Seb said, resolutely.

The most difficult part was the stairs. Each step sent a jarring pain into his bad shoulder. He closed his eyes.

When he opened them, he saw the slashed tyres on the van and the deep dark thing that had been sleeping began to unfurl. It whispered poisonously. He threatened it with *the knife.*

'We'll yomp out,' he said.

One foot after the other. These boots are made for walk-ing.

'Get a pack on me.'

'You won't make it,' she said.

'Of course I will,' he smiled, and eased himself back on to his knees.

It took a long and painful time to get the pack on his back. Madelene had to open the lid and remove many handfuls of heroin to lighten it. Pounds of gleaming white powder. He had to rock back and forth on the ground, with the nylon strap tightening on his torn underarm, to create the momentum to push him back on his feet. He staggered, bowed like a penitent. Gradually the pain straightened him up.

'See, no problem,' he gasped.

She pressed herself against him. He held her away for a few moments wanting to see her, to see the light on her face, wanting to know if she really, truthfully, felt for him – if it had been worth doing.

'To have done instead of not done, this is not vanity,' he said. 'To have gathered from the air a live tradition.'

Smiling, she drew herself up to his mouth and breathed life into him.

He was lifted.

'Dogs, would you live for ever?' he whispered, his voice failing. She silenced him with a finger to his lips. Whatever else, his love for her was genuine. They went out into the darkness and the rain, into a flurry of car horns and screeching tyres. Into the claws of bad dreams. Into a fusillade of shots.

It was a revelation. There was no ambush. It was obvious, now, looking at Torquil – alone, with the back-up probably stuck in a traffic jam and still minutes away. Torquil was working in deep cover, observing the garage and its occupants, not expecting this carnage.

Abandoned and afraid, Torquil speaking into his sleeve openly, now that his cover is blown. Emergency words. It made Seb profoundly happy: they had not penetrated his master plan. It was Truth's security that had failed, not Seb's. He had fooled them, every one of them. The SAS, MI5, 14 Company. The whole programme. An unconquered flame burned brightly in his almost sightless eyes.

He staggered across the road. Cars braked, tyres squealed. Madelene pointing her gun at the windscreen in front of her, screaming at the driver to get out of the car that had braked in front of her.

Torquil stood up, and rags of paper and black sodden cardboard, caught by the wind, cartwheeled away. To Seb it seemed that Torquil was falling apart. The world was imploding.

He tripped on the kerb and the weight of the pack pulled him over on his back. He opened his mouth in surprise at the sudden wrenching. He tried to stand without success.

The street-light hurt him. He raised a hand to shield his eyes.

'Ith finithed,' Torquil hissed, through the clots of his beard.

'No,' Seb said, in a burst of salivary laughing. 'Not till the fat lady things.'

Torquil took hold of the strap on Seb's shoulder and pulled down, brutally tightening it.

Pain within pain. Nothingness. He took a deep breath.

Torquil said, 'You'll burn.'

Seb gathered the tatters of his smile. 'Floreat Etona,' he whispered.

But Torquil wasn't listening, he was shouting at Madelene, telling her to put down the gun. The deep dark thing reminded him that he'd never liked Torquil. Kill, kill, kill, it urged. He brought up the pistol and emptied the magazine into the blurred and shifting mass above him.

3

C al walked. He walked westward through the early-evening darkness, moving from shadow to shadow between the orange street-lamps of the Shankill, staying intimate with the closed-up shopfronts and their cold steel grilles and shutters.

He crossed the darkened mass of Woodvale Park into the residential area beyond. He walked bowed, with the weight of complicity like a beast riding his back, sending him down into his boots for breath. He had heard the shots. On the Shankill people's faces had lifted miserably to the sound. A fragile peace shattered.

He could not believe he had been so blind and foolish, so gullibly led. He felt anger, and with it sorrow and a measure of self-pity and loss. He was not the only one to have been corrupted. He would not have believed that Seb would so easily abandon the one absolute that he had zealously adhered to; everything is permitted, he had said over and over again, except heroin. Heroin the fratricide.

It all led back to Madelene. There was something foul about her.

He had known it; he had always known it, but he had refused to acknowledge the truth of it. Between lust and misplaced loyalty, Seb and Madelene had him suckered from the very beginning, from his childhood. His face burned with shame and the plate in his mouth throbbed. He was a fool.

He had crossed the line.

He had followed the curve of the West Circular Road and, without realising it, had come back into the city – into a different place. Here the streets were flanked by tall galvanised railings with cruelly barbed points, and the murals on the shabby end-terrace walls were Republican. He had come to the area of his own religion, but it gave him no comfort. The shops were corseted in the same grilles and shutters. He was no less an unwelcome outsider. Brought out of their homes by the end of the ceasefire, young men clustered, like drug-dealers in any other city, on the street corners. They stared about them with an air of naked hostility.

He had no idea what he was doing or where he was going. He was turning his back on it all.

When he saw the black spires and corrugated walls of the army base on the slope of the mountain, he deliberately turned away from it, and went down the White Rock Road, with the grey mass of the 'bull-ring', the Ballymurphy housing estate, on his left and on his right the jumbled mass of the City cemetery, and beyond the ragged wind-blown Scots pines in the Falls Park. He stuck with the cemetery, and at the bottom of the hill he turned right and found himself sandwiched between two cemeteries, and he kept walking, and it felt as if the dead were boxing him in. The road forked ahead of him, and at the cleft of the fork, triangular like the prow of a ship, were the high walls and cages of an RUC station. It seemed to beckon. He hurried past its camera array with his head down. He went past an area of waste ground and beyond it a church, and another fortified post office.

He stopped. Arizona Street. He remembered a night stretched out in a narrow bed, with Oonagh beside him, her head on his chest, talking . . .

Arizona Street. The name, Arizona – suggesting some place different.

And he came to understand that all he wanted, that all he should ever have wanted, was to listen to Oonagh's wild and chaotic laughter. Images of her crowded him.

Jane, the manager at the veterinary surgery, picked up the receiver on the fourth ring.

'Jane, it's me, Calum.'

'Hello, Calum.'

'Can I speak to Oonagh, please?'

'I'm sorry, Calum.'

'Tell her I want to speak to her,' he said.

'I can't. She's not here.'

'She's not there?'

'She's on her way. Oh Calum, have you heard the terrible news?'

'What news?'

'About the bomb, down in England. It's a terrible shame.'

'Yes,' he said. 'It is.'

'I'll get her to call you.'

'Let me give you this number,' he said. She would recognise the code.

After he had put the phone down he crossed the street and stood opposite, at the darkened entrance to one of the cemeteries. He did not know if she would ring him.

After a while, the phone rang. He ran back across the road.

'You're in Belfast,' said the voice on the end of the line. The line was bad; the interference surged, and fell away, and surged again.

'I love you,' he said softly.

There was a long, empty crackling

'I wanted you to know, before the end. Before everything goes to pieces, I wanted to tell you, that I love you. I know it now, with certainty. Shit! Listen to me. I don't know how to say it so that it will get through to you. I love you. That's all. I don't know to say it.'

He had no way of knowing if she was listening, if she was even holding the receiver to her ear.

'I walked past Arizona Street. I remembered you speaking, beside me in bed, years ago, about wanting things to be different. About regrets. And hope. And escape.'

As the silence dragged on, the urge to scream grew in his throat and grew almost unbearable.

'I'm sorry,' he said. 'I'm so sorry.'

He put the phone down.

He was ten metres from the telephone box, walking towards the RUC Station, preparing to hand himself in, when the telephone rang again. He stopped. He went back.

She said, 'What kind of trouble are you in?'

'It was heroin. They were smuggling heroin. I didn't know. They lied to me. Everything went wrong. I heard shots. People are dead.'

'Seb and Madelene are dead?'

'Yes,' he said, certain that it was true.

There was a long pause.

'She had me beaten up, back in Edinburgh. When I ran. It wasn't your fault. It wasn't anything to do with you. It was me.'

He had brought everything down on himself. He had been stupid, not loyal. 'I believed their lies.'

'They were your family,' she said, her voice calm, revealing nothing.

She was right. In the midst of their tattered, broken-up families, the three of them had turned inwards, and formed a closer alliance, a different kind of family.

She said, 'They betrayed you.'

'I did it to myself.'

'Go back to Arizona Street,' she instructed him. She gave him an address and told him to wait fifteen minutes and then go there and do as he was told.

He didn't know what to say.

'I love you,' she said.

The phone clicked dead. He put it down and picked it up again and remained standing, with his hand on the receiver, for fifteen minutes while a woman's voice in his ear repeated the same refrain over and over.

'Please replace the handset . . .'

He didn't know if, in the worst of times, he deserved to be saved.

The door was opened by a young woman in her twenties, wearing a leather jacket zipped to the throat. A dark plait snaked out from under her woollen hat. He knew her, though for a second he could not place her. Then he remembered meeting her the first time he went out to Oonagh's cottage on the outskirts of Edinburgh, back when they were students. He remembered her holding a motorcycle helmet. He did not know if he had been told her name.

She gestured to him to enter. There was newspaper spread out on the cheap geometrically patterned carpet in the dim, narrow hallway. He stood on it. It was no warmer inside than it was outside.

'Take your clothes off,' she said brusquely, her accent Irish.

He stripped off, pausing briefly before removing his shorts.

'I've seen it all before,' she said. Shivering, he stepped out of her way and she bundled up his clothes in the newspaper.

'There's a bathroom at the top of the stairs on the right. Take a shower. There's a flannel for you. Scrub yourself thoroughly.'

He ran up the stairs. The bathroom was a narrow rectangle, with one window, divided into two panes, a lower frosted pane and an upper clear pane. There was mildew high on the walls. He drew the shower curtain round himself and switched on the shower.

The water was freezing.

He scrubbed furiously at his flesh, as if trying to rid himself of an unpleasant stench. He imagined Madelene's cold insect-like expression. The look of infinite sadness on Seb's face.

He wondered if they were really dead. It was difficult to imagine.

When he could stand the cold no more, he stepped out, wrapped himself in a towel and sat shivering on the toilet seat. After a few minutes he got up on to the seat, so that he could reach the upper pane in the window. He wiped the moisture off the glass with the towel and looked out at the concrete yard below.

The young woman was feeding his discarded clothing into a fire in a rusting oildrum. When she was done she came back into the house.

He heard her footfall on the stairs. She knocked on the door and he drew the towel around his waist and told her to come in. She had brought him some clothes, a pair of jeans, a clay-coloured vest, and a padded check shirt. Some underpants and socks. A pair of worn-out trainers. He had lost track of the number of times he had changed clothing in the past twenty-four hours.

'Put these on,' she said. 'Then come down for your tea.'

'What's going to happen to me?'

She shook her head and left him.

The jeans were a good two inches short and the trainers pinched his toes. Despite being scrupulously clean, they carried a musty aroma as if they had been folded away in a cupboard for a long time. Seeing himself in the mirror, with his shorn head and ill-fitting and faintly ridiculous clothing, he appeared somehow diminished, like a foolish child. It seemed more than apt.

He went cautiously down the stairs. She was in the kitchen, kneeling on the linoleum, stirring beans over a primus stove. The grimy unpainted corner that had once held an oven was clearly visible. There was half a pint of milk on the window-ledge, no fridge. The window looked out on the yard; a thin plume of smoke rose from the oil drum outside.

'Do you live here?' he asked.

'No.' She looked half-starved.

'Whose clothes are these?'

She shook her head. 'I don't know. Maybe his.' She didn't elaborate. 'Beans, OK?' she asked.

'Fine.'

There were two chipped dinner plates on the table. When he closed his eyes he could see Seb's face, with Death's voice coming out of it: 'Let vengeance take the wicked . . .'

She spooned out the beans and slid a plate across the table towards him. Cal sat down and started eating. He tasted nothing.

There was a knock at the door. The beans calcified in his mouth, a hard indigestible lump.

'Stay here,' the woman said. She got up and went out into the hallway, closing the door behind her. Cal heard the front door being opened, and then the low murmuring of a conversation on the doorstep; a man's voice, his words inaudible.

Cal got up out of his seat and went over to the bin and spat the mouthful of beans into it, and after that he opened the back door into the yard, and crossed it in three steps and scaled the wall, intent on escape.

There was the outline of a man standing in the darkness of the churchyard beyond. 'Get back inside,' he said, in a low and menacing voice.

Defeated, Cal eased himself back down off the wall. In less time than it took him to cross the yard, the woman had returned to the kitchen and discovered his absence. He was cornered. He stared at her.

'You're safe here,' she told him. Her features softened somewhat. She held out her hand to him. He hesitated and then allowed himself to be drawn back into the kitchen.

'We're both safe,' she said. 'That's what they came to say. Word has come down to leave us unharmed.'

'Unharmed?'

'Oonagh's father must have fixed it.'

Oonagh's father? He tried to remember what she had told him

about her father. He was a businessman; that was all he could remember. He didn't know what to say or do. Everything was out of his hands.

She asked him if he was tired and he replied that he was, and she led him up the darkened stairway to a room with a single bed and a pile of thin blankets. There was a half-melted candle in a saucer, its light flickering on the walls.

She stripped down to a T-shirt and her underwear and climbed under the blankets. 'Come on,' she said, in the same dispassionate tone.

He took off his trousers and joined her; they lay side by side, shivering in the candlelight. After a few minutes she eased herself in against his chest and they clung to each other; a sexless trembling. She matched his fear with her own. Pressure swelled against the inside of his skull.

She woke him by laying her hand on his shoulder. She was dressed. Morning was visible through the thin net curtain. 'Get dressed,' she said. 'There's someone waiting.'

He lifted himself on to his elbows. The last thing he remembered was the pain behind his eyes. He had slept without dreaming.

'It's time for you to go,' she explained.

He wanted to know her name, but it seemed pointless asking, somehow dishonest. 'Go where?' he asked.

She shrugged. There were dark lines under her eyes, and she did not look as if she had slept. 'Home.'

Home?

He got out of bed and put on the clothes that she had given him. 'Thank you for helping me,' he said.

She did not acknowledge that he had spoken. He used her toothbrush to clean his teeth and then he followed her down the stairs. A well-groomed man in his fifties stood out in the street beside a gleaming white Mercedes. He was tall and sinewy, with reddish-grey hair and a smattering of freckles across the bridge of his nose.

Without once looking at Cal, he gave the woman a perfunctory nod and then went round and got into the driver's seat. Cal stood motionless beside the car, aware of people watching from behind the curtains masking their front rooms.

'Go,' the woman said. She went back into the house and closed the door.

Once again there was nothing for it but to do as he was told. He climbed into the passenger seat and did up his seatbelt. He stared at the immaculately clean dashboard. The man pressed a button and the doors were locked.

The man drove single-mindedly, his head darting back and forth as he muscled through the Belfast traffic, speeding northwards.

'My name is O'Hara,' he said.

'I know who you are,' Cal replied. 'You're Oonagh's father.'

He watched the man's knuckles whiten on the steering wheel. They drove on in silence for a while.

'Back in the eighties, during the hunger strikes, I was responsible for a line of communication between the Army Council of the IRA and the British government,' O'Hara explained. 'I have connections.'

'I don't know what you're talking about,' Cal said.

'When you get back, I want you to remind my daughter that she made a deal with me, and I expect her to honour it.'

A large Rover came up fast behind them on the road to Larne and flashed its headlights. O'Hara pulled over to the side of the road and switched on his hazard lights, leaving the engine idling. Cal turned round in his seat and watched as someone advanced towards them from the Rover behind. A small man in a mackintosh.

Clunk. The doors unlocked.

The man slid on to the back seat, removed his glasses and started wiping them fastidiously with a white handkerchief. His lopsided mouth hung slackly open.

'My name's Holdfast,' he said. He was English, without any trace of regional accent. He continued to work on his glasses.

'It's not a name,' O'Hara explained, his attention fixed on the oncoming traffic. 'It's a label. A bar-code.'

'How was your coronary?' Holdfast asked affably.

'Coronaries,' O'Hara corrected him.

Holdfast replaced his glasses. 'That's better,' he said. His eyes swam indeterminately behind the bottle-thick lenses of his glasses. There was no way of judging his point of focus. He spoke out of the corner of his open mouth. 'I want your opinion of our young friend?'

'I don't hold an opinion,' O'Hara replied.

'Not in a position to, I suppose. After all, you're offering protection to a heroin-smuggler.'

O'Hara directed a suspicious glance at Cal.

Holdfast allowed himself a small chuckle. 'An uncomfortable truth?'

O'Hara scowled. 'Say your piece, then let me on my way.'

Holdfast nodded thoughtfully, then his face seemed to brighten. He tapped Cal on the shoulder with one of his small, slightly pudgy fingers. 'You'll never guess what I've just been reading. I was just reading your play.'

Cal's skin crawled beneath the pressure of the man's finger; he felt a sudden wave of fascinated indignation. 'I didn't know that it was in print,' he said.

'We have it,' Holdfast said. 'Along with pictures. Somewhere called Claremont Road. Twyford Down. I rather enjoyed it. An interesting diversion at four o'clock this morning. Your file, I mean. Not the play.' He seemed to await some response. 'The play seemed rather pointless,' he went on, after a pause. 'They never did stop the road. I found it difficult to sympathise with the characters.'

'Not everyone did.'

'Frankly, it is astonishing to me that some people see you as a ringleader. I think I know you better than that. You're a parasite. Nothing wrong with that. As long as you keep your eyes closed, and your mouth shut.' He smiled opaquely. 'That's all. I expect you will want to get back to your woods and wetlands.'

'I don't know what you mean,' Cal replied.

'I'm sorry. I'm not making myself clear. The meat of it is that I'm here to be persuasive. You see, we don't want it all resurfacing in print. Even in drama. Gulf War hero turns round and smuggles heroin, that sort of story. Kiss and tell, you know. Do I make myself clear?'

'I think so,' Cal said.

'I have had to draw strongly on a reputation for efficiency and rectitude. It is untidy, but fortunately there is no compromising evidence, nothing that can't be written off as an internal feud. So, you see, we can turn a blind eye. No point, as I see it, in dragging you down to "nick" at Paddington Green and grilling you under the Prevention of Terrorism Act. No point at all. We can accommodate you, if you can accommodate us.'

A scintillating new pattern had emerged that was not visible to those with focused eyes. The city as a moving field of light, as a fluid wash of monochrome shot through with streaks of orange and red and green. It filled his retinae with brilliance. Seb was transformed.

At one point he thought that a large chunk of himself had come away in his hand and slipped away across the back seat of the car; it took him some time to realise that it was the backpack. There was so much blood, more than he had ever expected. It hurt very much each time she took a corner. There were so many corners. So many racing lights and filaments and galloping strobes.

The pack slid menacingly back towards him. For some reason he looked inside, and what he saw there terrified him. An open beak filled with crackling white noise. A voice and its plausive giggle. *Somebody's done for*, it warned.

A nauseating stench filled his nostrils. The voice in the bag, which was the same as the voice in his head, invited him to look at his arm. It was burnt black, its skin turned to ash. He had to fight the urge to scrape it away.

The car slammed to a halt. The field of light swelled and contracted like a kaleidoscope.

'You keep passing out,' Madelene told him.

He gripped the headrest in front of him with his strong arm. He resolved not to look at his bad arm again or listen to that voice – wherever it came from. Not if he was going to survive.

'Where are we?' he gasped.

She read off the street names. From memory he visualised the layout of the city, and then let his eyes search out the pattern in the field. It was good to concentrate. Concentrate and survive.

These fragments I shore against my ruin. Whadyathink?

'We need to stop somewhere,' she said.

After a few seconds he smiled, or at least he tried to; cajoled the muscles of his face to arrange themselves that way. All might not be lost, after all. He barked directions.

Counting.

The moon had risen by the time they turned off the Glen Road, and went up between steep banks of bare and littered rock on the approach road to the gypsy camp. They circled the car-park. The moonlight made his wound throb. He could count to the rhythm of it. He gritted his teeth. 'Do you see a Nissan pick-up? Next to a caravan?'

'Seen.'

'Park beside it.'

If anyone could move weight on spec, Seb reasoned, the gypsies could. They were resourceful; and they had little respect for the law or the paramilitaries. It was the only chance.

Madelene helped him out of the back of the car. He paused before going up the loose pile of breezeblocks that served for steps. The curtains were drawn on the windows. He slipped his gun into his jeans; the bloody stock was visible against his belt. She held him by his good arm.

'Don't lose your rag,' he cautioned. 'This is not a good place for a shoot-out.'

'I don't think you'd survive another,' she said.

'I'll drink to that.' Smiling was getting more and more painful. He was relieved that she hadn't asked him to explain his plan.

He knocked loudly on the door. He didn't want to cause too much surprise. He pushed the door open and walked a few steps inside.

From where he stood he should be able to see all of the caravan. He was careful not to squint, or give them any clue that he was almost blind. He moved his head slowly from side to side, trying to generate an impression of implacable threat. He wished he had his Ray-Bans.

Formless colour; a bright orange-red smudge was a portable gas heater and a yellower light was an oil lamp on a table in the corner. Two small brightly coloured lozenges were playing with brightly coloured toys in the middle of the linoleum floor. Children.

Two blurred, hulking shapes at the table were men. He imagined them gaping at him. His bloody arm. He located a chair and sat down in it. He flung the pack on the floor in front of him. Heads dipped and shifted. They were watching his stuff.

Vultures.

One of the men climbed to his feet and took a few slow, predatory steps towards him. He was not sure, but Seb felt that he was the one who had been at the window when he had been first brought here. Bob, the SAS man, had called him Anthony. He was overweight, and short of breath. The caravan was filled with the lumbering whistle of his breath.

'That's close enough,' Madelene hissed.

The people in the room were looking towards the door behind him where Madelene stood. He imagined her looking cool and arrogant with her Moss Side gun in her hand. He shivered.

'You're Brits,' Anthony said.

'That's right,' Madelene replied.

'The agreement we have is that you don't come in the door.'

'Things change,' Seb said.

'You're bleeding on my floor,' Anthony said. The other gypsy said nothing.

'It'll add a dash of colour,' Seb said.

'I hear there's been shooting up on the Shankill.'

'You have good ears.'

The other man, who he thought must be younger, seemed to smile and shake his head slowly.

'That's smack,' Anthony said, opening the bargaining.

Seb said, 'Get me some water.'

Anthony nodded to one of the children, who brought him a beaker of water from a plastic cylinder. It was a girl. Her eyes were huge as she looked at his wound.

'Go over and sit down,' Madelene said. 'All of you.'

She came forward and knelt beside the pack. From somewhere she produced her works, a syringe and fresh needle still in its wrapping. There was a dropper, some cotton and a spoon. She dipped the spoon into the pack.

Seb was puzzled. 'What are you doing?'

'Giving you a shot,' she said. 'Watch them.'

He was beyond caring. She took the beaker out of his good hand and used the dropper to draw off enough water to fill the spoon.

'You're not army,' Anthony said.

Seb laughed, a painful spasm. 'It's complicated.'

He drew out his gun as Madelene cooked up using his bronze Zippo. When the heroin had melted she loaded a shot in the needle.

'Goodnight, sweet ladies,' Seb said, gesturing with the gun.

She gave him the shot in his limp left arm. When he had the shot he passed out briefly. When he came back he found Madelene winding strips of torn bedding round the wound. The other occupants of the caravan were still seated at the table.

'You've lost a lot of blood, you know that?' Madelene said.

'I don't need blood. I've got determination.'

He put a hand on Madelene's shoulder to move her out of the way and vomited explosively on the floor.

'It's a beautiful wound,' he thought she said, as she was finishing the bandage. It reminded him of when she had stuck her finger into MaColl's head. He wished he could see her face clearly.

He lifted his chin and directed his voice at the men hunched expectantly at the table. 'I can sell you the smack,' he said. 'At a good rate.'

They let it float for an unsettling length of time.

'There's no call for that stuff here,' Anthony replied, eventually.

Seb laughed. He wasn't surprised by their lies or their cunning. He expected it. They could smell the carrion in his wound. For a split second he wondered if they could hear the voice in the bag; but it was impossible.

'If you fuckers think you're going to bluff me out of my shit, think again,' he said.

'Smack's a Brit thing,' Anthony replied in a reasonable voice. 'Not our thing.'

'It's indiscriminate,' Seb said.

'People take a dim view.'

'You're the people the IRA are frightened of.'

Anthony shook his head impatiently. 'It's too difficult.'

'What do you mean?'

'I mean' – he eyed the pack – 'we don't want it.'

'Bollocks,' Seb sighed.

There was a pause.

'You're dying,' Anthony said. 'You're bleeding to death.'

'Shut the fuck up!' Madelene screamed.

'It's all right,' Seb told her. He took a deep breath. The voice in his head was giggling, heedlessly. He saw now that it was a test. He must be decisive. There was only one true option. 'We'll take it home. All the way.'

Slowly and painfully they went through the business of getting the pack on to his back. When it was done he drew himself up and closed his eyes. He would have to be strong. There would be roadblocks on all the roads, the voice reminded him. He backed up towards the door.

'You won't make it,' Anthony called out.

'I've got this far,' he said, backing down the steps.

The sky was clear and the car-park was bathed in excruciating moonlight, but he had the drug to ward it off. He struggled purposefully across the tarmac.

'Where are you going?' She hurried after him.

He pointed at the mountain above them. The voice giggled.

'There. The Black Mountain.' He gritted his teeth. 'It's not over yet.'

'You're delirious,' she said.

'I'm strong. We'll walk.'

The first part of the ascent was through gently sloping pasture; obstinate snow gleamed in the corners of the fields and the ground was sucking and boggy. The hedges were the most difficult part. He fell several times, and she had to pull him out of the mud.

They were tense as they crossed the Upper Springfield Road, walking slowly, ready to crouch and bring up their weapons. There was one field beyond the road and then the mountain. The green-black of the ground gave way to the unearthly twinkling of snow on the upper slopes. The summit seemed an unattainable distance away. He resolved not to look up again. He watched his footsteps appearing in the snow. They seemed to keep one step ahead of him. Crisp white outlines. The limit of his old bad vision.

They followed a chattering stream up a narrow re-entrant. It chattered with the same voice as the deep, dark thing.

An icy wind began to claw at the heat in his wound. He tried counting, but he kept losing track of the numbers. Suddenly he could no longer remember where he had begun counting. Or when? Was it back at the Fort? Chechnya? Iraq?

This was no time for reason.

Instead, he concentrated on *the knife*; mentally licking the palp of his thumb and running it along the blade. He found that it helped with the climb. He was making good ground. Left foot, right foot. He fought the urge to look up and check his progress.

He saw it now. It was all in *the knife*; a savage bulwark to hold back the pain. The blade was heated in the wound and quenched in the wind. Heated and quenched.

Hard. Brittle. Hatred.

The knife held the pain. Provided it did not shatter, he was confident that it would carry him all the way back to Cual.

'They're following,' Madelene said.

He didn't understand.

The wind was making the snow drift. Flurries of it kicked up in front of him. Sparkling torrents that tried to distract him. It was getting much colder. Debris swirled around him.

'Where are you going?' asked a voice beside him. It was the Iraqi with the stiff hair and the moustache. He had a bayonet sticking out from between his ribs. Then it was a giant needle.

'I'm climbing this mountain. One step at a time,' Seb replied.

The lever mechanism of an L2 grenade spun away over his head. He was in a trench. A tunnel. A hole.

The voice was bubbling with pleasure. He couldn't tell if it was coming from the bag, or whether it was back inside him. There was grit in his eyes. *The knife* was white-hot now, barely holding the pain. It swelled and vibrated to the rhythm of his steps. He was climbing a Glasgow stairway with murder in mind. Indiscriminate violence; collateral damage. The entrenching tool swinging loosely in his palm.

Knock knock.

'Who are you, and why must I kill you?'

He fell flat on his face in the snow. Clouds of boiling steam embraced him. *The knife* shattered.

Unmanageable pain.

Nothingness.

After a few moments, he licked at the snow to find some balance to the pain. Get back on your feet, MacCoinneach. He took a deep breath and gathered up the pain. He rolled over and looked down at himself. His left arm was enormous, swollen and blackened. The knuckles of his left hand were dragging in the snow. The line of footsteps behind him was black with blood.

As he looked out over the snow it began to glow. The field of light expanding like an atomic reaction. Like the end of the world.

Mother?

'Sebastian?'

It was his mother's voice, and it filled him with terror. She told him that it was the beginning of term. Her voice rasped like a saw.

No.

The first two years at Eton, and he's still wetting the bed; wakes each morning to a urinous tangle of sheets. Mercilessly teased.

Why don't you have a mother, MacCoinneach?

She's dead and burnt.

Why do you wet your bed?

Family holiday; his father dragging him screaming to the high diving board of the Olympic-size Beirut swimming pool, shouting, 'I'll teach you to be a coward, boy.'

He groped around for *the knife*. He found the haft and the broken blade. He concentrated on it. It required metal and heat to mend. Or a whole new one.

'Cold baths and grit and graft,' his father said. 'Pull yourself together. Remember, you are a MacCoinneach.'

'Poor little Thebathtian. Thomebody thumped him.'

'Fuck you!' Seb screamed. 'Fuck you all!'

Which was enough mettle. Enough mettle for a mountain. There was power in hate; he used it to forge a new *knife*. He worked on this new *knife*, honing its edges. It levered him on to his feet, and set him in the right direction. One step at a time. Conquering Everest.

'What are you carrying?' someone asked. It was Rory, walking beside him. Bright steel braces gleaming on his teeth.

'What's the knife for? What's in the pack?'

'Its mine,' he said defensively.

'It's not necessary,' Rory said, in gentle reproof. 'Not any more.'

'Of course it is,' Seb protested. 'It's the Freedom to Live.'

'It's an illusion.'

He reached behind his right shoulder and patted the pack. It was real enough. He couldn't remove it if he tried.

'Goodbye . . .' Rory said, his voice dissolving into the sound of falling waves. Way out in front of him, Seb saw whitecaps from waves falling over in the sea. There was pitch darkness between him and the waves. Looking back he could see no sign of the

BLIND

mountain. The rest of the world was nowhere; once again his eyes had failed him.

'Rory?'

Water lapped at his ankles. He could hear Madelene singing, away to his right. She must know the way. He was going in deeper to reach her. A small wave buffeted his thighs. In the deeper water he felt kelp shift against his knees.

Waves pulled and sucked at his legs. He felt light-headed and shivery.

He cupped a handful of water and let it trickle across his forehead. Some of it touched his lips and it was not salty. A voice reminded him that he was thirsty. As he lowered his face to the water, the backpack slid forward over the back of his head and the strap pulled at his wound. The pain was excruciating. A wave came and lifted him off his feet. He slipped under the inky surface of the water. The water hurt at first, but within a short time it felt very good.

He opened his eyes and watched the bubbles of air from his mouth drifting towards the surface above him. His legs hung away in the huge depth beneath him.

He could still hear singing. Madelene came for him, wreathed in streamers of red and brown seaweed. She drew him down to her tiny breasts, to the smooth oily surface of her lower body. Her mermaid's tail.

Her voice: Is this not worth a ten-year war?

She took his hand and dived down into the darkness. A wave of much colder water surrounded him and there was pressure in his ears. The water funnelled him downwards.

Into the whirlpool.

4

Cal followed the coastline, working his way between stippled pools of water and slick nodules of stone. It was raining. It had been raining for a week now, without respite. A steady falling of rain from the metal-coloured sky like a spell cast over the island. He had not passed a single car on the road from Port Claganach. Only the twists of peat smoke in the trees indicated a living presence.

He had walked in from the Celtic cross, careful to avoid any of the paths that the travellers used. It had not taken him long to work his way around to the smuggler's cove. He located the two green-black boulders that marked the entrance to the defile and squeezed between them, sinking into the sodden drift of leaves beyond. All around him the thick, iridescent moss sparkled with fat drops of water. He waded forward, going deeper into the trench. He was wet to the skin and shivering.

Carefully, he eased himself between two rusty strands of barbed wire. There was no sign that anyone had been in the trench before him. He found the gouge marks in the rock that marked the spot and knelt down in front of the broad, flat stone and traced its outline with his fingers as he had done many times before. When he had shifted it he reached down and lifted out the old ammo box. Many-legged bugs milled around at the bottom of the hole it left. He popped the catches on the box and pushed back the lid.

He listened for a while. Drips of rain snaked down his backbone. He half-expected Torquil's voice, but Torquil was dead. His name added to the list on the bell tower at Stirling Lines in Hereford.

Cal retrieved the waterproof bag, unrolled it carefully and removed the contents. Two British passports, slightly used. Russian visas stamped Entry and Exit. Familiar faces attached to unfamiliar names. A wad of twenty-dollar bills. More Brink's money. Birth certificates, insurance and share certificates, bank accounts, credit cards; all the carefully constructed data of two fake identities.

The Freedom to Live.

He put it all back in the bag, rolled it up and dropped it back in the box. When he was ready he kicked in the sides of the hole, picked up the ammo box and carried it with him out of the trench. He threw it into the sea. It sank immediately, and left no trace.

The rain stopped that afternoon. The sun stripped the clouds away into vapour and made the sky as brilliant and austere as ice. He had thought the rain would never end.

The next day it was freezing out on the Og. Even the act of breathing was painful. Cal stood waiting by the graveside, in a storm of spindrift rising off the whirlpool, and with it the smell of goat from the cliffs behind him. A punishing wind.

The MacCoinneach had insisted on the observance of the ancient island tradition that the cortege take the longest route to the grave-site: files of kilted officers, their scabbards clanking, struggled up the hill from the sycamore wood towards the cemetery, bearing the flagged coffin between them. With each step they broke through the thin crust of ice – their spats and brogues and bare goosebumped legs were already black with mud, their faces red with the strain. Soldiers with rifles at the shoulder followed, and behind them a regimental piper in tartan plaid, and behind him the Commanding Officer and his Adjutant, in mud-spattered pinstripe.

Shuard and the other travellers from the Murbhach site, in their own mud-coloured plumage and with their own barefoot piper and didgeridoos, retreated before the oncoming cortege, hissing in protest. Two different worlds had collided, and there was no telling what the outcome would be. Seb would have loved it.

Children moved jerkily around Cal, up to their knees in the quagmire. Organ's dog Kali yelped at the heels of the soldiers. One of the black-skirted ladies from the Port Claganach Hotel went over in the mud and her trayful of oatcakes and cheese was dispersed to the wind. Only The MacCoinneach, standing at the grave's head, seemed impervious. He held himself ramrod-straight despite the wind, his calculating eyes half closed, as if he was expecting some further disaster.

As the coffin-bearers crested the hill and came wading through the gravestones, Cal fell back from the hole. He stumbled against a spade. A hand gripped his elbow. It was Andy. In his other hand Andy held Seb's lump of the Berlin Wall; each of them, in his own way, participating in this bizarre theatre. At the gate at the foot of the Og the island's single policeman struggled to contain a posse of tabloid photographers. Initially overshadowed by the Canary Wharf bomb, the death had received some late interest. The stories read like the end-product of a game of Chinese whispers: the truth transmogrified, villain to hero, smuggling operation to undercover sting.

With knees bent, spines bowed and feet braced against the lip of the hole, the soldiers lowered the coffin into its watery trench. Colonel Hector Macleod, OBE, MC, stood at the other end of the grave from The MacCoinneach, and with the granite line of his jaw he seemed to challenge anyone to disagree with his interpretation of events.

A coat of whitewash had been slapped on everything.

The Murbhach estate was no longer up for sale. A well-placed article in a broadsheet newspaper hinting that ex-MI6 agent Hugh MacCoinneach was considering an offer from an Australian publishing firm to print his memoirs, had resulted in a flurry of activity at Murbhach and a near-miraculous revival in the family's financial fortunes. Hugh had ridden the blows like the old boxer he was; and struck back with his own lethal counterpunch.

Somewhere a priest was speaking some irrelevance. All Cal heard was 'To die is life.'

'Aa chlann na sunn,' someone muttered.

Coffin-bearers stumbled back and riflemen stepped between them, their rifles an interlocking arch over the grave.

An officer cried, 'Take aim.'

Hugh MacCoinneach lifted his head to ninety degrees. An oddly disciplined movement.

'Prepare to fire.'

Drew breath.

'Fire.'

Whatever he said, The MacCoinneach's words were drowned by the fusillade of shots, and their answering echo from the unsettled ocean beneath them. He strode away down the hill towards the woods.

There was a brief hiatus. No one went after the old man, no

one rushed to comfort him. There was no sign of Breeze. At the grave-side the military had its say; and the initiative had passed into the hands of the crowd beyond them.

Andy was the first. He stepped up through the ranks of soldiers and dropped Seb's lump of the Berlin Wall into the grave; it struck the coffin with a hollow thud. After him Organ, with a cloth-wrapped chillum, and Shuard with a tartan rug, and after him someone flung in a silver coin in accordance with custom, and after that Seb's Action Men, and his American bayonet from the Gulf.

Calum was the last.

Everyone gave him space; as if acknowledging a special bond that he was no longer sure had even existed. It had all been bad wiring. Misplaced loyalty and dumb arrogance. Doing for the sake of it, because not to have done would be diffidence. Now it seemed that it had been swallowed up – transformed into something heroic. It was as irreconcilable as Seb's Double Life had been. It could make you laugh or scream.

There was even talk of awarding Seb a posthumous medal.

Everything was contradiction. In death Seb had achieved what he had hoped to in life. The biggest fucking thing. Cal said, 'Whadyathink?'

It was his only offering. Someone passed him a spade and he started to backfill the grave from the mound beside it. Clods of earth from other spades thumped down on the coffin. A flask of whisky was passed from hand to hand. Spindrift whirled like soda water around them and stung their faces. The whisky burned his throat. When the grave was filled with earth they stamped it down with their boots and by the time they had finished the soldiers and photographers had all gone. The spectacle was over.

He leant breathlessly against a spade. A joint went around but he refused it. Something made him look up. He saw Oonagh. She was beautiful and pale in a slim black dress and wellingtons, silhouetted against the cliffs behind her. He had not seen her since he had returned back from Ireland.

She rubbed his mud-caked shoulder. 'Come on,' she urged.

He left the spade standing and followed her down the hill, through the sycamores, to the car park.

'Get in the car,' she said. 'Let's go somewhere.'

He got into the passenger seat. He wiped his palm across the condensation on the windscreen.

Oonagh studied him, her arms crossed and resting on the wheel. 'I'm sorry he's dead,' she said.

He watched the sea. 'Where are we going?' he said at last.

'I don't know,' she replied.

He wound the window down and rested his arm on the frame. They took the road off the Og, and Fly craned forward, neck outstretched between them, as she watched for rabbits on the verges.

They caught up with The MacCoinneach on the airport road. He was walking in the opposite direction from Murbhach.

'Where's he going?' she asked.

'I don't know.'

'We'll take him home,' she said.

Oonagh slowed the car as they came abreast of him and Cal reached behind him to unlock the rear door. As he did so, he was aware of a shadow falling across his face. A mouth, the bared teeth savaging its lower lip, spitting.

'Swine.'

Oonagh slammed on the brakes. As they came to a sudden halt, The MacCoinneach reached out and struck the bonnet with his fist. Then he turned his back on them and started striding purposefully out across the moor, away from the road.

'Jesus,' Oonagh said.

Cal reached up and wiped the spittle off his face with the palm of his hand. Oonagh switched off the engine and they sat for a minute.

'It's understandable, I guess,' she said. 'His second funeral in a week.'

'You make allowances for everyone,' Cal said.

'So do you,' she reproached him.

'Let's go to the Big Strand,' Cal said.

'OK.'

The roads were empty. They parked on the edge of the rabbit grounds, and when he opened the door, Fly leapt out from the back seat, scrabbled across his lap, and streaked away.

They climbed to the top of one of the highest dunes, and stood amongst the frosty maram grass, looking down on the beach and the unceasing Atlantic waves. The pale bleached-out orb of the sun seemed to float just above the horizon. His clothes, soaked through with mud, had gone stiff on his body.

'You've been avoiding me,' she said.

He stood there, with his lips caught painfully between his teeth. He was freezing. 'I thought you'd be angry.'

'Where's the point in it?' she shrugged. 'It's such a waste of time.'

She took off her jacket and wrapped it round his shoulders. She sat down and hugged her knees, her cold red nose peeping out above her scarf.

'I don't think that Seb meant for it to be heroin,' he explained. 'Not at the beginning. I still believe that.'

'It's important to you, isn't it? The distinction?'

'Yes. Yes, it is.'

'Why?'

He shifted self-consciously. His big-knuckled hands hung from the end of his sleeves, heavy as joints of meat from the freezer. 'I've never really believed in much. Not since my mother died. I guess I got things out of proportion.'

'Why?'

He searched the breaking waves for some kind of answer. 'When you're a child,' he said, 'you think your mother is inde-structible. After it happened it was like we were marked and set apart. It was scary. Taboo, even. It was as if people thought everything we did was determined by being a boy without a mother. We could do anything. There weren't any limits.'

'So you made one?'

'Yes. That's it. Exactly it. It was meant to be the limit, the edge of the precipice. Everything except heroin. I thought it was a joke at first, but Seb was serious. He really believed in things like that. Oaths of fealty.'

'Not enough, it seems.'

'No. He did believe. He just . . . just . . . lost it. Somewhere. I walked out of his life at a crucial time. I shouldn't have. He relied on me.'

'You weren't his keeper,' she said, reasonably.

She was right. He breathed in the cold air. Sand shifted on the surface of the beach like cigarette smoke.

'I thought I could redeem him. I was arrogant and stupid.'

He rubbed his face. Together they watched the afternoon plane banking, and approaching out of the west. For the briefest time it seemed like a crucifix hanging in front of the sun.

'I wish it wouldn't land,' she said grimly.

He looked across at her. 'You don't think it's over do you?'

'Do you?' she asked. Her sharp, evaluating gaze was on his face.

He shrugged. 'They made threats. They paid out money. They look after their own.'

'Come on, since when did one of their cover-ups hold?'

'Let it fall apart,' Cal told her. 'I don't care.'

'That's a dangerous attitude,' she said. 'I'd keep it to yourself.'

'Don't worry. After all, what would I say? I'm not even sure what happened, and I was there.'

'We have to be careful,' she said.

'What did you have to do?' he asked her. 'What was the deal you made with your father?'

'Sile. I sent Sile back.' She shook her head at the expression on his face. 'Just for a couple of weeks, stupid. She was curious to meet her grandparents. Where's the harm in that?'

'Thank you,' he said. 'You saved me.'

'Don't mention it,' she replied.

'I wish we had just met,' he said. 'I'd get it right this time.'

'Mrs Greechan has gone to stay with her sister,' Oonagh told him.

A lengthy pause. 'You have an empty house,' he said.

'And a big heart.'

He did not dare believe her. 'Which chance is this?' he asked.

She finally laughed. 'I'd say it was your last chance but you're bound to fuck it all up again.'

He grinned.

'Come on,' she said, 'before I change my mind.'

He rolled across the bed with Oonagh astride him and struck his head, a smart blow against a bulky metal object.

'Shit!' he said. He squeezed closed his watering eyes, and gripped the emergent lump on the back of his head. Oonagh was squatting back on the bed, laughing. He reached over his shoulder, under the haphazard spread of pillows and came out clutching a tarnished steel tube with a button at one end, and the head of a spring-loaded punch at the tip. He recognised it as a captive bolt, used for killing cattle.

'Where the hell did you get this?'

'From Dylan, at the abattoir. He lent it to me.' She was still laughing, and shaking her head. 'I'm sorry, but you looked so indignant.'

He lifted himself on to his elbows. 'Why?'

She became serious. 'Because he escaped from Whitemoor, and I thought he was coming here.'

He considered this. 'What were you going to do? Fuck him and whack him?'

Her eyes narrowed. 'I don't know. Probably.'

'Jesus!' He got up off the bed and started walking back and forth under the eaves, teeth gritted.

'What is it?' she asked, drawing her arms across her naked chest.

'I'm just,' he struggled, exasperated. 'Just. Sick of . . . people knocking chunks out of each other.'

'Calm down,' she said softly.

'What . . . ?'

'Calm down.'

He stopped pacing and stood facing her. Everything they had, the moments of happiness, the brief instances of ecstasy, had been achieved despite the full weight of everything against them. They had something, but almost nothing. It was fragile as glass.

'It's over,' she said, softly. 'Nobody is going to hurt anybody else.'

The summons to Murbhach came the next morning. Cal woke to find the telephone ringing. It took him a second to remember where he was, and another second to realise that Oonagh had already left for work. He scrambled out of bed and grabbed the receiver.

'I'm coming to get you,' Shuard told him, and hung up.

Cal sat on the side of the bed and rubbed furiously at his face as if that might strengthen him for whatever lay ahead. He dressed quickly, and paced the length of the house until he heard the sound of Breeze's Discovery on the gravel outside.

It was raining. The airport road was awash.

'There's a storm coming,' Shuard yelled over the torrent of

water hammering on the roof, as the gateposts of Murbhach loomed above them, some twenty minutes later. Cal had been thankful for the rain. It offered a measure of protection from difficult conversation.

Shuard stopped the car in the courtyard. 'Pepil huv bin askin fir ye,' he said. 'They wan youse to write aboot it.'

Cal's hands stiffened in his lap. He listened to the wipers sloshing back and forth on the windscreen. He wondered if he was being made an offer, something else to keep him quiet.

'I don't know what I'm doing,' he said. 'I haven't made up my mind.'

'You've goat to decide where yir sympathies lie,' Shuard told him.

Cal found that all he could think about was Oonagh. All he cared about was her.

'Let's get this over with,' he said.

Shuard sloshed barefoot across the cobbles with Cal following, and mounted the steps. He grasped the rusting door-knocker and hammered on the door.

'I'll leave you to it,' he said, and went off in the direction of the stable block.

Presently, a woman's voice addressed Cal from the far side of the door. 'Who is it?'

'Calum,' he called.

'Are you alone?'

'Yes.'

He listened to the clatter of a chain been drawn, and a key turning in a heavy lock. The door opened. He stepped on to flagstones in a dark hallway. There was a strange, sharp smell in the air like cat piss. A single light bulb burned at the end of a length of antique braided flex; by its light Cal recognised the diminutive figure of Breeze MacCoinneach standing amongst yellowing stacks of newspapers. She wore a green velvet dressing-grown buttoned to the collar and had her long black hair brushed down her back. She held a small child on her hip. A girl.

'You are Calum,' she said, in her Americanised accent, and he realised that it was the first time he had heard her speak; that he knew nothing about her beyond the notoriety of her marriage. He had a picture of her life, but no understanding of it.

'Follow me,' she said and they went through an archway and down a dimly lit corridor past pale rectangles that marked the places where paintings had once hung. He remembered horses. Her footsteps barely made a sound.

The drawing room existed in a kind of mournful twilight, the windows blocked with thick brocade curtains, the darkened corners suggesting stacks of boxes; the light coming from a couple of weak standing-lamps and the huge fireplace where logs were spitting and popping.

There was a small door in the corner of the room that led out on to the balcony. Breeze paused for a few seconds at the door. Her eyes shone brightly in the firelight.

'He wants you to tell him that he has time enough for a son,' she told him.

She opened the door for him.

The MacCoinneach was sitting in a wicker chair on the bleached wooden decking, facing out to sea.

'The only good thing about old age,' he said, without looking up, 'is that nobody gives a damn, including you. You can do anything you care to; make all manner of threats. Everything is negotiable.'

Grasping the arms of the chair, The MacCoinneach lifted himself on his thick, grizzled forearms and the rug slipped off his knees. He turned to face Cal. The wrinkles round his eyes, the only visible indication of his age, were like the ancient fracture-lines left by water on rock. His eyes were the same cold and unsettling blue as Seb's had been.

He motioned to Cal to draw nearer.

'You were Sebastian's friend,' he said, in a voice that would brook no contradiction. It was more of an accusation than a statement.

'Sit down,' he said, returning to his own chair.

Cal sat with his back to the wall of green-tinged window panes, which were running with water.

'You were also my daughter's lover,' Hugh told him, leaning forward over his knees. And Cal received a hint of the deep and awesome hatred that the old man nurtured.

'You were with them at the end?'

'Not at the very end,' Cal replied, softly.

'Why?'

'I walked out. I didn't like what were they doing.'

'You didn't see them die, did you?'

'No . . .' Cal faltered. 'I heard shots.'

'You presumed.'

'When I left they were pointing guns at each other.'

'And they just let you walk away?'

Cal said, 'Yes.'

The MacCoinneach sneered derisively. 'I've seen you,' he said. 'On my land. I can see more up here than you might think. From certain angles everything is clear. What did you throw in the sea?'

Cal swallowed. 'Passports. Some money.'

'Why?'

'I agreed to get rid of the evidence.'

'You betrayed my son.'

'No. I made a deal,' Cal said, his voice rising. 'Like you made a deal.'

Hugh MacCoinneach stared at him. 'This is my home,' he said.

'What do you want?' Cal demanded. He stood up.

'Sit down.'

Cal remained standing.

'Sit down. Please.'

Cal watched while Hugh MacCoinneach rummaged in a pile of bills and letters on a low table beside him. He retrieved a copy of the *Telegraph* and offered it to Cal. 'Inside page. Small paragraph.'

Reluctantly Cal took the paper and returned to his seat. He had to search for a few seconds before he found the report. His eye quickening, he read the whole paragraph at once and his skin began to tingle and his throat became so dry that he did not know if he would be able to speak. A former executive of Tarmac and master of the hunt found dead in the charred remains of his rebuilt medieval house in East Sussex. Arson suspected. Mention of a previous history of attacks, including a fire-bombing, and years of anonymous hate mail. Police would neither confirm nor deny reports that the Justice Department, an extremist animal liberation organisation, was suspected of involvement.

A death with which to mark her passing; like graffiti. A stopover en route to somewhere else.

She was alive. Somewhere out there, Madelene was alive. Their precious cover-up was falling apart.

'Why?' The MacCoinneach demanded, and suddenly he was his real age, his cheeks and neck as crisp as parchment, with crevices like the indiscriminate slashes of a knife. Whatever it was that had kept him so young for so long, strength of will or a store of hatred as deep as Seb's, it was beginning to fail him.

'She wants you to know,' Cal replied, handing back the paper.

'You know where she is, don't you?'

'No.'

'She's coming here, isn't she?'

'I don't know.'

'For Christ's sake,' The MacCoinneach muttered. 'There's no need to go over the top. I'll give you both money. Whatever you want. We can be reasonable. Just keep her away from my family.'

'I'm leaving now,' Cal told him.

'I mean it,' The MacCoinneach appealed, desperately. 'We can make a deal.'

'There's no deal to be made,' Cal told him, before he left.

They lay, with her head resting in the hollow of his shoulder, listening to the sound of the storm outside. The scattering shadows on the ceiling. He had tried to explain his fears to her.

'She won't come here,' Oonagh said. 'Just like Sile's father never came. It just doesn't happen. It'll be all right.'

'Will it?' he wondered aloud. 'Will it be all right?'

She said, 'Yes.' Her eyes had filled with tears. She continued to stare at the storm's track across the ceiling. At last she blinked and a single tear ran straight across her temple and vanished into the hair above her ears.

He imagined her waiting, in the nights following the break-out from Whitemoor prison, in this same bed, paralysed by a sense of impending disaster.

More than anything else, he did not want to lose her. They groped together, avoiding silence. There was a desperate edge to their coupling.

He dreamt of Madelene that night. He lay on a smooth skull of rock at the water's edge, staring into an oily pool. She rose from the deep with her head back and arms thrown out. His ears filled with rushing. The dark liquid slid off her face as she broke the surface. Her hair snaking and floating with the water's movements.

'Come to me,' she whispered.

He felt her cold breath on his face. Her wet, trembling body, sleek as a seal's, pressing down on his. The icy zero at the end of the gun puckering his inner thigh.

He opened his eyes.

'Lover,' she whispered. Her eyes gleamed, tormented.

Oonagh shifted in the bed beside him, her breathing shallow and steady.

Madelene pressed a finger against his lips. She smelled of ashes and of brine, of fire and of the sea.

'I burned Murbhach,' she said.

Carefully she insinuated her finger into his mouth. The end of the gun travelled across the meat of his thigh and came to rest alongside his penis.

'You betrayed us. It had to be you.'

He gave no reaction. He watched her face, in silent fascination. She was methodically working her finger across the plate in his mouth, following the contours of her artwork. Small, almost imperceptible spasms moved like tides across the skin of her face.

'I've decided to forgive you.'

The storm outside swelled menacingly against the windows. She slipped her finger out of his mouth and traced the latticework of scars on his nose and cheeks. She began to caress the side of his jaw.

'If you come with me . . .'

He detected a certain stiffness in Oonagh's thigh where it rested against his own. He imagined her hand under the pillow.

No.

'Where are the passports?' Madelene whispered. Her finger on the trigger.

He wanted to shout, even to scream; as if by making a loud enough sound he might prevent what was about to happen, but in the end all he could do was whisper, 'No.'

Oonagh struck.

Thunk.

The abattoir bolt punched clean through the case of Madelene's skull, into the soft tissue of her brain.

He gasped. Her head hung down like a punctured melon. Water seeped out of her on to him, and washed across his thighs.

As suddenly, it was all over. Oonagh had backed off the bed into the corner of the room, dragging the covers with her.

'No,' he said, his voice fading away into nothing.

The stretched-out body was incredibly heavy. The bolt still protruding from its head. A red plush of blood. Everything was quiet.

She had come from nowhere. Without trace. She could be returned there. He saw it clearly. The whirlpool. His lips formed the words that would be the sequence of events. Oonagh was on her hands and knees, scrubbing the pine floorboards with bleach. From the kitchen, he could hear the sound of the remaining bedclothes revolving in the washing-machine.

'I'm not going to prison,' she told him.

The body was on the bed, wrapped in a sheet. There was an open bottle of whisky by Oonagh's knee. When he bent down to pick it up, she flinched. The windows were open and rain was coming in.

'It was self-defence,' she said.

'Stop doing that,' he snapped, regretting the harshness of his words as soon as he'd said it. She had everything to lose.

She stared at him.

'Please,' he said.

They sat on the bed, with their backs to the body, and passed the bottle back and forth without their fingers touching. He wanted to touch her, just for a moment. He didn't dare.

'The whirlpool,' he said.

It was painful to bear her gaze.

'We throw her in the whirlpool,' he said. 'No one will know.'

He had to work the bolt back and forth in Madelene's skull to get it out. It made a sickening crunching noise. When he got it out it was sticky with hair and pieces of other matter. He rinsed it in the shower. Oonagh would sterilise it in the autoclave at the surgery in the morning. There would be no evidence.

He went back into the bedroom. There was a flush of red on Oonagh's cheeks. The bottle was almost empty.

'Ready?' he asked.

She nodded.

He took the head end and Oonagh took the legs. They lifted the bundle and backed out of the room. The body lolled and thumped on the steps as they dragged it down. They had to put it down so that she could open the door and switch the porch light on.

The white Discovery was parked beside Oonagh's Subaru; inside it stank of bonfire. They lifted the body into it.

It was like travelling down a tunnel, through great sheaves of spray from the wheels. Into the underworld. Always his eyes flicked across to her, seated beside him. She was staring out of the window, into the spray. Madelene's body was curled up in the boot.

He turned off on to the Og and followed the tarmac road past the last dark outline of a farm, to where the road ended; not caring if they knew a car had passed. One car only; there was no going back.

When the road ended he dropped into low ratio, and took the track through the sycamores. The torrent of water was so thick that it was as if they were rising through a mud-slide.

The first lightning flash lit up the cemetery, and wild goats scattered among the gravestones. He bounced across the verges of the path that went through the centre, and struck the side of a headstone. His ears were filled with the squeal of rending metal. Oonagh was screaming. Each turning of the steering wheel seemed more likely to deliver hurt and damage. It was a chaos of sparks, and ripping metal and lightning flashes.

At last he made it to the end of the cemetery. Beyond the railings the grass fell away in a gentle slope towards the cliffs. Suddenly he saw the gap in the fence, the half-rusted spikes of the gate. He accelerated towards it, and it was bent beneath the car and dragged with it as they raced across the soft ground.

He kicked open his door.

'Jump!' he screamed.

He flung himself out of the door, struck the ground and started to slide.

He lay, fighting for breath at the edge of the cliffs. He raised his head and saw Oonagh standing over him, with the black sky whirling behind her. There was blood in her hair, and running down the side of her face.

'You're fucking crazy,' she screamed at him. 'Stupid. Crazy. Fucker!'

There was such rage in her eyes, he could not meet them. He struggled backwards, trying to gain his feet. He couldn't get a purchase. The ground was smooth as grease.

'I hate you!' She picked up a stone and threw it at him. It struck his cheekbone. He groaned and rolled over, cupping his face.

'Fuck you!' she screamed.

She grabbed at his hair, but it was too short and she spun away, slipped and fell. He pinned her down.

'It's all over,' he shouted. 'Finished!'

Eventually she stopped struggling.

When he awoke, he was sodden and bone weary. On his knees, he crept out from under the tarpaulin beside Seb's grave. The sky was blue. It had stopped raining, and the wall of thick black clouds was retreating in the direction of Ireland, casting its shadow across the sea.

There was water everywhere, pools of it as bright as mirrors on the grass, and drops of it glistening on the headstones and railings.

He pressed his fingertips to the tender flesh of his cheekbone. There was no energy in him for fear or regret.

He walked across the hilltop through the headstones, and went down the slope to the edge of the cliffs. On a lower slope, the goats were rooting amongst the rocks and heather. The billy-goat looked up at him briefly, and then returned to its foraging.

He stood at the very edge of the steepest cliff. There was no sign of the Discovery; just the vast ceaselessly roiling eye of the whirlpool. The salt-spray.

He might have preferred some other solution, some other ending, but really, given the way the MacCoinneachs led their lives, it fitted. It was apt.

He remained at the edge until his eyes stung from the salt. Then he turned away. On the far side of the Og the pale yellow strip of beach, the Big Strand, stretched away into the distance. It wasn't long past dawn.

He went back to Oonagh. When he heard her groan he folded back the tarpaulin and helped her sit up. Her hair was matted with blood.

'I ache all over,' she said.

'Me too.'

She blinked, as if unsure of her surroundings.

'We should think about getting started,' he said. 'It's a long hike back on the beach.'

'You fucked up again,' she said.

He glanced down at his hands and nodded slowly. 'Yes.'

When he looked up, he saw her staring past him towards the edge of the cliffs.

'Is she gone?' she asked.

'Yes. There's no trace.'

She smoothed her matted hair.

He said, 'We need to get our story straight.'

She swallowed hard and nodded. 'Yes,' she said. 'I guess we do.'

She put her arms round him, and rested her head on his shoulder. After a minute or so she raised her head and looked into his eyes.